Best Wishes
C Risenhoover

A NOVEL

TRESTLES OVER DARKNESS

C. C. RISENHOOVER

Contrary Creek Publishers

Also by C.C. Risenhoover

DEAD EVEN
BLOOD BATH
CHILD STALKER
DEATH ANGEL
LETHAL RAGE
WHITE HEAT
WINE, MURDER & BLUEBERRY SUNDAES
MURDER AT THE FINAL FOUR
SATAN'S MARK
HAPPY BIRTHDAY JESUS
LARRY HAGMAN

Printed in the United States of America

FIRST EDITION

Library of Congress Cataloging-in-Publication Data

Risenhoover, C.C.
Trestles Over Darkness / C.C. Risenhoover. – 1st ed.
p. cm.
ISBN 1-930899-04-1
LCCN 00-107537

AUTHOR'S NOTE

The individual characters who appear in this book are wholly fictional. Any apparent resemblance of a character to any person alive or dead is purely coincidental.

DESIGN BY JEFF STANTON

Published by Contrary Creek Publishers

For my wife

Georgia

ONE

Summer is about the same as any other season in Walla, Louisiana. There's never much going on. The exception was that August in nineteen forty-nine, the year little Sadie Scott came up missing.

Of course, that was also the same month and year the Williams family was murdered, only they were coloreds so white folks didn't give much thought to the significance or reason for the killings.

Except for Johnny Tobin.

He gave a lot of thought to it. Most say he was a strange boy, born out of his time, without explaining whether his time should have been earlier or later. Some even like to say he was a tad off center, maybe just to try to justify what happened to him. Johnny would probably have agreed that he didn't subscribe to the same standards of sanity as most folks.

Whatever the case, he was different. He didn't march to the same drummer as did most folks in the parish. Nor for that matter did he march to the same beat as the majority of those who lived in Louisiana.

Sadie was a beautiful child, a little short of five years old when she disappeared. Those who can remember the time say her eyes were bluer than a passionate sky, her hair as fine and golden as cornsilk colored by a caring sun. They can also recall the haughty tilt to her chin and the arrogant walk that belied her age.

Sadie was bright; no mistake about that. Most attributed her unusually large vocabulary for a child so young to the fact that her folks were teachers at the local school. Those who knew, of course, say the child's intelligence came from the mother's genes, even though there was a strangeness to the mother that is still talked about.

Sadie's father, Vernon, was a clod. He was paid to be a football coach first, a teacher second. If he had known anything to teach, they say, it would have been way down on his list of priorities. Despite that, he was not as unfeeling a man as many thought him to be. He just had difficulty expressing himself. Then, too, a lot of people in Walla had difficulty expressing themselves.

But little girls just didn't come up missing in Walla. It wasn't that kind of town. About the worst the parish sheriff or town police chief ever had to contend with was a couple of good old boys getting drunk and fighting over some girl at a Saturday night Catholic church dance.

The Catholics had one of their wingdings about once a month. Some said it was for the purpose of upsetting Brother Marvin Baker, pastor of the First Baptist Church. When fired with righteous indignation, Baker could preach a mean and passionate sermon against dancing. Of course, he was never one to let scripture get in the way of his opinion. His reasoning made the thinking people who lived in the town scratch their heads in bewilderment. Of course, there weren't that many heads that got scratched.

Brother Baker attributed a minimum of fifty percent of the evil in Walla to the Catholic dances. His flock didn't argue and the Catholics didn't care.

Johnny Tobin, twelve going on thirteen, was fishing beneath the railroad trestle that ran over Sandy Creek when he heard Sadie Scott was missing. He wasn't pleased that the news came from his friend Bobby Milam, who had come down to the creek to fish with him. Johnny liked to be the first to know what was going on, not the other way around.

"Who told you about it?" Johnny asked.

"My mother. You'd have knowed already if you hadn't got up so early and come fishing'. Your mom told her."

Johnny grunted. "They bite better early. You can't drag down here in the middle of the morning and expect to catch a mess of fish."

"How many you got?"

"Two. They ain't biting."

Bobby laughed. "Looks like I don't have a whole lot of catching up to do."

Johnny scowled, then grinned. He had a disarming smile. And, he enjoyed teasing and being teased. "Guess not. I think I had a big bass on a few minutes ago, or a hog bream. Whatever, it took me in the brush and hung me up."

While carefully threading a wriggling worm on the barb of his hook and up its shank, Bobby said, "You always say that."

"Always say what?"

"That you had a big bass on. You ever catch a big bass down here under the trestle?"

"You know I ain't. But they're here. They always pull me in the brush and get off. And, you can't expect to catch a big bass on a perch hook anyway."

Bobby spit on the worm, then tossed it out next to a brush pile that was close to where Johnny's bobber was resting. "Well, I ain't never had a big bass on down here under the trestle. Seems to me that I would have had one on if they were here. I don't think there's anything here but perch and catfish."

Before Johnny could say anything, Bobby's bobber disappeared and he set the hook. He was soon showing off a big perch, its colorful red and yellow underside glistening in the sunlight filtering through the railroad ties of the trestle. While removing the hook Bobby asked, "You been spittin' on your hook?"

"No, I ain't been spittin' on my hook."

While putting the fish on his stringer Bobby said, "Makes a difference. Dad told me to always spit on my hook."

"That's a bunch of bull. The water washes the spit off."

Bobby grinned. "Then how come that fish bit my hook and not

yours? Answer me that."

"It had nothin' to do with spit. You just dropped the bait on his head is all I can say."

"The only reason you say spit don't work is because you didn't think of it first."

Johnny let fly a few expletives and said. "That stuff about spittin' on your hook. . . it's as old as the hills."

"You sure been cussin' a lot lately."

"No more than I always did."

"Seems you didn't cuss as much last year, especially after you was baptized." Bobby set the hook and landed another big bream.

Johnny grumbled something indiscernible under his breath, then in a normal voice countered, "You were baptized same time I was. I can't see it's made much difference in the way you talk."

"I never did cuss as much as you did," Bobby said.

"Well, ain't you the pious one. It ain't like I take the Lord's name in vain. I don't say much that you could call profane. In fact, I don't say anything using God's name."

"You don't figure those other words are takin' the Lord's name in vain?"

"Not unless you put God in front of one of those words."

Bobby pondered his friend's interpretation of the Bible for a few seconds. He knew it wouldn't do any good to argue. Johnny was so hardheaded and opinionated that it would be an unwinnable effort. So he asked, "Your mom try to get you to go to Vacation Bible School?"

"Yea, but not too hard. Be a little hypocritical since she and daddy don't ever darken the door of the church. . . unless it's the Catholic Church when there's a dance. She used to go. . . back when the war was on. . . when dad was fightin' the Germans. Back then I remember goin' to tent revivals where the preacher would wash your feet."

"Why?"

"I don't know. There's something in the Bible about it, that's all I know." The truth was that Johnny did know the scripture passage about Jesus washing the feet of His disciples, but didn't want to have to explain it to his friend. There were times when he liked to flaunt his Biblical knowledge, other times when he didn't.

One

Bobby landed another big perch and Johnny scowled. "Why are you coming on with all this stuff about Vacation Bible School anyway?"

"Well, it's going on now. We went last year, you know. . . when both of us got saved and baptized. My mother's pressuring me to go."

Johnny laughed. "Vacation Bible School would cut into my fishing'. You can go for both of us."

"I ain't going unless you do."

"Then you ain't going."

They both concentrated on fishing for a while. It was very peaceful under the trestle, the gurgling rush of creek water playing its own special symphony. The water where they fished was pure and clean, not like a mile downstream where the town dumped its sewage.

Then Bobby asked, "What do you think might have happened to little Sadie?"

Johnny shrugged. "She'll probably show up. . . probably over at some neighbor's house."

"If she was over at some neighbor's house, don't you think they'd have let the coach and Mrs. Scott know? She's been missing since yesterday."

"You didn't tell me that. I thought she'd just come up missing this morning."

"No, since yesterday. They just didn't find out about it until this morning."

"If they didn't know she was missing until this morning, how do they know she was missing yesterday?"

The question took Bobby back a bit. "I don't know."

"Well, I don't have a clue about where she is and ain't got time to worry about it."

"What you got to do besides fish and play baseball?"

Johnny grinned. "That's enough to do. But I got lots of chores to do around the house, too. I've got to pick peas, milk the cow and all that kind of stuff."

"I figured you'd want to try to find her since you're always reading those detective books and listening to *Mr. District Attorney* on the radio."

The books Bobby referred to were pulp novels purchased by Johnny's father, who was an avid reader. And, while Johnny devoured the books, too, he was much more curious and interested in a detective's relationship with women than in whodunit. But, Bobby's statement did hit a nerve, causing Johnny to conjure up some visions of himself as a detective.

"I could probably find her if I wanted to," he said.

Bobby laughed. "I figured you'd say that. If the law can't find her, what makes you think you can?"

"Because the law in this town don't know its rear end from a hole in the ground. They're the most ignorant folks who ever walked on two feet."

"That go for Billy Burton, too?"

Burton was a parish sheriff's deputy. He had taken the boys for a ride in his car and familiarized them with his gun. Johnny figured he was not the brightest guy around, but grudgingly admired him because he could shoot the head off a match at twenty paces.

"Billy ain't a bad guy. I don't think he's much of a detective, but he's not a bad guy. I was talking about Sheriff Merrick and Chief Crossland."

"Well, I think everybody is out looking for little Sadie."

"We ain't."

"Well, maybe we ought to be. . . especially since you've already bragged you can find her. But, I figure they'll find her before we could even get started looking."

Johnny looked at his friend with disdain. "If you want to go look for the kid, we'll go. I was just counting on catching a big mess of fish for supper."

"You don't even like fish."

"They ain't bad. . . if they're cooked right. But, what the heck. They ain't biting. We'll go see what we can find out then come back here later. I figure they'll bite this afternoon."

"What are we gonna do with our fishin' poles? You want to take them to your house?"

"No, but we need to hide them so the colored boys won't find them."

"You're a big one to talk about niggers. . . much time as you spend with Ben Jim Cade."

"Ben Jim's different."

One

"I don't know how you figure that. He's as black as the rest of them."

"Maybe so, but color ain't what makes him different."

"What does then?"

"You wouldn't understand if I told you."

Bobby knew the conversation regarding Ben Jim Cade was over, so he took another tack. "You think maybe the niggers got Sadie?"

Johnny gave Bobby a disbelieving look. "Now why in the dickens would they want her?"

Bobby shrugged his shoulders. "Dad says they're out to cause trouble."

"Some of them. . . maybe. But, not the ones from around here. He's talking about them from up North. And, I don't know of one around here that's from up North."

"Where's Ben Jim from?"

"Well, he ain't from up there."

After hiding their fishing poles, the boys walked down the railroad tracks to where the combination of rusty and shiny steel rails spiked on creosote crossties went across the street leading to the downtown area. Walla was a dinky town of slightly less than four thousand people. At least half the population was black, drawn to the heavily wooded area to work at the big sawmill or in jobs related to it.

It was mid morning, hot and humid. The air was stale. Smoke from the sawmill hung in the air, looking for a place to go. But there was no breeze to give it a ride.

As they moved along, dust kicking up with every step, Bobby asked, "You got any money?"

"No, why?"

"I could use a cold soda pop."

"Mr. Bernstein would probably let me charge a couple at the store."

"Bernstein's a Jew, ain't he?"

"Yeah. . . what about it?"

"Dad says they're part of the problem."

"What problem?"

"The nigger problem."

"I don't see how he figures that. Jews are white."

"He says they're agitators."

"Well, Mr. Bernstein ain't never been nothing but nice to me. I sure don't think he's an agitator."

Sol Bernstein's General Merchandise Store was a large gray clapboard building where most of the sawmill workers bought their groceries on credit. Johnny worked there on Saturdays with the owner and his two daughters, Ruth and Ruta. His salary was two dollars a day. The store had a long porch across its front, and dust-covered plate-glass windows on either side of its big double doors. Those doors were wide open, but the screen doors were closed, which was an effort to keep the flies out.

Johnny's and Bobby's feet resounded across the wooden porch, then there was the loud squeaking of one of the screen doors as they opened it and entered. Overhead, attached to the high ceiling, a couple of fans knocked and creaked, providing an eerie feeling to the dimly lit interior. But if the place had been spooky as a graveyard, it wouldn't have mattered to the boys. It was several degrees cooler inside than out and their taste buds were anticipating the cold pop.

Bernstein looked up from where he was stacking some canned goods and smiled. "Johnny. . . how you doing? You, too, Bobby?" He was a small man with kind eyes and gray hair that looked as if it had been puffed up by the wind.

Bobby nodded acknowledgment and Johnny replied, "Fine, Mr. Bernstein. I was just wondering if I could charge a couple of pops until Saturday?"

Looking over small wire-rim glasses balanced precariously on the end of his nose, the grocer said, "Of course you can. Just help yourself."

The boys walked over to the big red metal soda pop case and lifted its lid. Inside beverage bottles were lined up smartly, their caps looking up through little chunks of ice. Johnny chose a Coke and Bobby took an orange. After getting the lids off the cold, glistening bottles they went back to where Bernstein was working. Except for the three of them the store was empty. Most of the establishment's trade came in early morning and late afternoon on weekdays.

Johnny said, "Bad about little Sadie, huh?"

The grocer frowned. "Terrible. Is there any news?"

"None I know of," Johnny said. "I just heard about it this morning. . . thought maybe you'd heard something."

The storeowner shook his head. "All I know is that Sheriff Merrick and Chief Crossland are recruiting every available man to look for her. A lot of the sawmill people will be out looking, including your fathers."

"I didn't know that," Johnny said.

"Neither did I," said Bobby.

Bernstein said, "I wanted to go, but the sheriff told me to stay here. . . said he had plenty of searchers and that people would be needing supplies."

Johnny gave his best bewildered look. "Wonder why they didn't conduct an all out search last night?"

"They didn't know she was missing last night," the grocer said. "They didn't know she was gone until this morning. Mr. Scott told the sheriff he put her to bed about nine o'clock last night and they didn't realize she was missing until about seven o'clock this morning."

"So they figure she wandered off during the night?" Johnny asked.

"Or was abducted," Bernstein replied.

"Why would anybody want to take a little girl?"

The merchant shrugged. "There are some terrible people in this world."

Johnny took a swig of his Coke. "Bobby here thinks a colored might have got her."

Bobby grimaced and looked at the floor. "Now I didn't say that exactly."

"Yeah you did."

"That would surprise me," Bernstein said. "Most of the Negroes here are very nice people."

The boys exchanged knowing glances, then Bobby said, "There's a bunch of them live in the woods. Those are the ones we don't exactly know."

Bernstein said, "Well, let's just hope that no one took her. . . that she just wandered off and will be found safe and sound."

"That's a good thing to hope," Johnny said.

The two boys talked to the merchant a while longer, finished their beverages and left the store. As they ambled down the sidewalk Bobby said, "Did you notice that Mr. Bernstein called niggers

Negroes?"

"That's what they are."

Bobby gave Johnny an annoyed glance. "Then how come you call them niggers?"

"I don't call them that. I call them coloreds. And, what I call them and what I know are two different things. I know it's best to call them Negroes, but most of the people around here don't know what's best. They're too ignorant to know."

Bobby snorted. "If you know better and still don't call them Negroes, don't that make you ignorant, too?"

"No, it don't. I talk the way I do so the people here will understand me. I know better than to say *ain't* but I say it. I don't want to be talking over people's heads or they'll think I'm strange. I don't have time to explain everything to you."

Bobby laughed. "You're full of bull. . . and you are strange."

Main Street in Walla was the two-lane state blacktop highway running through the town. On one side was a cluster of frame buildings and the movie theater, which had a balcony, making it the tallest structure in town. The theater regularly featured cowboy stars like Lash Larue and Big Boy Williams.

On the other side of the blacktop were the railroad tracks and a dilapidated depot, its yellow paint peeling. Bernstein's store was on that side of the tracks, too, along with a few other old and worn looking buildings.

The two boys were attracted to the considerable activity in front of the combination police station, sheriff's office and jail. There were, they guessed, as many as a hundred men milling around. They joined the crowd.

As they threaded their way through the cars and pickups in front of the faded white building, they were stopped by a stern voice. "What are you boys doing here?"

It was Jake Tobin, Johnny's father. He was dressed, as always, in khaki pants and shirt. They were leftovers from his days in the Army. He was smiling.

"We were just trying to find out what was going on," Johnny said. "Don't usually see this many folks together unless there's a ball game."

Tobin's brow furrowed. "You know about little Sadie Scott, don't you?"

Johnny replied, "Yeah, we know about her. How did you get off from the mill?"

"The big boss shut the mill down until we find her. Company's paying all the white hands to look for her."

"What about the coloreds?" Johnny asked.

"They were just told to go home. . . to wait until something happens."

Johnny grunted. "Seems they could help look for her, too."

"Well," his father said, "you know how some people are. They don't want the niggers helping because they want to blame them if somethin' goes wrong."

"That's stupid, dad. Ben Jim Cade. . . he knows the woods around here good as you do."

"I ain't arguing it," Tobin said. "Ben Jim may know the woods even better than me. But, there's a lot of talk that a nigger probably took the little girl. Around here it don't take any proof to get people riled up about the niggers. The sheriff's already searched nigger quarters, but it'll be searched again. . . this time by a bunch a men. I don't think they'll find anything, but that don't mean some of them won't start a ruckus."

"You gonna be with 'em?"

"Nope. I don't want to be. I'm in charge of a group that'll be searching the bottoms along San Miguel Creek."

Johnny was glad his father wasn't going to be with the group who searched the quarters. "Bobby and me could come along. I know the creek bottom as good as anybody. . . better than most."

"I know you do, but why don't you and Bobby go back and do a little fishing'. Leave this kind of hunting to the men."

Johnny started to argue, but knew his dad wasn't the kind of man to take any guff. He also realized that Jake Tobin didn't want him along because he was afraid of what they might find. Johnny, of course, thought he was tough enough to handle anything, including seeing Sadie Scott's body. He was pretty sure that's what they were going to find.

He remembered seeing Raymond Gordon's body, all dressed up

and in a coffin. He had been five at the time. Raymond had been six when he died. They had been good friends. But Johnny hadn't cried when he saw the body in the casket at Raymond's folks' house. He had looked at the body while eating a piece of fried chicken. That's the thing he remembered most about his friend's death, all the food neighbors had brought to the Gordon house.

"Let's sit a spell," Johnny told Bobby.

They plopped down on the courthouse lawn, which was adjacent to the jail, and watched the proceedings. While the reason the men were there wasn't funny, Johnny found the fire drill atmosphere amusing. Parish Sheriff Nick Merrick, fat and dumpy, was in charge. Johnny figured he was a man who had trouble directing one deputy like Billy Burton. Trying to coordinate the efforts of almost a hundred men was overwhelming him. Sweat was pouring down from his greasy black hair, which was partially covered by a cowboy hat. It was washing his chubby and flushed cheeks, causing them to glisten in the bright sunlight.

Police Chief Roger Crossland, gaunt and scrawny, was the physical opposite of the sheriff. He stood to the left of his lawman counterpart smoking one cigarette after another. His face looked like a wrinkled leaf of tobacco hung and drying in a shed. There was no life in his black eyes. The snowy hair protruding from beneath his cowboy hat looked out of place and unreal.

The chief had no leadership ability, either. But, fortunately, he was a one-man show. He didn't have anyone working for him, unless one wanted to count his wife. She cooked meals for anyone unfortunate enough to end up in the city jail. Of course, the parish also used the jail. The sheriff had his office in the building. So sometimes Mrs. Crossland cooked meals for the sheriff's prisoners, too.

After what seemed like an hour of confusion, but in reality was only a few minutes, Jake Tobin took charge. He was the kind of man others listened to, one whose calm and common sense restored order and initiated organization with urgency. Johnny figured his dad's leadership ability came from his time in the Army, when he was a sergeant and leading raw recruits against the Germans. He wasn't given much chance to use those leadership skills at the sawmill.

Jake Tobin seemed bigger than he actually was. He was two inches short of six feet, but carried himself like a much taller man. People were for the most part surprised when they learned his true height. This appearance of being taller was all the stranger because he walked with a limp, the result of a serious leg wound suffered during the Battle of the Bulge.

Tobin weighed around a hundred sixty pounds, but it was all honed muscle polished by the sun. He had piercing brown eyes, a prominent nose, and ears a little too large for a narrow face that showed numerous character lines. His hair was brown with streaks of gray.

After the men had left to conduct searches of various areas, Bobby asked, "You want to go back to the creek and do some fishing'?"

"No, they won't be biting until later," Johnny replied. "Let's go see if we can find out something else about little Sadie."

"Your dad told you to stay out of it."

Johnny grinned. "Well, he didn't say that exactly."

"Where you want to go?"

"Let's go over to First Baptist Church and see what's going on."

Bobby cringed. "You know Vacation Bible School's going on over there. They'll be asking why we ain't enrolled."

"Hey, don't worry about it. Just let me do the talking. We'll have some Kool-Aid and cookies, ask a few questions, then get out of there."

Bobby was reluctant, but as always gave in. Johnny, like his dad, was usually in control. Some said he had his dad's leadership qualities. His mother said he was simply stubborn and hardheaded. She said that about his dad, too.

The Baptist church was no more than an eighth of a mile away, so they walked the distance in short order. On arrival Brother Marvin Baker, who the previous year had baptized them, immediately accosted them. He was a pear shaped man who had, obviously, spent too much time at the dinner table. He had a Santa Claus belly and cheeks that were loose and drooped like a hound dog.

"Why ain't you boys in Vacation Bible School?"

Johnny replied, "We was planning to enroll today, Brother Baker, but this thing with little Sadie came up."

"What's that got to do with you enrolling?"

"Well, you know how well I know the woods around here. Billy Burton. . . he's a deputy sheriff, you know. . . asked me to do some looking around."

"Of course I know Billy Burton," the preacher said, "and he ain't got no business asking children to do his job for him."

Johnny knew Baker and Burton didn't like each other, which is why he made reference to the deputy. He figured the two wouldn't be having any conversations. And he didn't like being called a child. He held his tongue, though, and changed the conversation's flow. "The Scotts are members of the church here, ain't they?"

"You know they are. I just got back from visiting with them, praying with them. What's happened. . . it's a terrible thing."

Johnny wanted to ask the minister why he wasn't out looking for the little girl, but already knew what his answer would be. The fat man would simply say he could help most by praying and being available to console the Scotts. The truth, Johnny thought, was that he was too soft to do anything of a physical nature. It was one of several things he disliked about the preacher.

"Yeah, it's a terrible thing," Johnny said, "which, I guess, is why the Lord laid it on my heart to go looking for her instead of signing up for Vacation Bible School. And, he laid it on my heart to ask Bobby to help me."

Johnny knew his statement was one Baker couldn't argue with. The preacher was always talking about what God had laid on his heart. So did some of the deacons and others who made public pronouncements of their closeness to God. He figured it was all a lot of bull. But, whatever worked.

Baker made eye contact with Johnny and said, "Well, if the Lord laid it on your heart. . . "

"He did. . . which is why I'm here. I figured on talking to some of Sadie's friends, seeing if she told them about any secret places she liked to hide."

The preacher's eyes lit up, as much as they possibly could given his mental capacity. Johnny figured he had more than enough room inside his big head for his pea-sized brain. "That's a good idea, Johnny. Wonder why Sheriff Merrick and Chief Crossland ain't thought about asking?"

Johnny wanted to say, *Because they're stupid.* He, instead, said, "I'm sure they would've gotten around to it. Or, maybe the Lord planned it this way."

Baker's eyes flickered disbelief, which he tried to hide. "Probably best I talk to the kids. They may not feel comfortable with you two boys."

Johnny knew nothing could be further from the truth. If anything the preacher would scare the kids. He knew that from conversations with his younger sister. Baker frightened her because he was always yelling about sin, or what he considered to be sin.

But, with Baker choosing to intervene, there was nothing Johnny could do. Questioning the four and five year olds about Sadie Scott had suddenly become the preacher's idea. The ordeal lasted about thirty minutes, during which time Johnny and Bobby downed a couple of cups of Kool-Aid and some cookies. After it was over Baker acted like he was a little ticked about the results. The kids either didn't know anything or the preacher had scared them so much that they had clamed up. Johnny suspected the latter.

"Well, don't guess this was as good an idea as you thought it was, Johnny," Baker said.

"Never know until you ask, Brother Baker."

"You boys had best leave the finding of little Sadie to the men folk of this town."

Johnny asked, "Even if the Lord tells me to look for her?"

The question irritated Baker. "Maybe you misinterpreted what the Lord wanted you to do. Maybe you thought it was the Lord leading you when it was really Billy Burton."

"No, I don't think so," Johnny said. "Does the Lord ever mislead you, Brother Baker?"

The preacher's face turned a light shade of pink. "Of course not. But, I'm in contact with the Lord all the time."

Johnny deadpanned, "Ain't we all supposed to be?"

"Uhh. . . yes, of course. It's just that. . . well, never mind."

The preacher turned the conversation to Vacation Bible School and pressured them to enroll. Bobby gave in, but not Johnny. Baker was quite agitated by his reluctance. "Don't you think the Lord wants you in Vacation Bible School?"

"The Lord thinks it's more important for me to search the bottoms behind Ben Jim Cade's place. Since Bobby's gonna be in Vacation

Bible School, I'll get Ben Jim to help me."

"You better stay away from that old nigger," the preacher said. "He's no good."

"That's what I hear. Maybe the Lord wants me to help show Ben Jim the light. Maybe I can help him get saved. Don't the Lord want us to spread His Word?"

Baker grunted. "You better let the niggers bring salvation to the niggers. The Lord don't want us messing in their affairs."

Deadpan again, Johnny asked, "Am I reading the Bible wrong?"

"You may be interpreting it wrong."

"Interpreting? I thought everything in the New Testament was literal. You mean it ain't?"

The preacher was getting close to his anger zone. "It is literal, but some parts require a man of God for interpretation. You may lack understanding of certain passages."

"Gee, if something's literal I figured everybody could understand it."

Baker wanted to explode, to let the smart aleck kid have it with both barrels. But, everyone in town knew about Jake Tobin's temper. If someone messed with one of his kids, the preacher knew, he wouldn't care if the guilty party had a Reverend in front of his name. So he said, "We can discuss your views on the Bible later, Johnny. I have a lot of work to do."

Johnny left Bobby at the church and headed back toward what passed for downtown. He was amused by the exchange with the preacher, but his mind churned with more important things. He was now committed to the hunt for Sadie Scott, which took priority over everything else. He figured with the help of Ben Jim Cade, she was as good as found.

TWO

Brother Marvin Baker wasn't a man who appreciated subtle humor, possibly because he didn't recognize when it was being used. Make that more than a possibility. He was about as subtle as a charging rhino in everything he did. And, what was worse, he was deeply committed to the belief he had a monopoly on truth. He firmly believed there was no place for humor in religion, or any other area of life. He didn't believe in anything he couldn't understand, which meant he didn't believe in much. As for the Bible, he believed it but didn't really understand it. But he thought he did, which made him dangerous in terms of molding the minds of the young. For that matter, anyone who could be molded.

This failure to understand humor didn't mean Baker never smiled. Whenever he saw a platter of fried chicken he would put on a happy face. Banana pudding or any kind of pie made him grin like a Cheshire cat. He was addicted to food and would not leave the table until every morsel was gone. His appetite was legend; something that could not be said about his sermons.

But when it came to ranting and raving there were few that could hold a candle to Baker. His booming voice offset his other deficiencies, like knowing and understanding the Bible. He read the Good Book with a degree of regularity, but did not comprehend its meaning. Had he been able to comprehend its true meaning, he might have been forced to deal with changing some of his so-called religious convictions, all of which were based more on personal preference and opinion than scripture.

Baker liked to claim that he got all his information directly from God, which eliminated the need for a great deal of study and blocked any probing questions from his flock. After all, he had been called by God to preach the Gospel. To attack the calling was viewed as attacking God, which most church members were uncomfortable doing. The pastor counted on such bullying to keep everyone in line. And, for the most part, it worked.

Except when it came to Johnny Tobin.

Johnny's problem, Baker figured, was that he read too much. Doubly troubling to the preacher was what he read. The kid could quote Mark Twain like most people could quote a favorite poem. Baker was pretty sure Johnny had memorized everything Twain had ever written, which he figured was a bad thing. He had never read Twain himself, but from what he had heard the man was not exactly enamored with preachers.

Then, too, the boy also read those pulp books he had been trying to get the drugstore to ban. Had the owner been a Baptist, Baker figured he would have succeeded. But, the guy was a Catholic who, he opined, was hungry for the almighty dollar. Baker figured he'd have the last laugh on the drugstore owner. The way he interpreted his Bible, all Catholics would burn in hell. It would serve them right, too, for all the sinning they did at their Saturday night dances.

Baker was looking forward to a lot of folks burning in hell, including Johnny's parents. Jake and Mary Lou Tobin were known to attend some of those Catholic dances. He had heard they had parties at their house, too, where their guests danced.

What's more, the Tobins didn't give him the respect he deserved. Lack of respect for his calling, the preacher figured, was good enough reason for anyone to go to hell.

As for Johnny, Baker wasn't going to be all that upset if the kid didn't make it to the Pearly Gates. Johnny, he thought, had a real attitude problem. He suspected the kid wasn't really saved, that he had just succumbed to the pressure to be baptized with his friend Bobby Milam.

Of course, the preacher figured no one really knew what was going on in Johnny Tobin's mind. The kid claimed to have read the Bible through and through. Baker didn't believe it because he had never done it, but every time he tried to catch Johnny on a Biblical question the youngster knew the answer. It didn't please the preacher when the Sunday School teachers told him Johnny knew more about the Bible than they did. But they didn't have much opportunity to make such comments because Johnny was rarely in Sunday School. Most Sundays he was fishing or hunting with his dad or Ben Jim Cade.

Or both.

Johnny's friendship with Ben Jim Cade was another thing that bothered Baker. More than once he'd tried to warn the kid about befriending coloreds, but his counsel had fallen on deaf ears. That had made Johnny's friendship with Ben Jim Cade a personal affront. The preacher thought it was like the boy was trying to antagonize him. It never occurred to Baker that Johnny might really want Ben Jim Cade as a friend.

After Johnny left the church building, Baker went to his office to work on Sunday's sermons. But, his mind wouldn't allow him to concentrate on such preparation. It didn't matter, he decided. He'd just give the folks whatever the Lord laid on his heart.

The preacher blamed his lack of concentration on hunger. The cookies and Kool-Aid he'd had with the children had done little more than whet his appetite. It was close to lunchtime and he was craving something substantial. He'd had two eggs over easy, two slabs of ham, a bowl of grits and four biscuits for breakfast. But, the calories from the morning meal were waning. It was time to visit the Walla Cafe.

Baker could have walked to the cafe, but that would not have been in character. So he drove his new Chevrolet, which was his pride and joy. He had owned it for only a couple of months. Black and shiny, it was everything he had ever wanted in an automobile.

Main Street, with most of the townspeople out looking for Sadie Scott, was fairly barren of other vehicles. The preacher had no problem finding a parking spot in front of the cafe. He stepped out of his car, admired it momentarily, and then approached the cafe's screen door. A couple of flies rested on the screen, looking longingly at the eating establishment's interior. Baker chased them away, then stepped inside.

The change from bright sunlight to the dimly lit interior caused the preacher to hesitate. He eyes quickly adjusted and Baker scanned the customers. He was pleased to see Bailey Thompson sitting alone at a table. Thompson, the school principal, was one of his church members, though not one of the better ones. He was not regular in attending Sunday School and never stayed for the worship service, except when there was a visiting preacher.

Piously acknowledging the few other customers in the place, Baker approached Thompson's table. "I see you ain't ate yet, Bailey. Mind if I join you?"

"Glad to have the company, Brother Baker."

The wooden chair creaked under the preacher's weight, but the sound was somewhat cushioned by the squeaking ceiling fan struggling overhead. Baker smiled, anticipating a big plate lunch, a piece of pie, and Thompson picking up the check.

"Looks like you're dressed for the woods, Bailey."

Thompson's brow furrowed. "I've been out since early this morning. . . searching for little Sadie."

"Terrible thing," said Baker, changing to a more serious expression and, at the same time, checking the menu. "I was with Vernon and Marcie this morning. . . praying with them."

"This is killing Marcie," Bailey said. "That little girl is her whole world. I don't know what'll happen to her if Sadie's not okay."

The preacher agreed, then said, "I think Vernon's just as concerned as Marcie." He knew the gossip about Bailey and Marcie. The word was that they had been seeing each other for the past two years. He didn't know whether it was true, but wanted it to be. His psyche told him that if it was true and he could find out for sure, it could possibly give him some leverage over the man.

The waitress interrupted and took their orders. Baker ordered extra gravy on his chicken fried steak, plus a bowl of gravy on the side.

Two

The cafe's kitchen had a counter in the back where the colored cook served Negroes, allowed to enter the establishment by the back door only. When the waitress opened the door separating the dining area from the kitchen the preacher saw Johnny Tobin sitting at the kitchen counter with Ben Jim Cade.

"You ain't gonna believe this," he said, "but Johnny Tobin's eating back there with the niggers."

Thompson laughed. "Johnny Tobin. . . now there's a boy with a mind of his own."

"You approve?"

The principal shrugged his shoulders. "I'm not saying I approve or disapprove. I'm just saying he has a mind of his own."

"Well, I think he's heading for some real trouble. . . spending so much time with a nigger like Ben Jim."

"Maybe. . . or maybe he sees into the future better than most of us."

"What do you mean by that?"

"We're not always gonna be able to keep the Negroes eating in the kitchen."

"That's Yankee talk."

Thompson smiled and shook his head, though not in resignation. "A few years down the road the coloreds will be going to school with us. And, the First Baptist Church is liable to have Negro members."

Baker grunted and said, "Not while I'm pastor."

The principal figured no self respecting Negro would want to be a member of First Baptist Church while Baker was pastor. The Negroes he knew had some depth to their Christianity. He knew the preacher didn't.

"Well, there's no point arguing about it," Thompson said. "It'll either happen or it won't. I get the feeling, though, that the government's gonna make it happen."

"It'll be against every law of God."

"How do you figure that?"

"You don't find cows mixing with goats or dogs mixing with cats, do you? God made us different and He wants us to stay different."

Thompson wanted to say it wasn't exactly the same thing, but decided against it. He had never understood the preacher's logic, or lack of it, which is why he rarely subjected himself to the man's ranting and ravings on Sundays.

"What happens down the road is not as much my concern as what happens now. I'm talkin' about finding little Sadie."

The principal's attempt to change the conversation didn't work. Baker said, "Johnny will say the reason he's back there in the kitchen with Ben Jim Cade is because they're trying to find little Sadie."

"The two of them know the woods around here as well as anybody. Probably better. Course, I don't know why everybody is so convinced she's gonna be found in the woods."

"That's not the point," Baker said. "I'm not talking about them knowing the woods and all that."

"Does it matter who finds Sadie. . . as long as she's found?"

The question stymied the preacher temporarily, which pleased Thompson. "No. . . no, it doesn't matter who finds her. But, I don't think Johnny's all that serious about looking. I think he's playing some kind of game."

"I doubt it. He's a smart kid. Right off, I'd say he's probably about the smartest kid we've got in school. Of course, he pulls some stunts I don't exactly approve of. . . especially during hunting season."

"What kind of stunts."

"Well, last season I warned him about playing hooky to go squirrel hunting, but it went in one ear and out the other. He was absent the first day of squirrel season. And, when I got home from school there was a mess of squirrels on my doorstep."

"What did you do?"

"Cleaned and ate them."

"No. . . I mean about Johnny."

"Well, I gave him a good paddling. So did his dad. But, he'll probably do it again."

"See. . . that's what I'm talking about. Chances are he went hunting with that no good nigger. . . Ben Jim Cade."

"Probably did. But, I can't agree with you about Ben Jim. He's a smart fellow. He's just sometimes misunderstood."

"Smart aleck, you mean."

The waitress brought their food, which distracted the preacher from continuing his verbal tirade. He insisted on saying a quick prayer, making Thompson feel a bit self-conscious. Then the principal marveled at the way in which Baker attacked his lunch, how quickly he devoured it. By the time Bailey was half through with the food on his plate, the preacher was ordering pie. The dessert also disappeared quickly. Then Baker ordered coffee and leaned back in his chair, causing it to groan.

He said, grinning, "That was a mighty fine meal, Bailey. . . what little there was of it."

The principal shook his head in dismay. "You can sure put away the groceries."

"Always been a healthy eater."

Baker's contented mood shifted when the door separating the kitchen and dining area opened and Johnny Tobin came walking up to their table. "How you doing, Mr. Thompson. . . Brother Baker?"

"What are you doing. . . eating back there with the niggers, Johnny?" the preacher asked.

The kid grinned. "If I was being particular, I'd rather sit by one than eat what one cooked. Course, I don't mind doing either. . . cause that old colored woman back there can cook greens almost as good as my mama's."

Thompson knew Johnny's logic went right over Baker's head. He was sure the youngster knew it, too, which made it all the more humorous.

"You been out looking for little Sadie?" the principal asked.

"Not yet. I had some stuff to do first. . . like tracking Ben Jim down. We're gonna check the bottoms behind and to the south of his house."

Baker grunted. "Ben Jim's liable to be more concerned with protecting his own than in finding a little white girl."

Johnny pondered the statement before answering. "Now I asked Ben Jim about that and he told me that no colored had her. He suggested something, though, that I think might be worth looking into."

"What's that?" the preacher asked.

"He thinks maybe the Catholics got her."

Bailey had to struggle to keep from snickering. He knew Johnny was lying, understood how he was playing with Baker's bigotry. But, the preacher didn't catch it. In fact, it was obvious he liked the idea. Baker hated Catholics and Negroes. It was a toss up as to which he hated most. The principal knew the preacher would be satisfied if either group was found responsible for Sadie Scott's disappearance.

"What makes him think it's the Catholics?" Baker asked.

Johnny shrugged. "I don't know. Maybe it's something that just appeared in his mind. You know how some of these colored people are. . . they see visions. Maybe it has to do with voodoo."

Baker snarled. "What it has to do with is the Devil."

"I don't know about that, either. All I know is that Ben Jim has visions about where squirrels and fish will be hiding. That's why we kill so many squirrels and catch so many fish. He sees where they are in his mind."

"That's nonsense," the preacher said. "If he has these visions, why can't he tell us right off where little Sadie is?"

"I asked him about that. Ben Jim's never claimed to have visions about people. . . just about squirrels and fish."

The preacher, grumbling, got up from his chair. "This is ridiculous. I have to go."

Bailey didn't endear himself when he said; "You forgot your check."

The principal left the waitress a tip. The preacher didn't. The two men paid their respective bills and Johnny walked out the door with them. Outside the cafe in the bright sunshine they saw Ben Jim Cade leaning up against Baker's shiny new Chevrolet. The preacher's face turned crimson.

Ben Jim came to an upright position. "How are you, Reverend Baker. . . Mr. Bailey?"

The preacher didn't respond, but the principal said, "I'm fine, Ben Jim. And you?"

"About as well as can be expected. You ready, Johnny?"

"I'm ready, Ben Jim. Let's go find that little girl."

They walked down the street together, the tall black man with stooped shoulders and a defiant look in his eyes. And, the tall for his age white boy with freckles across the bridge of his nose and mischief in his eyes. Bailey watched the two move away and smiled. There was something about the friendship between the Negro man and white boy that made him feel good.

"That's one uppity nigger," Baker said.

"Oh, I don't know about that," Bailey said. "A lot of people think that because he doesn't grovel, but he's never been anything but nice to me."

"The nigger's living with a woman thirty. . . forty years younger than he is."

The principal laughed. "What's that got to do with being uppity?"

Baker didn't have a suitable answer. "I've got to go. But, you mark my word, Bailey. The Tobin boy is gonna get in trouble because of that nigger."

Walking about a quarter mile to the apartment he rented that was over Winston Railey's garage, Bailey had opportunity to ponder the preacher's prophecy. He liked Johnny Tobin, especially his spirit and self-esteem. True, Johnny sometimes prodded his teachers and took them to the limits of their patience. But, he wasn't just rebellious. He was bright and different. He had the smarts to break out of his nowhere existence, to really be somebody.

As for Johnny's friendship with Ben Jim Cade, the principal saw it as more than just another act of rebellion. He'd had enough contact with Ben Jim to know the black man was also bright and rebellious. So the two had something in common.

He figured Ben Jim had been a lot like Johnny when he was the same age. He'd just had the disadvantage of being born black in a white man's world. But, he appreciated the fact that Ben Jim kept his head up and walked with a great deal of pride. It told him the man wasn't going to be a doormat for anybody.

Another thing Bailey appreciated was that Johnny's parents hadn't thwarted his creative rebellion. Of course, he wouldn't have expected anything less from Jake or Mary Lou Tobin.

Jake, he knew, was no saint. He'd been around the horn a few times and had told enough people in town to stick their opinions where the sun didn't shine. He wasn't the most tolerant man around so couldn't expect his son to always adhere to what was socially acceptable in Walla.

As for himself, Bailey had been around enough to know that the socially acceptable in Walla was far different from what it was in other parts of the country. He, like Jake, had been in the Army. He hadn't seen as much action as Jake had, but he'd had a chance to see what was going on in the rest of the country. His eyes had been opened quite a bit.

A native of Louisiana, Bailey had ended up in Walla because there weren't any teaching jobs available in Shreveport, which was his first choice as a place to work. He'd kept his bag packed since moving to the little town of four thousand, but was beginning to settle in. First there was the thing with Marcie Scott. Then he'd been named principal. And, he liked playing third base for the town's semipro baseball team.

It was through baseball that he had come to really know Jake Tobin, who was the team's best pitcher. There were rumors that Jake had been on his way to the Yankees when he up and volunteered for the Army. He'd never substantiated those rumors, had simply told Thompson he volunteered to keep from being drafted into the Navy. "Never liked the idea of bouncing around on a ship in the middle of all that water," Jake had said.

Anyway, a crippling wound had ended any chance Jake had to play in *The Show*, but he still had enough stuff to be one of the best semipro pitchers in Louisiana.

Bailey had also gotten to know Johnny better through baseball. The kid practiced with the men's team. And, no matter the age differences, he asked no quarter and gave none.

Bailey loved the game, but had no illusions about his baseball ability. He looked more like a player than he actually was. He was six feet tall and a muscular two hundred pounds. He had a rifle arm, but was a mediocre hitter and only an adequate fielder.

The walk to his apartment gave Bailey sufficient time to think about Mary Lou Tobin, too. He figured she had a lot to do with Johnny's independent spirit. Like her husband, Mary Lou wouldn't back down to anyone.

It was stifling hot inside the small and neatly furnished apartment. Bailey turned on a fan and stripped down to his underwear. He planned to rest a while, call the Scott residence, and then take up the hunt again if little Sadie hadn't been found.

Three

Ben Jim Cade and Johnny walked down the lane leading to the colored man's house. It was really an old logging road, filled with chug holes and grown up with weeds and briars. But Ben Jim called it *The Lane.* It intersected with the highway leading from Walla to Shreveport. There were a lot of little towns in between, but nobody paid much attention to them. Shreveport was the big city closest to Walla. New Orleans was bigger, of course, but it seemed a lifetime away.

"That preacher man. . . he sure don't like me," Ben Jim said. "Why do you think that is?"

Johnny laughed. "Well, he ain't exactly partial to me, either. Maybe he don't like you because you don't kiss his rear end."

The black man grinned. "Maybe he wants me to call him master. The man thinks he's the Lord God himself."

"Yeah. . . and that's funny. I don't think he knows the Bible all that well. I'm always catching him messing up on certain verses."

"I'm afraid that's why you read the Bible, Johnny. . . so you can catch somebody making a mistake. And that ain't a good reason for reading the Good Book."

"You're probably right, Ben Jim. My reason for reading it ain't what you'd call noble. But, I do believe in God and the Lord Jesus Christ. I believe every word in the Bible is true. I just don't believe everything Brother Baker says is true."

It sometimes bothered Johnny that his Negro friend could see right through him. But, when Ben Jim admonished him, and he did it often, it didn't make him angry. When other people tried it, even his parents, it angered him.

Johnny's mother was the one actually responsible for his relationship with Ben Jim. Mary Lou Tobin worked part time as a cook at the Walla Cafe. It was one of the reasons Johnny felt so comfortable eating in the kitchen with the Negroes. He always ate in the kitchen when his mother was working.

Sally, the dishwasher at the cafe, was Ben Jim's wife. Mary Lou Tobin was always saying, "Sally ain't no bigger than a washing of soap," whatever that meant. Sally was short and thin, no more than five-foot two inches tall. It's doubtful she would have tipped the scales at a hundred pounds. She looked especially small up beside Ben Jim. And, because of the difference in his or her ages, it was easy for someone to think she was his daughter.

Anyway, Mary Lou was talking to Sally one day about how upset Johnny and his dad were that their squirrel dog had died. That's when Sally told her Ben Jim had a fine squirrel dog named Jack, and that he'd probably welcome the chance to hunt somewhere other than the woods around their house. Ben Jim didn't have a car. When he or Sally wanted to go somewhere they had to walk or hitch a ride.

Jake Tobin, of course, wasn't about to ask a colored man to go hunting with him. He didn't dislike colored people, but he accepted the way things were. The prevailing attitude was that coloreds had their place and whites had theirs. Work was a different matter. He worked with Negroes, respected a colored man for the work he did, but that was the end of it.

Johnny didn't suffer from the same social malady, so had been first to invite Ben Jim to go hunting with them. And, to bring his dog.

Three

Jake didn't object to his son's invitation to Ben Jim, because squirrel hunting was actually a lot more important to him than any social issue. Having his new untrained dog hunt with Jack was the quickest way to train him.

While Jake sometimes talked like a racist around other white people, he didn't act the part. The coloreds who made up his crew at the sawmill said he was more than fair. He expected a man to give a full day's work for a full day's pay, but never asked anyone to do anything he wouldn't do himself. In fact, the Negro workers said he was generous to a fault, that he would give them the shirt off his back if they needed it.

Even after Jake's dog got to where it could tree squirrels as well as Jack, the threesome continued to hunt together. They were no longer just hunting companions, they were friends. Ben Jim even started fishing with Jake and Johnny when hunting season was over.

To some extent Jake actually came to feel he owed Ben Jim a debt of gratitude. His time for hunting and fishing was limited by work and he had always worried about Johnny going alone, which he knew was inevitable. But, he didn't worry when his son was with Ben Jim. He had come to trust the colored man completely.

Sally was fond of saying her husband thought of and treated Johnny like his own son. They had one boy, Bobby, who was six years old.

As to Ben Jim's age, he never shared that information with anyone. Just like he never told anyone about his past. He had just shown up in Walla about ten years earlier, bought a little piece of land from one of the timber companies in the area, then built his shack out of scrap lumber. He did some odd jobs around town, but never anything regular. Almost everyone who cared knew he got a small government check every month because he cashed it at Sol Bernstein's store.

Guessers figured Ben Jim was past sixty-five and that Sally was in her twenties. That bothered some, along with the fact that the older man had sired her child.

Sally had been married to a man named Isaac Simpson, who was just a few years older than she was. The younger man, however, was abusive and beat her. He would even do so publicly, but one day made the mistake of beating her in front of Ben Jim.

Though Simpson was heavier and looked much stronger, Ben Jim gave him a good old-fashioned whipping. Then he had offered Sally the opportunity to be his wife and she had accepted. There hadn't been a divorce and she'd never gone through a marriage ritual with Ben Jim. They just had an understanding.

As they continued walking along the lane Johnny asked, "You know the Bible pretty well, don't you, Ben Jim?"

"You know I do. Why are you asking?

"Cause I was trying to get the preacher to tell me what's literal and what ain't. He talks about him having to interpret on the one hand and it being literal on the other. I think it's just what ever is convenient for him."

"What difference does it make? The main thing to believe in is the Lord. . . not worry none about how all the folks down here messing up what He done said."

"Well, Brother Baker just tees me off with his pious attitude. . . like he's the only one who really understands the Bible."

Ben Jim grinned, which was something he didn't do around all that many people. "You're gonna run into lots of people what tees you off. I done learned not to worry about them people. But, as far as the Reverend Baker teeing you off, I figure you tees him off just as much as he tees you off."

Johnny laughed. "You think so? I sure hope so."

The house came into view. It had never been painted. The lumber had turned gray with age and some of the boards were warped. They were working hard against the nails, trying to pull loose from the framing. The tin roof was shiny, except for a few spots of rust. A hog-wire fence surrounded the structure.

As they got closer, Jack came running down the lane to meet them. Ben Jim simply gave him a pat on the head, but Johnny hugged the dog and stroked his coat with genuine affection.

"You're gonna ruin that dog."

"Nah. . . no way."

Jack was black and tan. He was part hound and part of a lot of other kinds of dog. He had a good, friendly disposition until he got on the trail of a squirrel, coon or possum. Then he didn't have time for anybody. He was all business.

Three

"Is Jack gonna go down in the bottoms with us?"

"Best he not go. He'll just start treeing squirrels and we can't be shooting none because it's out of season."

Johnny laughed. "You telling me you ain't never shot a squirrel out of season?"

"No. . . I ain't telling you that. But, this ain't the time to be doing it. . . not with the woods crawling with people looking for that little girl."

"You're gonna carry your shotgun, ain't you?"

"Yeah. . . but that's in case we run into one of them big old boar hogs what would just as soon eat a man as look at him."

They went inside the house, which had a hodgepodge of broken down furniture most people would have taken to the city dump. Johnny figured that's where Ben Jim and Sally had probably gotten most of it. Yet the place was immaculately clean, a testimony to Sally's work ethic. He knew Ben Jim wasn't into scrubbing floors.

The important thing, Johnny figured, was that he felt very comfortable in Ben Jim's house. After all, there wasn't all that much difference between it and where he lived. His folks were poor, too, just not quite as poor as Ben Jim and Sally.

Ben Jim took his single-shot twelve-gauge from a crudely made gun rack above the door, then got some shells from a bureau drawer and stuffed them in a pocket of his faded overalls. They walked outside where, with a rope, the older man leashed Jack to a tree. The dog didn't like that they were going to the bottoms without him and let it be known.

Johnny sympathized. "That's okay, boy. It ain't long until squirrel season."

"I done told you. You're gonna ruin that dog. . . babying him the way you do."

As they walked toward the even greater humidity of the bottoms, the heavy rays of the sun attacking them through the foliage, Johnny said, "I bet we find her."

"Ain't likely."

"Why do you say that?"

"Cause it's true. That little girl. . . I ain't believing she's gonna be found in the deep woods."

"Well, where do you think she's gonna be found?"

"If she's gonna be found around here, it's gonna be in a ditch beside the road. If that little girl is around here they ain't no way she's gonna be alive."

Ben Jim's statement was unsettling to Johnny. He figured little Sadie was dead, too, but what his mind told him and what his heart wanted were two different things. And, where little Sadie was concerned, he wanted his heart to be right.

"Well, we can't just give up hope."

"I ain't giving up no hope. We're looking, ain't we? There's a chance I'm wrong. I want to be wrong."

"Is there something you ain't telling me?"

Ben Jim pondered the question before answering. "I had this dream last night. . . about a little white girl that was taken way. I ain't seen the little girl's face. . . or the face of the one what took her. But, in the dream they put her in a car and drove away."

Johnny shivered, which was amazing given the heat and humidity. Ben Jim's dreams gave him the willies. In the time he'd known the colored man, he'd learned to believe in his dreams. Too often they had been right on target. His friend had often told him of dreams or premonitions that came true. It was like he could see into the future.

Johnny warned, "I wouldn't tell nobody about the dream if I was you. There are people around here who want to blame whatever happened to Sadie on a colored."

"I ain't in the habit of telling everybody about my dreams. I tell you. . . Sally. . . that's about it. And, folks round here could be right. Some bad nigger might've got her."

"You don't believe that, do you?"

"You need to always remember, Johnny. . . bad folks comes in all colors and sizes. There's plenty of bad niggers in the quarters."

"Well, there's some white people around here who want to blame you for everything they don't like. They think you're a smart aleck because you don't Uncle Tom them."

"I leave folks alone. . . figure them to do the same to me."

"It don't always work that way around here. . . not if you're a colored."

"You always been a lot more worried about the way things is than

I am."

They combed the bottoms until dusk, but found no sign of Sadie. And, while they didn't come under attack from a wild boar hog, they did have to kill a couple of rattlesnakes and three cottonmouth moccasins. The snakes in the bottoms got awfully irritable in late summer.

Having had time to think about it, Johnny knew Ben Jim was right. The person, or persons, who took Sadie, if they'd killed her, wouldn't take her some place they couldn't drive. There wouldn't be any reason. If Sadie was dead, the killer, or killers, would dump her in a ditch or bury her in a shallow grave a short distance off a road. Of course, that didn't make things any easier. There were dirt logging roads carved in the woods in every direction.

Jake Tobin arrived home about the same time Johnny did. He reported that no one had found any sign of the missing girl. The rest of the family had already had supper so Johnny and his dad ate the leftovers. Johnny contemplated telling his father about Ben Jim's dream, but decided against it. He figured it wouldn't serve any worthwhile purpose.

FOUR

There were three days of intensive but futile searching for Sadie Scott. Concerned citizens from throughout the parish, plus state law enforcement officers, joined local people in the search. Some of the state's finest trackers and dogs were used in the hunt. They combed the area as if it was tangled hair that had to be made smooth and silky.

Nothing.

Not one clue.

The majority was ready to concede that the little girl, whatever her fate, was not going to be found around Walla. They wanted to believe that she was alive and well, that her abductor had taken her to another city or town.

Of course, the more morbid suggested that she was on the bottom of one of the small area lakes or ponds, some sort of heavy weight holding her down. Or that her body was in the current of a local stream, and that what was left of her would someday be found in a drift.

Even the most optimistic knew the searchers could have missed a shallow grave covered with leaves. Men who knew a lot about tracking had conducted the hunt. The trackers were men who were as comfortable in the woods as in their living rooms. But, there was just too much territory.

The majority had abandoned the search by the fourth day. The diehards continued searching, though, as if failure to find the child was an insult to their manhood. Ben Jim and Johnny were among those who would not quit. So was Jake Tobin, who now had to do his searching before and after work. The lumber company called its employees back to work after the third day.

On Saturday Johnny worked at Bernstein's General Merchandise Store and on Sunday the town's baseball team was scheduled to play Zwolle. There was talk about calling off the game, but after considerable discussion it was decided that to do so wouldn't solve or prove anything. Brother Marvin Baker, of course, was all for canceling the game. He often preached against Sunday baseball. Johnny mentioned to Ben Jim that he couldn't remember Baker ever preaching for something, that he always preached against something.

"How do you know that for sure?" Ben Jim asked. "You ain't at the church every time he preaches."

"Dang it, Ben Jim. . . I just know, that's all. I may not always be sitting in a pew, but I know the man. Besides, you're a fine one to defend him. He treats you like dirt."

"He may think he do. But I ain't paying him no never mind."

"Maybe you ought to. I'd like to kick his rear end."

Ben Jim grinned. "You just let things bother you too much, Johnny. The man not liking me ain't gonna kill me."

"He's supposed to be a man of God."

"What a man's supposed to be and what he is. . . that's two different things."

It bugged Johnny that Ben Jim was just too forgiving. It was strange, too, because most people thought him to be arrogant and uppity. That, he figured, was because Ben Jim didn't grovel. And most white people thought Negroes were supposed to grovel. But, he'd never seen Ben Jim be discourteous to another human being.

Johnny went to the ball game with Bobby Milam, who complained about being drafted into Vacation Bible School. His words fell on unsympathetic ears.

Johnny grumbled, "If you don't want to go. . . don't go."

"That's easy for you to say."

"Sure, it's easy for me to say. I ain't going, am I?"

"Yeah. . . but you lied."

"About what?"

"All that stuff you told Brother Baker about the Lord telling you this and that. . . how He told you to look for Sadie Scott. Lightning's gonna strike you."

Johnny grinned. "How come you think I'm lying about the Lord talking to me. You sure as heck don't tell the preacher he's lying when he talks about the Lord talking to him."

"Course I don't. The Lord's supposed to talk to him cause he's a preacher."

"That's bull. There's stuff in the Bible about how we're all responsible to God. . . stuff about the priesthood of the believer. The Lord would come as close to talking to me as he would to the preacher. You mean He don't talk to you?"

"You're crazy. . . you know that? You're a good example of a little learning being dangerous."

"Maybe. But if the Lord wants to give a test on the Bible, I bet I can make a better score than Brother Baker."

Bobby shook his head in dismay. "It's hanging around that old nigger that's doing it to you. You're getting where you act like him."

If you're saying Ben Jim's influencing me. . . better him than the preacher. He's a whole lot smarter than Brother Baker. . . and a heckuva lot more Christian. And, you don't know how Ben Jim acts. You've never been around him."

"I hear things."

"Like what?"

"How uppity he is. . . how he don't act like no nigger."

"Now that's the stupidest thing I ever heard. How's a nigger supposed to act? Maybe he's acting right and the rest of them are acting wrong. And, who are we to say how a colored is supposed to act?"

Their argument wasn't going anywhere and both knew it. That's why Bobby abruptly changed the subject. "You go fishin' this morning?"

"Yeah. . . I went down to the trestle for a while. Didn't see you there."

"Mama made me go to Sunday School. You catch any?"

"Caught thirty big bream. . . lost a couple of big bass."

"There you go again, claiming some big bass broke off on you. You know good and well there ain't no bass under the trestle."

"I know darn good and well there are. . . and, I'm gonna prove it to you. I'm gonna take some minnows down there one of these days. . . and a bigger hook."

"I ain't believing you caught no thirty big bream, either."

"Believe what you want to. You're just teed off because you had to go to Sunday School."

They argued a bit more, until Bobby finally gave up in disgust. Johnny was satisfied. He'd have argued until doomsday rather than give in.

Johnny believed there was something pure and clean about a Sunday afternoon of baseball, something even God could appreciate. He'd never bought Brother Baker's ranting that the godly should exercise righteous indignation over a game being played on a Sunday afternoon. He figured if Jesus was still physically on earth, Sunday or not, he'd be right in the middle of a baseball game, probably pitching and batting cleanup.

He noted that Father Walter Ingram, the local Catholic priest, was at the game doing some glad-handing. It made him want to join the Catholic Church. He had heard, though, that there was a lot of study a person had to do when converting to Catholicism. There was more to it than just walking down an aisle, saying you believed in Jesus, then being baptized. His public confession of faith at the First Baptist Church had been hard enough. He wasn't prepared to do more. Not now. The nice thing was that since joining, nobody had been bugging him about being a Christian. That was worth a lot.

Bobby, noting the faraway look in Johnny's eyes, asked, "What's on that mind of yours?"

"I was just thinking about maybe becoming a Catholic."

"Now what brought that on?"

Johnny shrugged. "Lots of stuff."

"There's talk that the Catholics may be responsible for little Sadie being missing'."

"Where did you hear something like that?"

"Brother Baker was talking to my dad."

Johnny laughed.

"What's so funny?" Bobby asked.

"Nothing. Nothing at all."

Because of the early French influence in Louisiana, many outsiders figured it was a stronghold for Catholicism. The southern part of the state was, but not the northern half. North Louisiana belonged to the Protestants, more specifically the Baptists.

The baseball field at Walla was owned by, and maintained by, the lumber company. Local merchants provided the uniforms, the name of the provider emblazoned across the back of an individual player's flannel top, part above and part below his number. The letters, numbers and piping on the gray uniforms were maroon. The team name was Bulldogs, though there was nothing on the uniforms to give evidence of such. The town's name was scripted across the front of each top, nothing else. Indeed, the best minds in town couldn't recall anyone in the entire parish ever owning a bulldog, nor could they remember who gave the team its name.

It really didn't matter. The important thing was that the team was a winner, a source of pride for the entire populace. In the summer occasional Saturday afternoon, and always Sunday afternoon, baseball provided an escapism from the mundane that couldn't be found in any other activity.

The team didn't always play in Walla but, fortunately, every little town in the parish fielded a team. So many townspeople attended the road games of their beloved Bulldogs. The trips were short and provided still more escapism from the drab of small town life.

The baseball field in Walla was manicured to perfection, excellent by even minor league standards. The players did most of the work on it. About the only deficiency was the limited seating, though only visitors complained about it. There were bleachers behind the home plate backstop, a tall wire fence that was rusty with age. The hogwire fence around the rest of the playing field was low, no more than four-foot high.

Fans liked the low fence and didn't care about the limited capacity of the stands. They liked to ring the field in their cars, sit in or on the vehicles and watch the game. It was convenient because they could keep a jug of cold lemonade in their car.

Or, some home brew.

Or, a jug of Muscatine wine.

Or, a jar of white lightning'.

Mild drunkenness and baseball went hand-in-hand for some, which, Johnny noted, didn't seem to bother Father Ingram. Johnny had, of course, agitated Brother Baker more than once with questions as to why Jesus had drunk wine. Baker had never satisfactorily answered his questions. He had, as always, just gone off on another tangent.

Tangents were his forte.

As for Johnny's own attitude about alcohol, he hated the stuff more than Baker professed to hate it. He didn't like it that his parents drank. He considered drinking and smoking weaknesses, cowardly support devices. And, he didn't like to think of his parents as needing crutches to face the difficulties of life. He wanted to think of them as being stronger and more morally upright than the parents of his friends were.

Despite some perceptions to the contrary, Johnny was morally upright. He tended to joke about things, even mislead folks a bit, but he believed in absolutes where right and wrong was concerned. So in his mind any type of addiction, such as alcohol or tobacco, was wrong. No one could argue that he was a complicated youngster, one whose abstract mind and way of thinking was difficult to comprehend.

Ben Jim had come to watch the game. He and Alto Jackson had found themselves an unoccupied spot along the left field fence. Alto was a husky colored sawmill hand that worked in Jake Tobin's crew. He looked as broad as he was tall. He only measured about five-foot seven inches, short for a man tipping the scales at better than two hundred pounds. But, he was all muscle, not an ounce of fat on him.

When Johnny decided to go out and talk to Ben Jim and Alto, Bobby chose to stay back by the bleachers. Johnny knew it was because Bobby was afraid his daddy might whip him if he thought he was associating with a couple of Negroes. His daddy was like that. Johnny was glad his father was more lenient.

"What's happening, Ben Jim. . . Alto?"

Ben Jim shrugged. "Ain't nothing happening, Johnny. I'm just here on this hot afternoon hoping to see a good baseball game."

"It's a scorcher, ain't it? Dad tell you that you had to come to the game, Alto?"

Alto kind of semi-laughed, which was what Johnny wanted. The man had a big head and teeth that reminded him of the front grill on a Buick. "Now you know your daddy ain't never made nobody come to the game. I'm here because I likes to see him pitch."

"Don't pay no never mind to Johnny," Ben Jim told the younger man. "He always trying to start something."

Johnny grinned. "You know better than that, Ben Jim. I just happened to notice that Father Ingram was here. . . figured you and me might go over to the Catholic Church and sneak a peek. . . see if they're hiding little Sadie there."

Ben Jim frowned. "Now, Johnny, you done started a bunch of stuff that's liable to rile up the wrong folks. You know good and well that little girl ain't over at no Catholic Church."

Johnny shrugged. "Well, Bobby said his daddy. . . "

"And, that's all because you done went and told that preacher a big tale. You start spreading tales and you're liable to cause some serious harm to folks that don't deserve it."

Johnny figured Ben Jim was right, but it was hard for him to leave well enough alone. He liked to stir things up, just to see how people would react. Otherwise, life in Walla would have been pretty boring.

Make that more boring.

"So you won't help me search the Catholic Church?"

"I sure won't. I ain't messin' with no church."

"I guess I'll get Bobby to go."

"Well, you do that if you're bound and determined, cause I ain't going. And, I'm telling you that you ought to let well enough alone. Now the game's about to start, so you better get back with your own kind. Just enjoy the day. . . stay out of trouble and watch your daddy pitch this game."

Four

Ben Jim's scolding didn't bother Johnny. He wasn't amused by it, of course, but accepted it more graciously than he would have from most people. That's because he had great respect for Ben Jim's counsel, though he didn't always adhere to it. What bothered him was Ben Jim's reference to your own kind. It called attention to the differences between them, differences Johnny preferred to forget.

Johnny passed the time with Ben Jim and Alto a few minutes longer, talking about the possibilities of the game. As he started walking back toward the stands he heard Alto say, "That Johnny. . . he's a mess, ain't he?"

Ben Jim chuckled and replied, "You ain't wrong. . . he's a mess and a half."

Johnny grinned and hurried over to where Bobby was standing. He was greeted with, "Figured you might stay out there with your nigger friends."

"Thought about it, but figured it would be more fun to watch the game with a chucklehead like you."

Bobby frowned. "If you feel that way, you don't have to hang around with me."

Johnny laughed. "Don't get your tail in an uproar. Can't you take a joke?"

"It's hard to tell with you. . . what's a joke and what ain't."

"What's to tell? Let's go over to the concession stand and I'll buy you a snow cone."

Bobby could get over his mental hurt quickly with the aid of a snow cone. Johnny knew it, just like he knew Bobby didn't have a nickel in his pockets. He never did. Johnny, on the other hand, almost always had a few coins. Having money to spend on a friend, as well as himself, was one of the most pleasant perks of working for Sol Bernstein.

The minute granules of ice covered with a syrupy strawberry flavored concoction tasted good beneath the blazing sun. Johnny enlisted Bobby's help in carrying snow cones to his mother, sister and brother, who were sitting in the family's nineteen thirty-eight Ford parked behind the wire fence adjacent to the first base bag.

With the completion of their deliveries it was time for the game to start, so Johnny and Bobby leaned against the front of the car to watch the game and finish their snow cones.

In the first inning Jake Tobin baffled Zwolle's hitters with an assortment of curves, fastballs and knucklers, striking out two of the first three hitters. The third popped to short. As always, Jake exhibited pinpoint control with his curve and fastball. His unpredictable knuckler wasn't always in the strike zone, but darted around it closely enough to frustrate batters into swinging wildly.

From his vantage point Johnny could see Ben Jim and Alto, who were unable to hide their glee when a Zwolle player swung foolishly at the acrobatic white spheroid delivered by Jake's fingernails. The knuckler was, indeed, a pitch to reckon with, not only by a batter but also the catcher. For Johnny it was easy to see that his dad had special stuff on this day, that it was going to be a tough afternoon for Zwolle's hitters.

The game moved into the home half of the seventh with no score. The opposition's pitcher, obviously, was no slouch either. He had scattered seven hits, struck out five, walked none, and had been aided by three doubleplays.

But, his performance paled in comparison to Jake Tobin's.

Johnny's dad had struck out fourteen, walked none, and had allowed no hits. The crowd was buzzing with anticipation at the prospect of a no-hitter, a perfect one at that. While not all the people at the game understood the significance of what was happening, many were knowledgeable baseball fans. One of the most knowledgeable was Father Walter Ingram.

He walked up to the car and said, "Mary Lou. . . looks like Jake's really on top of his game today." Then the priest greeted Johnny, Bobby, Sister and Sonny Boy. Sister was Johnny's eight-year-old sister, whose real name was Louise. Sonny Boy, his brother, was four. His given name was William.

Mary Lou, sitting in the front seat of the Ford with the doors open, beamed with pride. The priest was only one of many who had stopped by to compliment her husband's performance. However, religious sanction, no matter what the source, was appreciated. It was a lead pipe cinch that the Brother Marvin Baker would never have paid such a compliment, even if he could have brought himself to be at a Sunday game.

"I'm kind of surprised Jake's pitching so well," she said. "He ain't worked out any this past week. . . spent all his spare time looking for little Sadie."

Ingram's brow furrowed. "The whole town's in shock about little Sadie. I been out searching with the men all week, too."

Johnny hadn't known about the priest being one of the searchers, but it made him appreciate the man. Ingram had been at the Catholic Church for only a short time, less than a year. Reverend Baker had told anyone who would listen that the old priest had been replaced because he was a drunk. Anyway, from what Johnny had heard Ingram had come to Walla from up North, not New Orleans, which made most of the folks in town suspicious of him.

The priest continued, "This game. . . it's not much comfort to little Sadie's parents, but it's a help to the folks here. None of us are going to forget little Sadie, but the town's been in a state of depression. People have been scared for their kids. . . locking their doors at night. This game. . . what's happening here. . . it's uplifting for the whole town. I know Jake was concerned about even playing with what's happened, but it was the right thing to do. If I don't get to tell him. . . I'd appreciate it if you'd do it for me."

Mary Lou said she would, then Johnny interjected, "We was just wondering where you're from?"

"Johnny. . . " his mother scolded.

Ingram laughed. "I'm from Rhode Island. I'm one of those awful Yankees you've heard about."

Mary Lou said, "Father Ingram. . . I'm sorry. Johnny. . . he's just so nosy."

"To tell you the truth, it's good to have someone ask me about myself. Most of the people around here. . . even the ones who come to the church. . . treat me like I'm from another world."

"They just have respect for priests and preachers," Mary Lou said. "They think they're special."

"It's not me who's special," Ingram said, smiling. "It's who I represent."

Johnny had never before had any contact with the priest, but he liked his manner. He also liked his looks and easy smile. Ingram was, he guessed, in his late thirties. He had a ruddy complexion, was about six-feet tall and had a decent build. He certainly looked more fit than

Brother Baker did, Johnny thought, but that could be said about almost every living thing.

And some that were dead.

"You go to college up in Rhode Island?" Johnny asked.

"No, I went to Notre Dame."

Johnny was impressed. "Yeah? They got a heckuva football. . . "

"Johnny," Mary Lou warned.

Ingram laughed.

"Sorry. Like I was saying, they got a good football team, but I ain't never heard nothing about their baseball."

"It's good," Ingram said. "At least, it's been good since I quit playing."

"You played?"

"Afraid so. But, I wasn't much shakes as a player."

"You ought to be playing for the town team."

Mary Lou said, "Johnny, you got no business telling Father Ingram what he ought to do."

"It's okay," Ingram said. "To tell you the truth, I thought about it. But, I'm not sure how my parishioners would feel about it. Or, my superiors. But, if you boys want to come by some time, we can play a little catch. . . maybe even toss the football around."

Johnny said he would take the priest up on his offer, but Bobby didn't say anything. In fact, he didn't say anything the entire time Father Ingram was at the car. When the priest left, Johnny asked him why.

"Cause my daddy said the Catholics are part of the nigger problem. . . especially them that's from up North."

"According to your daddy everybody is part of the nigger problem. Father Ingram seemed like a pretty good guy to me."

"You think anybody who likes baseball is a good guy."

"That may be carrying things a little far," Johnny said, grinning. "Maybe I just think them that like baseball are smarter than them that don't."

Walla managed a run in its half of the seventh and Jake again shut Zwolle down in the eighth without a hit. He took a one to nothing lead and a perfect no-hitter into the ninth. That's when things fell apart.

Jake struck out the leadoff hitter, but the second batter ricocheted a grounder off the second baseman's glove. It was a routine play, so the infielder was charged with an error. The Walla fans groaned, their anticipation of seeing a perfect no-hitter down the drain. But, a win and a no-hitter were still possible, dangling in front of them like a carrot enticing a hungry rabbit. They shook off their disappointment and shouted encouragement.

The third hitter in the inning struck out, but the fourth guy hit a little grounder to short. The shortstop decided to get the lead runner, but overthrew the second baseman covering. When the dust had cleared runners were at second and third.

With Jake's fielders feeling the pressure of his no-hit effort, the seemingly inevitable happened when the next hitter blooped a single to right-center, breaking up the no-hitter and driving in two runs.

The once festive attitude of the Walla crowd was now one of gloom. Only the elation of Zwolle's players and supporters shattered what would otherwise have been a funeral-like quietness. The Walla fans had come to the game sharing a reserved despondency about their inability to find little Sadie, a remorsefulness that begged for an outlet. For a couple of hours they had been caught up in a flight of fantasy that helped them temporarily forget the events of the past week, but now all illusion had been stripped away.

When Zwolle's next hitter popped out to Bailey Thompson at third, it was like an afterthought. So was the bottom of the ninth. The Walla players and crowd knew the game was already over. They knew they wouldn't tie or win in the bottom half of the inning.

It was over.

FIVE

Sheriff Nick Merrick was feeling the pressure of not being able to find little Sadie Scott. And, he wasn't making life too pleasant for Deputy Billy Burton.

Billy was a good old boy, one whose idea of the good life was a cold bottle of beer in his hand and a few coins in his pocket. He didn't ask much, but then he didn't contribute much, either. He was satisfied being what he was and was totally devoid of ambition.

He did aspire to holding the office of sheriff when Nick Merrick retired, but that was a ways down the road. And, of course, being the parish sheriff didn't require a great deal of ambition. All it required was kissing up to the right folks and following their directives, the primary directive being to keep the colored folks in line.

Billy was expert at that. Every Friday when the blacks at the sawmill got paid he was right there to keep an eye on their activities and to collect fines they owed for drunkenness and what not. The sheriff didn't think he was doing his job if he didn't get at least twenty-five percent of a colored man's salary for the town's coffers. Much of the money never made it to those coffers. It ended up in Merrick's pocket.

Charges against a black man could range from taking up too much space on the sidewalk to what the sheriff perceived to be a discourteous reply to a question. Basically, a colored man had to pay for the privilege of working at the sawmill and living in Walla.

Billy didn't see anything wrong with the system. It was just the way things were and he didn't see any reason for change. He liked a lot of the colored folks, but figured God had a reason for making them black and subservient to white people. In other words, Billy Burton, thirty-five going on adolescence, was neither a mean man nor an overly bright one. He was simply a man who was a product of his environment, one who didn't have the wherewithal upstairs to question the way he was raised.

"Dang it, Billy, we've got to do something'," Sheriff Merrick said in the midst of some well-chosen expletives. "People around here. . . they're gonna think we ain't doing our jobs if we don't find that little girl."

"I don't know what else we can do, Sheriff. We looked everywhere anybody can think to look. . . and folks are still out looking."

Merrick snarled. "I still think the niggers are behind it. I want you to go out and scour niggers quarters. . . scare the living daylights out of somebody. . . but get me something."

Billy whined, "I been out there a half dozen times. Ain't nobody out there knows nothing."

"They know. . . they just ain't telling. So, you get out there and you find something. I hope I ain't gonna have to find me no new deputy."

The sheriff was always threatening Billy's job, most often when he was drunk. That was most of the time since Merrick usually started drinking about mid morning. It was his way of escaping the reality of who he was. Having to be who he was would have been tough on anybody.

"Wouldn't surprise me if that smart aleck nigger Ben Jim Cade wasn't behind the whole mess," Merrick continued. "You find me something on Ben Jim Cade, Billy, and I'll see to it that the town gives you a bonus."

Billy didn't respond because the sheriff didn't expect a reply. When he talked he usually answered all his own questions. He liked an audience, but only one that nodded agreement to everything that he said.

Billy escaped the sheriff's drunken maundering by leaving the office, positioning his muscular six-foot, two-inch frame behind the steering wheel of the black Ford assigned to him and heading for the Negro section of town. He didn't want to make the trip, but knew he had to find someone who would tell him something. Even in his drunken state the sheriff would remember he had sent him on a mission.

Billy had driven a couple of blocks when he saw Johnny Tobin. He pulled over and Johnny walked up to the driver's side of the car.

"Where you headed, Johnny?"

"No where in particular. Just killing some time until the fish start biting, or until I can find somebody to play a little baseball with."

"Bad deal. . . your dad losing that game yesterday. Wasn't his fault, of course."

Johnny shrugged. "Dad says it's just the way the ball bounces. He ain't blaming nobody."

"Wouldn't expect him to. . . not Jake Tobin. He's a man doesn't blame another. . . no matter what."

Johnny didn't want to talk about the game. His dad wasn't mad about it, but he was. His dad had a greater tolerance for stupid plays. "Pretty hot. . . figured you and the sheriff would be holed up in his office. . . dozing and staying close to the fan."

Billy laughed. "That's what he's doing, but he wants me over in nigger quarters trying to find out something about little Sadie."

"Why is he sending you to the quarters?"

"He's bound and determined that a colored man got her. He'd like to blame it on Ben Jim Cade."

"The sheriff's being stupid. Ben Jim ain't never bothered nobody. He sure wouldn't hurt no little girl."

Billy laughed. "You ain't wrong, but he's the boss. I got to do what he says."

"I figure little Sadie's dead, don't you?

"It ain't something I like to think about."

Five

"People around here don't want to think about anything, but sometimes you got to. I figure whoever got her took her out of the parish and killed her. . . liable never to find her body. Killer probably threw her in a swamp somewhere. . . gators probably ate her up."

"You got some kind of imagination."

"Maybe it's imagination. . . maybe it ain't."

"You hear anything, Johnny? I mean. . . heck, a lot of the niggers like you. I figure they might have said something."

"What would they say? They don't know anything about Sadie. Some of the white people from town have been in the quarters causing them grief. . . that's all I know. I ain't figured out why some white people want to blame the coloreds for everything that goes wrong. I guess for the same reason Hitler wanted to blame the Jews."

Billy didn't know a lot about history. In fact, he didn't even know the name of the first President of the United States. But, he liked Johnny and figured the kid knew a little too much history, and often felt compelled to warn him about such knowledge. "I wouldn't be spouting off that kind of stuff to just anybody, Johnny. Folks in the town are pretty uptight right now. They might take what you're saying wrong."

"I don't care how they might take it."

"Now that's the problem with you, Johnny. You just fly off half cocked. What I'm tellin' you is for your own good."

"I know you mean well, Billy. It's just that the people who run this town treat poor folks like trash, especially the coloreds. I mean. . . what can a poor Negro or poor white boy from this town do? He can work at the sawmill or join the Army. It's enough to make you puke."

"I didn't join the Army."

"No. . . you didn't. But maybe you should have."

"They wouldn't take me. . . medical reasons."

It bothered Billy Burton he hadn't served in World War Two, made him feel like a coward. He felt obligated to explain when anyone mentioned the Army, but never bothered to explain the medical reason he hadn't served. Everyone suspected Billy had been turned down for mental reasons, which seemed a bit inconsistent with letting him strap a gun on to enforce the law.

Johnny didn't have anything against Billy, figured he was an all right guy even if he was a bit slow. He knew that in spite of what he was forced to do as a deputy he wasn't cruel and uncaring.

"Billy, you know darn well Ben Jim doesn't have anything to do with little Sadie being missing."

"Oh, I don't think he did, neither. . . but you know the sheriff. He doesn't like Ben Jim. . . thinks he's a smart aleck. He'd like to put Ben Jim under the jailhouse. And, you've got to admit. . . nobody knows nothing about Ben Jim."

"What's to know? He's a colored man who minds his own business. . . who likes to hunt and fish. I don't see where that's a crime."

"I ain't saying it is. But, you need to watch your step, Johnny. The sheriff's looking for something to pin on Ben Jim. . . and, if he finds it even your daddy can't save Ben Jim."

"What's daddy got to do with it."

"The sheriff thinks your daddy likes that old nigger as much as you do. . . cause y'all all hunt and fish together. And, the sheriff's scared of your daddy. Most folks are. . . myself included. But, if he gets the goods on Ben Jim, gets the town to support him, then he ain't gonna be as scared to do something."

They talked a while longer, then Billy said he'd better get on over to the quarters to try to get some information for the sheriff. He left Johnny pondering their conversation, worrying about why the sheriff was so down on Ben Jim. Of course, a lot of people were, which didn't make any sense. The way things were, the attitudes of the townspeople toward any colored who didn't kowtow got Johnny's dander up. There were times he got so angry about things that he stood on the trestle bridge and yelled at the sky.

Johnny walked about a quarter of a mile to the Catholic Church, not really sure why he felt the need to go there. All he really knew was that the brief conversation he'd had with Father Ingram made him want to know the man better. He was standing in front of the church, probably a good fifty yards from its front doors, when the priest came around the left corner of the building and greeted him.

"Oh. . . hey, Father Ingram. I was just killing some time. . . heading down to Bennett Lake."

The priest smiled. "Going swimming?"

"You kidding? Bennett Lake has more big water moccasins in it than fish. I don't cotton to the idea of swimming with snakes."

"I take it you don't like snakes?"

"I didn't know anybody did."

"Well, they're God's creatures, too."

"I always figured God made all the other stuff and the Devil made the snakes."

Ingram laughed. "Why don't you come on in. It's hot out here and I've got some cold lemonade inside."

"I don't want to bother you."

"It's no bother. I'd enjoy the company."

The priest led him back around the front corner of the church to one of its wings. They entered through double doors, turned left down a hallway, and then went right through a doorway into a moderately large room. The walls were adorned with books.

"Dang, you got. . . oh, excuse me Father Ingram. What I was going to say was. . . you got more books than the town library."

"Look around," Ingram said, smiling. "I'll check on the lemonade."

The priest left and Johnny's eyes devoured the book titles. With the cursory examination he determined the majority had nothing to do with religion. There was, in fact, an outstanding collection of fiction. When Ingram returned Johnny expressed his surprise, said that he figured a priest didn't read anything other than the Bible and books about religion.

"Depends on how you look at it," Ingram said. "In my view all these books have religious significance because everything is in some way connected to God."

Johnny's mind pictured Brother Marvin Baker's office, how few books it held, and how those that were there were definitely of a religious nature. Not that he thought Baker even bothered to read those he displayed.

"I see you got all of Mark Twain's stuff."

"Oh, yes. . . I'm a big fan of Mark Twain."

"That kind of surprises me."

"Why?"

"He's kind of irreverent."

Before Ingram could respond a large black woman entered the

room. She was carrying a tray holding a pitcher of lemonade and two glasses filled with ice.

"Hey there, Aunt Bessie," Johnny said. "I didn't know you were working here."

She laughed, showing white teeth that were accentuated by her dark skin. "Didn't expect to see you here neither, Johnny."

"How's old Alto?" Bessie was Alto Jackson's mother.

"He's doing fine. He says he saw you at the ball game. Your mama. . . she all right?"

"She's fine, Aunt Bessie. . . just fine."

"That's good."

After she had waddled out of the room the priest said, "You seem to know Bessie pretty well."

"Yeah. . . real well. She took care of us when mom was having Sonny Boy. Cooked for us. . . did the washing. . . all that kind of stuff. Of course, I could've done it."

"She's a nice lady," Ingram said. "Just started workin' here a month or so ago."

"Aunt Bessie's a hard worker. . . believes in giving a day's work for a day's pay. Good cook, too."

"I can't argue with you there," the priest said while pouring each of them a glass of lemonade. They each savored a taste of the cool liquid, then Ingram said, "I take it you like books, Johnny."

"Some. . . not all."

"You read a lot?"

"Book or two a week. . . sometimes more. Not much else to do round here when the sun goes down."

Ingram laughed. "I'm sure you go to the movies. . . listen to the radio."

"Yeah. . . usually go to the movies on Saturday night after work. Sometimes the whole family goes to the tent movie during the week."

"Movies under a tent? That's new to me."

"Y'all didn't have them up where you're from?"

"Not that I recall."

"It's just here in the summer. Guy comes here and sets up the tent. . . gets sawdust from the sawmill for the floor." Johnny paused and laughed. "I guess it looks like a big tent revival's going on."

The priest smiled. "I haven't been."

"You ought to come. Course they don't show much except westerns. . . Big Boy Williams and Lash Larue. Lash Larue even came to the regular theater last year. Showed me how to use a whip out in the alley behind the picture show."

"I'll try to make it to the tent movie before the summer's over," Ingram said. "But, before I forget. . . if you want to borrow any of my books, you're welcome."

"You're kidding."

"The priest laughed. "Why should I be kidding?"

"These books. . . they're expensive. How do you know I'll give them back?"

Ingram laughed again. "I'm not really too worried. I know where you live. For use of the books, though, I've a favor to ask."

"What is it?"

"Maybe you can teach me a little about fishing."

"Well. . . sure. You got a pole?"

"No, but I figured I could pick up one at Bernstein's."

"That ain't necessary. I cut a whole bunch down in a canebrake about two weeks ago. . . got them dryin' on top of the chicken house. I'll give you the best one I got."

"That's real nice of you."

"You'll have to buy you some line, hooks and sinkers, though. Mr. Bernstein will tell you what you need."

"Good," the priest said. "We're in business then. You borrow any of my books you like. . . and in exchange you teach me to fish."

Johnny stuck out his hand. They shook and he said, "Deal."

They drank the rest of the lemonade and Johnny asked the priest if he would like to start learning to fish that very afternoon, join him underneath the trestle. Ingram declined, said he had other plans, but would let Johnny know when the lessons were to begin.

Moments later he watched as Johnny walked briskly away on the dusty road that led past the church, carrying an armload of books. *What an unusual kid*, he thought.

SIX

Deputy Billy Burton spent a good three hours talking to folks in the quarters. He didn't expect to find out anything, but any report to the sheriff was better than none. He could never predict what kind of mood Nick Merrick was going to be in. It all depended on what he was thinking about when he was drinking.

Merrick's life and disposition was pretty well known to all, which made it all the stranger that he could be elected sheriff election after election. He was a good Democrat, of course, which pretty much precluded any opposition. His platform had never been spelled out, but was understood. He never hesitated to tell his constituents, *I'll keep the niggers in line.*

The sheriff had been born and raised in the parish. His daddy had made a living doing a lot of things, including stealing. The elder Merrick had been, supposedly, a farmer, though he never raised more than a small garden. He also trapped game for the hides and netted fish, in season and out. During Prohibition he had a still. After Prohibition he kept operating it. He sold bootleg whiskey until he died.

Old man Merrick had always figured the law never applied to him, an attitude he passed on to his son. For Nick Merrick, it had been easier to become the law than to abide by it.

Like his daddy, Merrick enjoyed bullying women. He had beaten his wife regularly until she up and left him, which didn't bother him all that much. He didn't have much use for women. To him they were all like the prostitutes who operated in the parish.

The most important thing was that there was also plenty of whiskey available. Good bootleg whiskey. The bootleggers operated openly because they let Merrick share in their profits.

Merrick loved whiskey more than anything other than himself. He was a bona fide alcoholic, but didn't know it. In fact, he prided himself on being able to hold his liquor. He was always bragging about how much he could drink without getting a buzz. The truth was he couldn't hold an ounce without getting that buzz, and the more he drank the more he wanted to drink. Also, the more he drank the more incoherent and unreasonable he became. He was not a pleasant drunk, at least around people over whom he had some control. Around potential voters and people with a little prestige he could be patronizing and lapdog like, but he just wasn't a likable man.

When Billy Burton came back to the office to give his report on what he had learned in the quarters, Merrick was in one of his ugly moods. Though he would never go so far as to fire Billy, fearing he couldn't find anyone else who would so blindly carry out his often-ridiculous wishes, he loved to hammer the deputy with verbal abuse. This time Billy didn't give him a chance. He had some information.

"Isaac Simpson. . . he told me some stuff about Ben Jim Cade that you ought to know."

"Then why don't you tell me, Billy? I ain't no mind reader."

Simpson, the man Sally had been married to before she moved in with Ben Jim, was a low-life who hung around the quarters most of every working day trying to charm the wives of men who were employed at the sawmill. When the five o'clock whistle blew he was long gone. His evenings were spent at a couple of colored barbecue places, trying to entice customers into a dice game. He thought he was a whiz with dice.

"Isaac says Ben Jim came here from Mississippi. . . that he had some trouble over there and had to leave the state."

"That's the big news?" the sheriff said, sarcastically. "Any nigger like Ben Jim Cade is gonna have trouble anywhere he is. Sounds to me like Isaac's just wanting us to lock up Ben Jim cause he whipped him and took Sally away from him."

Billy shrugged, despondently. "Well, I thought. . . "

"Now that's a first. When are you gonna learn, boy, that all niggers lie and steal? And, if they have their druthers, they'll lie about and steal from each other. Fact is, they'd rather lie about and steal from each other than lie about and steal from a white man."

"So what he said ain't worth nothing?"

"I ain't saying it is and I ain't saying it ain't. Maybe I'll look into it if I get the time. I sent you over to nigger quarters to see if you could find out anything about little Sadie. You come back here telling me that maybe Ben Jim Cade got in trouble over in Mississippi, which is why he's here now. You want to tell me what that's got to do with little Sadie being missing?"

"Well. . . "

"Well what?"

Desperate, Billy said, "Well, I thought maybe Ben Jim's trouble might've had something to do with a little girl being missing in Mississippi."

The sheriff liked the possibility, though he wasn't about to tell his deputy. That uppity nigger Ben Jim Cade being in trouble because a child was missing in Mississippi would be too good to be true. It was sure worth checking out. It was something to hope for.

"You sure are reaching, Billy. Something like that ain't likely, is it?"

"Don't guess it is, but figured I ought to tell you what Isaac said. Up to now ain't nobody ever knowed where Ben Jim was from."

"We still don't know," the sheriff said. "At least not for sure. One nigger telling on another. . . now that ain't what I'd call reliable evidence, especially when one's mad at the other cause he took his woman."

Billy asked, "You ever come right out and ask Ben Jim where he's from?"

"No. . . can't say that I have. Never liked to talk to that uppity nigger any more than I had to."

Merrick wasn't lying. Being around Ben Jim always made him nervous, though he wouldn't admit that even to himself. The colored man emitted an intelligence and breeding that subconsciously was both foreign and frightening to him. The way Ben Jim carried himself, the way he really listened when someone else was talking, the way he talked with such assurance, the way his eyes looked right into a white man's without even wavering, all that was enough to cause the sheriff to label him an uppity nigger.

"Well, you got any more use for me?" Billy asked. "Anything else you want me to do?"

"No. . . nothing in particular. Just get out there and sniff around like an old hound dog. . . see what you can come up with."

"What about Ben Jim?"

"What about him? I'll make a few calls over to some people in Mississippi. . . see if they know anything about him. I doubt anything will come of it, though. Isaac. . . he's just blowing smoke. If I find out Isaac's lying, I'm just liable to bring him into the jailhouse and work his black back over with my hose."

Billy laughed. "You ever whip Isaac before?"

"Can't say. Might have. . . when I was drunk. To tell the truth, most all the niggers look alike to me even when I'm not drunk."

Billy wanted to ask, *When has that ever been*? but didn't. He was just grateful Merrick was thinking about jumping on someone else's back other than his.

Even though the sun was unbearably hot when Billy exited the sheriff's office, he felt cooler away from the man's foul breath. Merrick liked garlic and onions as much as he liked booze. The three combined, plus the sheriff's constant belching, could make even a big room seem awfully small.

Billy drove over to Bernstein's store and picked up a couple of cold pops, then drove down as close as possible to the trestle and parked. He took the cold pops and walked down the tracks, then under the trestle. Sure enough, Johnny Tobin was fishing there.

"Figured on finding you here."

"Ain't that hard to find me on a summer day before school starts," Johnny said, smiling. "Might say this is my office."

Billy extended a hand with one of the bottles. "Brought you a cold grape pop. . . figured you could use it."

"Thanks," Johnny said, taking the bottle and then a long swig from it. "It is a bit hot today. Almost too hot for the fish to bite."

"Caught any?"

"Yeah. . . thirty, forty big perch. Had a couple of big bass on, too, but lost them."

The deputy didn't ask to see the fish, just figured Johnny had them staked out on a stringer. "Surprised Bobby ain't fishin' with you."

"He's probably over at the church trying to make points with Brother Baker."

Billy laughed. "You sure ain't much of a fan of Brother Baker's, are you?"

"Can't say that I am. Something fishy about that man."

"Well, if there's something fishy about him you'd know it. . . being as how you know more about fish than anybody else I know."

Billy's teasing statement pleased Johnny. He stuck his pole in the bank and said, "Let's sit a spell. Like I said, fish ain't biting much right now anyway."

They moved up the embankment a bit, away from the water, and stretched out in some short trampled grass. The trestle and trees along the creek kept the place shady, though it couldn't keep the heat and humidity away. Billy sipped his pop, then said, "Hope I don't get covered up with chiggers."

"Ain't likely. To hear Bobby tell it, all the chiggers that was down here got on him."

Billy laughed.

"Chiggers ain't no problem anyway. I guess maybe I've had more chiggers on me than anybody alive, but they can't stand a good washing with lye soap."

"Is that right? Does your mama still make lye soap?"

"Used to, but ain't for a long time. Sally. . . Ben Jim's wife. . . she makes it. Ben Jim always brings us some meat when he kills a hog and when Sally gets around to making soap she brings us some."

"Sally and Ben Jim. . . they ain't married, are they?"

"Far as I'm concerned they are. Colored folks. . . they do things different than we do."

"Law's the same for everybody."

"Now if that ain't a bunch of bull I've never heard it. You know better than that, Billy Burton. Law's never been the same for poor folks and coloreds as for the rich people."

Billy grinned. "Well, it's supposed to be."

"What's supposed to be and what is. . . that's two different things."

"You know Isaac Simpson, don't you?"

"Sure. . . I know that no good nigger."

"How come you call Isaac a nigger and Ben Jim a Negro?"

"Cause they're different. . . that's why."

"They're both black."

"Ben Jim's soul is whiter than yours and mine put together. Isaac's is as black as the darkest night. Besides, what I call people is my business. Far as I'm concerned you're okay, but Sheriff Merrick is the biggest nothing I've ever known. I'd rather be a nigger than be like the sheriff."

Billy laughed again. "Sheriff says you and your folks are nigger lovers."

"I bet he ain't never said it where my daddy could hear it."

"No. . . and he ain't likely to. I hope you ain't going to say nothing cause I shouldn't have told you. It could get my rear in a sling."

"Don't worry, Billy. . . I ain't gonna get you in trouble. I ain't gonna tell daddy cause he might just whip the sheriff and end up in jail."

"Don't it bother you none that somebody calls you a nigger lover?"

Johnny laughed. "No. . . it don't. Now I might get real upset if they called me a sheriff lover."

"Well," Billy said, chuckling, "I can sure as heck understand that."

They shared a good guffaw and Johnny said, "Ain't much danger of the sheriff getting chiggers on him. They couldn't stand the smell."

Billy smiled and then his faced turned grim. "I got a feeling the sheriff is going to get Ben Jim." He then told of the events of the afternoon, what Isaac Simpson had said.

"I don't know if Ben Jim's from Mississippi or not," Johnny said. "Ain't never asked him. I figure he'd tell me if he wanted me to know. But, I can't see as it makes much difference where he's from."

Billy shrugged. "Maybe it don't. I don't have anything against Ben Jim. . . just doing my job. But, you might want to tell him that he'd better watch his step."

"Ben Jim and me. . . we're planning to do some catfishin' tonight. So I'll tell him. Doubt it'll bother him, though. Ben Jim. . . he just takes things as they come. He might decide to whip Isaac's rear again, though."

"I'd pay to see it."

"If Ben Jim decides to do it. . . it'll be free."

SEVEN

With his little girl being missing, most townspeople didn't expect Vernon Scott to start high school football practice on schedule. But, he did. Some people talked about how brave he was, starting practice when Sadie had been missing for such a short time. Others said he was an unfeeling clod, a man with a piece of pigskin for a heart. People were divided about fifty-fifty as to whether what he was doing was right.

Regardless, football practice started that same night Johnny and Ben Jim went catfishing. The coach and the players preferred night practice because it was too hot during the day. But, there were other reasons, too. Several of the better players worked at the sawmill or in the logging woods during the summer. The start of school was still two weeks off and they needed to earn as many paychecks as possible.

School principal Bailey Thompson was grateful for night football practice because it gave him opportunity to see Marcie Scott. A few people knew about it, but since they liked Thompson a lot more than the coach they kept their mouths shut.

The lovers had not been together since Sadie had come up missing. Bailey had gone by the Scotts house a couple of times to pay his respects. Vernon had always been there. Vernon had also been with him on a couple of occasions when the heavy searching for Sadie was going on. The number of people continuing to search had dwindled considerably. Bailey, though, could still be counted among the few.

Marcie usually attempted to sneak into Bailey's apartment, though it was all but impossible for her to go anywhere without being seen. She always carried books and papers in an attempt to create the impression that they were meeting on school business. As to whether she fooled anyone is subject to speculation. A small town does, of course, have more than its share of naive people.

On that first night of football practice, Bailey and Marcie embraced immediately after she entered his apartment. There was passion in their kisses, but there was also something far deeper. Then she began to cry and he tried to console her.

"Why, Bailey, why?" she asked through her tears.

"I don't know, baby. . . I just don't know."

"I can't eat. . . I can't sleep. It's driving me crazy."

"I know. . . I know."

"I keep thinking it has something to do with us."

"Why are you thinking something like that?"

"Maybe God's punishing me for our sin."

He didn't respond immediately. The last thing he wanted to hear was that what they were doing was a sin. He searched for the right words. "I don't claim to know much about God, but from what I do know. . . well, I know He wouldn't be responsible for something like Sadie being gone to punish us. You've got to quit thinking that way, Marcie. What's happened. . . it's not your fault."

"That's easy to say. . . about not thinking about it. But, I can't help the way I think."

Bailey knew he had a problem with the woman he loved, one that wouldn't be easy to solve. They both had a religious upbringing, one that promised punishment for wrongdoing. And when it came to wrongdoing, adultery ranked right up near the top of the list. Among Baptists, it ranked above murder.

Seven

"What we're doing. . . it isn't wrong."

"How can you say that?" she asked, a touch of anger through her tears.

"We love each other."

"I know. . . but is that enough?"

"I think it is," he answered with conviction.

"I'm not so sure."

Bailey wanted to get away from the subject, but knew he had to exercise care in doing it. "Why don't you sit down on the couch. . . let me make us some iced tea. . . and we'll talk."

Her eyes showed appreciation for his gentle approach. He would, of course, readily admit that he was not as noble as she thought. He knew, though, that he really had no other choice.

While getting the tea ready, Bailey could see her through the door that opened into the kitchen. She sat on the couch in a helpless pose, like she was totally at the mercy of forces she could not understand. He guessed she was, though he figured some of the demons torturing her might have been planted in her mind by Brother Marvin Baker.

For some reason his mind went to Johnny Tobin. Picturing the kid, thinking about the way he was always putting the preacher on the defensive, forced the corners of Bailey's mouth to turn up into a wry smile. Such pleasure was short lived because his thoughts quickly went to his guest. The tea was ready.

Back in the living room he handed Marcie a cold, sweating glass. "Just the way you like it. . . two spoons of sugar and a slice of lemon."

"Thank you, Bailey."

They sipped the golden liquid and his eyes devoured the lovely woman who sat beside him. Her eyes were green, like pools he had seen in San Miquel Creek, and the creamy skin of her oval face was accentuated by short-cropped blonde hair that glistened like corn silk. He loved her more than life itself, and hated himself for it.

"I understand Brother Baker's been spending quite a bit of time with you and Vernon."

"Yes. . . he's done his best to comfort us. But nothing he says seems to do much good."

"A lot of people here. . . good people. . . they want to say something to comfort you, too, but don't know what to say."

The tears came back. "I know. There really isn't anything to say. Everybody's been so nice. Everybody's tried so hard to find her. But I don't think I'll ever see her again, Bailey."

He put an arm around her shoulders to comfort her, was disgusted with himself because her tears and vulnerability stirred him. "Don't say that, Marcie. Don't ever give up hope."

"I don't want to. It's just so hard to keep hoping. I just wish I knew for sure. . . knew what had happened to her."

"If there was anything in the world. . . "

"I know, Bailey. No one's looked for her any harder than you have."

"And, I'll keep on looking."

"I know you will."

He kissed her then. He couldn't help it. She responded momentarily, then pulled away.

"Bailey, I hope you. . . "

"Sorry."

"You got nothing to be sorry for. It's me. Right now all I can think about is Sadie."

He sighed. "She's all you should be thinking about. But, that doesn't keep me from loving you and wanting you."

"I love you, too, but. . . "

"No buts. It's okay. I understand."

"You always do."

They talked until about eight-thirty, knowing that was about the time Vernon Scott would end football practice and turn out the field lights. It would be another thirty or forty-five minutes before he left the dressing room to go home.

After Marcie left, Bailey drank some more iced tea and tried to read. It was a good novel, but his mind wouldn't let him comprehend the story. The words on the page became a blur and he finally gave up. He thought about going to bed, but knew he wouldn't be able to sleep. It was too hot and the sound of chirping crickets penetrating the screens on his open windows was maddening.

Bailey knew he was a fairly intelligent man, but where Marcie was concerned all that went out the window. She was different, unusual, a woman whose moods required more interpreting than the hidden meaning of the most difficult poem. He often found himself wondering about a future life with her, whether or not he could afford her. Such thoughts involved not only the financial, but also the mental. Marcie was capable of wreaking havoc with a man's mind. And, probably with his soul, too.

He decided to go for a walk, something he found himself doing with increasing frequency. The walks were inadequate in combating his loneliness, but if he walked fast enough and far enough there was a chance that he would become tired enough to sleep. So he went out the door of his apartment with purpose, striding like a man on a mission.

Brother Marvin Baker, sitting in his shiny black Chevrolet and watching the apartment, saw Bailey leave. He had watched Marcie Scott leave earlier. The preacher, a self-satisfied smirk on his face, put the last piece of a moon pie in his mouth and savored its sweetness. He had eaten six, and had drunk three RC Colas. But nothing was as sweet as having seen Marcie Scott leave Bailey Thompson's apartment. He cranked the car and headed it back toward the parsonage.

EIGHT

There was a stretch of San Miguel Creek; maybe a quarter of a mile long, that Johnny Tobin thought provided the best catfishing in the world. It was where he and his dad often caught huge stringers of blue and channel catfish. The stretch of creek was hard to get to, but well worth the effort. It is where Johnny and Ben Jim planned to fish the night high school football practice began.

Johnny initially figured it would just be the two of them. That was usually the case when they went catfishing during the week. But, Father Walter Ingram had come down to where he was bream fishing beneath the trestle in mid afternoon and said he would like to go. Then Ben Jim showed up with his son, Billy Boy.

It was a good hour before dusk when the four of them started walking down the railroad tracks toward San Miguel Creek. It was a two-mile hike, but seemed longer in the heat. The humidity enveloped the quartet like a shroud.

Eight

To get to the fishing hole it was necessary to walk across a long trestle that stretched across the creek and bottomland adjacent to it. The trestle was probably a good two hundred yards long. Johnny knew the train schedules, knew nothing was scheduled to come down the tracks. But, walking to the other side on the creosote crossties was always a bit nerve racking.

When they arrived at the other side, they swung back underneath the trestle in order to hit a trail that led to the fishing hole. Before reaching the trail they had to jump a washed out ditch.

"Bet there's an old water moccasin in the ditch," Johnny said. "He's always there. But, this time I'm ready for him."

Johnny had brought a frog gig along. It had three sharp prongs and was mounted on the heavy end of a cane pole. He and Ben Jim had talked about doing a little frog giggling.

Sure enough, the snake was there. However, it slithered hurriedly away before Johnny could spear it. "Dang it," he shouted. Then he sheepishly said, "Sorry, Father Ingram."

The priest laughed. "If that's the worst you ever say, I won't complain."

"You're probably going to hear worse from him," Ben Jim said. "You can pretty well count on that."

Johnny grinned. "Now that ain't no way to talk, Ben Jim. You're gonna give Father Ingram the wrong impression of me."

There was a lot to be done before dark. Plenty of poles were already cut and down by the stretch of water where they would be fishing. Johnny planned to make about twenty of them fishable. For that purpose he had brought a board wrapped with the proper length lines, all with hooks and sinkers, that his dad had prepared.

"You know this is new to me," Ingram said. "How do you fish for catfish?"

Johnny replied, "We put a line on a pole, bait it, get the bait right off the bottom and stick the pole in the bank. We're gonna put out about twenty poles up and down this stretch of water, build us a fire, sit back and wait for the fish to bite."

The priest laughed. "Sounds to me like the poles are doin' all the fishing."

Johnny smiled. "Well, it ain't all that hard."

Johnny opened the jar of bait. The priest grabbed his nose and said through his hand, "Phew! What in the world is that?"

"Ain't no tellin' what he done come up with," Ben Jim wrinkled his nose and said. "I thought we was gonna use beef liver."

"We usually do," Johnny said for the priest's benefit, "but I was reading about this bait in a magazine. It's what's used to catch big cats out of the Mississippi River."

"What is it?" Ingram asked.

"It's beef heart covered with asafetida, red cake coloring and oil of anise. Mr. Bernstein gave me the beef heart. . . wants me to bring him a couple of good cats."

Ingram laughed. "You'll excuse me if I don't volunteer to bait a hook."

After the lines were set they had a supper of wieners roasted in the campfire, pork and beans and white bread. Johnny made boiled coffee in an old lard bucket.

"That's the best coffee I've ever had," the priest told Johnny. "But, aren't you and Billy Boy a little young to be drinking coffee?"

"Been drinking it since I was five. . . six years old," Johnny replied.

"Billy Boy. . . he's been having coffee since he was two," Ben Jim said.

"People in this part of the country. . . they start drinking coffee early," Johnny said.

They ran the hooks about thirty minutes after eating. Their flashlights revealed that the first two poles were as still as the hot night. The bait hadn't been touched. But, the business end of the third pole had been pulled down into the water. It was moving with frantic jerks and pulls.

"Looks like a nice one," Johnny said. "You take this one, Father Ingram. We want to break you in right."

The priest grabbed the butt end of the pole and started battling the fish. He soon had a five-pound channel catfish on the bank. Ben Jim took the hook out of the fish's mouth and put it on a stringer.

"Now that was fun," Ingram said.

They checked the rest of the poles and got three more nice catfish. Johnny and Ben Jim insisted that the priest and Billy Boy land the fish. Catching catfish on set poles was not new to them. Besides, catfishing in this manner was a group sport anyway.

Back at the campfire Ingram said, "So that's the way you fish for catfish."

"It's one way," Johnny said. "During the day you can sit by an old drift, hold your pole and fish for them."

"A drift?"

"Yeah, that's where a tree or something has fallen in the water. . . catches all the leaves and stuff floating down the creek and backs it up. It's like where we've got our last pole set. That's a drift just below it. Since the top of the water is all covered up with junk, it's dark underneath. The catfish like it dark."

Ingram questioned, "So you can't catch them during the day unless you fish in a drift?"

"Depends," Johnny said. "I've caught them after a rain when the water was muddy. But, I don't fish for them that much during the day except by a drift, so I can't say for sure. Some people catch them by putting out trotlines, throwlines and all that kind of stuff. Some people even get in the water and grab them."

"I don't think I want to do that," the priest said.

"I've heard that some people have been drowned doing it," Johnny said. "A big old cat clamps down on them and they can't get away."

Ingram asked, "How big do cats get anyway?"

Johnny replied, "I've heard of them weighing a hundred pounds or more. . . even seen pictures. But, I ain't never seen one that big. You ever seen one that big, Ben Jim?"

"Can't say as I have. I've seen cats that weighed fifty pounds and better, but I ain't never seen one that weighed a hundred pounds."

"Those kind of catfish. . . they come out of the river," Johnny said. "There's probably some of those big ones in the Sabine River. But, in this creek I figure there ain't any that will go over thirty pounds. What do you think, Ben Jim?"

"Hard to say about catfish. In some of the deep holes in this creek, there may be one that weighs more than thirty pounds."

For Ingram's benefit Johnny said, "Ben Jim has a feel for fish and game. He has visions about fish, squirrels. . . things like that."

The priest chuckled. "Is that right?"

Ben Jim smiled. "Well, Johnny may not be telling it exactly like it is. I just know the woods and water. . . can usually tell if there's squirrels or fish around."

"So it's not some vision?"

"Don't hardly know what it is," Ben Jim replied. "Sometimes I have dreams or something and they sure enough happen. Sometimes I don't remember a dream until it happens and then I remember dreaming it."

"Deja vu," the priest said.

"What's that?" Ben Jim asked.

"It's the illusion of having previously experienced something that's actually being encountered for the very first time."

Johnny said, "That's happened to me, too."

"It happens to all of us," the priest said. "At least, I think it does."

Johnny pondered the statement then stoked the fire with a stick. "Then Ben Jim has more than what you called it. He ain't one to brag about it, but he really sees in his head things that happened or are about to happen."

"You're talking about psychic phenomenon. It's a spiritual thing. . . something that happens outside of natural or scientific knowledge. Some people do have supernatural powers. . . the ability to see things others can't."

Johnny nodded agreement. "That's Ben Jim."

Ben Jim laughed. "Now Johnny, don't you go telling the Lord's man something that ain't so. He ain't wanting to hear that no colored man sees stuff in his head that only the good Lord knows about."

The priest smiled. "I believe the Lord speaks to us in many ways, including through men like you, Ben Jim. I happen to be one of those people who believe in psychics. There's lots of stuff in the world, including what goes on in the minds of men, that can't be explained."

"I told you, Ben Jim," Johnny said, nodding agreement. "I told you that what you had was a gift that ain't many people got."

Ben Jim frowned. "Maybe so. But, it ain't a good idea for a colored man to go around talking about how he's got some gift that other people don't. Ain't no good can come of it."

Johnny said, "I've been telling Ben Jim that every place ain't like here. Colored folks ain't treated like dirt everywhere."

"Well, I have to say there's too much of it everywhere," the priest said.

"Johnny. . . he's always telling me how much better things is in other places," Ben Jim said. "But, I know folks that went up to Chicago and almost starved to death. I ain't believing there's no Promised Land for a black man this side of the Jordan."

Ingram sighed. "You're right. It's nice to think that there are places where people accept people as people. . . don't discriminate against them. But, there's plenty of prejudice in the North as well as the South."

The mood of the fishermen turned somber. No one said anything for a minute or two. They just stared into the fire and sipped their coffee.

"There was this guy I heard about up in Oklahoma who was grabbing fish in a creek," Johnny said, breaking the silence. "You know, just running his hand down under rocks and stuff grabbing perch, bass and catfish. Well, he grabbed what he thought was a fish, brought it up and it was a big old cottonmouth moccasin. The thing bit him right in the throat. He died on the spot."

Ben Jim shook his head and said, sadly, "Cottonmouths got a mean streak in them. They'll go out of their way to bite something."

"There's a lot of talk about snakes down here," Ingram said. "There must be a lot of them."

"They're everywhere," Johnny said.

"You don't seem to let them keep you from fishing and hunting."

"Ain't no way I'm going to do that. We just learn to watch for them and kill them when we get a chance. There's no telling how many I've killed."

Ben Jim laughed. "Probably not as many as you say you have."

Johnny grinned. "Ben Jim thinks I exaggerate a little."

"Ain't so. I think you exaggerate a lot."

Johnny chuckled and said, "You can smell an old cottonmouth, especially when they get mad."

"Is that right?" Ingram questioned.

"Sure is," Ben Jim replied.

"What do they smell like?"

"Can't rightly say. It ain't like anything you ever smelled before, but you'll just know it when you smell one. You ain't never going to forget it, either."

Johnny grinned and said, "Squirrels got a special smell to them, too. Sometimes Ben Jim and me. . . we find squirrels by smelling them. Most of the time, though, we let Jack do the treeing."

"Jack?" Ingram questioned.

"He's Ben Jim's squirrel dog," Johnny said.

They bantered back and forth for several minutes. The priest was intrigued by the rapport between Johnny and Ben Jim. It was easy to see the two had a special relationship, one of depth and beauty. Their friendship, obviously, had overcome racial, educational and socio-economic barriers. Ingram felt himself in rarefied air that he had not experienced even with colleagues in the seminary.

"Ain't it about time we ran the hooks again?" Ben Jim asked.

"Probably is," Johnny answered. "Maybe we'll have a big old cat on that will drag Father Ingram or Billy Boy into the creek."

Billy Boy's eyes widened. "I ain't letting one pull me in the creek. I'll let go of the pole first."

The three older fishermen laughed, then they all headed down the trail along the creek bank single file, Ben Jim in the lead. Johnny warned Ben Jim to be on the lookout for snakes. The warning caused Ingram to recall camping out with his father and friends when a youth. They had sat around a campfire telling ghost stories. Now he was fishing with a youngster who preferred telling snake stories. Ghosts or snakes, either added an eerie element to nighttime in the woods along a creek.

The catfish, obviously, had dined about the same time as the fishermen. The line on the first pole was being tugged on frantically by something beneath the surface of the water. Ingram was called on to land the fish, which he did. It was a channel cat that went a good three pounds.

About every other set pole yielded a fish, all of which were landed by the priest or Billy Boy. Everyone was having a good time until they came to the last pole, which was by the drift.

As they approached the pole, Ben Jim's flashlight picked up its movement. The end of the pole had been pulled down into the water, indicating a good fish. The bank was steep, so it was decided that Ingram, not Billy Boy, would be responsible for putting the big cat on the bank. He had no trouble landing the fish, though it put up a good tussle. Ben Jim estimated that it weighed eight to ten pounds.

Johnny was feeling good because they already had a heavy load of fish to transport back to town. He had been worried that the fish wouldn't be biting and that Father Ingram would not have a good time. But, everything was going even better than he had hoped.

For some reason he started running the beam of the flashlight across the drift while Ben Jim was again setting the pole. What he saw made the hot, muggy night disappear. He was suddenly blanketed with a cold chill. An unrecognizable cry escaped his throat, which startled his companions. But, then their eyes followed the beam of his light and Ingram cried out, his voice cracking with emotion, "Oh, my God."

Johnny was shaking so badly he couldn't keep the light steady, but the beam clearly revealed a little hand sticking up through the drift. Billy Boy started crying, which was all it took to get Johnny started. Ingram and Ben Jim couldn't fight back the tears either. Ben Jim took Billy Boy in his arms and tried to comfort him.

For a few moments they were all mesmerized by their grim discovery. Then Ben Jim choked out the words, "Somebody's got to go to town and tell the sheriff. You watch out for Billy Boy and Johnny, Father Ingram, and I'll go."

Johnny fighting to regain both his breath and composure said, "No, y'all stay here, Ben Jim. I'm the fastest. I'll go."

Ingram started to argue. "I don't think. . . "

"Johnny's right," Ben Jim said. "He's the fastest. . . and he ain't afraid."

Johnny knew Ben Jim was trying to bolster his confidence. The truth was that fear had made his legs rubbery. He was actually more afraid than he had ever been in his entire life. "Y'all wait by the campfire," he said. "I'll be back with help as fast as I can."

Flashlight in hand, Johnny started running along the trail that led past the campfire and to the trestle. Normally, fear of snakes would have caused him to walk the trail carefully. But, not now. He didn't even need the flashlight. He was soon past the campfire and jumping the ditch where the old water moccasin liked to stretch out. Then he was on the trestle, his feet finding the crossties like they were old friends. He didn't miss a beat.

The heat and humidity fought his lungs, tried to suck up his breath like a vacuum. But, he moved with such swiftness that it as though his feet never touched the ground. And, his heart raced in rhythm with his feet.

By the time he reached town his clothes were soaked in sweat and his legs felt as if they were dragging heavy chains, but there was no quit in his stride.

His first stop was not the sheriff's house. Jake and Mary Lou Tobin were awakened by their son, who tearfully spilled out his discovery. Jake got dressed and Mary Lou tried to comfort Johnny.

Johnny insisted on accompanying his father to the sheriff's house. Because of the circumstances, Jake didn't argue. Merrick came to the door, but was in a drunken stupor. It was obvious that he would be useless. So they went to the homes of Billy Burton and Police Chief Roger Crossland and rousted them from their beds.

"You think we ought to get Vernon Scott?" Crossland asked.

"No I don't," Jake replied. "I think we ought to get Bailey Thompson and the undertaker. And, we'll get a few men who work at the sawmill. Ain't no point in Vernon or Marcie seeing their little girl in this condition."

"I reckon you're right."

"Son, you go on home and go to bed, "Jake told Johnny.

"I've got to go back," Johnny said, defiantly.

Jake shrugged his shoulders. "I guess you got the right since it was you who found her."

Ruley Gaspard, who owned the funeral parlor, said he wasn't up to walking the tracks and crossing the trestle. "I'm too old for that kind of thing," he said.

Johnny's perception of Gaspard was that he was fat, greasy and pig-like, that he could have passed for the sheriff's brother.

"I've got a tarp you can put her in. . . and an old stretcher you can haul her on," Gaspard said. "Be careful with the body, though. It's probably decomposed quite a bit as hot as it has been. Turtles and fish probably been eating on her, too. If you've got a good seine, that may be the best thing to get her out of the water with. A tarp will catch too much water."

The way Gaspard talked, Johnny thought, little Sadie was not a person. She was just a thing.

Johnny and Jake Tobin led the men down the tracks. Several cursed the heat. All were nervous about how they were going to handle their emotions in front of each other. Bailey Thompson, however, didn't seem worried about appearances. From the moment he was told of the discovery, he had been tearful. He didn't say anything, just walked with a deliberate gait.

Billy Burton said to Johnny, "Well, you told me you and Ben Jim would come closer to finding her than anybody else."

"Ain't no pleasure in being right," Johnny said. "Not like this."

"I know there ain't," Billy said.

They crossed the trestle and went down on the other side. The beam of Johnny's flashlight picked up the old water moccasin in the ditch, but the snake slithered quickly out of sight as the men started jumping across the depression. They greeted Ingram, Ben Jim and Billy Boy at the campfire, then silently made their way single file along the trail that led to the drift.

The little hand reaching up through the drift still sent a chill down Johnny's spine, but this time he was more prepared. His knees were still weak, but there were no tears.

"How are we gonna handle this?" Crossland asked Jake. "How deep do you figure the water is?"

"Water's no more than five- or six-feet deep," Jake said. "I'll go in and get her."

His volunteering caused a collective silent sigh of relief. But, then he said, "I might need some help."

Billy said, "I'll help, Jake. You want to take the seine out in case. . ."

"Yeah, we'd better."

I'll help, too," Bailey Thompson said.

The deputy and school principal followed Jake into the water. Then they began working their way through the drift to where the little hand was sticking up.

Before discovering the hand, Johnny and his companions had, earlier in the evening, discussed an unusual odor near the last set pole. They attributed the smell to a dead animal. And, of course, Ben Jim and Ingram had kidded Johnny about the bait he had prepared for catfishing. Now knowing what the sickly odor was, it was all that Johnny could do to keep from vomiting. He wondered how his father, Billy and Bailey Thompson could keep from throwing up.

Jake, the beams of a half-dozen flashlights on him, reached the little hand. His hand felt the flesh beneath the surface. "It's bad," he said. "Real bad."

Johnny had to quit watching what was happening in the water, but didn't want anyone to know he didn't have the stomach for it. He had been raised to believe that even at a young age a male child had to be manly, which equated to not showing tearful emotion no matter what the circumstances. He had mentally cursed himself for crying early on.

Ingram put an arm around him and squeezed his shoulder. He knew the priest understood, appreciated the reassurance and was grateful for his presence.

Finally, after what seemed an eternity, Jake's voice and those of others mumbling in the darkness caused Johnny to know that the body was in the seine. Moments later his father, Billy and Bailey Thompson had the body on the creek bank. That's when he heard the police chief swear and say, "That ain't little Sadie. It's a little nigger boy."

NINE

Jake Tobin and Bailey Thompson manned the stretcher on which the small body was carried to Gaspard's Funeral Home. It was at the entry of the white building where an explosion of emotion occurred.

"I ain't taking in no dead nigger kid," Ruley Gaspard said. "Find some other place to put him."

Jake didn't say a word. His fist caught Gaspard in the nose with all the force he could muster. There was a sickening sound as the undertaker's nose flattened and blood spurted. The man's big belly shook, his knees buckled and his eyes turned glassy.

Billy Burton, Ingram, Thompson, Ben Jim, Billy Boy and Johnny witnessed the punch. The other men, including the police chief, had gone home.

Billy, shocked as the others were by the suddenness of Jake's punch, cleared his throat and said, "It's a shame about old Ruley walking into a door like that. He probably won't remember it that way, but

I sure ain't seen nothing."

Even though the body of the child was in the process of decomposing, Ben Jim identified the little boy as belonging to Vernell and Clarice Williams, who lived several miles up the creek. Crossland, when told, said it was out of his jurisdiction, that it was up to the sheriff to investigate the matter. Strangely, the little boy had not been reported missing.

They put the body in the icehouse. Billy said he figured the boy's parents would want the colored funeral home in Zwolle to pick it up. The deputy shook his head in resignation and said, "I can't figure out why his folks ain't come in and told us about him being missing."

Ben Jim said, soberly, "Unless they're the ones who killed him."

His statement shocked the others. Billy said, I ain't thought about that. "I guess I'd better get the sheriff and go out there."

Jake grumbled, "Good luck. He's drunk as a skunk."

"That ain't exactly surprising," Billy said. "Well, I guess I can go out there by myself. . . unless you'll go with me, Ben Jim."

"If we can drop Billy Boy off at the house, I'll go with you," Ben Jim said.

"That's no problem."

"Maybe I'd better go, too," Ingram said.

"Me, too," Johnny said.

Jake grunted. "You ain't going nowhere but to bed."

So Ben Jim and Father Ingram accompanied Billy to the Williamses house. Their approach was down a winding dirt road filled with chug-holes. Billy's car dragged in a couple of places. By the time the gray structure was in sight the light of day was filtering through the trees.

"Something bad here," Ben Jim said.

"Why do you say that?" Billy asked.

"Just a feeling I got."

Before getting out of the car Billy unsnapped the strap on his holster that kept his gun secure. His right hand was on the grip of the gun. "That smell," he said, "it's like. . . "

Ben Jim nodded. "Something's dead all right."

The stench was awful, filling their nostrils with an odor that defied description. In Ingram's mind it was the smell of Hell.

Nine

Buzzards picking at a carcass were frightened by their presence. The winged flight of the scavengers up through the trees provided an ominous sound to the otherwise dead-like silence. Vernell Williams' body was face down a little south of the small front porch. The big birds had torn the clothing from his back and feasted on pulpy flesh, exposing bones. Ingram lost it, vomiting and retching. Billy followed suit.

Regaining his composure, the priest performed a ritual over the body that neither Ben Jim nor Billy understood. They had seen him do the same thing over the child's body.

The three men entered the house, each dreading what they were sure would be a grim discovery. Even before opening the door they heard the buzzing sound of thousands of flies. And, the odor intensified.

The bodies of two children were in the front room in pools of blood that had dried. They were covered with flies. The body of the mother was found in the bedroom, her eyes open wide and a huge hole beneath her breasts.

Billy swatted the flies away from his face and muttered, "Shotgun." He and Ben Jim then went back outside, leaving the priest in the house. "What do you think?" he asked.

"Don't rightly know," Ben Jim replied.

"How well do you know these people?"

"Seen them in town some. The mama. . . she was a fine looking woman."

"That all the kids they had?"

"Far as I know."

"What's going on around here, Ben Jim? Little Sadie comes up missing. . . and now this. We ain't never had this kind of stuff around here before."

Ben Jim shook his head in resignation. "Ain't no accounting for the meanness going on."

Ingram came out of the house, his face ashen, and asked, "What do we do now?"

Billy shrugged. "Ain't nothing to do but get the colored undertaker from Zwolle out here."

"Aren't you going to get somebody out here to take pictures. . .

look for clues and stuff like that."

"Oh, yeah. . . that's probably a good idea. I ain't ever come up on something like this before, Father Ingram, so I ain't got a real good handle on things. I figure the sheriff will want to look around a bit."

When they got back to town Billy dropped the priest off at the Catholic Church, then said to Ben Jim, "The sheriff will probably be at the cafe by now. He may want to talk to you."

"Ain't nothing I can say."

"Yeah. . . I know. But, you knowing Vernell and Clarice. . . well, he might want to ask you some questions about them."

"I don't know nothing about them."

"Well, Ben Jim, would you mind just going to the cafe in case he wants to talk to you. I'll buy you a cup of coffee. . . breakfast if you want it."

Ben Jim grinned. "The sheriff ain't going to like you buying me no breakfast or no cup of coffee."

"It ever occur to you that I don't care what he likes and don't like." When the sheriff wasn't around Billy could talk bravely.

When they got to the cafe and parked, Ben Jim went to the back door and Billy walked in the front. The place was buzzing with talk of the events of the night and the sheriff, as was his custom, was holding court at his usual table. Billy was besieged by questions as he made his way toward the sheriff's table, but didn't acknowledge them. His stride was that of a man on a mission.

With what could have passed for either a snarl or smile, the sheriff said, "It's about time you got here. Find anything?"

Roger Crossland was at the sheriff's table with four other men. They were all smoking and there was a sort of bluish haze hovering above and around the table that wasn't being pushed away by the movement of the creaking ceiling fan. Billy cleared his throat and said, "Whole family's dead. . . worse thing I've ever seen. Buzzards was eating on the man and flies were blowing the woman and kids."

The chatter in the cafe died. There was an eerie silence for a few seconds before Merrick uttered a few expletives and said, "I figured the kid just drowned and his folks were scared to tell us about it."

"Murder," Billy said, his voice quavering. "They was all murdered. Been a long time since there was a murder in the parish."

Nine

The sheriff laughed. "Don't get all choked up, Billy. It ain't like they was white."

His matter-of-fact statement bothered even some of the avowed racists who were listening. They shuffled uneasily and murmured to each other, words that were indiscernible to the sheriff and his cohorts.

Crossland asked, "What's it been. . . four. . . five years since Ready James killed his old lady with an ax?"

Merrick chuckled again. "At least that long. I was hoping the niggers would do a better job of killing each other off by now."

Those at the sheriff's table laughed. A few others nervously joined them.

"I figured you'd want to go out and take a look," Billy said. "I left everything like it was."

"You did good, Billy," the sheriff said. "And, I guess I'd better go out there and look around. But, I ain't going until I get some breakfast and have a few more cups of coffee. From what you tell me. . . ain't anybody going nowhere. Besides, I don't like looking at dead niggers on an empty stomach."

Merrick was never more obnoxious than when trying to be funny. Still, he could always count on a few people to chuckle at what passed for his sense of humor, especially when it was derogatory toward Negroes.

Billy said, sheepishly, "I figured you might want to talk to Ben Jim Cade."

The sheriff frowned. "Now why would I want to talk to that old nigger?"

He knew Vernell and Clarice Williams."

Merrick uttered an expletive and said, "Everybody knew them. Leastwise, they seen him around here enough times."

"Well, Ben Jim's in the kitchen if you want to talk to him. He went out to the house with me. . . him and Father Ingram."

Merrick grunted. "Don't know why you'd take some nigger out there with you. By the way, Ruley Gaspard got me out of bed this morning wanting to swear out a complaint against Jake Tobin. . . says Jake broke his nose and you saw it happen."

"I ain't seen him do nothing. Ruley probably slipped and banged his nose on the door. Father Ingram and Bailey Thompson was with me over at Ruley's place."

The sheriff, who had no desire to confront Jake Tobin, grinned. "Well, Ruley's been known to drink a little too much. His nose looks as if it was run over by a truck. . . and he can't hardly see because his face is so swoll up his eyes is about closed."

Billy managed a half-hearted smile. "Well, I wish he wouldn't try to drag me into some beef he's got with Jake."

The sheriff grunted. "He said Jake was mad because he wouldn't put the nigger kid in his funeral home."

"Yeah. . . Jake was mad. So was I. Didn't seem right."

"Well, it was right. And, you ain't got no reason to be mad."

"Can't see as there would be any harm in it."

"That's the trouble with you, Billy. You don't think. You start sticking a nigger corpse in a white funeral home and they're going to start taking over everything."

Billy didn't understand the sheriff's logic, but Crossland laughed and said, "The dead ones ain't going to start taking over nothing, Nick."

Merrick chuckled. "That's a good point, Roger, but you know what I mean. I ain't sure Billy ever will. And, I ain't just thrilled about the kid's body being stuck in the icehouse. I'm probably going to be drinking warm water and tea for quite a while. Now, Billy, I want you to call that nigger funeral home over in Zwolle and have them come get the body right away. The niggers need to take care of their own."

"I'll call them before we go out to the Williams' place," Billy said.

Billy hadn't had any sleep and was dead tired, but the sheriff piddled around for a good hour drinking coffee and smoking with Crossland and some of the good old boys. He was thoroughly enjoying the murders because the bizarre butchery had given him a chance to pontificate, something he often did with limited or no knowledge of a subject.

The deputy paid for Ben Jim's breakfast and made his way back to the kitchen to tell him he wouldn't be needed. Ben Jim shrugged his shoulders and said, "I figured he wouldn't be needing something from me."

The words had barely escaped his mouth when Johnny came in the back door and asked, "What did y'all find."

Nine

"They was all dead. . . murdered," Billy replied.

Johnny's mouth flew open in surprise. "How?"

"Shotgun," the deputy said. "It ain't pretty, Johnny. Just be glad you wasn't there."

"Y'all already brought them in?"

"No. . . the sheriff ain't been out there yet. He is going as soon as he quits talking. Who knows when that will be."

"Are you going back?" Johnny asked.

"If you're asking me, I ain't," Ben Jim said.

"I've got to go," Billy said.

"How about letting me go with you?"

"It ain't something you want to see, Johnny."

Ben Jim agreed, but Johnny was adamant. "Dang it, I do want to see. You guys treat me like I'm just a little kid."

"You are," Ben Jim said.

Billy shook his head in resignation. "It ain't like that at all, Johnny. Besides, your daddy might just whip my rear end if I took you to see a bunch of dead people for no good reason."

"I ain't gonna tell him."

"Somebody would. It ain't like you can do something in this town without everybody knowing."

Johnny grumbled, "If people around here do so much all-fired talking, how come nobody has said anything about where little Sadie is?"

"That's different?"

"How's it different?" Johnny asked. He knew it was and also knew there wasn't much point in pressing Billy to take him to the murder site. Still, his curiosity was at a boiling point. "Guess y'all are going to call the colored funeral home over in Zwolle to pick up the bodies, huh?"

"That's what the sheriff told me to do."

"When is he going out there?"

"Soon as he gets his belly full of coffee, I guess," Billy said, sarcastically. He's just sitting in there bragging to his cronies. . . guys who would. . . Oh, well, never mind."

Johnny laughed, but not with amusement. "I told you he was a big nothing."

Ben Jim said, "Now don't you go messing with the sheriff, Johnny. Ain't no point in your talking about him at all."

"I'm just expressing my opinion."

"I know," Ben Jim said, smiling. "And, everybody's got one."

Johnny grinned. "Yeah, and that ain't all everybody's got one of."

"Now what are you two talking about?" Billy asked.

"Nothing, Billy," Johnny replied. "Are you going to ride out to the Williams place with the sheriff?"

"I hope not," the deputy said. "To tell you the truth, Johnny, I don't want to go back. I don't want to ever see anything like that again. It was a lot worse than fishing that little kid out of the creek."

Johnny's eyes clouded at the reminder, but his imagination was running rampant. Ben Jim knew how his young friend's mind worked, so he warned, "Don't you even be thinking about going out to the Williams' place. You go down to the creek and do some fishing and stay out of the sheriff's way."

"I ain't gonna get in his way."

"Then you ain't going out to the Williams' place, are you?"

Johnny didn't answer, but Ben Jim knew that what had happened at the Williams' place was drawing him like a magnet. And, he knew there wasn't anything he could do about it.

TEN

The sheriff took a swig from his ever-present bottle of whiskey and goosed the accelerator of the big Ford he was driving. Roger Crossland was in the front seat and Ozzie Guidry and Mouse Malone were in the back. Ozzie and Mouse, two of the sheriff's drinking buddies, had asked if they could go "see the dead niggers."

Mouse, a scrawny, wiry man in his forties, owned a service station. Ozzie, who had a weak chin, bug eyes and a long nose, was a barber. Both spent more time drinking with the sheriff than working.

Billy Burton followed the quartet in his own car. He was not as anxious to get to the site of the murders as those in the lead car. He was hoping he wouldn't puke again. He figured that if he did the others would ridicule him.

While the five men were en route to the scene of the murders, Johnny was having a conversation with Bobby Milam. He had caught Bobby leaving his house en route to Vacation Bible School. Johnny asked, "Why don't you skip today and let's go for a bike ride?"

"Where to?"

"Oh, I don't know. . . just out in the country."

"You're wanting to go out there where those people were murdered. Ain't it enough that you found that little nigger boy in the creek last night?"

"There's probably never going to be anything like this happen here again. Are you saying you wouldn't like to see it?"

"I ain't interested in seeing no dead people."

"I ain't either. I just figure we might go out there and find a clue or something."

"The sheriff don't need our help finding clues."

"The man wouldn't know a clue if it fell on him."

"And you would?"

"Dang right. We both will. We ain't stupid like the sheriff."

The statement pleased Bobby. He would never tell his friend, but he knew Johnny was smart. And, he appreciated being put in the same category. "I ain't never seen no dead people except at a funeral," he said.

"We ain't going out there to look at dead people," Johnny said. "We're going out there to look for clues. Chances are that they'll have moved the dead people before we get there."

"Well, I don't know. I don't think. . . "

"You're a baby. I'll bet you still sleep with your mama."

Bobby's face flushed crimson. "Don't neither. And, I was considering going. Everything's a test with you, ain't it? Everybody's got to do what you want or they ain't worth nothing."

"I ain't saying you ain't worth nothing. I'm just saying you're a sissy."

"Well, say all you want. I ain't no more scared than you are."

"Well, I'm going whether you go or not. Does that sound like I'm scared? I know you wouldn't go out there by yourself."

Johnny usually got the best of Bobby in an argument and this time was no exception. Bobby angrily agreed to go along, but his heart wasn't in it. Johnny wasn't all that sure they should be going, but his curiosity always overwhelmed good judgment.

Finding the little boy's body in the drift had been a nightmare that hadn't gone away when he went to bed. He hadn't been able to sleep. He had been replaying the discovery over and over in his mind. And, he hated the fear that he had experienced. He thought the only way to combat the fear was to face something that was possibly worse. He was too tired to think clearly.

Bobby told his mother he was going bike riding with Johnny and she said, "Now don't you be late for Vacation Bible School."

"I won't, mom." Then he turned to Johnny and said, "See what you done made me do. I lied to my mama and daddy is probably going to give me a good whipping."

Johnny laughed. "I ain't never had a *good* whipping. It'll be worth it, though. You just wait and see. And, I'd rather get a whipping everyday than go to Vacation Bible School."

"My daddy must whip harder than yours does."

"Ain't no way. My daddy swings the meanest belt in town. But, I can take it."

Johnny had an old Western Flyer bicycle. Bobby had a newer model. They mounted up and headed out the gravel road that would eventually lead them to the cutoff to the Williams' farm. It would be a long, hot ride, up and down hilly terrain.

In the meantime, Sheriff Merrick had arrived at the Williams place. He braked his car to a stop and turned off the engine. The heat was oppressive, the smell worse.

For all his talk, Merrick had never before encountered death the way he was going to see and smell it. Neither had the others in the car. They had all been able to avoid the war.

As the sheriff had so aptly put it to his companions while en route to the site, his comments spiced with expletives, he could care less about a bunch of dead niggers. But, when he saw Vernell Williams' body, he puked up his guts. Crossland, Ozzie and Mouse followed suit.

This time Billy Burton only retched. He had lost everything earlier. Despite the discomfort caused by his retching, he thoroughly enjoyed what happened to the sheriff and his cronies.

ELEVEN

Johnny and Bobby were topping the crest of a hill when the sheriff's car came speeding past them en route to town. Billy Burton was close behind, but screeched to a stop when he saw the boys. He got out of his car and leaned against the door. Johnny and Bobby brought their bikes to a halt and dismounted.

Muttering an expletive, he said, "What are you two doing out here? As if I didn't know."

Johnny grinned. "Can't a couple of guys ride their bikes without being hassled by the law?"

"You're going to think hassled. I'm telling you, Johnny. . . where you're heading, it's not something you want to see."

A chill ran down Bobby's spine. "You mean the bodies are still there?"

"Of course they are. Where did you think they'd be?"

Bobby looked at Johnny and said, "You told me the nigger

funeral home was going to pick them up."

Johnny shrugged. "They are. . . ain't they, Billy?"

"It's gonna be a while before they get there. The sheriff had to go out and see if he could find some clues before anybody started messing with the bodies."

"He find anything?" Johnny asked.

Billy grinned. "No. . . but he lost something."

"What are you talking about?"

"He puked up about a week's worth of whiskey."

Bobby was pale and silent, but Johnny said, "I'd like to have seen that. But, I can't believe he didn't find anything."

"He didn't stay long enough to look. When he and his bunch got through puking, they were ready to leave. They didn't even go into the house."

The news pleased Johnny. He figured it would be easier to find a clue since the sheriff hadn't messed things up. "Why were Ozzie and Mouse out there with the sheriff?"

"They got as much business there as you do," Billy said.

Johnny grinned. "Can't argue with you there."

"I ain't going," Bobby said. "Not if the bodies are still there."

"Now you're talking sense," the deputy said. "You boys go down there and you ain't going to be able to sleep for a month of Sundays. I ain't had no sleep last night but I couldn't sleep now if I wanted to."

Billy's warning was a challenge to Johnny. "I ain't worried about losing no sleep. Somebody needs to find out who killed those folks."

The deputy muttered, "And, you think you might just be the one to do it, huh?"

Johnny asked, sarcastically, "Is the sheriff going to do anything?"

"Ain't likely. You know how he feels about niggers. He just figures, good riddance."

"How do you feel?"

"Ain't nobody ought to be killed that way. Ain't nobody got a right to take somebody else's life, no matter what color they are."

Johnny was glad to hear that. Until that moment, he hadn't been sure about Billy. "That's the way I feel. It doesn't matter that these people were coloreds. They got as much right to live as you and me. Now the one that killed them. . . I don't figure he has any rights at all."

Bobby countered with, "I don't think it's any of our business."

Johnny frowned. "If it's not our business, whose business is it. Ain't anything going to be done unless folks like us does it. The sheriff ain't gonna do nothing. And, most of the folks in town don't care."

"I think we ought to leave well enough alone," Bobby said.

Johnny gave him an incredulous look. "*Well enough alone.* Evidently they ain't teaching you no Bible in Vacation Bible School. I don't care what the preacher says, the Bible says we're responsible for our fellow man. . . and it doesn't specify color."

Billy nodded agreement. "You're right, Johnny. I'd like to do something, but I don't know where to start. And, the sheriff will be all over me if he thinks I'm looking into the murders without his permission."

"What he don't know ain't gonna hurt him," Johnny said. "And, if you're wondering where to start, Billy, that's obvious. You start at the scene of the crime. You know that I read a lot of books about this stuff and that's where the detective always starts. It's where Sherlock Holmes always starts because the killer always leaves a clue. Ain't no such thing as a perfect crime. . . unless, as my daddy says, you want to call an election in this parish a crime."

The deputy wasn't quite ready to take the bait. "Books might not be the same as real life."

"That's why I'm going to the Williams' place to look around," Johnny said. "I'll find a clue. You can count on that."

"What if the guy that killed them is still hanging around there," Bobby said. "You could get yourself killed, Johnny."

"I guess that means you ain't going with me."

"Not while the bodies are there."

Billy sighed. "What Bobby says about the killer still being around bothers me, too. Are you just bound and determined to go, Johnny?"

"Ain't nothing or nobody going to stop me."

"Then I'm going with you," the deputy said. "Just don't tell anybody I took you, especially your dad. He wouldn't like it no little bit. You can keep a secret can't you, Bobby?"

Bobby vowed that he could, then Johnny said, "I guess you're going on back to town, huh?"

"Reckon so."

Eleven

"Did it occur to you that if there's a killer roaming these parts, he might attack somebody who's alone?"

Fear flickered in Bobby's eyes, as Johnny knew it would. Johnny continued, "There's safety in numbers. You might want to consider coming with us, Bobby.

Billy knew what Johnny was doing to Bobby and it was all he could do to keep from laughing. "Oh, I think Bobby will be all right in broad daylight."

Johnny said, "Could be the Williamses were killed in broad daylight, couldn't it? We don't know, do we?"

Billy shrugged. "No, we don't."

Bobby asked, timidly, "What are we going to do with our bikes?"

"We can put them in the trunk," Billy said.

• • •

Billy's third trip to the murder site was no charm. On seeing Vernell Williams' body again, he vomited until he had the dry heaves. So did Johnny and Bobby. What surprised the deputy was Johnny's resolve. Tearful, he was more determined than ever to find a clue.

Bobby, crying, wanted to leave but Johnny wouldn't hear of it. His face ashen, Bobby laid down in the back seat of the car as Johnny walked with determination toward the front door of the house.

Billy warned, "It's worse inside the house. The smell. . . the flies."

"Let's get on with it."

For Billy the second time inside the shack of a house was worse than the first. It had been bad in the eerie early morning light when he had been there with Ben Jim and Father Ingram, but now it was hotter and the smell and flies was worse.

Working their way through the house like zombies in a bad movie, neither knowing what they were looking for, Johnny and Billy surveyed the horror. Each held a hand over their mouth as a defense against flies, fanning with the other hand to keep them away from their eyes.

"Don't touch anything without a hankerchief or something," Johnny said. "The killer might have left fingerprints."

Billy mumbled, "Now who do you think is gonna check for fingerprints?"

"I think you ought to call the state police."

"Me call the state police? That's up to the sheriff."

"Then it won't get done. If you won't do it, Billy, I will."

"I can't tell you what to do and not to do."

Keeping his eyes off Clarice Williams' body as best he could, Johnny found an old ragged towel and began pulling open the drawers of a rickety chest next to the bed. In the top drawer he found a piece of paper with a name and phone number. The name surprised him. There was no phone in the Williams house, but he figured the name and phone number might be important. He shoved the piece of paper in his pocket just prior to Billy entering the room.

"Find anything?" the deputy asked.

"No. . . did you?"

"Might help if I knew what I was looking for."

"You see Vernell Williams' shotgun anywhere?"

"How do you know he had one?"

"There's a gun rack over the door. . . and a man don't live in the woods around here without having a shotgun."

"Makes sense."

"I figure the killer used the shotgun on the family."

"If that's the case, he probably took it with him."

"Maybe not. I'm betting he tossed it somewhere in the woods. . . or threw it in the creek."

"Why would somebody throw away a good gun?"

"Wouldn't want to be caught with it."

The smell of death in the house was getting to Billy. Johnny, too. They could have looked more, but both felt the need for some fresh air. It was bad enough outside where Vernell Williams' body was rotting, but worse in the house."

Billy asked, "Do you want to check the woods a bit to see if we can find the gun?"

"It would be like looking for a needle in a haystack. We need help."

Billy grunted. "Well, it ain't likely we're going to get any."

"You're right. But, somebody really ought to check for fingerprints before the colored funeral home comes for the bodies."

"You know the sheriff ain't gonna ask for help," Billy said. "I don't know nothing about fingerprints and he don't either."

"Like I told you, I may put in a call to the state police and to the newspaper in Shreveport."

"That's up to you, but I ain't got nothing to do with it."

Bobby was still stretched out in the car seat; his face still drained of color. "You okay?" Billy asked.

"I'm fine."

"You don't look fine," Johnny said.

Bobby brought his body to an upright position and Billy said, "I hope you boys remember what you promised. . . not to tell anybody I came out here with you."

"Don't worry," Johnny said. "We ain't gonna tell."

Johnny took another look at the rundown shack and the woods surrounding it. The sun was shining brightly; its rays filtering through the foliage, but the woods around the house now looked foreboding. Maybe the killer is watching us, he thought. Even in the oppressive heat, he felt a sudden chill.

He knew he would never be able to forget the gruesome crime committed here, what he had witnessed. He wasn't sure he ever wanted to forget. Burning inside him was a desire to see the killer of these innocent people roasting in the fires of Hell.

TWELVE

Johnny didn't call the state police or the newspaper in Shreveport. He might have called if his folks had a phone, but they didn't. And, shortly after returning to town he learned that the colored funeral home from Zwolle was already en route to the Williams place to pick up the bodies.

Another reason for delay was the piece of paper he had found in the bureau drawer. The name and phone number, what it might mean, intrigued him. That's why he immediately sought out Ben Jim Cade, who was drinking coffee in the kitchen of the Walla Cafe.

"What do you think it means?" Johnny asked.

"Don't rightly know. I guess you'll have to ask the one whose name is on the paper."

"I don't know, Ben Jim. What if this is a clue. . . has something to do with the murders?"

"I doubt that it does."

"Another thing is that this might not be the best time."

Twelve

Ben Jim smiled. "So what are you gonna do with it?"

"I'm gonna have to think about it."

The town was buzzing with talk of the murders, and how it was Johnny Tobin's discovery of the little boy's body that had led to the grisly discovery of the rest of the family. That Johnny was involved didn't surprise anyone. He was, most believed, the kind of boy who attracted trouble.

The murders had, temporarily at least, given people something to talk about in addition to little Sadie Scott's disappearance. Some wondered, of course, if there might not be a connection between the killings and little Sadie's disappearance. It seemed a logical assumption, though most people were reticent to voice it. The talk was that a colored man killed the Williamses, which would mean that he also took Sadie. What he might have done to the child was too horrible to contemplate.

Johnny asked, "Why do you think someone would kill a whole family?"

"Hard to say," Ben Jim replied. "People give all kinds of reasons for their meanness."

"People been saying they were probably killed by a colored."

"Might have been. Dark souls come in every color."

"None of it makes any sense."

"Killing never does."

"I don't think the Williamses had anything worth stealing, do you?"

"What might not be worth nothing to you might be worth something to somebody else."

"I figure the killer used Vernell Williams' shotgun to kill them with," Johnny said. "It was missing."

"How do you know the man had a shotgun?"

"Just seems reasonable. And, there was a place above the door to put one."

"I saw that, too, but it might have been a place to put a twenty-two. We don't know for sure the man had a shotgun. But, you're probably figuring right, Johnny, because whatever gun he had ain't in the house no more."

"There's another thing, too."

"What's that?"

"Vernell Williams bought twelve-gauge shotgun shells at Mr. Bernstein's store. I remember getting a box for him one Saturday when I was working there."

Ben Jim grinned. "I might've known. You're way ahead of everybody else, Johnny."

"The killer took the gun with him. . . probably tossed it somewhere in the woods or threw it in the creek."

"That's probably what a thinking man would do, but there ain't no telling what caused this man to go off and kill all these folks. He may not be thinking the way you are. If it was a poor colored man. . . well, he might not want to throw away a good gun."

"If the man was colored," Johnny said. "Ain't nothing I saw out there that proves to me he was colored."

Ben Jim countered, "Ain't no proof either way."

"The killer might not have come out of the woods. He might have driven right up to the house. Of course, after Billy and the sheriff drove up it messed up any chance of seeing if there were other tire tracks."

"It's been awful dry, Johnny, but there was other tracks. I don't know if they were the killer's, but I noticed them when I was there. Vernell Williams. . . he didn't have no car or pickup truck, but that don't mean he didn't know somebody who had one."

Johnny's eyes showed excitement. "You know, I saw a wagon in back of the house but I didn't see a horse or mule or nothing."

"Can't swear to it. . . didn't know him all that well. . . but I think the man owned a mule. When I seen him and the family in town they were in a wagon pulled by a mule. When I was looking around out there, I saw where he might have owned a cow, too."

"I never paid much attention," Johnny said, "but now I seem to remember the Williams family coming to town in a wagon pulled by a mule. Of course, so many folks still use wagons that you just don't notice. So a mule, cow and gun are missing. Do you think somebody would kill for that?"

"People been killed for a lot less."

"I guess I'd better tell Billy."

The deputy's car wasn't parked at the sheriff's office, just

Merrick's car. So Johnny decided to go to Bernstein's for a cold pop. He wasn't willing to share any information with the sheriff.

Ozzie Guidry was at the counter paying for cigarettes when he walked into the store. The bug-eyed barber looked down his long nose and said, "Finding that nigger kid in the creek last night. . . you sure stirred up a hornets nest, Johnny."

"Can't help what I stirred up. Wasn't exactly planned."

Guidry's smile bared tobacco-stained teeth. "Oh, I ain't complaining, mind you. Nice to have a little excitement around here besides little Sadie being missing. Won't hurt my feelings none if a bunch more niggers is sent to meet their maker."

Sol Bernstein showed discomfort at the statement and Johnny said, matter-of-factly, "He's your maker, too."

Guidry, however, didn't seem to comprehend Johnny's comment. He rambled on with, "Yeah, Nick wanted me to go out there with him. Mouse went, too. Never seen anything like it."

"I heard it was pretty bad."

"You wouldn't have been able to handle it, Johnny. It wasn't anything for a kid to see. If it had been white people, it would have bothered me. But, since niggers is thicker than seedticks around here, it didn't bother me none."

Johnny frowned. "Don't think I could feel good about anybody being murdered. . . no matter what color they were."

Guidry lit a cigarette and said, "I ain't saying I feel good about it. I just ain't gonna lose any sleep over a bunch of dead niggers."

Johnny wanted to ridicule Guidry in front of Bernstein, to say something about him puking up his guts, but knew it would get Billy in trouble. He just wanted the man to leave, to quit running his mouth. "What kind of man is it that kills little kids?" Johnny asked.

Guidry shrugged his shoulders. "Them kids was liable to have grown up mean."

The man's logic stymied Johnny. "I need a cold pop," he said, going to the cooler and pulling a Coke from the bed of ice. He opened it and took a drink.

"You reckon that ice covering them pops was in the ice house when that dead nigger kid was in there, Sol?" Guidry asked, grinning.

Johnny looked at the merchant, who looked helplessly back at him and stuttered, "No. . . no, I don't think so."

His mind going to the little body in the drift, Johnny knew he couldn't swallow any more Coke at the moment. However, it wasn't because of what Guidry said about the ice. He was just feeling queasy over all that he had seen in so short a time. Guidry's comment, of course, didn't help. The barber had lit Johnny's fuse. It was short, sizzling, and he was about to explode.

"When are you gonna come by the shop and let me cut your hair, Johnny?" Guidry asked.

"Mama cuts my hair."

"You're getting old enough that you need a professional haircut."

"She cuts it professional enough for me."

Guidry left and Bernstein asked, "You okay, Johnny? You don't look so good."

"I don't feel so good, Mr. Bernstein. I'd better go out back a few minutes."

Out in the alley Johnny vomited and started having the dry heaves again. He wondered if he would ever again be able to hold anything on his stomach. He figured the only way would be to shut out the memories of what he had seen. But he wasn't sure he ever could.

Back inside the store Bernstein said, "Finding that little boy. . . it must have been bad."

Johnny nodded in the affirmative and wanted to tell the grocer he had seen the bodies of the boy's family, too. He didn't, though, because of his promise to Billy Burton. "It was bad, Mr. Bernstein, but it's people like Ozzie Guidry who make me sick."

"He doesn't know any better."

"Everybody ought to know better than the way he talks. Ain't nobody been raised that bad."

Bernstein shrugged. "You might be surprised the way some people are raised."

"I'm surprised you didn't say something."

The merchant's eyes showed sadness. "I have to live among these people, Johnny. And, some of these people. . . they don't like Jews any better than they like Negroes."

"Well, it's a crying shame that anybody has to listen to Ozzie Guidry."

Twelve

When Johnny left the store there was a gnawing pain in his stomach, but not from hunger. His emotions were running rampant. He liked Bernstein a lot, but wished the man had more backbone. He realized that he didn't know or understand all that the merchant had gone through in his life, but the man had not been born in some foreign country. He was an American, and that gave him a right to stand up and be counted.

Feeling the way he did, there was only one thing to do. He went home, dug a few worms, got his fishing pole and went down to the creek. It was only after he was under the trestle that he started feeling a little better.

There were times, like the present, when Johnny preferred being alone with his thoughts. He put a fat, wriggling night crawler on his hook and flipped it in the water. The bobber had no sooner touched the water than it disappeared beneath the surface. He set the hook expecting the pull of a perch on the other end of the line. But, whatever was there didn't give.

Johnny's mind immediately cleared of anything other than combat with the fish. He was using a small perch hook and realized that there would be little chance of landing a big catfish or bass. Still, as long as there was a chance he planned to do everything he could to put the fish on his stringer.

The fish lunged for a partially submerged brushtop, but Johnny was able to turn it. Whatever species was on his hook, it fought valiantly, bringing the end of his cane pole dangerously close to the breaking point. The fish intensified its efforts to reach the submerged brush, but Johnny turned back each of its surges. His heart beat faster with the realization that there was actually a chance that he might land the fish.

Finally, he was able to lead the fish into the clear, shallower water near the bank. It was a big bass, the largest he had ever seen.

His heart pounded even harder. He had never seen a fish he wanted so much. He would, at last, be able to prove Bobby Milam wrong. There were big bass under the trestle.

The bass made some last frantic tugs before Johnny brought it to bay. He managed to get its bottom lip between his thumb and forefinger and lifted it out of the water.

It was beautiful. The hook was barely stuck in its lip. One more surge and it would, possibly, have gotten away.

Johnny removed the hook and held the fish up to the sunlight, admiring the distinctive stripe down its side. He looked at the big bass for a few seconds, then gently placed it back in the water. For a split-second the fish didn't move, then with a rush swam away.

Johnny wasn't sure why he let the fish go, especially since Bobby would think he was lying about catching it. He just knew he didn't want the fish to die, that he wanted it to live and be free.

THIRTEEN

Just before suppertime Johnny found Billy Burton alone in the Walla Cafe and told him about the possibility of a mule and cow being missing from the Williamses place. The deputy was having pie and coffee and offered to buy Johnny the same.

"Probably ruin my supper, but what the heck," the youth said. "It's hard to turn down apple pie and coffee."

"Coffee's gonna stunt your growth," the surly waitress said.

"I'll take my chances. I sure don't want to get as big and ugly as Billy."

The deputy grinned. "You'd better just hope you grow up to be as handsome as me."

The waitress allowed a hint of a smile to disrupt her craggy face and shook her head in mock dismay. "You want some ice cream on top of that pie, Johnny?"

"Sure. . . as long as Billy's buying."

When she left to fill the order, Johnny semi-whispered, "In all those detective books I read, there's always a motive for murder."

Billy, his voice as muffled as Johnny's, said, "I'll take your word for it. You know I ain't never read no book, except for the ones they made me read in school."

"Well, Ben Jim remembers. . . and so do I. . . that when the Williams family came to town they were in a wagon drawn by a mule."

"Yeah. . . I did see a wagon at their place but I didn't see any livestock. You'd have to figure he had something to pull the wagon with."

"Ben Jim said he saw signs that they had a cow, too."

"So you're saying a cow and a mule are missing."

"The shotgun, too. Mr. Bernstein remembers Vernell Williams buying twelve-gauge shells. And, I remember getting a box for him one Saturday when I was working at the store."

Billy mused, "A shotgun, mule and cow. Don't seem like much to kill folks over."

"I ain't saying those things are the motive. I'm just saying they're missing, which gives us something to look for."

"Whoa, now. The sheriff told me not to worry about a bunch of dead niggers, just to keep looking for little Sadie."

The waitress brought Johnny's order, interrupting their conversation. When she left Johnny doctored his coffee with a couple of spoons of sugar before saying, "Why ain't I surprised the sheriff said something like that."

"He's the boss."

"So he just ain't concerned at all about who killed the Williams family?"

"Guess not. Far as I can tell nobody's that concerned. . . not even the niggers who live around here."

"They're just scared to say anything."

"What have they got to be scared about?"

Johnny gave Billy an incredulous look. "Stupidity most likely. I don't understand why you can't be looking for whoever killed the Williams family at the same time you're looking for little Sadie. After all, some people think the murders and her disappearance are connected."

Billy thought about it for a moment and said, "Guess I could. . .

as long as the sheriff don't know."

"I sure ain't gonna tell him. If I never speak to him again it'll be too soon."

"Only problem is. . . what if I catch the killer? What am I gonna tell the sheriff then?"

Johnny sighed. "Let's cross that bridge when we come to it. If you find out who killed them, you don't have to tell him anything. Just tell me and I'll take care of it."

"What are you going to do?"

"I ain't figured it out yet, but I'll think of something."

Johnny figured there wasn't much chance of Billy finding the murderer, especially if it took actual detective work. The deputy might, however, hear about somebody trying to sell a cow or mule. There were people in the area that talked to Billy about any number of things. He was likable and most people didn't take his connection with the law all that seriously.

To Johnny the deputy could be frustrating when it came to comprehending things, which was why he hadn't told him about the piece of paper he found in the Williams' house. He also knew that Billy would just as soon not know about it. He was always saying that he subscribed to the adage that what a person didn't know couldn't hurt them. Johnny thought it was the most stupid of all adages.

"What are you going to do, Johnny. I know you're going to do something because you can't keep your nose out of anything."

Johnny grinned. "Right now I'm gonna eat my pie and ice cream. Then I'm gonna go home and eat supper."

"That ain't what I'm talking about."

"I know it ain't. If you have to know, I'm gonna try to get Ben Jim to go back down to the Williams place with me. . . see if we can find the trail of the mule and cow."

"I hate that you're going down there wandering around when there's a killer on the loose."

"I don't think there's any danger. The woods have been full of people looking for little Sadie. . . and about the only thing anybody's run into has been some nasty snakes. Of course, that has me wondering."

"About what?"

"It's kind of strange to me that those bodies laid out there so long before they was found, especially with people looking for little Sadie."

"Well, they live pretty far up the creek. And, maybe they were alive when people were searching that area."

"Could be that one of the searchers killed them."

"Oh, no. . . I can't believe that."

Johnny said, "We've got some people around here who are bound and determined that a colored took Sadie. Maybe some of the searchers thought the Williamses had something to do with it and just killed them on the spot."

"You've got a big imagination. . . I'll give you that."

"Maybe. . . but in all the books I've read about murder, it's always the least likely suspect who did the killing."

"Maybe you read too much."

"I know some people say that, Billy, but that's just ignorance talking."

"Just don't be getting yourself in no trouble Johnny. Don't be getting Ben Jim in no trouble either. The sheriff wants him real bad."

"We'll be careful. Thanks for the pie and coffee, Billy."

• • •

It never occurred to Vernon Scott that his wife might be cheating on him. His passion for Marcie had died shortly after their marriage, but his ego wouldn't allow him to believe that she might find comfort with another man.

Vernon was the definition of machismo only in his mind, not in the perception of others. He was big, muscular and quick-tempered, but there was something about him that didn't strike fear in the hearts of men with lesser physiques. Maybe it was his sad eyes, the uncertainty that resided in them.

There was also the problem of the quaver in his voice when he got excited. It was a rather weak voice that should have belonged to an English teacher who seemingly pulled the waist of his pants up under his armpits.

When he was out of earshot, all the football players made fun of Vernon's voice. That's because he spent considerable time threatening them without being threatening.

Born and raised in Arkansas, Vernon graduated from one of the state's many second-rate colleges. He achieved a degree of stardom as a high school tackle, but never rose above mediocrity in college football. He had always wanted to be a coach, but never had any desire to teach. In his heart he knew that he didn't know anything to teach.

At Walla it didn't matter. The school board figured ninety-nine percent of the students were going nowhere anyway, and that what Vernon didn't teach them wouldn't hurt them. So his duties required that he teach math to students from sixth grade through high school.

Johnny had taken sixth grade math from the coach and wasn't looking forward to another wasted year in seventh grade math. He didn't dislike the coach. He just didn't have any respect for him as a teacher.

As for Marcie Scott, Johnny thought of her as an average English teacher. He gave her high marks in the looks department, though. He thought she was almost as beautiful as his mother.

He had heard she was seeing Bailey Thompson on the sly. The thought of it was downright distasteful to him. It made him uneasy. He liked Thompson a lot and hoped it wasn't true. Of course, there was a lot adults did that was distasteful to him, even stuff his parents did.

After supper Johnny listened to *The Green Hornet*, *The Lone Ranger* and *Mr. District Attorney* on the radio. Then he walked to the football field to watch practice.

Though all the players were three to seven years older than Johnny, he was well known to them. Some liked to tease him, but knew not to take the teasing too far. They knew he would fight at the drop of a hat, that age and size difference meant nothing to him. Johnny was known as a boy who would fight a circle saw. He was, many believed, a bit crazy.

Also, the older, bigger boys figured that fighting Johnny was a no-win situation. If they fought him they were expected to win. If he happened to inflict damage on them, which he was capable of doing, it enhanced his reputation and hurt theirs. He fought like a wildcat and had already given bigger, older schoolmates reason to wish they hadn't crossed him.

The coach had his charges doing a head-on tackling drill when Johnny walked out on the field. Scott, crouching with his hands on his knees, turned slightly and asked, "How are you doing, Johnny?"

"Fine, I reckon."

"Won't be long before you can have one of these uniforms. . . be doing what these boys are doing."

"Reckon so."

Scott smiled. "Don't sound like you're all that excited about it."

"I ain't."

The coach didn't respond because he didn't know how to read Johnny. So he went back to watching his players bang into each other. Johnny often left Scott in a dilemma as to how to respond to his statements. It was that way in class, too, where the youngster always seemed to be ahead of him. Vernon knew that wasn't hard in math, or in any other subject for that matter. He wasn't offended by it. After all, it wasn't as if Johnny was trying to put him down. To the contrary, the boy was polite and only responded to questions when asked. It was just that when someone asked him a question, he didn't always answer as expected.

Johnny was standing away from the drill, arms folded, watching the players crash into each other. Scott finally tired of the carnage and gave the players a short break prior to a full contact scrimmage.

"You boys can put some water in your mouth and swish it around, but don't swallow it," the coach said.

That seemed a stupid order to Johnny. All the players were sweating profusely in the humid evening air.

"Why can't they swallow the water?" he asked.

Scott gave him a bemused look. "If you drink a lot of water when you're hot, you'll get stomach cramps."

"If you don't drink it, you'll dehydrate."

Miffed, the coach said, "It's the way I was taught."

Johnny wanted to say, *Maybe you were taught wrong.* He didn't, though, and Scott walked away from him.

Elmer Guerdat swished some water around in his mouth and then spit it on Johnny's shoe. Johnny gave him a hard look, but Elmer didn't care. He let fly an expletive and said, "You come out here with your smart-aleck questions, he gets riled and takes it out on us. Why don't you just bug off?"

"I don't figure it was a smart-aleck question. . . just a logical one."

Elmer sneered. "You're a little too smart for your own good, Johnny, and you think you're real tough. Well, I heard you turned green around the gills when you found that little nigger boy in the creek."

"At least I was there, which is more than I can say for you. I imagine you'd have done more than turn green."

Elmer tried to intimidate by quickly moving his face close to Johnny's and taking a combative stance, but the youngster didn't flinch. He just looked Elmer up and down like he was sizing him up. Guerdat was six-feet two inches tall and weighed a hundred and ninety pounds. Nineteen years old, he was considered the stud of the high school football and basketball teams, which didn't cut much mustard with Johnny. He figured Elmer couldn't handle a real sport. He had tried out for the town's baseball team but couldn't hit or field.

"Why don't you hit me you little smart aleck?"

"Because I might get dumb all over my hand."

"That's just like you. . . got an answer for everything. But, I ain't likely to throw up because I see a dead nigger."

"Well, what can I say, Elmer? You're just a lot tougher than I am. Flesh rotting and falling off a human being's bones is probably gonna make me sick every time. . . whether the dead one is black or white."

The players gathered around wondered where Elmer's confrontation with Johnny would lead, but before anything could happen the coach blew his whistle. It was time to scrimmage.

Five minutes into the scrimmage Guerdat, who was playing halfback, took the ball through a hole off-tackle. He stiff-armed a linebacker and cut toward the sideline. The closest defensive back had a bad angle on him, so it looked as if he was going to score easily. He glanced back at the pursuit and smiled, his long stride rapidly eating up ground.

Johnny came from nowhere, hit Guerdat at the knees and sent him somersaulting onto his back. The wind swished out of Elmer. He sat up for a split-second, a stunned look on his face, then fell back gasping for air.

Lying there on the ground he saw Johnny get up, brush himself off and walk away. He also heard the laughter of his teammates. He was thinking about giving Johnny the whipping of his life, but he couldn't breathe.

• • •

Johnny thought football was stupid, but figured he would have to play the game. It would be expected. While he didn't always do what was expected, there were some things that weren't worth getting bent out of shape over. Football was one of them.

He figured on being the quarterback, since no other position required much thinking. And he figured it didn't take much genius to play quarterback.

The tackling and being tackled wasn't bad, he thought. It wasn't as satisfying as a good fistfight, but there could be some pleasure in it. He had, he decided, achieved a degree of satisfaction from busting Elmer Guerdat. The fact he had taken on a much bigger opponent who was dressed in football armor was not a consideration. He figured tackling was all a matter of leverage, like stacking green lumber. He played tackle football with other kids all the time without pads. It was no big deal.

Johnny wasn't sure why he took the route home he did, but it took him past Bailey Thompson's place. He saw a light was on and thought about talking to the principal about the piece of paper he had found at the murder scene. Then he saw the black Chevrolet parked just ahead of him. He was approaching it from the rear.

His immediate thought was that Brother Marvin Baker was visiting Thompson, which was a good reason to steer clear of the principal's place. But, he was curious as to why the preacher would park so far away from Thompson's door, given Baker's aversion to walking.

Then he saw the back of Baker's head through the car's rear window and wondered, *What in the dickens is he doing?* He decided it might be worthwhile to hang around and see. He backed away so the preacher wouldn't see him, found a place where he could observe and probably wouldn't be seen, sat down and waited, his back against a utility pole.

Fishing and hunting had taught Johnny the importance of patience. He had spent considerable time sitting on the bank of a creek waiting for fish to bite. Eventually, he had always been rewarded. The same was true in hunting. He had sat quietly in the woods for hours waiting for a deer to appear. He had not always seen a deer in those instances, but it hadn't spoiled his commitment. The solitude of the woods, the time he had to think and reflect, was as important as any game he might see.

Thirteen

Johnny had been sitting for about fifteen minutes when the door to Bailey Thompson's place opened. Marcie Scott came out. She was carrying some books and papers. The sight of her shocked Johnny momentarily. He had heard the stories, but didn't want to believe them. Maybe her being at the principal's apartment had something to do with school, he thought.

Marcie Scott walked hurriedly away and Johnny's mind went back to the preacher. *The jerk*, he thought. *The no good jerk.*

He knew what he had to do. He had already gotten up from where he had been sitting. Before Marcie Scott passed out of sight he walked over to Baker's car and stood quietly just off from the driver side door. Baker, who was slumped down in the seat, never saw him.

"How's it going, Brother Baker?"

The startled preacher, muttering something indistinguishable, launched from his lowered position and banged his head on the car's roof. When he saw Johnny, his eyes turned mean and angry.

"Sorry if I scared you," Johnny said.

"You didn't scare me. You just surprised me."

"Hey, I'm surprised, too. . . seeing you here. What are you doing here anyway?"

Baker was taken aback by the question. "I. . . I'm here to see Bailey Thompson."

"Guess you was waiting for Mrs. Scott to leave before going in, huh?"

The preacher knew he was caught cold. His hatred for Johnny Tobin increased tenfold. "I just got here. . . didn't even know she was visiting Bailey. School business. . . I guess."

Johnny flashed a maddening grin. "Probably. I was thinking about seeing Mr. Thompson myself. Hope you don't mind if I go up with you."

"What I was gonna see Bailey about. . . it isn't important. And, there was some stuff I was gonna bring him that I left at the church. I'll just come back tomorrow."

"I hope I ain't running you off."

"You ain't," Baker said, while turning the car's ignition. He drove off quickly.

What a jerk, Johnny thought. He walked over to the stairs leading to Thompson's apartment, walked up and knocked on the door. The principal answered, filling the door with his frame.

"Johnny. . . what are you doing here?"

"I needed to talk to you. Hope you don't mind."

"Of course not. C'mon in."

Johnny stepped inside and took in his surroundings. He had never before been in Thompson's apartment. It was nice, though certainly not pretentious. The furnishings had come with the place, so it spoke more of landlord Winston Railey's taste than that of Bailey Thompson's.

"Would you like a Coke?" Thompson asked.

"I don't want to be any trouble."

"You're not. To tell you the truth, I don't think a student has ever visited me before."

"I guess most would be afraid to."

Thompson laughed. "But not you?"

Johnny shrugged. "What's to be afraid of."

The principal suggested Johnny take a seat on the couch. Then he went into the kitchen and moments later emerged with two cold bottles of Coke. "You don't mind drinking out of a bottle, do you?"

"It's the way I drink them most of the time."

Thompson sat down in an easy chair and asked, "Now Johnny. . . what did you want to see me about?"

"Well, it's about a problem I've got."

"What kind of problem?"

"If my daddy knew about it, he'd whip my rear end."

Thompson chuckled. "That is a problem. I imagine Jake gives pretty decent spankings."

"I wouldn't call it decent. . . and I wouldn't call it a spanking. When he pulls off his belt it's an old fashioned whipping."

"Before you say anything else, Johnny, I'm not sure I could promise to keep something from your parents."

"I figured you'd say that, but this has something to do with one of your teachers."

Puzzled, Thompson questioned, "One of my teachers?"

"Yeah. . . and the murders."

"Maybe you'd better tell me what you're talking about, Johnny. I can't say I won't tell your folks, but I'm not looking for a reason to tell them something either."

So Johnny told Bailey Thompson about going out to the Williams place and seeing the bodies. He didn't mention Billy Burton, because if the principal told his folks about it he didn't want to get the deputy in trouble.

"Given your curiosity, I don't guess I'm surprised that you went out there," Thompson said, "But I don't understand why you'd want to see the bodies of those poor people. . . especially after being there when we fished the little kid out of the creek."

"I was looking for clues."

"Now why would you be looking for clues? That's the sheriff's job."

"Well, you know he ain't gonna do it."

"What do you mean, *he ain't gonna do it?*"

Billy Burton told me the sheriff didn't care that some niggers got killed. He told him to forget about the Williamses and concentrate on finding little Sadie."

"Seems to me he could do both," the principal said.

"You know all the sheriff cares about is whiskey and whores."

Thompson laughed. "Well, I wouldn't be going around calling the sheriff a whoremonger and drunkard if I was you."

"I don't have to go around calling him that because everybody already knows it."

"I still don't know what you going out to the Williams place has to do with one of my teachers."

"I searched the house while I was there."

"My god, Johnny. . . why would you do something like that?"

"Like I said, I was looking for clues."

"And what did you find?"

"I found a piece of paper in a bureau drawer. It had Mrs. Scott's name on it. . . and a phone number."

Thompson's eyes turned troubled at the mention of Marcie Scott's name. "You have the paper?"

"Yeah. . . I got it."

"Mind if I see it."

Johnny pulled the piece of paper out of his pocket and handed it to Thompson. The principal knew immediately it was Marcie's handwriting. "This is the school's phone number," he said. "I'm sure there's some logical explanation."

"I'm sure there is, too," Johnny said. "I thought about asking Mrs. Scott about it, but with all she's been through lately I figured on waiting. Or, I figured you might be able to ask her about it."

A look of understanding passed between the boy and man. Then Thompson said, "She has been through a lot. Hearing about the Williamses. . . the fact that a killer's on the loose. . . it's bothering her a whole lot. She can't help but wonder about little Sadie."

"What I can't figure is why the sheriff can't see that there might be a connection," Johnny said.

Thompson sighed. "I'm afraid our sheriff isn't the brightest man in the world. Unfortunately, our police chief leaves a lot to be desired, too. But, I'm surprised the sheriff didn't find this piece of paper."

"He didn't stay around long enough. He saw Vernell Williams' body and started puking up a storm. So did Chief Crossland, Ozzie Guidry and Mouse Malone."

"Ozzie and Mouse? Why in the world were they out there?"

"They were drinking coffee with the sheriff when Billy Burton reported in on the murders. They thought it would be fun. . . and I'm quoting Billy. . . *to go out and see some dead niggers*. At least, that's the way Billy tells it."

"I'm sure Billy's telling the straight of it. He's got some faults, but lying isn't one of them."

"You gonna tell the sheriff about the piece of paper?" Johnny asked.

"Not unless you want me to."

"I don't see where it would serve any worthwhile purpose. I'm just curious about it. . . that's all."

"What else did you find out at the Williams place?"

"Vernell Williams' shotgun was missing. I know it to be a fact because Mr. Bernstein told me he sold him twelve-gauge shotgun shells more than once. And I remember selling him some shells, too. I figure the killer used the gun."

"To get hold of the gun. . . maybe he knew the family."

"Could be," Johnny said. "I think a mule and a cow are missing, too."

"They shouldn't be too hard to find."

"Hope not. I'm gonna get Ben Jim to help me look for them."

Thompson shook his head in resignation. "I don't mind telling you, Johnny, I don't like the idea of you roaming the woods looking for a killer. . . even with Ben Jim along. Whoever did this. . . he's already killed all those people and probably won't hesitate to kill again. I'm guessing your folks don't know what you plan to do?"

"No. . . and I'm hoping you ain't gonna tell them."

"I'm kind of torn about that. I don't know what to do. If something happened to you. . . then I don't know if I'd like myself much for not telling them."

"Ain't nothing gonna happen to me. . . not with Ben Jim along."

"You ought to have taken him with you when you went to the Williams place, instead of going there by yourself."

"Probably," Johnny said, still protecting Billy Burton. "You mind letting me know what you find out from Mrs. Scott."

"I owe you that."

"When are you gonna talk to her?"

"Soon," the principal said. "Very soon."

Johnny swallowed the last of the Coke and got up to leave. As he started to go out the door, he paused and asked, "Did you know Brother Baker was sitting out in his car watching your place?"

"He was what?" Thompson asked, shocked.

"Yeah. . . he was sitting out there watching."

"How long had he been there?"

"I don't know. He was out there when I got here. He said he was here to see you, but had forgot some stuff at the church he was going to bring. He seemed real agitated when I said hello to him. He took off real fast."

Thompson knew what Johnny was telling him. The kid didn't have to tell him the preacher was spying on him, that he had seen Marcie leave his place. "I appreciate your telling me about Brother Baker," he said. "I'll try to get in touch with him tomorrow. . . see what he wanted."

"I hope I did the right thing in telling you."

"You did the right thing, Johnny. I appreciate it."

FOURTEEN

Bailey Thompson couldn't sleep. He tossed and turned. Any brief snatch of slumber he might have obtained was not worth the bad dreams that accompanied it. He couldn't get the dead child in the drift out of his mind. And, he worried about Brother Marvin Baker spying on him. What did the man hope to accomplish?

While shaving, he looked at his bleary eyes in the bathroom mirror and wondered what the immediate future held. Would he and Marcie finally be exposed? How would he handle Vernon Scott when the situation finally came to a head? Would he and Marcie be able to stay in Walla?

He knew the answer to the latter and, for some reason, it bothered him. When he had first come to the town he had looked at it as a temporary thing. In fact, he could hardly wait to leave. Then Marcie happened, he made some friends, got the chance to play some baseball and suddenly small town life had become more appealing.

He still didn't like the small minds that ran things, but knew he was going to encounter them wherever he went. For the most part, he liked the winds of change that were blowing in the South and wasn't afraid to be caught up in them.

Bailey made coffee, doctored it with two spoons of sugar, stirred and sat down at the small dining table adjacent to the kitchen. He was still dressed in only his underwear. He sipped the coffee, thought about making oatmeal, then decided against it. He decided, instead, to go to the Walla Cafe for breakfast.

Johnny Tobin came to mind. *What a kid?* If he ever had a son, he hoped he would be like Johnny. He wondered if Jake and Mary Lou realized how bright Johnny was. It seemed likely they did. They were bright people themselves, even if they were trapped in a dead-end existence with no way to escape. They were as trapped as the Negroes who depended on the sawmill for their livelihood. Johnny, though, was sure to somehow break out.

Bailey now knew that Johnny knew about Marcie. How many more knew? How many more knew that when she came by his apartment it was not on school business?

He figured nobody could really know what went on between them. They had never made an outward show of affection. The guessers could just speculate. As for the Reverend Marvin Baker, the man made him want to puke. He, obviously, was more interested in digging up dirt than in preaching forgiveness.

There I go, trying to justify my actions, he thought. He wasn't sure he was all that glad Johnny had told him about the preacher's spying. Now that he knew, he wasn't sure he could be civil to the man again. He wondered if he ought to confront Baker, then thought better of it. After all, what did he really know?

The hour he had spent with Marcie before Johnny showed up had been one of the best they had ever spent together. It had been wonderful, but strange, too. Not once while they were together had she mentioned little Sadie. That bothered him a bit, though he just figured it was because she didn't want to spoil the magic of their time together. With what had happened to the Williamses, he thought, she was probably on the verge of a breakdown and seeking some sort of relief from reality.

But she had seemed happy, almost too much so for the circumstances in her life.

The coffee and reflection helped. Bailey dressed and went to the Walla Cafe, where he was greeted by what seemed to be the omnipresent clientele. The sheriff and his cronies were filling their usual table, in competition to see who could smoke the most cigarettes.

He ordered eggs over medium, bacon, biscuits and a bowl of white gravy. Coffee was a given, served the moment he sat down at a table. He had a copy of the Shreveport paper and was scanning the headlines when a familiar voice startled him by asking, "Mind if I join you?"

"No. . . not at all, Vernon. Have a seat."

The coach, whom he saw more as Marcie's husband, sat down across from him. "Figured on gettin' a decent breakfast. Marcie. . . she's not much of a cook, you know."

Almost defensively, Bailey responded, "No. . . no, I didn't know that at all."

"Take my word for it. She's the only woman I know who can't even make chicken-fried steak."

The waitress came and took the coach's order. He duplicated what Bailey was having.

When the waitress left, Bailey, wondering where the conversation was going, said, "Well, good chicken-fried steak isn't that easy to fix." Then he hoped he wasn't defending Marcie too much, not to where Vernon might suspect something. He was pretty sure the coach didn't, that he wouldn't unless someone brought it to his attention. He wasn't the most perceptive guy around.

Scott shrugged and his eyes teared up. "Whether she can cook or not. . . now that ain't the most important thing, is it?"

"No, I don't guess it is."

"I been needing somebody to talk to, Bailey. I know you come in here a lot, so I took a chance on you being here."

The way he said it made Bailey uncomfortable, put him on guard. "Well. . . sure, Vernon. What do you want to talk about?"

"About little Sadie."

Bailey let his defenses down. "I know it's been tough on you and Marcie."

"Tough ain't the word for it. You don't know how much I loved that little girl."

"I know how much both of you loved her." He didn't like that the references to Sadie were in the past tense.

"Marcie's handling her being missing a lot better than I am," the coach said. "I guess she's really the strong one in the family."

That surprised Bailey. "What do you mean?"

"She's able to function. Me. . . I'm just going through the motions. I thought starting football practice might help, but it ain't. I can't sleep and it's hard for me to keep anything on my stomach."

"That's understandable."

"I wouldn't tell just anybody this, Bailey, but I think Marcie blames me for Sadie being missing."

"Why's that?"

"I don't know. I just think she does."

"I'm pretty sure you're mistaken about that, Vernon. There's just a lot of pressure on the two of you now. When something like this happens, we all start looking for reasons. . . and we look for somebody to blame. But, there's no way Marcie could be blaming you for what happened."

"You don't know her."

Bailey was taken aback by the statement. He paused, then said, "No, I don't guess I do know her like you do. But, you may be reading something into the way she's acting because you feel so badly about what's happened."

The waitress brought their breakfast and fresh coffee. Bailey salted and peppered his eggs. He used an excessive amount of pepper. He did the same to the gravy, after he broke open the biscuits and poured it over them.

"You sure use a lot of pepper, Bailey," Scott said. "I don't know how you taste the eggs for the pepper."

Bailey smiled. "I think I like pepper better than eggs. I've been told I use too much salt and pepper on everything, but I like the taste."

Scott started cutting his eggs with his fork and said, "What you said about reading something into the way Marcie's talking and actin'. . . you're probably right. Sadie being missing, it's not like there's a right way to handle it."

"I think you're both handling it better than most people would. And I don't mean that in a bad way, either. I think you're both being pretty brave."

Scott's eyes looked up from the food and his fork quit working. "There ain't no bravery in me, Bailey. I feel like my guts have been ripped out. But I ain't giving up hope."

"You shouldn't. There's always hope. Has the sheriff been keeping you informed?"

Scott grunted. "Informed of what?" he asked, sarcastically. "The drunken jerk ain't done nothing. . . and ain't doing nothing. People like you. . . they're the only ones been doing anything. That jerk sheriff of ours didn't even call the FBI. We finally asked about it, found out he and the police chief hadn't bothered. They didn't want any federal people in here."

"I had no idea. I figured. . . "

"Everybody did. It wasn't until a couple of days ago that an FBI agent came to see Marcie and me. He said they would try to do something."

It was not just the sheriff's failure to contact the FBI that bothered Bailey. Marcie hadn't mentioned the FBI agent to him. Maybe it was because she was preoccupied, he thought. He had to remember that she had too much on her mind to tell him everything.

"I have to agree with you that Nick Merrick is an jerk," Bailey said. "And, Roger Crossland's just a miniature of him, though I don't think he's as much of a drinker. The truth is. . . we have a poor excuse for law around here. I hear they're not even bothering to look for the killer of the Williams family."

Scott's eyes flashed both fear and recognition, causing Bailey to regret mentioning the murders. The coach, Bailey figured, had to think Sadie might have suffered a similar fate.

"Hard to believe what happened to them," Scott said. "Clarice was gonna take care of Sadie and the house when school started."

Bailey felt relief. So that's why the piece of paper with Marcie's name and the phone number was in the bureau drawer at the Williams place. Now it all made perfect sense. "Did you know the Williamses very well?"

"Not really," Scott said. "I will say that Clarice was one fine looking woman. . . for a nigger, that is."

Bailey wanted to say, *What did that have to do with her looking fine or not?* Instead, he said, "You ever been out to the Williamses place?"

The coach acted as though he didn't want to answer. He hesitated, then said, "Marcie and I drove out there a couple of times. . . when we was considering Clarice for the job. Sadie went with us. The place is really back in the boonies. . . couldn't get there in a car after a rain."

"I think they had a wagon and mule, didn't they?"

Scott shrugged. "I don't know. . . probably."

"I guess Brother Baker has been a big comfort to you and Marcie."

"The man's a jerk."

Bailey wanted to laugh, but didn't. Maybe Vernon Scott was more perceptive than he had thought. "I had no idea you felt that way about him. I thought he'd been spending a lot of time with you and Marcie."

"He has. Too much. . . if you ask me. I think he just wants to be around Marcie. Hope I'm not offending you by talking about the preacher this way."

"Oh, no. . . you're not offending me in the least. I'm not one of Brother Baker's fans. I don't talk about him the way some people do. Like little Johnny Tobin, for instance. . . "

Scott laughed. "Johnny Tobin. You know what that skinny little rascal did last night?"

Bailey wondered if the coach was talking about before or after Johnny had visited with him. "I have no idea," he replied.

"Came out to the football field and watched us practice some. I guess maybe Elmer Guerdat said something to him when I gave the boys a break. Anyway, we were scrimmaging and Elmer broke through the line and was running for a touchdown. Johnny came off the sidelines and busted him. Dangdest thing I ever saw."

"Without pads? He could've been hurt."

"He hurt Elmer. I can hardly wait to get the little rascal in a uniform. He's got a mean streak in him. I think he's gonna be a heckuva football player."

Bailey laughed. "He's an unpredictable kid."

They talked about this and that for the better part of an hour, ate their breakfast and had several cups of coffee. Finally, Scott said, "Bailey, you don't know how much I appreciate the conversation. It's nice to have somebody you can talk to."

The coach's words made Bailey feel all the more guilty for being in love with the man's wife.

FIFTEEN

Ben Jim didn't want to search for Vernell Williams' gun, mule and cow. But, he didn't want Johnny doing it alone. He tried to argue the youngster out of the hunt, suspecting from the get-go that it was an exercise in futility. Once Johnny set his mind on doing something, nothing was going to stand in his way.

"Now this time maybe we'd better take ol' Jack," Ben Jim said.

"Fine with me," Johnny said. "Far as I'm concerned, Jack can go everywhere with me. It's you that leaves him home."

Ben Jim grumbled under his breath and then asked, "Now how are we gonna get all the way out to the Williams place?"

"I was figuring on walking."

"That's what I was afraid you was figuring. These old legs ain't what they used to be."

Johnny laughed. "Now don't start that stuff with me, Ben Jim. When we're squirrel hunting you can walk me right into the ground."

"There's some reason for being in the woods when you're squirrel hunting."

"There's some reason now. Don't you want to find out who killed the Williams family?"

"I ain't sure I do."

"What do you mean by that?"

"Just what I said."

"Well, why would you say something like that?"

"What are we gonna do if we find out who killed them?"

"I figure on telling Billy Burton, who'll tell the sheriff."

"What do you think he's gonna do?"

"He'll have to arrest the killer."

Ben Jim shook his head. "The man don't have to do nothing he don't want to do."

"As big a jerk as he is. . . ain't no way he can walk away from arresting a killer."

"Now what if the killer is one of the sheriff's friends. He ain't gonna arrest no white man for killing a bunch a coloreds. And, there's plenty of colored folks the sheriff has got under his thumb that he ain't gonna arrest neither."

"You're talking about the ones that help him with the bootlegging."

"That's right. The man what killed the Williams family. . . he's a bad one. And. . . he ain't gonna take kindly to us stirring things up, especially when the sheriff ain't all that interested in who killed those folks."

"Well, then, I'll get in touch with the state police."

Ben Jim sighed. "You always think the right is gonna win, Johnny. . . and that ain't the way it is."

"All I know, Ben Jim, is that we're gonna get the guy who killed those people. . . one way or the other."

It was a long, hot walk to the Williams place. The heavy scent of death still lingered there. Even Jack seemed unnerved by the smell.

Both Ben Jim and Johnny had brought their shotguns, so Jack was anxious to tree squirrels. En route to the house they had to call him off trails a number of times until he finally got the message.

The doors and windows of the house were open, just as they had been when Johnny had been there with Billy Burton and Bobby Milam. The sound of the flies in the house was a steady hum. They continued to feast on the dried blood.

Even the oppressive heat couldn't dispel the chill that suffused Johnny's body. He shuddered, then said, "Ain't no reason to go in the house, I guess. We done seen what we needed to see in there."

Ben Jim nodded agreement. "The wagon's setting behind the house just like it was." He then pointed toward some trees about fifty yards behind the house. There was an opening behind the trees. "There's a pen back of them trees. Guess that's where he kept the mule and the cow."

They walked back to the pen. The fence had been built with a combination of pine and hardwood saplings. There was a tin-roofed shed inside the pen, a partial bale of hay beneath it. The shed and fence were falling down.

"Ain't much of a pen for a contrary mule," Ben Jim said. "Looks like the mule done kicked down the shed and the fence. I ain't figuring the man kept his cow in the shed with the mule neither."

"Where do you think he kept her?"

"Probably just let her wander around the place. A good cow doesn't need a fence. She's gonna show up for eating and milking time. If the man had put that cow in the pen with the mule, that mule was liable to kick the cow in the head."

"You saying they might've just wandered off after the killing?"

"Might have. Hard to say."

"Think you can track them?"

"It sure has been dry. It ain't gonna be easy."

"Yeah, but you can do it, Ben Jim. I've seen you track when it was drier than this."

"I ain't never remembered it being drier than it is now. How come you always remembering something I can't remember?"

Johnny grinned. "I got a memory like an elephant."

Ben Jim grunted. "You got more imagination than memory."

"I just know there ain't nobody better at tracking than you, unless it's my daddy."

"You right about that. Your daddy's as good as they come when it comes to tracking. He's a lot better than me."

"He ain't that much better."

Ben Jim flashed an incredulous look. "You sure are full of compliments when you want something. You don't have to worry none. I ain't gonna suggest you go get your daddy to do the tracking, because if you was to go tell him what you has in mind he'd just naturally whip your rear end."

Johnny laughed. "You're right about that."

"I ain't wanting to do it myself, but I know you're bound and determined. . . that you're gonna do it whether I help or not."

"I appreciate what you're doing."

"That ain't the point. We ought not to be doing it. This is the sheriff's job."

"But you know he ain't gonna do it."

Ben Jim sighed. "I know. Let's get on with it."

Whether Jake Tobin was a better tracker than Ben Jim Cade was subject to debate. Both men were good. They could follow sign even when a good dog couldn't pick up a scent. Ben Jim's dog, Jack, had an exceptional nose. But, it's doubtful his interest could have been piqued to where he would be interested in trailing a mule or cow. He was too busy checking on squirrels, coons and possums.

Ben Jim tried first to find sign of the killer, around the house and near the pen. "Too many people been around the house for me to know which is which," he said. "We're just gonna have to try to trail the cow first, because maybe she ain't wandered as far off as the mule."

"Can't you tell if somebody. . . say the killer. . . is driving her?"

"Ain't that easy if the man knows what he's doing'. A man can hide his tracks, especially if he's trying and it's dry as it's been. A cow ain't gonna be worried about hiding her tracks."

Tracking the cow was tough because of the dry ground, but Ben Jim kept finding sign where Johnny couldn't see anything. The process was slow and the day wore on. Ben Jim had told Johnny to keep his eyes peeled for movement in the woods, that his eyes were going to have to be pretty much glued to the ground. Johnny knew what his friend meant, that he wasn't talking about movement from a cow or mule. The killer might be in the woods and might not take kindly to what they were trying to do.

Finally, Ben Jim said, "Look over here, Johnny. Here's where a man is walking with the cow."

"The killer?" Johnny asked, trying to see what Ben Jim saw. He didn't see anything."Hard to say. At first the cow just seemed to be walking around by herself. Then this man just kind of showed up."

"Maybe he was hiding his trail at first and finally decided he was far enough away from the house that it didn't matter."

Ben Jim pondered the situation, then said, "It's hard enough to read sign without trying to figure what's in somebody's mind. Don't make a lot of sense, though, because now the man is as easy to track as the cow."

Excited, Johnny said, "Let's see where they're headed."

"You keep your eyes open now, because I got to keep mine on the ground. Don't you let somebody sneak up and surprise us now."

Ben Jim trailed the man and cow down an old logging road, then through a pinoak bottom along San Miguel Creek. They hit another logging road after getting out of the bottom, then a better road. A house appeared in a clearing.

Ben Jim quietly cautioned Johnny to keep in the trees so they would not be detected. Then they circled the house from a distance. Out back was what passed for a barn. A cow stood grazing in a fenced area. In another fenced area was a mule.

Johnny whispered, "You know who lives here?"

"Sure do. The house belongs to Mr. Willard Jordan."

Johnny's mind conjured up an image of Jordan, whom he had seen at Bernstein's Store. He was a thin, stooped man, not very tall. He had large ears and slicked-back hair. His eyes were deep-set. He had eyebrows that looked like caterpillars, a long hooknose and yellow teeth. Johnny had never seen him without a hand-rolled cigarette in his mouth.

"I know him," Johnny whispered. "Never figured on him being a killer, but it figures. He. . . "

"Whoa," Ben Jim said. "You getting way ahead of the wagon. We don't know that the man done killed anybody. Maybe he just found the cow wandering around in the woods."

"What about the mule?" Johnny asked.

"We don't know for sure that the mule out in Mr. Willard Jordan's pen belonged to Vernell Williams. For that matter, we don't know that the cow belonged to Vernell neither."

Johnny wanted to argue. "We trailed the cow and Willard Jordan here."

"We done trailed a man and a cow here, but we don't know for sure that the man we was trailing was Mr. Willard Jordan."

"Well, what are we gonna do?"

Ben Jim shrugged. "Ain't nothing we can do."

"We could go up there and arrest him. We got our guns."

Ben Jim chuckled. "You want us to march the man into town on the front end of our shotguns. That'll be the day. . . a colored man arresting a white man and marching him into town."

Johnny was downcast. "So you don't want to do nothing?"

"Ain't a matter of wanting. We just got to use the sense God gave us. We can go on back to town and you can tell Mr. Billy what you done found out. Be fine with me if you leave my name out of it."

"Why's that?"

"Can't do me no good if the sheriff thinks I'm out here trying to do his job for him."

"He ought to be glad somebody's doing it."

"It don't work that way."

SIXTEEN

Johnny thought Billy Burton would be ecstatic when he told him about Willard Jordan. To the contrary, Burton seemed to be downright angry about it. Johnny had waved the deputy down and got in the car with him.

"What do you know about Willard Jordan?" the deputy asked.

"I know he's probably got Vernell Williams' cow and mule. . . that he probably killed the whole family. Of course, he might've had help."

"If Willard had caught you spying on him your rear end would probably be in a sling right now."

"Well, I didn't get caught, Billy. . . and if I had been he probably would've killed me to keep me from telling about the mule and cow."

"How do you know it's Vernell Williams' mule and cow?"

"Cause I trailed the cow right up to Willard Jordan's house."

Billy gave him a look of disbelief. "Now, Johnny. . . if you'd told me your daddy trailed the cow I'd believe it. But. . . with the weather being so dry there's probably only two men around here who could follow an old trail like that. The two would be your daddy and Ben Jim Cade."

"I'm pretty good at tracking myself," Johnny said.

"I ain't saying you ain't. But I figure if you trailed a cow from where those folks got murdered all the way to Willard Jordan's place. . . then Ben Jim was with you. Am I right?"

"What difference does it make who did the tracking. I got the killer for you. All you got to do is go out there and arrest him."

"Everything's easy for you, ain't it?"

"Well, I sure as heck can't see what's so hard about going out and arresting the man. With the cow and mule being there, you got reason."

"Didn't you know that Willard Jordan is the sheriff's kin?"

Johnny muttered something under his breath before saying, "No. . . I didn't know. What kin are they?"

"I don't know. Cousins. . . I think."

"Cousin, uncle or daddy. . . the sheriff can't let the man run around killing people."

"You don't know that he killed anybody," Billy said. "He could've just found the cow and mule."

Johnny gave his best incredulous look. "Oh, yeah. . . sure."

"Well, you don't know for sure."

"I got reason to be pretty darn suspicious."

"Do me a favor, Johnny, and just don't push this thing. Everything will work out for the best in the end."

"Now you know that's a bunch of bull. What's best usually requires a push."

"I'll see what I can do," Billy said.

"You ain't gonna tell the sheriff, are you?"

"Not now. I'll look into it. . . see what I can find out."

Johnny shook his head in disapproval. "Not long ago I was talking to Bobby Milam about you and saying, Billy Burton. . . now there's a man who has some hair on his chest. But now, I don't know. How long are you gonna let the sheriff dump on you, Billy?"

Billy's face colored. "Now that ain't fair, Johnny. I've got to bide my time. Ain't I always been straight with you."

Johnny sighed. "Yeah, you have, Billy. Sorry about what I said. I'm just frustrated by this whole mess."

"Let me tell you about Willard Jordan," Billy said. Then he proceeded to tell Johnny everything he knew about the man, which was a bunch. Jordan had spent some time in the pen. Maybe, Billy said, for refusing to go into the Army. Whatever the reason, it didn't matter. The man was a mean one, dangerous as they came. There was a rumor that he had killed a couple of coloreds over in Texas with a knife.

He had been raised around Walla, but never bothered to get a real job. He had made his living for a long time by helping Nick Merrick's daddy make and sell whiskey. Billy said he figured he was probably still doing it, along with some illegal fishing and hunting. He had heard that Jordan also did some work as an enforcer for a man in Beaumont who loaned money to coloreds.

"He's the kind of man who could've killed them. . . no doubt about that," Billy said.

"If you want to go out there and talk to him, Billy. . . I'll back you up."

The deputy chuckled. "Well, I'd just about rather have you backing me up than anybody I know, Johnny. But I don't think it's a good idea for me to go out there right now. Fact is, I've got to figure a way to talk to the sheriff about Willard without bringing you into it."

"I don't care if you bring me into it."

"You want your daddy to know you was out there snooping around?"

Johnny pondered the question. No doubt Jake Tobin would give him a good whipping if he thought he was sticking his nose where it didn't belong. But, he also knew his dad believed in justice. He even favored the eye-for-an-eye variety. "I might get a whipping out of it, but it'll be worth it if we get the killer."

"Well, let's just say I'd rather the sheriff didn't know a Tobin or Ben Jim Cade was the one who found out his cousin was a murderer. He don't like Ben Jim and he don't like the Tobins."

"Ben Jim didn't have nothing to do with it."

Billy gave him a look of disbelief. "The sheriff ain't gonna believe you did the tracking anymore than I do."

"So when are you gonna talk to him?"

"When the time's right."

"Willard Jordan's liable to have sold the mule and cow before you get around to it."

"It ain't gonna be hard to find out who he sold them to," Billy said. "Besides, I doubt Willard's gonna sell them. . . especially if he stole them."

"Well, Billy, I figure that's why he stole them. . . so he could sell them. Ain't no other reason makes sense. Living out there by himself. . . I doubt that he needs a mule and cow."

"Maybe he's gonna sell milk. . . do some plowing."

"From what you told me, Willard Jordan ain't the kind of man to do no milking or plowing. He's the kind who'll kill a man, take what he has and sell it."

"Well, you just stay away from Willard. He's a dangerous man."

Johnny laughed. "You ever knowed me to get myself in a dangerous situation."

Billy grinned. "Only when there's one around."

SEVENTEEN

The FBI man was Carter Duncan. He was in town again to talk to Vernon and Marcie Scott about little Sadie's disappearance, and complained to Billy Burton about the lack of cooperation he was getting from the sheriff. The deputy just happened to mention that, overall, Johnny Tobin might know more about what was going on than anybody else in town.

Duncan questioned, "A twelve-year-old kid?"

"Well now, he ain't your normal twelve-year-old kid."

Billy wasn't sure why he told the agent about Johnny, except that Johnny wasn't one to hold back when it came to unloading on Sheriff Nick Merrick. Billy might not have been the smartest man around, but he was devious. He figured it might be good for a federal officer to know about the sheriff, and he also figured nobody in town would have the guts or be as honest as Johnny in giving Duncan the real low-down on Merrick.

So the agent asked Billy to have Johnny meet him at the Walla

Cafe at about three o'clock. Billy picked the time. He knew the sheriff would be drunk by mid-afternoon and not visiting the cafe. He couldn't be sure, though, about some of the sheriff's cronies.

Billy found Johnny fishing under the trestle and told him Duncan wanted to see him. "What for?" Johnny asked.

"I don't know. But you've been wanting to tell somebody that nobody's doing anything about that nigger family being murdered. This is your chance to tell somebody important."

"What have you told him?"

"I ain't told him nothing, except that I been looking for little Sadie."

"Well, I'll sure as the devil give him an earful."

Billy grinned. "I figured you would."

It was easy enough for Johnny to pick Duncan out of the patrons of the Walla Cafe. He was the only one wearing a suit. Johnny introduced himself, then said, "Ain't you about to burn up?"

Duncan grinned. "Maybe I'll pull off the coat." He did, and his shirt was wet with perspiration. "We're supposed to wear a suit and tie."

"Figured you were," Johnny said. "Didn't figure somebody was doing it of their own choosing in this heat. Besides, the suit makes you look like an FBI agent."

Duncan laughed. "You mean I wouldn't look like one if I wasn't wearing a navy blue suit?"

The agent was, Johnny guessed, about five-feet ten inches tall. He was clean-shaven, had a good haircut and skin that hadn't been constantly exposed to days in the sun. He couldn't have passed for a sawmill worker or logger.

"Be pretty hard to tell," Johnny said. "Of course, just about anybody around here would have known you weren't a working man."

Duncan's laugh had turned to a grin. "I take it you don't think people who wear suits work?"

"Brother Baker. . . he's the Baptist preacher here. . . he's the only one around other than the banker who wears a suit kind of regular. I know Brother Baker doesn't work."

"Billy Burton told me you were kind of opinionated."

"Daddy and Ben Jim Cade both say opinions are like noses. Everybody's got one."

"I heard that put a different way. But, it sounds like your daddy and this Ben Jim are wise men."

"Ain't many smarter."

"That's kind of a different attitude for a kid. A lot of kids think their folks are dumb."

"That's because most kids are stupid themselves."

The waitress came over and the agent ordered a Coke. "You order anything you like, Johnny. You want some ice cream?"

"That wouldn't be bad. I like to pour Coke over vanilla ice cream."

She left and Duncan said, "I been hearing you're not that fond of the sheriff."

"What's to be fond of? He's a jerk. I don't care if you tell him I said so."

"Don't worry about that. I'm not interested in telling him anything. I'm just here to investigate Sadie Scott's disappearance. I'm here because it was probably a kidnapping."

"Could've been. Ain't nobody been able to find hide nor hair of her."

"Billy said you had a theory that her disappearance might've had something to do with all those colored folks being murdered."

Bailey Thompson had told Johnny what Vernon Scott had told him, that Clarice Williams had been supposed to take care of little Sadie when school started. So as far as Johnny was concerned the note wasn't evidence anymore. "I ain't saying one has anything to do with the other. But, it seems kind of strange. . . what with Sadie disappearing and the Williams family being murdered so close together. I just thought it was worth the sheriff looking into, but he ain't got the brains God gave a goose."

"What's your impression of Billy Burton?" Duncan asked.

"Billy's a good guy. He just doesn't have much say in what goes on. The sheriff keeps him on a short rope."

"I wish someone had contacted my office earlier about Sadie being missing."

"I guess everybody thought the sheriff was doing it. Most everybody I know was busy hunting for little Sadie. The woods was searched high and low."

"Billy tells me you and an old colored man did a lot of searching."

"Yes sir. . . he's the Ben Jim Cade I mentioned a minute ago. And, Ben Jim ain't no old man. We searched just about everywhere we could think to look, but there were lots of people doing just as much. My daddy. . . he's the best tracer in these parts. . . he looked and looked but didn't find nothing."

"Then you found the little colored boy in the creek."

"That's right. If I hadn't, I guess those folks would still be laying up there rotting and being blowed by flies."

"Billy says you're the only one seems very concerned about finding the murderer of those people. He says the sheriff isn't interested."

"That seems to be the fact of it. I think I know who the killer is, but can't get the law to do anything about it. What do you think I ought to do?"

Duncan shrugged. "Murder like that. . . it's up to the local law to handle it. Now if we thought the murderer had kidnapped Sadie Scott, then we could step in."

Johnny shook his head in despair. "I don't understand the way the law works. It seems to me that what's right is right, but nothing is being done about Willard Jordan because he's related to the sheriff. I don't think Billy's even told the sheriff about it."

"Why don't you tell him?"

"I guess I been hesitating to do that because I know he ain't gonna do nothing about it. He thinks that because the people who were killed were colored, it don't matter."

"Lots of people think like that."

"Do you?"

"I haven't given it much thought."

"Well, the way I read my history book our forefathers wanted everybody to have a decent shot. And, that's the way the Bible reads, too. What's right is right."

"Johnny, I don't want to tell you what to think, but down in this part of the country thinking like you do could lead to some serious trouble."

"Maybe so. . . but I can't help the way I think."

The waitress brought Duncan's Coke, along with Johnny's Coke and ice cream. The agent took a long drink from the cold, perspiring bottle and asked, "You know anything about Sadie Scott's disappearance that might help me?"

"Like what?"

"Oh, I don't know. . . just anything."

"All I know is she was a cute little girl. . . went to the same church I go to. . . sometimes."

"That would be. . . "

"The First Baptist Church."

"I thought you said you didn't care much for the preacher."

"I don't. But, I ain't blaming God for somebody who calls themselves a preacher. When I go, I just go to Sunday School. And, I ain't exactly set any attendance records. Dad and me. . . we do a lot of fishing and hunting on Sunday. Oh, every once in a while I go on Sunday night, but that's just to be with my friend Bobby. I ain't interested in anything Brother Baker has to say."

"Why do you feel that way about him?"

"You know him?"

"No. . . I haven't met him."

"When you do, you won't have to wonder about the way I feel."

"What do you know about Vernon and Marcie Scott?"

"Nothing much. I've had them both for teachers. She's okay. He ain't much. I guess he's a good coach."

"Is there any kind of problem between them. . . Mr. and Mrs. Scott. . . that is?"

Johnny's defenses went up. He wondered if someone had talked to Duncan about Bailey Thompson and Marcie Scott. "If there is I don't know about it. Somebody say something to you?"

"No. . . just curious. She's one fine-looking woman."

Johnny grinned. "Lots of people think that." Then his grin turned to a frown. "People said that about Clarice Williams, too. . . that she was one fine looking woman."

"Why are you so concerned about those darkies being killed?"

"Ain't nobody ought to die that way. It don't matter the color of the skin."

"You think the killer's ever gonna be brought to justice?"

"I was hoping you'd help."

Duncan dropped his eyes from Johnny's. "There's nothing I can do."

"Can't somebody from the state or federal government do something'?"

"It's a local matter, Johnny. Folks here are gonna have to take care of it."

"Folks here are me, I guess," he said. "I ain't gonna rest until the one who killed those people pays for it."

Duncan started to protest, but Johnny's eyes told him it wouldn't be a good idea. He was a strange youngster, the most unusual one the agent had ever met. Though he was just a kid, Duncan decided he wouldn't want Johnny Tobin as an enemy.

"Look, Johnny, I'm here to check on Sadie Scott's disappearance. . . possible kidnapping. But I'm willing to check on the guy you think killed the colored family. Maybe there is some connection between the murders and Sadie's disappearance. It'll give me a reason to talk to this man. What did you say his name was?"

"His name's Willard Jordan."

"All right. . . now tell me why you think he's the killer?"

So Johnny told Duncan all he could about Vernell Williams' shotgun being missing, and about the cow and mule, without bringing Ben Jim and Billy Burton into it. After he was through the agent said, "That's a pretty good piece of detective work. But you took a real risk being out there by yourself with a killer on the loose."

"I had my shotgun with me. I can take care of myself."

Duncan laughed. "I'll bet you can."

"You want me to go out to Willard Jordan's place with you?"

"No. . . you'd better just let me take care of it."

EIGHTEEN

The Reverend Marvin Baker was in the Walla Cafe working on a platter of ham, biscuits and gravy when Johnny Tobin showed up. It was eight o'clock on a Friday morning. Jake Tobin had to work until five, then Johnny and his dad planned to go to a favorite spot on San Miguel Creek to fish for catfish in an old drift. They hadn't decided whether they would set out hooks and fish into the night. Johnny had to work at Bernstein's store the next day.

"Mind if I join you?" Johnny asked.

The preacher frowned, gravy dribbling from the corner of his mouth, but nodded okay. Johnny sat. The waitress came over and he ordered a cup of coffee. She refilled Baker's cup.

"You're up bright and early," the preacher said, not particularly interested in a response.

"This ain't early. I've been up since four o'clock."

"Why did you get up that early?"

"Daddy gets up at four every morning, starts rattling around in the kitchen making coffee. Wakes me up. . . so I get up and have coffee with him."

"I've got to have my rest. . . don't usually get up until about seven."

Johnny wanted to ask, *Rest from what?* but didn't. Instead, he asked, "Did you ever see Mr. Thompson?"

"What do you mean?"

"I mean. . . when you were parked out close to his apartment the other night you told me you were there to see him."

"Well, no. . . I ain't seen him since then. It wasn't important anyway. Did you say something to him about me being out there?"

"Can't recall. We had some important stuff to talk about."

"Like what?"

"It had something to do with the colored family that was murdered."

Baker loaded up his mouth with biscuit and gravy, but that didn't keep him from talking. "You seem to have an unnatural interest in those murders."

"Why do you say that? I ain't never talked to you about them."

"People talk. I heard you've been snooping around."

"Everybody ought to be snooping with a murderer on the loose."

"Most folks figure it ain't none of their business. They figure if there's a murderer around he ain't interested in them."

"Meaning he's just interested in killing coloreds and that's all right. Am I right?"

"Well, I don't think any white folks here are in any danger."

"You might want to tell Mr. and Mrs. Scott that."

"That's different."

The waitress brought Johnny's coffee. He doctored it with a couple of spoons of sugar and said, facetiously, "Guess you been pretty busy, huh?"

Dull as he was, Baker knew the youngster was prodding him. "It may not be sawmill work," he replied, sarcastically, "but it's important work. It's the most important work in the world. You've heard the old saying, *The Lord's Work is never done.*"

Johnny laughed. "Can't say that I have. The way I heard it, *A woman's work is never done.*"

"Well, you heard it wrong."

Johnny knew it was time to change the subject and did, without batting an eye. "Talking about the Ten Commandments, which one do you think it would be worse to break?"

"You shouldn't break any of them."

"That's the way I see it, but looks to me like some would be worse to break than others. . . like killing and adultery."

Baker didn't want to get in a Bible argument with Johnny, not with so many people in the cafe able to listen in on their conversation. It was important, he figured, to come across as the compassionate and caring shepherd of the flock, which included being nice to Johnny Tobin. He really wanted to slap the kid. "Well now, Johnny, killing and adultery are bad. . . real bad."

"That's what I figured you'd say, which makes it strange to me that so many Christian folks don't seem to be interested in finding the killer of the colored family that lived up on the creek."

"I'm sure the law's looking into it."

"I don't think so. I don't think anybody cares."

The preacher looked around nervously. After all, a lot of Sheriff Nick Merrick's friends were in the place. "Well, you've got to understand that the sheriff can't just up and drop everything else when a few niggers is killed."

"They don't count, huh?"

"The important thing is taking care of your own."

"That's not something I figure Jesus would've said."

The statement angered Baker, but before he could say anything Winston Railey walked up to the table. He wore his pants hiked up higher than most and broad, colorful suspenders. He was, people thought, prissy. And, he was the only one in town who smoked his cigarettes through a sleek black holder. "Brother Baker. . . Johnny, mind if I join you?"

The preacher didn't like Railey any more than he liked Johnny, and was embarrassed that the man was a member of his church, even though he rarely attended. The man was more feminine than the most female member, though everyone tried to ignore it. "No, Winston. . . we don't mind. It's not like we was having an important conversation."

Railey signaled the waitress to bring him some coffee, then said, "I have to say you're one healthy eater, Brother Baker."

"Got to keep up my strength."

"And how are you doing, Johnny? I'm surprised you're not fishing under the trestle."

Johnny was neutral about Railey, who taught English, music and art at the school. He thought the guy knew his stuff, but wasn't interested in spending time alone with him. There was something different about him that bothered Johnny. "I just about wore out that fishing hole this summer, Mr. Railey. But I'll probably check it out again sometime today."

If Railey even heard his answer it didn't seem to register. He was too busy posing another question for the preacher. "Didn't I see your car parked out by my house the other night?"

"He was there to see Mr. Thompson," Johnny said. "Only he forgot some stuff he was bringing to him."

Baker gave Johnny a hard look and Railey said, pushily, "I don't believe you've ever visited me since you've been at the church, Brother Baker."

Johnny looked at the man with the thin lips and complexion that was whiter than the preacher's and loved what was going on. "Uh. . . uh, I'm sure I been planning to visit you, Winston," Baker said. "It's just that I've been so busy ministering to the sick and elderly. And, of course, little Sadie's folks."

"Oh yes. . . terrible, terrible thing."

"Besides, Winston, you never come to hear me preach."

Railey laughed. "Oh, I've heard you, Brother Baker. But Sunday School, occasionally, is about all the religion I can handle."

Railey was a little pudgy himself, Johnny noted, though a rail compared to the preacher. "Brother Baker and me. . . we were talking about the colored family that was murdered," Johnny said.

"That was terrible, too," Railey said. "I believe you found the body of one of the children in the creek, didn't you, Johnny?"

"Yes sir. . . I did."

"That had to be terrible for you."

"Yes sir. . . it was. But it got worse when Mr. Gaspard wouldn't take the little boy in his funeral home because he was colored."

"Oh, I didn't know about that," Railey said.

"Well, let's not get carried away here," Baker said. "Ruley did what was right. Most white folks don't want to be sharing their funeral home with niggers."

Gaspard was a First Baptist Church deacon, which was good reason for the preacher to defend him. He was also one of the church's most generous benefactors. But Baker was really defending him because they shared a common philosophy where coloreds were concerned.

"Frankly, Brother Baker, I think that's the most un-Christian thing I've ever heard," Railey said, haughtily. "Ruley Gaspard was wrong. We're going to have to share Heaven with the coloreds."

The preacher's face turned crimson. "I'm sorry you feel that way, Winston. I'm just telling you the way I read my Bible."

"We must not be reading the same Bible," Railey said.

For Johnny it was like Christmas had come early. What a wonderful August day, Winston Railey and the Brother Marvin Baker locked in verbal combat. Johnny already knew how the battle would come out. Baker was no match for Railey when it came to thinking.

I don't think he's a match for anybody, Johnny thought.

"Pigs and cows don't mix," the preacher said. "Neither do birds and horses."

Railey shook his head in dismay. "I'm sorry, Brother Baker, but I can't understand your. . . well, I can't call it logic. Whatever it is, it escapes me. I can't imagine Christ turning somebody away because of their color."

"You've got to look at the Bible as a whole, Winston."

"I look at the New Testament. . . at Jesus. . . and there's no other way to look at the Bible, Brother Baker."

"The way I interpret my Bible," the preacher said, "we ain't got no business being involved with the niggers. Just like we ought to stay away from the Jews. I been trying to straighten Johnny out here on being a nigger and Jew lover."

"Seems to me you're the one who needs straightening out. Johnny can think for himself. Is that right, Johnny?"

"I hope so." He hadn't been around Railey that much, hadn't realized he was so combative, but rejoiced in it.

"And, why are you so down on the Jews, Brother Baker?" Railey asked.

"Because they killed Jesus."

"Oh, for god's sake. . . you don't condemn a whole race of people for what a few did."

"It wasn't just a few."

"You think everybody wanted it to happen?"

"All the Jews did."

"That's ridiculous. Who do you think supported the ministry of Jesus? They were Jews. And the Romans were in control, not the Jews. Besides, the Bible teaches that He died for all our sins."

"Well, the Jews didn't lift a hand to stop it. And, I ain't got a whole lot of use for Romans, neither. . . especially the Roman Catholic Church."

By now a number of people at other tables were listening to and enjoying the conversation.

Railey said, "The way you talk there's not going to be anybody in Heaven but Baptists. And, knowing some of the Baptists I know, I'm not sure I want to be there."

Baker rose to his feet, his face as red as a beet. "I'm not gonna sit here and listen to you make a mockery of the Bible, Winston. You don't hardly never darken the door of the church anyway, so you ain't got room to talk."

Railey rolled his eyes. "Seems to me I got as much right to read and talk about the Bible as you do. The way I read it, the priesthood of the believer gives me that right."

"You don't have no understanding of God," the preacher screeched.

"Maybe not, but I have a good understanding of you. And, don't forget to pay for your breakfast. I'm sure not going to."

Baker stormed to the cash register, paid for his meal and rushed through the door. Johnny was having a difficult time staying under control. He wanted to laugh out loud. There was a rather loud mumbling of voices in the room, mixed with the creak of the ceiling fan, though Johnny couldn't make out what people at other tables were saying. He just knew that what he had witnessed was better than a Lash Larue movie.

Eighteen

Railey grinned and said, "Guess I kind of made the preacher mad, huh?"

"I reckon you did, but it didn't hurt my feelings none."

"I saw you sitting out there watching him the other night."

"What night?"

"You know when I mean, Johnny. . . the night he was spying on Bailey Thompson. I figure you were spying on him."

"Well I. . . "

"So you know about Bailey and Marcie Scott."

Johnny shrugged. "I don't figure it's any of my business."

"It's not any of the preacher's business, either. But he's an evil man and thrives on exploiting the weaknesses of others."

"I ain't never heard anybody talk about the preacher like that before."

"And, you ought not to be hearing it now," said Ozzie Guidry, who was standing by their table and seemed to be trying to tower over them. Given Guidry's small stature, that was a mighty tall order. "That what you said about the preacher just now. . . I heard it."

Railey kind of peeked around so he could see Mouse Malone, who was standing behind Guidry. Then he spoke ever so slowly. "I'm going to say this so you'll be sure to understand it, Ozzie. I don't care what you think about what I say. . . and that goes for Mouse and your buddy the sheriff. By the way, where is he. . . drunk as usual?"

Guidry colored up real quick. "You know, Winston, you'd better be watching what you say. There's lots of folks who ain't that pleased about you teaching at the school anyway."

Railey shrugged his shoulders. "Let them get me fired. I don't really need the money."

Everyone in town knew that to be true. Winston Railey had plenty of money. If he wasn't the richest man in town, he was close to it. The word was that he got his money from an inheritance. Whatever the source, in times past it had attracted some of Walla's more eligible females. It didn't take them long to find out Railey wasn't interested in women. And, it didn't take those shunned ladies long to inform the rest of the town about it.

Mouse Malone piped up. "You ain't never been part of this town, Winston."

Railey laughed. "Well, la de da, Mouse. That just breaks my heart. I do so crave your intellectual companionship. . . and that of others in this town."

"That sounds kind of like you're being a jerk," Guidry said. "You got no call to talk to Mouse that way."

"And you've got no reason to talk to me at all, Ozzie. Besides, I don't know why you're so concerned about what I say about the preacher. You never darken the door of the church."

Guidry took a long drag on his cigarette. "Maybe I don't go to church, but mama taught me to respect a man of God."

"I respect a man of God, too. . . when I meet one. Now why don't you and your little shadow go back to your table and let me talk to Johnny here. Go cut someone's hair. And you, Mouse, go change someone's oil."

Neither Guidry nor Mouse knew what to say. The barber decided to direct his words toward Johnny. "Well, Johnny, people are already talking about you being a nigger lover and Jew lover. I guess you want to get the reputation of being a. . . "

"That's enough," Railey said, standing to his feet.

"Oh, are you gonna stop me from saying something to Johnny, Winston?"

"No, Ozzie, you can say whatever you like. I figure Jake Tobin will be the one to say something to you about it."

Guidry's face flushed again. He wouldn't admit it, but was glad Railey had stopped him. It was one thing to get a little tough with Winston Railey, quite another to offend Jake Tobin. "Let's get out of here, Mouse," he said. "We both got work to do."

After they had left, Johnny asked, "What was he gonna say, Mr. Railey?"

Railey had sat down and was nursing his coffee. "No telling, Johnny. You know what a loudmouth Ozzie is."

"That was some argument," Johnny said, appreciatively.

Railey laughed. "It was, wasn't it? Must be my day. I've made the preacher and two of the town's leading citizens mad."

"I wouldn't call Mr. Guidry and Mr. Malone leading citizens."

"I was joking."

Johnny smiled. "Figured you had to be. Ain't you afraid the sheriff is gonna get on you for giving Mr. Guidry and Mr. Malone a bad time?"

"The sheriff and I. . . well, I don't like him but we get along. I can assure you he won't say anything to me."

"About Mr. Thompson and Mrs. Scott. . . I ain't gonna say nothing about that to anybody."

Railey smiled. "You like Bailey, don't you?"

"Yes sir, I do. He's always been straight with me. . . even when he's whipped my tail in school."

Railey's smile turned to a laugh. "Bailey does believe sparing the rod spoils the child."

"He and my daddy both."

"This thing with Mrs. Scott, though. . . it worries me."

"You think maybe Mr. Scott will find out?"

"That's not what worries me."

"What then?"

"Mrs. Scott. . . she's not what she seems."

"What do you mean?"

"I'm not ready to say."

"She sure is pretty."

Railey smiled again. "In time, Johnny, you'll learn that beauty is not the best way to judge a person. Beauty can be not only deceitful, but deceptive."

They talked on for a while about nothing in particular. Johnny had been told that Winston Railey was unusual, but had never before spent any time with him. He had never had him as a teacher, he had mostly just seen him in the library. From what he now knew, he liked the guy. Anyone who stood up to Brother Marvin Baker, Ozzie Guidry and Mouse Malone couldn't be all bad.

Johnny left the cafe before Railey, stepped out into the heat and drank in the August sunshine. The first day of school was in the offing, the freedom of summer fast disappearing. But, so far it had been a wonderful day. He hoped it would continue as such. Maybe, he thought, I'll just go down under the trestle and catch that old bass again.

Before he could make a move in that direction, though, he saw Ben Jim Cade walking toward the cafe, his brogans kicking up dust. He intercepted him.

"I've got good news."

"What kind of good news?" Ben Jim asked.

"I talked to an FBI agent. He's gonna go talk to Willard Jordan."

"Hmmm. Well now, don't you get your hopes up none. The fact that he's gonna talk to him don't mean nothing."

"I think it does. The agent. . . his name's Carter Duncan. . . he thinks maybe Willard Jordan might have something to do with little Sadie being missing."

"You sure you ain't planted that in the man's mind?"

Johnny grinned. "Now why would you say something like that?"

"Because you're bad about sowing seeds. One of these days you're gonna have to reap what you sow."

"You're heading for the cafe, huh?"

"Got to have some coffee this fine morning."

"You missed all the fireworks."

"What you talking about?"

So Johnny told Ben Jim about the confrontation in the cafe. He thought Ben Jim would be pleased, but his friend frowned. "Mr. Railey. . . he's a good man, but he starts raising Cain with the wrong people. . . he's gonna get himself in all kinds of trouble."

"I didn't know you knew Mr. Railey," Johnny said.

"Ain't nobody knows him all that well. But, I done some yard work for him. . . cleaning up around his place. He's different than most."

"What do you mean?"

"Well, when I work for him he always fixes a big dinner. . . makes me sit right down at the same table with him to eat."

"What's so strange about that? Mama makes you sit down at the table with us, too."

Ben Jim's mouth did what passed for a smile. "Your folks. . . I have to say they're different, too."

Johnny told Ben Jim that he and his dad were going to San Miguel Creek after Jake Tobin got off work, asked if he would like to come along. "It's a mighty tempting offer, but I need to do some stuff around the house."

"Like what?"

"Like hoe the garden. The weeds are about to take over my collard greens."

"Far as I'm concerned that wouldn't be any loss. I love turnip greens, but can't stand collards."

"That's your loss. Ain't anything any better than a good pot of collards greens with cornbread. Besides, another reason is that I'm about burned out on catfish. I don't want to clean no more of the things for a while. . . and I don't want to eat no more for a while."

After Ben Jim went in the back door of the cafe, Johnny thought about going down to the trestle. He decided, instead, to go over to the Catholic Church. He had seen Father Ingram only in passing since they had found the little boy's body in the creek. He figured on asking the priest if he wanted to go fishing with him and his dad.

Bessie Jackson answered his knock. "What you doing here this early in the morning, Johnny?"

"Father Ingram still asleep?"

"Oh, no. . . he has been up for hours. He in his library doing some studying."

"Well, I ain't gonna mess with him then."

"You just come on in. It's time for the man to have his coffee."

Johnny entered the door and asked, "You been doing okay, Aunt Bessie?"

"About as well as can be expected when you get my age."

"You ain't old."

She laughed. "I sure ain't no spring chicken. Now you come on in here to the kitchen table and let me pour you a cup of coffee. I'll go tell Father Ingram that you're here."

He followed the big woman into the kitchen, sat down at the table while she was getting him a cup and said, "Sure bad about the Williams family, ain't it?"

She paused before pouring the coffee. "Sure is. There's lots of meanness going on in the world, Johnny."

"Well, maybe the killer will be caught pretty soon."

"Ain't likely."

"Why do you say that, Aunt Bessie?"

"Seem like the bad ones just keep getting by with stuff."

"I heard there was an FBI man looking into the murders."

"He ain't got far to look."

"What do you mean?"

"Everybody know Isaac Simpson done it. He had his eye on Clarice Williams cause she was such a fine looking woman. She wouldn't have nothing to do with him, so folks figure Isaac done got mad and killed them all."

Johnny was shocked and it registered on his face. "You telling me all the coloreds think it was Isaac?"

"Sure am. Why, when Clarice was working for the Reverend Baker. . . "

"Wait a minute now, Aunt Bessie. You telling me Clarice Williams worked for Brother Baker?"

"She sure did. Didn't you know that?"

"No. . . I sure didn't."

"Well, she just worked a couple of days a week. Then she up and quit."

"Why?"

"She was gonna go to work for Mrs. Scott. . . take care of little Sadie. But that ain't the only reason."

"What's another one?"

"She said she liked Mrs. Baker, but she didn't like the Reverend at all."

"Can't say as I blame her. . . especially with the way he feels about colored folks."

"Oh, I don't think it had nothing to do with the way he feels about coloreds. It was something else."

"What?"

"You the most naturally curious boy I know. But, it ain't something I ought to be talking to you about. . . you being so young and all."

"Dang it, Aunt Bessie. . . you keeping stuff from me, how am I ever gonna learn anything?"

She rolled her eyes. "Hmmm. . . you already know more than a boy your age ought to know. Aunt Bessie ain't gonna be the one to tell you no more. Now you drink your coffee and don't be cussing none, cause if you do I'm gonna have your mama wash your mouth out with lye soap."

Johnny laughed. "It won't be the first time. I think you're gonna be surprised about who the killer really is, though, because it ain't Isaac."

"Now what you know about who the killer is?"

"I know there's an FBI man might be arresting the killer right now."

She feigned surprise. "And who this killer might be?"

"I can't tell you that. . . not until he's arrested."

"Won't be no need then. You know how word travels in this town."

"Okay, I'll tell you. . . but you've got to promise to keep it a secret."

"Ain't nobody can keep secrets no better than Aunt Bessie."

"It's Willard Jordan."

"What you talking about, child?"

"I think he's gonna be arrested for the killing."

"Ain't no way. The man's the sheriff's cousin. Ain't no white man gonna be arrested for killing no colored round these parts."

"Things are changing, Aunt Bessie."

"They ain't changing that much. Now don't you go spouting off this foolishness to other folks. Don't you be telling Father Ingram."

In his usual off-the-wall manner, Johnny asked, "You ever thought about becoming a Catholic, Aunt Bessie?"

She pulled her neck back into her chin until it almost disappeared. "Course I ain't thought about becoming no Catholic. I'm gonna be a Baptist until the day I die. Why do you want to ask something like that for?"

Johnny shrugged his shoulders. "Just thought I'd ask. You like Father Ingram, don't you?"

"Sure do. But liking the man ain't got anything to do with the way I worship the Lord. I've heard Father Ingram talk to the people and he talks too quiet to suit me. A preacher man. . . he's got to open his mouth and bellow like a bull. He's got to make sure the people and the Lord is listening."

"I kind of figure it makes a difference what he says, not just being loud."

"Course it do."

"Well, Brother Baker's a Baptist."

She grunted. "He ain't my kind of Baptist."

"And, what kind of Baptist is that?"

"I'm a shouting washed in the blood of the Lamb Baptist."

"Brother Baker's got the shouting part down. I don't know about the rest of it."

She laughed. "You just sit here drinking your coffee. I'll go tell Father Ingram that you're here."

She waddled out of the room and Johnny reflected on what she had said, especially about Clarice Williams working for Brother Baker and being anxious to leave his employ. Johnny's mental juices were flowing, his imagination running wild.

Ingram entered the room and said, "Johnny. . . pleasure to see you."

Johnny started to stand but the priest signaled him to remain seated. Then he took the chair across the table from Johnny. Bessie, who had followed Ingram into the room, poured him a cup of coffee.

"I feel I owe you an apology, Johnny."

"For what?"

"I thought you might want to talk to me about what happened at the creek. . . and maybe you think I haven't been available. I know discovering that child's body was hard on you."

"It was hard on a lot of people, I guess. Some, though, it didn't seem to bother at all."

"Well, I have tried to find you on a couple of occasions," Ingram said, "but you're a hard one to pin down. I guess I should have come over to your folks' house in the evening."

"Oh, you don't owe me an apology, Father Ingram. I've been pretty busy."

"Doing what?"

Bessie answered. "Putting his nose where it don't belong."

Johnny laughed. "To Aunt Bessie I'm always gonna be a baby."

She smiled, exposing pearly white teeth between her thick lips. "You're a baby all right."

The priest could see there was a special chemistry between his housekeeper and Johnny. It was something he had witnessed before in the South. He didn't understand it, but appreciated it. "I'm afraid the two of you have lost me," he said.

Eighteen

"Aunt Bessie. . . she thinks Isaac Simpson killed the Williams family. Oh, I don't guess you know Isaac, do you?"

"No. . . I don't."

"Anyway, I happen to know it wasn't Isaac."

"Johnny, he says it was a white man," Bessie said.

"Who?" Ingram asked.

"I ain't at liberty to say. The FBI man who's been here talking to Mr. and Mrs. Scott. . . he's probably gonna arrest the guy. I think he probably had something to do with Sadie being missing, too."

"They ain't no way a white man is gonna be arrested for killing no colored folks," Bessie said. "Now if the man done got little Sadie, that's a different story."

The memory of what he saw at the Williams house caused the priest to shudder. "I can't believe that, Bessie. Surely, the people here will not tolerate that kind of crime against anyone."

"That shows you ain't from these parts," Johnny said. "Aunt Bessie's telling the truth. . . if we was having to depend on the sheriff or police chief. But an FBI man has to look at things a lot different."

"What makes you so sure the man you're talking about committed the murders?" Ingram asked.

"Well, there's some evidence."

"What kind of evidence?"

"Well, I don't. . . well, it kind of. . . "

"What the boy is trying to say is that he's done been snooping around. And, they ain't any better than Johnny in doing that. But he ain't gonna say nothing because if his daddy found out he's gonna get one good whipping."

Johnny grinned. "Aunt Bessie can always get to the heart of the matter."

The priest frowned. "If I was your daddy, I'd be upset, too. There's a crazy killer on the loose and I don't think you should be putting yourself in unnecessary danger. Let the law handle it. Billy Burton. . . he's a good man."

"Ain't nothing wrong with Billy, but he can't do nothing without the sheriff telling him to do it."

"Nevertheless, this isn't something for a boy your age to be involved in."

Johnny knew Ingram was only thinking of his well being, but didn't like being told what he should or shouldn't do. So he changed the subject. "Daddy and me. . . we're going down to the creek late this afternoon to do some catfishing. You want to come along?"

The priest had not mentally recovered from their last fishing trip, which began with the discovery of the child's body and the carnage of his parents. "I appreciate the offer, but there's a lot I have to do around here."

"Like what?"

Ingram laughed. Bessie said, "I done told you that Johnny's the most curious boy I ever knowed."

"That's healthy," the priest said. "You don't ever want to lose your curiosity, Johnny."

They talked for a while longer and Johnny left. He was halfway home when he realized that Ingram hadn't answered his question.

NINETEEN

Billy Burton dropped by Bernstein's store about mid morning on Saturday for a cold Coke. While drinking it he engaged Johnny, who was stacking canned goods on a shelf, in conversation. "You and your dad catch any catfish last night?"

"I don't remember telling you we was going fishing."

"Not sure you did. You know how it is around here, though. People talk. Somebody must've told me."

Johnny laughed. "Then they ought to have told you how many fish we caught."

Billy grinned. "You got me there."

"You ever known me and daddy to fail catching some catfish?"

"No. . . to tell you the truth, sure ain't. But you might tell me how many."

"Well, I ain't sure how many. But they were too heavy for one man to carry. We tied our stringer to the middle of a pole and carried them between us."

Billy shook his head in appreciation. "I just never have that kind of luck when I go fishing."

"Luck ain't got nothing to do with it. You go with me and daddy sometime and you'll see."

"I'd like to do that."

"You got any news for me?" Johnny asked.

"News?"

"You know. . . anything happen with Willard Jordan?"

The deputy shrugged his shoulders. "Nothing that I know about."

"I figured Carter Duncan would have him in custody by now."

"Carter Duncan ain't here. He left town Friday."

Johnny's eyes filled with disbelief. "Didn't he go out and talk to Willard Jordan?"

"If he did, I sure don't know nothing about it. The man acted like he couldn't wait to get out of town. I think we've seen the last of him."

There was a bitter taste in Johnny's mouth. There always was when he found out someone had lied to him. Anger quickly enveloped his mind, then hardened to a steely resolve. "Well, dang it, I guess I'm just gonna have to go see Willard Jordan myself."

"Now you stay away from that man. I told you he was dangerous."

"I might've known nobody would mess with the sheriff's kin. Well, I'm sure not afraid of him."

Billy sighed. "Everybody knows you ain't afraid of nothing or nobody, Johnny. But you've got to promise me you ain't going out to Willard Jordan's place. The sheriff doesn't even go out there. I think he's scared of Willard."

"I ain't promisin' nothing."

"Then I'm gonna have to tell Jake."

"You wouldn't do that."

"To keep you from getting hurt, I would."

"Okay, I won't go out there."

"Don't you be lying to me. You've got to promise."

"Okay then, I promise."

"You ain't got your fingers crossed or anything, have you? I know if you did the promise wouldn't be worth nothing."

Johnny semi-laughed. "No, I ain't got my fingers crossed." However, he was thinking, *My toes. . . now that's another matter.*

"You gonna be at the baseball game tomorrow afternoon?" the deputy asked.

"Course I'm gonna be there, Billy. It's the last game of the season. I wouldn't miss daddy pitching against Leesville for nothing."

"Guess I'll see you at the game then. And you remember what you promised me."

"I ain't likely to forget. . . not with you threatening to tell daddy."

The truth was that Johnny had thought about telling Jake Tobin about Willard Jordan. However, if he told him he would also have to tell him that Ben Jim had done the actual tracking. He wasn't sure how his dad would react to learning Ben Jim had been with him, even though the older man had gone along to protect him. His dad's temper was legendary and there was no telling what might set it off. Johnny just knew he didn't want his dad mad at Ben Jim. Their friendship had come too far to have it destroyed for no good reason.

During an afternoon lull in business, Sol Bernstein asked Johnny to have a cold drink with him. Johnny chose a Coke, the grocer a grape. "So, Johnny. . . how you doing?"

Johnny shrugged. "Can't complain, Mr. Bernstein. Looks like we're running a little short of potatoes."

"Truck'll be here Monday. But when I ask *how you doing*? I'm wondering about how you're feeling since finding the little boy in the creek."

"Oh, I'm doing okay."

"Something like that. . . it would give me nightmares."

"Well, I ain't slept all that well since it happened," Johnny said. He thought, of course, part of that has to do with seeing the whole Williams family dead.

Bernstein said, "This has been a bad summer. . . all those people murdered and little Sadie missing. I don't like what's happening here."

"Do you know Willard Jordan, Mr. Bernstein?"

The question caught the grocer off guard. "Why do you ask?"

"Oh, no reason. Just curious. Billy was talking about him and I don't guess I've ever seen him in here."

"When Mr. Jordan comes in it's usually the middle of the week," Bernstein said.

"What kind of guy is he?"

"Mr. Jordan?"

"Yeah."

"Quiet. He doesn't say much."

"What does he do?"

"I don't know."

"Does he have credit here or anything?"

Bernstein laughed. "You sure are a curious boy."

Johnny grinned. "Can't help it. . . just my nature."

"Well, Mr. Jordan doesn't have credit. . . never asked for it. He always pays cash for everything."

"Would you give him credit if he asked for it?"

"Probably. No reason not to."

"What kind of stuff does he buy?"

The grocer laughed again. "Same as anybody else. Just groceries. What's this all about, Johnny?"

"Nothing. . . just curiosity. He ever buy shotgun shells?"

"I think so. Everybody around here buys shotgun shells. Is there anything I should know, Johnny?"

"Nothing I know about. Ruth and Ruta going to the dance tonight?"

The grocer was taken aback by the question. It was just like Johnny, though, he thought, to suddenly switch from talking about Willard Jordan to the Catholic dance that was being held that night. "No, I don't think they have any plans to go. I'm not sure they'd be welcome."

"I thought everybody was welcome, except kids like me."

"Our religion bothers some people."

"You talking about being Jews?"

"Yes. . . I guess I am."

"Pretty as Ruth and Ruta are. . . I figured a lot of guys would be camped on your doorstep."

"I'm afraid they don't have much of a social life here."

"If I was old enough, one of them would."

Bernstein laughed. "Which one?"

Johnny grinned. "Be kind of hard to choose."

Later that afternoon Father Walter Ingram stopped by the store to buy tobacco for his pipe. "I ain't never seen you smoking a pipe," Johnny said. "Didn't know you smoked anything."

"I don't usually smoke in public," the priest said.

"Do you think people will think less of you for smoking?"

Ingram laughed. "Well, no. Then again. . . yes, I guess I do."

"I smoke a little myself," Johnny said.

"Well, I don't think I approve of a boy your age smoking cigarettes."

"Oh, I don't smoke cigarettes. Bobby and me. . . sometimes we smoke Muscatine vine."

"Muscatine vine?"

"Yeah, you know. . . Muscatine grapes. People around here pick them and make wine. My folks do it."

"Does your dad know you're smoking grape vine?" the priest asked, laughing.

"You kidding? He would tan my hide."

"So you're ashamed of your smoking, too?"

"More scared than ashamed."

Then Johnny told him about Ruth and Ruta, and how they didn't feel welcome at the dance. "I'll invite them right now," Ingram said.

TWENTY

While Johnny was talking to the priest there was an argument going on in the Scott house. "I want to go," Marcie said, angrily.

"I don't think it'll look good. . . Sadie being missing for such a short time," Vernon said.

"That didn't seem to matter when it was time to start football practice."

"That's different. . . that's my job."

"You could have waited. People expected you to."

"I ain't gonna argue with you, Marcie. I'm just telling you what I think."

"You do a lot of that, Vernon. Too much if you ask me."

The coach sighed and threw up his hands in disgust. "I can't talk to you. . . about anything."

"You don't talk. . . you preach. You tell."

"Well, suit yourself. I ain't gonna argue about it anymore."

Twenty

"You coming?"

"That means you're definitely going?"

"It sure as does."

"Then I ain't got much choice. . . do I? You go to the dance by yourself and people are really gonna talk."

She smiled. "Oh, c'mon, Vernon. . . it'll be good for us to get out. We can't just quit living because Sadie's gone."

"You surprise me, Marcie. It ain't been that long ago you was so upset and crying that I wasn't sure you was ever gonna be able to get out of bed. I just don't understand the sudden change."

"I just got it in my mind that Sadie's all right."

He shook his head in dismay. "I wish I could get it in mine. Who told you to start thinking she was okay. . . the dang preacher?"

Marcie smiled again. "Well now, he did encourage us to have faith. But, I don't think he'd want that faith to lead to dancing. You know how he feels about dancing."

"I don't like dancing myself, but not for the same reason. I always feel like I've got two left feet."

"You don't have to dance."

"Ain't a matter of not having to. . . I can't."

"You always enjoy talking to people. . . and drinking."

"Yeah. . . and then the preacher makes me feel guilty as the dickens. You reckon he knows I drink a little?"

She shrugged. "I don't know. I doubt it. Who's gonna tell? Everyone I know who'll be at the dance drinks a little. If they're Baptists they're sure not going to run tell the preacher on you. They're probably afraid you'll tell on them."

He sighed. "I guess you're right. Maybe Bailey'll be there. Then you'll at least have a dancing partner."

Marcie looked at her husband and wondered if there was any hidden meaning in the mention of Bailey Thompson. She decided there wasn't. *He doesn't know*, she thought. *He's too preoccupied with football to know what I do.*

There was considerable truth to her thinking. Vernon Scott lived and died football. There was rarely a time when some aspect of the game wasn't running through his mind. He was possessed by the sport.

"Okay, I'm going, Marcie, but I ain't gonna dress up," he said, defiantly. He needed to try to assert authority in some small way.

"You wear whatever you like, Vernon. I don't know what you call dressing up, but I've never seen anyone around here do it." *It doesn't matter what he wears*, she thought. *You can't make a silk purse out of a sow's ear.*

"Some guys wear ties to the dance."

"Well, you don't have to."

"Don't intend to. . . hate wearing one to church."

She sighed. "Like I said, Vernon, I don't care what you wear."

"You wouldn't like it if I wore my coaching gear."

"If you want to look like one of these yokels. . . fine and dandy with me. I'm gonna take a bath now and start getting ready."

"It's early."

"Well, I'm a little more concerned about how I look than you are."

She left him in the living room sitting in his favorite chair, fuming. It was hot in the house, even with all the windows open and a fan working at full capacity. Summers were awful in Walla. The heat during part of the fall could be awful, too.

Vernon picked up a book Marcie had been reading, looked at the first page and threw it down. He didn't like to read, though he mentally tried not to admit that to himself. After all, he was a teacher. For a teacher not to like to read was like a preacher who didn't believe the Bible.

He wished he had scheduled football practice for the evening. Some of the parents would have complained about that, though. He had practices Monday through Thursday nights, but some parents would object to Friday, Saturday and Sunday night practices. That's what Vernon really wanted, practice seven nights a week, then practice seven days a week when school started. It wouldn't have bothered him if they practiced the afternoon before a game.

Some people, he thought, *just don't understand the game. They don't understand what it takes to be good.*

Vernon didn't know beans about what it took to excel in the classroom, but thought he knew what it took in athletic competition. He figured the key was repetition, just to keep doing something over and over again. Whether what was being done was right, now that was another matter.

People in Walla may have had a lot of doubts about Vernon in some areas, but the one thing they couldn't doubt was his dedication. Not as football coach, at least. They could have searched the nation and not found anyone more dedicated to football.

Sitting there in his modestly furnished rented home, Vernon pondered his wife's mood swings. She had always been a bit strange to his way of thinking, even mysterious. Now, however, the changes in her were not only more pronounced but were also more frequent. It seemed almost that her personality went to a new mood every day, with her whims and attitudes running an emotional gauntlet.

God knows I've never understood her, he thought. *But lately it's been worse than ever before.*

Vernon knew Marcie was beautiful. People had told him often enough, though that was the one thing he didn't need to be schooled in. From the time he first met her until the present, he had thought she was the prettiest woman he had ever seen.

The problem was that he didn't desire her. There had been some moments early on in their marriage when the wanting her was there, but not now. He wasn't sure when the desire had died, but didn't care to rekindle it. It just didn't bother him.

What did bother him was Sadie being gone. He loved Sadie. Too much, some said. They said he had what might be called an unnatural love for the child.

There did seem to be a correlation between Sadie's arrival in the world and his desire for Marcie depreciating. It seemed the older Sadie got the less interested he was in Marcie.

Now Sadie was gone and he wasn't sure he would ever see her again. He had maintained his composure in public, but had cried much in secret. He wished he could have the kind of faith Marcie had, the faith that she was okay. He wasn't sure, of course, that it was real faith. Maybe it was just one of her many mood swings. Maybe she would wake up Sunday morning, be contrite for having gone to the dance and go to pieces.

He knew Marcie was fragile mentally, that it would not take much to set her off. He had been witness to her explosions before, many of which had been directed at him.

Her new attitude, though, this idea that Sadie was okay, was both puzzling and frightening. He mentally cursed Brother Marvin Baker for putting such a notion in her head, if, indeed, the preacher was guilty. Marcie, he thought, often misinterpreted what people told her. He did not consider himself a genius in defining a conversation, but didn't try to read more into what people said than was there. Marcie, he believed, made what people said conform to what she wanted them to say.

Oh, well, maybe the dance will calm her a bit, he thought. *As far as I'm concerned, though, it's a poor way to spend a Saturday night.*

• • •

While Vernon was doing his pondering, Marcie was soaking in the tub. She had added a generous portion of bubble bath to the water, which was deep and hot, and was enjoying the way the combination felt to her skin.

Marcie was anticipating a good time at the dance, a few drinks to lighten her mood and seeing the jealousy light up in the eyes of other women when they saw her. She liked the latter as much as anything, seeing and talking to women who envied her beauty, whose possessive attitudes toward their husbands heightened when she was around.

She liked how they tried to treat her just like one of them, like a dowdy housewife with nothing to talk about except her kids and husband and what she planned to cook for Sunday dinner. *But, they know I'm not like them,* she thought. *They know it all too well.*

Marcie appreciated her beauty as much as anybody. From the time she was able to comprehend as a child, she had been confident of it. Her father had started calling her his pretty girl the day she was born. He still did. No man had ever been, or ever would be, as important to her as her father. There was no one else with whom she could talk so freely and honestly.

Her mother was more like the dowdy housewives she would see at the dance. She was repetitious in conversation, with nothing, really, to talk about. She felt sorry for her father, that he had for years been chained to a woman whose thinking was on par with that of the most ignorant, boring person imaginable.

Marcie was as confident of her intelligence as she was of her beauty, though there had been a setback or two that tortured the subconscious of her mind. In high school she would have been valedictorian had it not been for Amos Taylor. He beat her out by a point. She hated Amos Taylor for stealing an honor that she believed was rightfully hers. But, she didn't hate Amos as much as she hated Mrs. Doris Gibson.

Doris Gibson was the home economics teacher whose grading of her work had caused Marcie to lose the valedictorian plum. Marcie thought to lose was bad enough, but to lose for something as worthless and suspect as home economics as an academic subject was ludicrous.

Like her husband, Marcie had been born and raised in Arkansas. Her origin, however, was Little Rock, where her father was a successful retailer. She had a sister who was ten years older, whose age had negated any competition she might have felt for her father's affection. Marcie's father had always been partial to her, said he didn't have any other children because he couldn't improve on the perfection that was his youngest daughter. Marcie believed that.

She had planned on going to the University of Arkansas, but had let a girlfriend talk her into going to a teachers college in Arkadelphia. There were some advantages to the place, though her intelligence had never been challenged there. She figured it would be easy enough to graduate at the top of her class, but this time a boy named Harry Stinson beat her by a fraction of a point. It galled her because she believed no man, other than her father, was on par with her in terms of intelligence.

As to why she had married Vernon Scott, who played football at the college, she wasn't sure. Some of her catty friends said it was because he would never challenge her intellectually, that she would be able to reign over him. Maybe they were right. All she knew was that she would never find a man like her father, and Vernon seemed like a good idea at the time.

She wasn't sure whether she loved Bailey, but if it wasn't the real thing it was better than what she had known up to this point. Bailey was tender, caring, and possessed a few of her father's attributes.

Soaking there in the tub she wondered if she and Bailey would be able to snatch some time alone and away from the gossipy eyes of those at the dance. She had gotten word to him that she was going, with or without Vernon. She knew he was surprised by her decision to go, that most people would be. Many townspeople, she thought, wouldn't dare to say anything but would let their eyes speak for them.

Oh, well, it all has to come out in the wash sooner or later, she thought. *Vernon will probably be relieved when I'm not around. He doesn't care about me anyway. . . just Sadie.*

Thinking about her daughter, she smiled. *If Vernon only knew*, she thought. Then she frowned. She had never been jealous of another woman. But Sadie, that was a different story. From the time Sadie was born Marcie's father had called his granddaughter *my pretty girl.*

TWENTY ONE

Hillbilly, or country, was the music of choice for most of those in the parish. Even the coloreds sang country songs, probably because that's all the big radio station in Shreveport played. The Negroes changed their tune in church, though, turning to a foot stomping, rocking gospel. The country and gospel kind of intertwined.

Anyway, a hillbilly band from Shreveport was featured at the Catholic dance. The band had at times even played on the *Louisiana Hayride* in Shreveport, which to folks in Walla was the equivalent of playing at Carnegie Hall. People lucky enough to go to the *Louisiana Hayride* had something to talk to their neighbors about for months. Even a lifetime.

This dance was going to be special.

Father Walter Ingram had little, if anything, to do with the dance. The kind of music played at the dance was alien to the priest's upbringing, though he was accepting of it. The actual event was handled by some of his more devoted parishioners, a percentage of the money going to the church coffers.

Eyes turned when Marcie Scott entered the large hall where the dance was being held. She was wearing a white sundress. No one noticed what Vernon Scott was wearing, if, indeed, they noticed him at all.

Marcie, most men thought, looked like a movie star. Their wives had a different opinion.

There was a moment of awkwardness when no one seemed to know what to do. Then Mary Lou Tobin, whose own beauty, though not as flashy, made her the equal of Marcie, came up and said, "I'm glad to see you and Vernon here."

Marcie smiled. "Maybe we were wrong to come, Mary Lou."

"No you weren't. You've got to go on living."

There was a lot about Mary Lou that bothered Marcie. The fact that Johnny's mother was her equal in beauty was the primary thing, though Marcie wasn't about to admit that anyone came close to her in that department. She also sensed Mary Lou wasn't shabby intellectually, another mark against her. Marcie believed she was the smartest person in Walla, maybe the whole parish. She didn't like competition from any source.

My god, she thought, angry at herself. *Mary Lou didn't go to college, probably didn't even finish high school.*

Vernon asked, smiling, "You hear about what that boy of yours did the other night, Mary Lou?"

"If you're talking about Johnny. . . there's no telling."

"He was just standing on the sidelines watching us practice when Elmer Guerdat broke through the line and was running for a touchdown. Johnny came on the field and blind-sided him. Dangest thing I ever saw."

Mary Lou sighed and shook her head in resignation. "I don't guess Johnny said why he did something like that?"

"I think Elmer was teasing him about something earlier."

"Johnny's temper is gonna get him in trouble one of these days. I sure do like that dress you're wearing, Marcie."

"Oh, it's just something I picked up in Shreveport. It's cool. . . feels good on a hot night like this."

Twenty One

Mary Lou's dress was plain and homemade. She had never shopped in Shreveport. Marcie did all her shopping there and didn't have any homemade dresses. With Vernon's and Marcie's combined salaries from the school, they had a better than average monthly income for the area. However, Marcie also received a monthly check from her father.

"Well, you look good in it. . . no doubt about that," Mary Lou said.

Jake Tobin walked up and put his arm around his wife. He gave her an affectionate squeeze and said, "Are you gonna talk all night or are we gonna dance?" He nodded and smiled at the Scotts and said, "Howdy. . . Marcie, Vernon. . . good to see you."

Vernon shook Jake's hand and Mary Lou said, "I been waitin' to dance ever since we got here. I ain't been the one outside smoking and drinking."

Jake grinned. "I ain't much of a dancer until I get a drink."

"I ain't much of a dancer even if I'm drunk," Vernon said. "Some boys outside got a bottle, do they, Jake?"

"Be harder to find one that ain't got one," Jake replied, laughing. "But, if you have any trouble just look on the front seat of my car."

"Ain't you gonna dance with Marcie?" Mary Lou asked.

Vernon grunted. "She ain't gonna have any trouble finding someone to dance with her."

"I'm sure she ain't. I just thought. . . "

"Mary Lou, you just quit your thinking and come on and dance," Jake said.

"Go on," Marcie said. "Vernon's right. I'm not gonna have any trouble finding a partner."

The Tobins went out on the dance floor and Vernon said, "Nice people."

Marcie agreed. "Yes. . . they are."

"There's Bailey," Vernon said, motioning for the principal to come join them. When he arrived the coach said, "Good to see you here, Bailey. You want to take my wife off my hands so I can go get a drink?"

Bailey didn't know how to reply. "I guess that's up to Marcie. Would you like to dance, Marcie?"

She smiled. "I certainly would. You go along Vernon. Drink all you want and talk football all you want. Bailey'll take care of me."

When she was on the dance floor in Bailey's arms and her husband was gone from sight, Marcie whispered, "People are looking at us."

"You knew they would be."

"You think they know?"

"I don't know. People always want to think the worst."

She laughed. "You're a cynic, Bailey."

He smiled. "I guess I am. Whatever I am, you look especially beautiful tonight."

"Thank you."

"I like your dress."

"I hope that's always the case."

"Why wouldn't it be?"

"Things change."

"The way I feel about you, Marcie. . . that's never gonna change. You know how much I love you."

"What are we gonna do about it?"

"I guess that's up to you."

She liked his answer, the fact that he acknowledged she was in control. "I guess it is. When the time's right. . . I'll tell you."

He looked into her eyes and saw the mystery there. However, he didn't have a clue as to what she was talking about.

"You're surprised, aren't you?" she asked.

"About what?"

"My being here. . . with what happened to Sadie. . . it not being that long ago that it happened."

"Yeah. . . I guess I am."

"She's okay."

"Sadie?"

"Yes."

"What do you mean? How do you know that?"

"I just have faith. . . that's all. I'm at peace about it."

He couldn't understand this woman that he loved, couldn't understand how her moods could change so quickly and dramatically. But, as always, he was reluctant to question her too intensely. His greatest fear was that he might say something that would drive her away. He knew he couldn't handle that.

• • •

Marcie was right in thinking her presence at the dance was being discussed, and by practically everyone there. There was a group who felt her presence violated some standard of decency in regard to a particular vague period of time required for mourning the loss of a loved one. The other group felt such a period of time had been observed and that she had every right to get on with her life.

Almost all agreed that her close dancing with Bailey Thompson was shameful, and more a violation of morality than simply being at the event. Some even lamented poor Vernon Scott's burden. For most, however, Vernon didn't conjure up much in the way of pity.

When Bessie Jackson went to the hall's kitchen area to get more ingredients for the punch bowl, she was almost scared out of her wits by Johnny Tobin and Bobby Milam, who were hiding there. "What you boys mean being in this kitchen and the lights all out, Johnny Tobin?"

"Heck, Aunt Bessie, we didn't mean to scare you," Johnny replied. "We was just hiding in here watching our folks get falling down drunk."

"Well, you ain't got no business being in here. And don't you be cussing none cause this is the same as the church house."

Johnny rolled his eyes. "Now I don't think you mean that, Aunt Bessie. I don't think the Lord would approve of this kind of stuff going on. Besides, all I said was heck."

Bobby laughed and Bessie frowned. Then a big smile spread across her face. "You right, Johnny. I don't imagine He would."

"You know people are pouring whiskey in the punch you put out there, don't you?" Johnny asked.

"Sure, I know it. Ain't nothing I can do about it, though."

"I was telling Bobby a while ago that I'd like to load that punch bowl up with castor oil, give a lot of people a good case of the runs. They'd be running for the toilet instead of begging forgiveness for their sins tomorrow."

Bessie laughed. "You're one naturally mean white boy, Johnny Tobin. But that sure enough would be funny."

"You got any castor oil around here?"

"No I ain't. And if I did, you ain't gonna get Aunt Bessie mixed up in none of your meanness."

"You ain't gonna tell our folks we're here, are you?" Bobby asked.

"Now what would I want to do that for? If I go out and tell Mr. Jake. . . he's gonna come in here and give Johnny a good whipping. I expect your daddy would do the same. They're both having too good a time to have to come in here and whip your lily white butts."

Johnny laughed. "You're a pal, Aunt Bessie."

She grunted. "You just don't get into any meanness, Johnny."

When she left they went back to their hiding place, which had an opening that allowed them to see all that was going on. Johnny whispered, "Man, that Mrs. Scott is something, ain't she?"

"What do you mean?"

"Now what do you think I mean?"

"I don't know. Why don't you tell me."

"Look at her. . . she's a beauty."

"Well, it ain't right. . . you looking at a teacher like that."

Johnny grumbled, "You been hanging around Brother Baker too much lately. There ain't no fun in you."

"Just because I got some respect don't mean I can't have no fun. I have as much fun as you do."

Johnny laughed. "I kind of doubt that. And I got respect, too. I think Mrs. Scott's an okay teacher."

For a while they watched the dancing and listened to the music without saying anything. Johnny didn't like hillbilly music, even though his folks didn't seem to know any other kind. "Did you know my folks want me to be a hillbilly singer?"

"No," Bobby replied. "I thought they wanted you to be a baseball player."

"They do. They want me to be both. . . a ball player and a hillbilly singer."

"I ain't never heard you sing no hillbilly songs."

"I don't sing them. I don't like them. My voice is too good to be that kind of singer."

"Now that's the dangest thing I've ever heard. . . and I kind of like hillbilly music."

"Fine with me if you like it. Don't mean I have to."

• • •

Vernon Scott was standing by Jake Tobin's car, having a drink from Jake's bottle, when Billy Burton walked up. "Hey, coach. . . how you doing?"

"Fine, Billy. . . just fine."

"Kind of surprised to see you here."

"You ain't any more surprised to see me than I am to be here, Billy. Marcie's idea. I imagine a lot of folks are wondering why we're here."

"Oh, I didn't mean anything by it. I just ain't never noticed you being at one of these dances before."

"I've been to a few. . . just don't get out on the dance floor. Marcie now, she likes to dance. But me. . . I can't dance a lick."

"I'm the same way. Makes me nervous."

"You want a drink of this whiskey, Billy. Jake won't mind."

"No. . . better not. I've got to try to keep my head clear. Sheriff wants me out here in case there's trouble."

Vernon laughed. "You know for sure he ain't got a clear head by now, don't you?"

Billy shuffled his feet and fidgeted. "Well, I don't know. . . "

"You don't have to try to protect the jerk, Billy. Everybody knows he's a drunk. Bet he's passed out drunk somewhere."

"You know I can't say stuff like that, coach."

"You don't have to. Everybody says it for you. Now. . . you sure you don't want a drink of Jake's whiskey?"

Billy hesitated, then replied, "Well, maybe a little sip. Don't figure that's gonna cloud up my head too much, do you?"

Vernon laughed again. "Living around here. . . people be better off if they all kept their heads cloudy."

Billy grinned, took a swig from the bottle and said, "Ain't it the truth."

"What do you know about my wife, Billy?"

The deputy was taken aback by the question. "Can't say that I know nothing, really. I just know she's awful pretty."

Vernon snorted, took a swig from the bottle, sighed with resignation and said, "She's that all right. Now Mary Lou Tobin. . . she's just as pretty, don't you think?"

"I reckon so."

"I ain't trying to put you on the spot asking you about Marcie, Billy. I just thought you might've heard something. . . noticed something."

Billy was scared that Vernon was going to ask him directly about Marcie and Bailey Thompson. He shrugged. "Coach, I ain't heard or seen nothing."

"The reason I'm asking. . . she's been acting awful strange lately. At first she was almost sick to death about Sadie being missing. Now she acts like everything's okay. She made me come to the dance tonight, said she had faith Sadie was all right."

"I guess it's good she feels that way."

"I don't know whether it is or not. I figure that dang preacher. . . you know, Brother Baker. . . put some notions in her head. I guess it's fine for now, but what if. . . what if Sadie. . . "

The tears started streaming down Vernon's face. Billy was again caught in the dilemma of not knowing what to say or do. "Coach, I wish. . . "

"I'm okay, Billy," Vernon said, wiping his eyes with the sleeve of his shirt. "It's just that I really miss my little girl. I don't like acting like everything's okay because it ain't. It ain't gonna be all right until we get her back. . . if we ever do."

"You know I've done looked every place I can think of, coach. Everybody's done everything they could."

"People have been nice, Billy. . . no doubt about that. Everybody's worked real hard at finding her. . . except for maybe the sheriff. The man's useless."

Billy wanted to laugh, but it wasn't the time. "I'll take another drink of Jake's whiskey. . . if you're sure he won't mind."

"He won't mind. Jake ain't gonna go wanting because the punch bowl inside has more whiskey in it than punch."

Billy smiled. "Funny how that happens, ain't it?"

Vernon forced a smile. "Yeah. . . sure is. Nice there's a few Catholics in town that don't mind us Baptists having a drink in public now and then."

"Mama's a Baptist. I ain't one."

Twenty One

"Guess that's about the way it is for me, too, Billy."

"The preacher. . . Brother Baker. . . he don't like me at all."

"Well, I wouldn't lose any sleep over it. What's he got against you?"

"I'm not sure. But, I think he thinks I'm a bad influence on Johnny Tobin."

Vernon downright laughed. "You a bad influence on Johnny? Might be the other way around."

Billy grinned. "That Johnny. . . he's a cutter, ain't he?"

"Oh, he's that okay." Vernon then told Billy what had happened at the football field, what Johnny had done to Elmer Guerdat. "The little devil's not afraid of anything or anybody."

"All the Tobins are like that," Billy said. "You know Jake don't take nothing from nobody."

"Well, I sure as heck don't want to get him riled."

Somberly, Billy said, "Johnny. . . he's looked for Sadie as hard as anybody. Him and that old nigger. . . Ben Jim Cade."

"Yeah. . . I heard. Lots of people think Johnny ought to be more careful about who he associates with."

"Ben Jim's okay."

"I never heard anybody call him a good nigger."

"I ain't calling him that either. He's different than most."

"Oh, I wasn't trying to imply anything, Billy. I was just saying people don't call him a good nigger because he ain't as predictable as some of the others."

"That's for damn sure. The sheriff hates his guts."

"Better not be telling that around. A lot of people will start liking Ben Jim if they learn the sheriff don't like him. He might just become the most popular man in town."

Billy laughed. "Let me have another shot of that whiskey. . . if you're sure Jake won't mind."

"He told me to help myself. I don't know who made this stuff, but it's good. Real smooth."

Billy took a long drink, then said, "Reckon Jake might've made it? I'll bet he knows how."

"I imagine he does, but I doubt he has a still. I ain't never heard anybody say anything about him making whiskey."

"Closemouthed as Jake is. . . nobody would know."

"If you really want to know, why don't you ask him?"

"Not me. I ain't gonna pry into Jake Tobin's business. That ain't healthy."

Vernon laughed. "You're probably right. This trouble between you and the preacher, it. . . "

"Ain't no trouble as far as I'm concerned."

"Well, I guess it's safe to say you don't like Brother Baker?"

"I wouldn't want that floating around neither. My mama's a member of his church, you know. And she's like a lot of others. She thinks preachers are perfect."

"Well, I'm a member of Brother Baker's church, too. . . but I don't think he's perfect. If you want to know what I really think, I think he's a jerk. I wouldn't want that getting around neither. Lots of folks around town feel like your mother does about preachers."

"Oh, I ain't gonna say nothing."

Vernon seemed to be preoccupied in thought. Then he said, "Could be that Brother Baker put a lot of foolish notions in my wife's head. If I find out he did, you're liable to have to come after me, Billy. I'm just liable to kill the jerk."

• • •

As the night went on the music seemed to get louder and faster, the dancers slower. Maybe it was the alcohol, or tired limbs giving up after a hard week's work in the heat and humidity. Whatever, people just seemed to be going through the motions and smiling without purpose.

"She ain't trying to hide it none," Mary Lou Tobin said.

"Who are you talking about?" Jake asked.

"You know darn well who I'm talking about. Marcie and Bailey."

"I ain't been noticing. Maybe it's because you've got all my attention."

Mary Lou smiled. "I'm supposed to. I'm your wife. I wouldn't be noticing if Marcie was with Vernon."

"Don't think I'd want to be with Vernon myself."

She laughed. "I sure hope not, Jake Tobin. And, I hope you wouldn't want to be dancing with Bailey, either. I hope you ain't that drunk."

Twenty One

"I ain't drunk."

"I just wonder how your head's gonna feel tomorrow afternoon when you're pitching in the afternoon heat."

"I ain't gonna be pitching with my head."

"You'd better be pitching with it or you're gonna get beat."

"Mind if I cut in?" The intruder was Father Walter Ingram.

"Not at all Bro. . . Father Ingram," Jake said. "I need some punch anyway."

Ingram laughed. "I got dizzy just smelling the punch."

Jake started weaving his way across the floor toward the punch bowl as Ingram and Mary Lou started dancing. She said, "I've never danced with a priest before."

"That makes us even."

"How's that?"

"I've never danced with you before."

She laughed and he liked the sound of it. He also liked the way she looked. Three children, but she hadn't let herself go. *Even a priest has the right to appreciate a beautiful woman*, he thought.

He didn't have a right, he knew, feeling the way he often did around a beautiful woman. Mary Lou stirred him, caused some of his old passions to rise. He had hoped all that was over, that his renewed commitment to the church would put his desires to rest once and for all.

It hadn't happened.

Even escaping to this godforsaken place called Walla hadn't helped. He had hoped the women wouldn't be as pretty or as desirable when he accepted the assignment to the backwoods of Louisiana. Mary Lou Tobin and Marcie Scott, however, were two of the most beautiful women he had ever seen. The two Bernstein girls were not far behind. Clarice Williams had been beautiful, too.

All these women brought back memories of his priesthood in Boston, where the parish to which he was assigned was like a candy store of tantalizing sweets. He had not been as discreet as he should have been, had been caught and in shame had confessed his sins to the bishop. He had doubted his salvation, whether he had what it took to be a priest, but the church had generously given him an opportunity to do penance in Walla.

"You better be careful talking like that," Mary Lou said. "There are a lot of young women around here who. . . oh, I forgot. Priests don't. . . "

He laughed. "You're right. . . they don't."

Mary Lou blushed. "Maybe I should have said it's too bad you're not a Baptist preacher. If you were, though, I don't guess you'd be dancing with me."

"I don't understand why Baptists in this part of the country are against dancing."

"Obviously, not all of them are," she said. "There are quite a few here who are sashshaying around on the dance floor and hanging around the punch bowl who'll be sitting in a pew at the First Baptist Church tomorrow."

"But not you?"

"No, I won't be there. I ain't proud of it, mind you, but listening to Brother Baker takes more Christianity than I've got. . . or will ever have."

He laughed again. "I've never had opportunity to have a conversation with the man."

"You probably never will. He thinks all Catholics are of the Devil. He thinks the three evils in the world are Catholics, coloreds and Jews."

"You can't be serious."

"Ask anybody. They'll tell you the same thing."

"The Bernsteins. . . they're the only Jews in town, aren't they?"

"Far as I know."

"I personally invited Ruth and Ruta to come to the dance. I haven't seen them, have you?"

"No. . . and we won't."

"Why not?"

"Even with you inviting them, they wouldn't feel welcome here. Most of the people here feel just like Brother Baker about the coloreds and Jews."

"That's hard for me to believe."

"After you've been here for a while, you'll believe it."

The priest danced to a couple more songs with Mary Lou before Jake, who was feeling no pain, returned to the dance floor. Ingram went to mingle with some of the other people and to lament the rush of persistent passion in him that Mary Lou had caused.

• • •

"Let's go some place, Bailey. . . some place where we can be alone."

"You think that's a good idea, Marcie. I mean. . . with Vernon here and all."

"Vernon's drunk by now. If he hasn't passed out he's too busy talking football with some of these idiots to notice that we're gone."

"Where do you want to go?"

"We'll find a place."

She led him off the dance floor like a dog on a leash, past dozens of sets of prying eyes and minds with multiple questions and answers about what they were doing. Bailey smiled sheepishly and nodded to a number of people. Marcie ignored them.

They went out a side door into the darkness, the only light coming from the glass in the door they had exited. She put her back against the building, just to the right of the door, and pulled him up against her. They began kissing.

They were locked in an embrace when the door opened.

It was like a rush of cold air hit them as they separated. The couple who came out the door paid no attention to them. They were much more interested in each other.

"Let's go some place else," Marcie said.

"Where?"

"Just follow me."

She took his hand and led him across the lawn to the door of the church sanctuary. He balked. "We can't, Marcie."

She laughed. "Yes we can."

Bailey wasn't all that religious, but what she was asking went against every tenet of decency he knew. He also knew he couldn't deny her, which is why he soon found himself in the confessional booth. What neither knew was that two other people were in the other side of the booth, frozen with fear.

Johnny and Bobby had been exploring the sanctuary of the church when they heard someone opening the door. They immediately jumped into the confessional booth to hide and were horrified when they heard Marcie and Bailey coming toward them. Bobby looked like he was about to run but Johnny grabbed Bobby's arm and covered his mouth. They waited and hoped that Marcie and Bailey would leave.

Instead, the couple squeezed into the other side of the booth. A moment later the terrified boys were the unwilling witnesses to a chorus of kisses, whispers and moans. The entire booth throbbed with the couple's passion. After what seemed like an eternity, but was really only a few minutes, the couple became quiet and Bailey whispered, "We need to go. Someone is going to find us."

Marcie giggled and they quietly slipped out of the other side of the booth and walked out of the sanctuary.

Marcie and Bailey had been gone for several minutes before Johnny broke their stunned silence. "Whew. . . you ever hear anything like that?"

"I thought my heart was gonna blow up. I told you we ought not to be messing around in here."

"I just wanted to see what it was like in a Catholic Church. I didn't know Mr. Thompson and Mrs. Scott were gonna come in here."

"What are we gonna do about it?"

"I ain't gonna do nothing, Bobby. If I told somebody about this and it got back to my folks, I'd get a whipping like you wouldn't believe."

"You think I wouldn't get my rear whipped, too?"

"Best thing for us to do is just forget it."

"How are we gonna do that?"

"I don't mean really forget it. . . just don't tell nobody about it."

"That ain't gonna be hard to do."

They stealthily exited the sanctuary and were making their way back to the kitchen area of the hall where the dance was taking place. That's when Johnny noticed a familiar car parked just outside where the others were clustered. "Well, I'll be darn," he said.

"What is it?" Bobby asked.

"C'mon. . . I'll show you."

Using the other cars to shield their approach, Johnny led Bobby close to the car he had spied. Then he boldly walked over to the open window on the driver's side, Bobby close behind, and asked, "How are you doing, Brother Baker?"

The preacher, who hadn't seen their approach, was startled. His big body jerked like he had been bit on the rear by a rabid dog. Quickly gaining his composure, he asked in a growl, "What are you boys doing here?"

"We was just passing by," Johnny said. "You just out here listening to the music?"

"No, I ain't just out here just listening to the music. I'm out here keeping an eye on the Devil's work so I'll know how to fight it. And you boys ought to be home in bed."

"We was just going," Johnny said. "You got any ideas?"

"Ideas about what?"

"About fighting the Devil. That's what you said you was out here for."

Baker grumbled under his breath. "Course I got some ideas."

Johnny, who loved playing dumb to agitate, asked, "The music help you think of ways to fight the Devil?"

"The music in there is the Devil's work."

"Golly, I didn't know."

"If you'd come hear me preach once in a while, you'd know."

"I'll have to do that."

"I've got to go," Baker said, cranking the car. "Am I gonna see you boys in church tomorrow?"

"Yes sir," Bobby replied.

The preacher looked at Johnny for a response. He said, "I'm gonna give it some serious thought. . . if I can get my chores done."

Baker shook his head in resignation, angry, and drove away. "If I'd knowed it was Brother Baker sitting over here, I wouldn't have come with you," Bobby said. "I don't know why you treat him the way you do."

"I thought I treated him pretty nice. I was just being friendly."

"Oh, sure. Why do you always lie? You're always looking for some way to make him mad."

"I don't know why you always want to kiss his rear. I thought you was going with me in the morning."

"I was. Now I don't see how I can. It's your fault. If I hadn't seen him, I wouldn't have promised him I'd be at church."

They went to the kitchen area where Bessie was busy washing cups. Billy Burton was sitting at a table there, his face on it, a cup of coffee beside his left ear. He was passed out.

Bessie provided an unnecessary explanation. "The man's drunk as a skunk."

"I ain't never seen Billy drunk before," Johnny said.

"He done been out there drinking your daddy's whiskey with Mr. Vernon."

"Where's the coach?"

"Billy say he done puked and passed out in the back seat of your folks' car."

Johnny laughed. "I've got to see this."

"No, you ain't. You just sit your little white fanny down and stay in here with Aunt Bessie."

"Dang it, Aunt Bessie. . . you ain't as much fun as you used to be."

"You gonna think fun," she said, smiling. "You boys want a cup of coffee?"

"I could use one," Johnny said. "Then I better get home before my folks do."

"I'd rather have some punch," Bobby said.

"I'll give you some of this punch in here. Ain't no way you need some of that punch the grown folks is drinking."

They sat at the table with Billy and she served them. While Johnny was adding sugar to his coffee, she asked, "What you know about Mr. Billy and one of Mr. Sol's girls?"

"Which one. . . Ruth or Ruta?"

"I don't know which one. . . they looks the same to me."

Johnny laughed. "I don't know nothing. Why you asking?"

"He came in here talking about one of the girls like he all lovesick or something. I couldn't tell all he was saying cause he wasn't talking plain."

"Mr. Bernstein. . . Ruth and Ruta. . . none of them have ever said anything about Billy to me. You reckon he's dating one of the girls?"

"Maybe he just wants to. He's a grown man. . . and far as I know, he ain't got no woman."

After finishing the coffee and punch the boys headed home. They made just one stop en route. Johnny insisted on walking past his folks' car, so he could see Coach Scott passed out in the back seat.

TWENTY TWO

Jake Tobin didn't get up early Sunday morning. He was not in the best of shape. He and Mary Lou hadn't gotten in until about two o'clock. His head felt bigger than the state champion watermelon. And, he had to pitch a game in the afternoon.

Johnny, who got up just before six, was pleased his dad was not his usual early morning self. He didn't want to have to explain where he was going and what he was going to do. In fact, he would have had to lie about it because Jake Tobin would never have allowed him to do what he planned.

He dressed in what he usually wore hunting, excluding a coat. He hadn't worn his boots since hunting season and they felt strange to his feet.

Quietly, so as not to wake anyone, he got his single shot sixteen-gauge off the gun rack, rummaged in a closet and got nine shells, which he stuffed in his pockets. Then he went out the door, tied the shotgun to the handlebar of his bicycle and rode off.

It was already hot and muggy. He knew he would be drenched with sweat before arriving at his destination. He wondered what Ben Jim would say if he knew what he was up to and decided it would probably be pretty much what his dad would say.

I'll probably get my rear blistered, he thought, *but it'll be worth it. Somebody has to do something and it might as well be me.*

Riding up and down the hills of the dusty gravel road he decided a bicycle was an overrated method of transportation. After a couple of miles his legs ached and his stomach muscles seemed to be chewing at his calves.

As he pumped on he mentally cursed the sun, which, he thought, was taking great pleasure in beating him with its rays. He had read about cooler climates, but this was the only one he had ever known. The winters here were too short as far as he was concerned and he promised himself that he would someday move away from the stifling heat and humidity of Louisiana.

He finally arrived at a logging road, rode down it a short piece, then dismounted the bicycle. He hid it in some brush off the road, put a shell in the shotgun and began walking.

Johnny wasn't sure how long he walked before the house in the clearing came into view. He was in the trees, could only see a side of the structure, but it looked very foreboding. *What in the dickens am I doing here?* he asked himself. *If I left now, nobody would know. Nobody knows I'm here.*

For the first time since deciding on the mission, the fact that no one knew where he was bothered him. He could disappear and no one would know where he had been, or what had happened to him. Maybe they would find his body. Or, like little Sadie, maybe they wouldn't.

He remembered then that Bobby knew he had planned to bicycle out into the country. Bobby had planned to go with him until they had accosted Brother Baker and Bobby had promised to be in church. Of course, he hadn't told Bobby what he actually planned to do, or where he planned to go. If he had, there was no way Bobby would have agreed to accompany him.

Despite the heat, a chill ran down his spine. There was a temptation to break and run, to escape whatever danger lurked in the area.

But, for some reason, the very fascination with danger kept him there. It was not a matter of courage, because a combination of fear and bravery clashed in his mind. It was as if destiny had brought him to this place and that even if he ran there would be no escape.

So with sweat bathing his body and fear shooting chills through it, Johnny sat down with his back to a tree and waited. He waited for the better part of an hour, though he had no way of knowing the exact time.

At a distance he could see through a window of the house, but saw no movement there or any outside. The house, he believed, was deserted. He relaxed a little.

The mule and the cow were in their respective places, doing what such animals do when men aren't interrupting their lives. There was a kind of serenity to the entire setting.

Well, he thought, *I came here to check things out. If I'm gonna do it, I'd better do it now.*

The truth was that he wasn't quite sure why he had come. He had some vague idea about finding a clue that would tie Willard Jordan to the murders, plus a stranger idea about arresting the man and marching him back to town at shotgun point. *If I ain't the stupidest kid around, I'm darn close,* he thought.

He got up and started moving toward the house, ever so slowly. *If he's here, I'll just tell him I'm hunting and stopped by for a drink of water.*

He was pleased with the plan. Nothing was in season, but a lot of people in the parish didn't pay any attention to the game laws. He figured a guy like Willard Jordan would probably approve of hunting out of season.

The exterior of the house was plain and gray, not from paint but from the elements. It, obviously, had never been painted. The slanted tin roof showed traces of rust. The fireplace chimney had been built with native stone.

Wood stacked on an end of the covered porch that ran across the front of the house kept him from seeing the other part of it. As he came around the house and his line of sight cleared the wood he was taken aback with fright, frozen with fear.

On the porch were two coffins.

Johnny wanted to turn and run, but his legs wouldn't go. He

sucked air, tried to fight off the chills and thought he might wet in his pants before a voice asked, "What you doing here, boy?"

He wanted to lift the shotgun, to turn toward the voice behind him and shoot. But his arms felt paralyzed. "I. . . I was wondering about getting a drink of water."

"Well sure. You see the well down there at the far end of the porch. Just help yourself."

Johnny turned and looked at Willard Jordan, who suddenly seemed to be right on top of him. The man reached over and took the shotgun out of his hands. "You'll need both hands free if you're gonna draw a bucket of water. I'll put your gun right up here against the porch."

He again sucked air and turned away from Jordan, whom he was sure was going to shoot him in the back. He cringed, waiting for the sound of the shotgun blast. Glancing back, furtively, he saw that Jordan had actually put his gun's barrel against the floor of the porch, its stock on the ground.

"Awful hot, ain't it?"

"Yes sir. . . it is."

"Well, go ahead and get your water, boy. . . I don't want to hold you up."

Johnny reluctantly walked up the porch steps and by the coffins, which were perched on sawhorses, to the well at the other end. He lowered the bucket down into its darkness until he heard it hit water. Then he cranked the filled bucket back up and set it on a portion of the well's lip that had a wide board for just such a purpose. He took a dipper off a nail stuck in the well's upper structure, submerged it in the cool water, then lifted it and tried to drink. The water felt good to his mouth, but he had trouble swallowing it.

"Ain't you Jake Tobin's boy?"

"Yes sir. . . I am."

"You was pointed out to me a couple of times when I was in town. . . and I saw you in Bernstein's store."

Johnny didn't know how to respond, so he tried to drink some more water. "You look flushed, boy, like you're about to pass out. . . face all red and all. Why don't you sit down here on the steps and rest a spell?"

Twenty Two

"I've got to be getting on."

Jordan grinned. His mouth, Johnny was sure, looked just like the Devil's. "What's the all-fired hurry? If you're out here looking for squirrels, they ain't going nowhere. They ain't gonna be moving much in this heat anyway."

Resigned to his fate, Johnny's eyes finally focused on Jordan. The man was small and wiry, with big ears and a burned face wrinkled by the sun. He had bushy eyebrows, deep-set black eyes between slits in his skin and a prominent nose. He needed a haircut, Johnny thought. He was wearing an old grease-stained hat over his gray hair. He was attired in old overalls, a faded blue shirt and scuffed brogans.

"I guess I could sit a spell," Johnny said.

"You do that, boy. I'm gonna have some of that water you just drawed up."

Johnny sat down on the porch steps and Jordan walked up the steps past him and across the porch to the well. Johnny thought about running for and grabbing the gun, but he was afraid to make the move. If I make a move toward the gun he might pull a knife, throw it and stick me right in the back, he thought. He had seen a lot of *Tarzan* and western movies where that had happened.

After having shown his pleasure at a drink of water from the dipper with a prolonged *ahhhhh*, Jordan asked, "You had any breakfast, boy?"

"I ain't hungry."

"Course you are. Man out hunting gets hungry. I ain't ate myself, so you come on in and I'll fix us some bacon and eggs."

"No sir. . . I better be getting on. My mama'll be expecting me."

Jordan laughed. "You're actin' awful nervous, son. I'll bet it's because of these coffins on the porch."

Johnny didn't say anything, so Jordan continued. "That's one of the things I do. . . build coffins. I build them for the state prison. They don't want anything fancy. . . not like the undertaker in town. Just these plain wooden boxes. . . that's all they want."

The man talking about the caskets bothered Johnny, but he tried not to let on. "I guess somebody's got to build them. . . might as well be you."

"That's the way I figure it. Now come on in the house and I'll fix us some bacon and eggs."

"I better be getting on."

"I ain't taking no for an answer."

Johnny didn't know whether it was a threat or not. He was too scared to try to interpret the meaning of what Jordan said. He had never been so scared.

"Well, okay. I'll get my shotgun and. . . "

"Just leave it where it is. Ain't nobody gonna bother it. Ain't nobody ever comes around here."

Jordan opened the front door and Johnny reluctantly went in the house ahead of him. All the windows in the front room were open, there were no curtains, but it was still semi-dark. And, there was a musty smell to the place, as if it had been closed up for a long time.

The furniture, Johnny decided, wasn't as good as what Ben Jim had in his place, which he had always figured came from the town dump. The room had a dilapidated easy chair, an old rocking chair with the paint peeling, and a small table with a battery radio on it.

They went on back to what passed for a kitchen. An old black wood stove set out from the wall and close to a window. There were some open shelves on the wall that held a hodgepodge of dishes and canned goods. There was also a homemade table and two battered chairs.

"Sit and I'll stoke up the fire," Jordan said. "Probably still some coals left from last night." He took a lid off the stove and put in a few pieces of kindling and three pieces of wood. "There. . . that ought to do it. You like coffee, boy?"

"Yes sir."

"Pot here's full. Soon as the fire heats up I'll pour you a cup. You just set still and I'll get some eggs and bacon from the smokehouse."

When he went out the back door Johnny was tempted to go out the front. *What if he's waiting for me to do something like that?* he thought. *He may just be waiting for an excuse to kill me.* So he just sat there waiting, too numb to even be bothered by the heat in the room.

Jordan came back a few minutes later with some eggs and a slab of bacon. He put the bacon on a small table near the stove and started slicing it with a butcher knife. "You like your bacon thick, boy?"

"Any way's fine with me."

Twenty Two

When he had finished slicing the meat, Jordan put the butcher knife aside and put a cast iron skillet on the stove. He tossed the bacon in it and straightened it with a fork. "There. . . fire's going pretty good now. Won't be long now until the bacon's done and I'll fry you up a couple of eggs. How you want them?"

"Any way's fine with me."

"You sure are accommodating. Ain't you got no likes or dislikes on how things is done?"

"Got lots of them. How eggs are cooked ain't one of them."

A few minutes passed with no conversation. Jordan looked out the smoke stained window by the stove, like he was watching something far off. Johnny nervously watched his captor, wondering what was going to happen next.

"That coffee ought to be ready," Jordan said. He checked. "Yea, it's ready." He brought the pot over to the table and poured the hot liquid in a cup he had put in front of Johnny earlier. It was an old but sturdy cup, chipped a bit in places.

Johnny spooned some sugar in the coffee, stirred and took a sip. Then he thought, *Maybe he poisoned it.*

He was relieved when Jordan poured himself a cup from the pot and started drinking it. Then he started worrying because Jordan was drinking his coffee black. *Maybe the sugar's been poisoned*, he thought.

The smell of fried bacon, then the eggs frying in the bacon grease, caused Johnny to realize he was hungry. He had left home early in the morning without eating a bite and without a cup of coffee. He decided that if he was going to die it might as well be on a full stomach. The truth was that Jordan was becoming less frightening, or Johnny was just becoming resigned to the fact that whatever happened would happen, that he was powerless to stop it.

Regardless, when Jordan put the bacon and eggs in front of him, plus a couple of biscuits that had been cooked the previous day and reheated on top of the stove, he was ready to eat. He cut up the eggs, salted them, then added pepper until there seemed to be more black than yellow or white.

Jordan, who sat down across from him with his bacon and eggs, said, "You sure do like pepper, boy."

"Truth is. . . I like pepper better than eggs."

His host laughed. "Don't let my laying hens hear you talk that way."

For a split second Johnny, who was caught off guard, started to exchange a quip with the man. Then he remembered what Jordan had done to the Williams family. It became hard to swallow his food.

When they had finished the meal, Johnny eating out of fear, Jordan poured them another cup of coffee, sharpened a matchstick with a pocketknife and started picking his teeth. "Hear tell you was the one that found the little Williams boy in the creek," Jordan said.

Johnny nodded in the affirmative, not really knowing how to respond. He didn't know where the conversation was leading, but hated whatever direction it was taking.

"Vernell and Clarice was good folks. . . the kids, too. If I ever find the man who killed them, I'm gonna butcher him like I would a hog."

"You knew them. . . the Williams family, I mean?"

"Yeah, I knew them. Vernell and me. . . we were kind of partners. He was one of the best niggers I ever knew. . . helped me build the coffins. I went over to their place ever once in a while to tell Vernell when we had an order for coffins. . . probably would've been the one to find them dead. . . if we'd a had any orders for coffins. We were caught up, so when he didn't come around I just figured old Vernell was catching up on work at his place. Course I never went around his place that much anyway."

Johnny was shocked, but tried not to show it. "When did you find out?"

"I think it was the afternoon after they was found that morning. I went to town and somebody told me. I think it was Mouse Malone."

"From what Billy Burton told me, it was awful."

"I expect it was. I went over there to pick up the mule and cow I loaned to Vernell. . . and there was a smell of death about the place. The bodies was gone but there was still plenty of blood and flies."

"You loaned Vernell a mule and cow?" Johnny asked, elated.

"Yeah, but they was broke out by the time I got there. I found them wandering in the woods."

"I thought. . . Billy said he thought Vernell had a mule and cow. And a shotgun."

"Well, when you see Billy you tell him that the cow and mule belong to me. I let Vernell use the cow because his kids needed milk. . . and I ain't got use for much of the stuff. He always saw to it that I had butter and buttermilk. Now I do like my buttermilk. . . usually keep a syrup bucket full of it down in the well to keep it cold for drinking and to make cornbread with."

"The wagon at Vernell's place belongs to me, too. I let him use it and the mule because he didn't have any transportation. I got myself an old pickup truck out in the barn. I ain't got around to going over and picking up the wagon."

"Did you loan him a shotgun, too?"

"No. . . but he had one. I don't know what happened to it."

"I'll bet. . . Billy said he figured the killer used Vernell's shotgun."

Jordan shrugged. "Might've. All I can say is that he killed a mighty fine man. Vernell might've been colored, but I'd have been proud to have him as a brother."

"I never met him. People keep telling me what a fine looking woman Clarice was."

"She was surely that. . . looked to be about half white. Caused her lots of grief, too."

"How's that?"

"Lots of folks took an unnatural interest in Clarice."

"Like who?"

"The ones that Vernell told me about was that woman teacher whose little girl came up missing. That priest feller, too. . . and the Baptist preacher."

Johnny was stunned. "Priest fella? You talking about Father Ingram?"

"Guess so. Ain't no other priests around here, are there?"

TWENTY THREE

By mid morning Johnny and Willard Jordan had become pals. Johnny learned that though Jordan was a relative of Nick Merrick, he hated the sheriff passionately. His new friend didn't go into any detail about why he disliked Merrick so much, but Johnny gleaned that there had been some sort of bootlegging deal the two had been involved in that had gone sour.

Jordan said he had spent ten years in the pen for a killing that was justified, but he wasn't angry about it. "Best thing ever happened to me was going to the pen. Learned me a trade there. . . and made the contacts for my coffin business. I would've just passed off them ten years anyway."

Johnny learned that Jordan had been born in the parish, had a third-grade education and hated towns about as much as he disliked his cousin. "You spend time in a cell and around a bunch a men like yourself," he said, "and you ain't gonna be in the mood to be crowded like townfolks are. That's why I like living out here. I don't go to town any more than I have to."

Jordan said he was hunting wild hogs when he first met Vernell Williams. "We hit it off right away," he said. "I think Vernell was out trying to kill a rabbit or squirrel to feed his family with. He was carrying that old twelve-gauge shotgun of his. Course I had my shotgun with me.

"I told old Vernell he ought to come long with me, that if we found us a big old hog I'd split the meat with him. Well, we found that old hog. . . must've weighed nigh onto six hundred pounds. I killed it, then we walked to my place and got the mule and wagon.

"We got the wagon as close to where the hog was as we could. Then we took the mule and pulled the hog to the wagon, loaded it on and took it here to butcher it.

"Vernell couldn't carry all the meat back to his place so I drove him there in the wagon. We got there and Clarice just about had dinner on the table. They were having collards and cornbread. Vernell asked me if I wanted to eat with them.

"Well, I ain't one to turn down a good bait of collards, so I said, *Yeah, I'll eat.* Clarice fried up some of that fresh hog meat and I ate so much I darn near made myself sick.

"When I saw them kids and found out Vernell didn't have a cow I asked him to borrow mine. I hate milking a cow about as much as anything, so I told him he would be doing me a good turn by taking the cow. . . which he was. First thing I knowed I was making Vernell take the wagon and mule, too.

"They was such dang nice folks."

Jordan's eyes had misted while he talked about his late friend. "Vernell. . . he wouldn't take something for nothing, though. He made me let him work around the place here. . . helped me build caskets. I had to make him take money for helping me.

"I told him, *Vernell, I ain't got no use for it.* I make my own liquor and don't buy much in town except a little tobacco. He wouldn't take as much as I wanted to give him, so sometimes I gave it to Clarice without him knowing."

Jordan told Johnny that in dry weather a car could get to the Williamses place and that he knew of three that had been there. The priest had visited. So had the Brother Marvin Baker and Marcie Scott.

It bothered Johnny that Father Walter Ingram had said nothing about knowing the Williamses. Maybe there was a good reason, but he couldn't think of one.

Bailey Thompson, of course, had explained to him about Marcie Scott's relationship with Clarice. She was going to be taking care of little Sadie while Mrs. Scott was teaching. But, there was still some mystery about Brother Baker's involvement with Clarice. Aunt Bessie had triggered his curiosity about that.

Despite Johnny's protest, Willard Jordan insisted on driving him back to town. They stopped and picked up Johnny's bicycle, put it in the back of the man's pre-World War II vintage Ford pickup, then Jordan deposited him right in front of his house. When he walked in the front door his mother had asked, a little more angrily than he thought was necessary, "What are you doing with that ex-convict?"

"He just gave me a ride."

"From where?"

"I was out close to his place."

"Why?"

When it came to thinking Johnny was fast on his feet, but his story broke down with his mother. There were just too many whys that he couldn't answer. His daddy gave him a good whipping for leaving without telling them where he was going. Johnny figured he deserved it, but also figured it was worth it because of what he had discovered.

He could understand the whipping. What he couldn't understand was what his daddy always said before doing it, which was "This is gonna hurt me more than you."

Jake Tobin was not in the best of moods. He had a hangover and a headache as big as Texas. It didn't help that when he complained Mary Lou said, "I told you what was gonna happen."

Jake had his baseball uniform on, except for the shoes and cap, hadn't shaved, and after punishing Johnny sat down at the table to work on a pot of hot, black coffee. The whipping didn't bother Johnny all that much. It hurt, of course, but he didn't get all worked up about it. So he joined Jake at the table, doctoring his own cup of coffee with a generous helping of sugar.

"You ready to pitch?"

"There's probably some things I'd rather do. . . my head feeling the way it does. But, yeah. . . I'm ready. Last game of the season. . . might've knowed it'd be a hundred degrees in the shade."

"It's gonna be a hot one okay."

"Johnny, your mama and me. . . we worry when you go off and we don't know where you are. I figured you was down at the trestle, so I walked down there. . . didn't notice your bicycle was gone right off. Then you show up with Willard Jordan. Now I'm pretty sure you went out there where those coloreds was killed."

"No. . . I didn't go out there."

"Then why in the world were you out around Willard Jordan's place?"

"I was looking for sign."

"Sign? What kind of sign?"

"Squirrel sign. You know it ain't long until the season starts."

"I ought to give you another whipping for lying," Jake said. "I know dang well that ain't why you was out there. You were carrying your shotgun thinking you might run across the man who killed those folks. You just don't know when to leave well enough alone. I don't mind you going fishing by yourself down at the trestle because that's safe enough, but I don't want you wandering around in the woods unless Ben Jim's with you.

"Snakes get blind and mean this time of year. If one bites you and you're way off like that. . . hot as it is. . . you could die before you got any help. And, you sure don't need to be looking for somebody who killed a grown man like Vernell Williams."

"I was kind of sticking to the roads," Johnny said.

"There you go. . . lying again. You ain't never stuck to no roads. And, I don't want you hanging around with no ex-convict."

"Mr. Jordan. . . he ain't a bad guy. He acted like he knowed you."

"Course he knows me. He tried to get a job at the sawmill when he got out of prison. . . and he buys lumber from the company pretty regular."

"Yeah, he builds caskets."

"Caskets?"

"Yeah. . . he builds them for the prison. Said Vernell Williams helped him do it."

"Well, I didn't know Willard did that," Jake said. "You hear that,

Mary Lou."

"Yeah, I heard it," she said. "But it don't change my mind about him none."

"I dropped by there to get a drink of water," Johnny said, "and he had a couple of caskets setting on the front porch."

"I figured Willard was still making and selling whiskey," Jake said.

Mary Lou laughed. "Probably is. Those coffins was probably full of jars."

Jake grinned, but quit rather quickly. Even that much movement of the mouth made his head hurt more. "Somebody's making bad whiskey in these parts. . . and I must've drunk some of it last night."

"It ain't bad whiskey that done you in, Jake. It's just how much of it you drunk."

"Thanks for the sympathy, Mary Lou."

"How come I can't remember ever seeing Mr. Jordan in town?" Johnny asked.

"Since he got out of prison Willard's been what some folks call a hermit," Jake replied. "His daddy left him that place and he just stays out there."

"How come we ain't never hunted out there?"

"Ain't been no reason to."

"Mr. Jordan. . . he sure don't like the sheriff."

"Well now. . . I didn't know that. I understand they're related. Cousins, I think."

"If he don't like Nick Merrick, that speaks well of him in my book," Mary Lou said.

"That don't mean we want you hanging around him, Johnny," Jake said. "There are things about Willard Jordan nobody seems to know. Best he be left alone."

Despite his father's warning, Johnny found Jordan interesting and wanted to know more about him. Maybe it was the fact the man had been a convict, could describe prison life to him. Just as fascinating, however, was Jordan's relationship with Vernell Williams. It wasn't unusual for a white man to work with a black one, especially at the sawmill or in the logwoods. But from the way Jordan had talked about Vernell, Johnny got the idea the two were the best of friends.

Twenty Three

That was unusual.

Having been ostracized on many occasions for his friendship with Ben Jim Cade, Johnny realized that he may have found a kindred spirit.

A few minutes before the umpire said play ball that afternoon, Johnny found Ben Jim in his usual spot. Alto Jackson was with him. He told Ben Jim about the time he had spent with Willard Jordan.

"Uh huh. . . and you was ready to hang the man for murder the other day. Like I done told you so many times, Johnny. . . things ain't always what they seem."

Alto grunted. "I don't know why y'all was thinking the killer was Mr. Willard Jordan anyway. My mama done told you it was Isaac Simpson."

Johnny shook his head in resignation. "Yeah, Aunt Bessie did tell me that. Problem is she don't have any evidence."

Alto laughed. "Don't seem to me you had any evidence on Mr. Willard Jordan either."

"Well, there was the cow and the mule," Johnny said. "And Vernell's shotgun's still missing."

"Isaac. . . he's just liable to have that shotgun," Alto said.

Ben Jim shook his head in disagreement. "Ain't likely the man would keep it."

"Ain't no telling about Isaac," Alto said. "The man thinks he's smarter than any other nigger. He's liable to keep it and start bragging about what he done before long."

Ben Jim saw Johnny's eyes light up. "Now don't you be sneaking around trying to find out if the man has that shotgun, Johnny. Isaac. . . he's a bad nigger. The man wouldn't think nothing about hurting you if he thought nobody would know."

"He wouldn't be thinking about hurting me if you was with me."

"I ain't got no cause to be messing with Isaac. And, if I even think you're thinking about it. . . this time I'm gonna tell your daddy."

Downcast, Johnny grumbled, "Dang it. . . seems to me the coloreds would want to find out who killed the Williamses."

"Ain't nothing to find out," Alto said. "Isaac. . . he done it."

"Now you hush up, Alto," Ben Jim said. "Ain't no point getting Johnny here stirred up about something we can't do nothing about."

"You could tell the law," Johnny said.

Ben Jim spat. The snuff-laden missile balled up when it hit the dust. "The law don't care about a bunch of niggers that done got themselves killed. You told the law about Willard Jordan, didn't you?"

"Yeah. . . I told Billy Burton and I told that FBI man. . . when I thought Mr. Jordan was the killer."

"And what did the law do?" Ben Jim asked.

Johnny sighed. "Nothing. Billy. . . he was scared because the sheriff is Willard Jordan's cousin. He didn't know. . . and I ain't told him yet. . . that Mr. Jordan don't like the sheriff."

"That's what Mr. Willard Jordan told you," Alto said. "How you know he's telling the truth?"

"I don't guess I do," Johnny replied. "At least, not for sure. I think he was, though."

"Clarice Williams. . . she's the one that got the family killed," Alto said, "not knowing whether she was black or white."

"What do you mean?" Johnny asked.

Ben Jim gave Alto a hard look and the young man replied, "I don't mean nothing."

"Yes you do," Johnny said. "Aunt Bessie started telling me Clarice was having some trouble with Brother Baker, but she wouldn't finish telling me what it was."

Ben Jim said, "Ain't nothing to tell. . . nothing to know. You best just forget about it. That's what we all need to do. Just forget about all that stuff and enjoy the ball game."

The opposition was a team out of Leesville. On this day, despite the hangover, Jake Tobin was practically unhittable. He gave up no runs, just two hits and struck out sixteen. Walla scored seven runs in the first couple of innings to leave no doubt about the outcome.

The crowd was quietly enthusiastic. Many had been at the dance and their heads felt like Jake's. They much preferred sedate nods of appreciation to the head-busting experience of yelling.

Johnny found Bobby at the game. They ate snow cones and, as always, argued. Johnny told Bobby about catching the big bass and letting it go; but his friend didn't believe him. "If you would've caught a big fish like that you wouldn't let him go."

"If you'd been there you'd understand why I did. Come to think of it, though, I don't reckon you would."

Johnny and Bobby were weaving their way through the chatting fans when a voice snarled from the rear, "Where are you going, you little jerk?"

They turned and saw a menacing Elmer Guerdat. He was flanked by a couple of the other football players. "You talking to me?" Johnny asked.

"I sure ain't talking to that little jerk that's with you." Guerdat turned to his friends and they chortled on cue.

Bobby was so nervous he was almost shaking, but Johnny was just flat angry. He didn't like being called a jerk. "What's your problem, Elmer?"

Guerdat stuck his face close to Johnny's and said, "I ain't got no problem. You're the one with the problem. I'm gonna kick your butt from here to next Sunday, you little jerk."

The word jerk had barely cleared Guerdat's throat when Johnny hit him flush on the nose. Blood spurted and the bigger boy staggered backward, his face a mask of shock and surprise framed by a red tinge of running blood. His friends shared the surprise on his face.

Guerdat shook his head and screamed, "You little jerk!" He started toward Johnny, his fists clinched and ready. That's when Johnny, with all the power in his strong right leg, kicked his adversary right in the groin. Guerdat went down on his knees, his hands clutching his crotch, and Johnny butted his bloody nose with the top of his forehead. Guerdat went over on his back like a big tree that finally falls with the last swing of the ax.

Bobby was yelling, "Run," and a crowd was gathering. Johnny, though, had no intention of running. Instead, he jumped on Guerdat and started beating him in the face. The older youth's friends pulled Johnny off and held him until Guerdat was on his feet. Then they pushed Johnny toward him.

With a roundhouse swing Guerdat's fist found the side of Johnny's face and sent him sprawling. He bounced to his feet and charged, hitting Guerdat with a couple of good blows to the stomach. Size, however, was on Guerdat's side. He again decked Johnny and this time kicked him in the ribs while he was down.

Johnny rolled, but not quickly enough. Guerdat jumped on him and pinned him. He was on his back looking up and Guerdat's fist was cocked and ready to smash him in the face when a hand grasped it.

"That's enough," Ben Jim said, calmly, but in a commanding way.

Guerdat was as surprised by the one who had intervened as he had been by Johnny's first punch. He stood and said, angrily, "Who do you think you are, nigger?"

There was every indication that Guerdat and his two friends were going to turn their fists on Ben Jim, but Bailey Thompson came through the crowd that had gathered and stopped what could have become an even nastier situation. "What's going on here, Elmer?"

"I don't know, Mr. Thompson. Johnny Tobin. . . he hit me right in the nose for no good reason."

Johnny had gotten to his feet. His face was red from the punches Guerdat had landed. His hair and face were sweaty and had dirt caked to it. His shirt was torn, too, and he was sweaty and dust-caked. He looked as though he had been to war, but Guerdat looked worse. He had blood, dirt and sweat all over him. His nose was still bleeding.

Bailey asked, "Is that right, Johnny. . . you start this?"

"Reckon I did."

"Why?"

"Seemed the right thing to do at the time."

Guerdat was angry with Johnny, but the younger boy's answer earned a measure of respect from him. *The kid's crazy*, he thought, *but he ain't one to point a finger and fault somebody else.*

Bailey sighed. "Looks to me like you ought to apologize to Elmer, Johnny. Then the two of you ought to shake hands."

Guerdat quickly said, "Ain't no apology needed. Maybe part of it was my fault. Maybe I riled him."

"Well, you boys could at least shake hands," Bailey said. "I'm hoping this isn't gonna happen anymore."

"Fine with me," Guerdat said, sticking his hand toward Johnny.

For a few seconds Johnny didn't do anything. Then he grasped Guerdat's hand and muttered, "All right."

Peace is boring, so the crowd started breaking up. Guerdat asked one of his buddies, "Where did that nigger go?" His friend didn't know. Ben Jim and Alto had disappeared. "Ain't right. . . a nigger grabbing a white man," Guerdat said.

Out of Elmer's earshot, Bailey asked Johnny, "Do you want to come over to my place and clean up a bit?"

"No. . . I'll just go on home."

"What do you think your dad's gonna say? He wasn't feeling too good today. . . left the minute the game was over."

Johnny shrugged. "He's got a hangover. . . bad headache."

Bailey laughed. "Too much of the dance last night."

Usually, Johnny would have laughed. Knowing what Bailey and Mrs. Scott had done the previous evening, he was having difficulty maintaining eye contact with the principal. He didn't understand why. He had known about their affair, but knowing and almost being a witness to it was something else. He certainly didn't consider himself overly religious, but what they had done the previous evening, and where they had done it, bothered him.

"Tell me the truth, Johnny. . . did you start the fight with Elmer?"

"Yes sir."

Bobby, who had been standing by, said, "Johnny hit him when Elmer called him a. . . "

Johnny said, "Ain't no reason to bring that up."

Bailey said, "Well, maybe there is. If you were provoked. . . "

"Daddy always told me if it looked like I was gonna get in a fight, I ought to get in the first lick. Well, I figured it looked that way so I hit Elmer in the nose."

Bailey laughed. "I'll say you did."

"Elmer probably has good reason to whip my rear end."

"I heard what you did out at the football field the other night, so I can't argue with you."

"Sometimes I just do stuff for no reason at all."

"We all do," Bailey said.

On the way home Bobby said, "Kind of strange being around Mr. Thompson. . . knowing what we know."

"It's just strange if you want it to be."

"To tell you the truth. . . I wish I didn't know."

"There ain't no pleasure in knowing. . . that's for sure."

"Elmer was sure mad at Ben Jim."

"Ben Jim shouldn't have got mixed up in it," Johnny said.

"If he hadn't, Elmer would probably have knocked your teeth down your throat."

Johnny grinned. "Elmer can't hit hard enough to knock my teeth out."

There was less of a problem at home than normal because Jake had taken a couple of aspirin and gone to bed with a cold cloth on his forehead. Johnny wasn't too worried anyway. His dad didn't want him taking anything from anyone. He would more likely give him a whipping for taking stuff than for fighting. Mary Lou, who wasn't feeling all that well herself, said, "You've been in another fight. . . haven't you?"

"Not much of one."

"If you have to fight, I just wish you wouldn't get your clothes all torn up. Who were you fighting this time?"

"Elmer Guerdat."

"My god, Johnny. . . he's a grown man and twice as big as you."

"He ain't twice as big."

His mother's interest in the fight passed rather quickly, for which he was grateful. She fixed a good supper, which Johnny ate with Sister and Sonny Boy. Mary Lou wasn't hungry.

Johnny said, "I think I'm going to church tonight. . . if it's okay with you."

"Course it's okay with me," his mother said. "I ain't never kept one of my children from going to church, have I?"

He knew she didn't expect an answer to that question, so didn't provide one. He excused himself, went to the bathroom and filled the tub with water. He not only needed a bath, he figured one would help ease his aches and pain. Looking at his face in the small medicine cabinet mirror, it was obvious he was going to have a black eye.

It was too early for church when he left the house, but he had planned it that way. He knew Brother Baker left the parsonage early to allegedly study and pray in preparation for the evening service. He figured Baker was probably eating moon pies and drinking RC Colas.

He would have walked right on past Winston Railey's house, but the teacher was trimming some rose bushes in his front yard and hailed him. "That eye doesn't look too good, Johnny. Bailey told me you had a fight with Elmer Guerdat."

Can't do anything around here without everybody knowing, he thought. "Yes sir, it's probably gonna look pretty bad tomorrow."

"You going to church?" Railey asked.

"Way things are going. . . figure I need it."

Railey laughed. "Something tells me you have more on your mind than Brother Baker's sermon. Some little girl?"

Johnny figured it was pretty important to let Railey know he liked girls, so said, "There's two or three I like."

"For some reason I got the idea you had your cap set for Lynn Gutherman."

The reference was to the local doctor's daughter, who was, in Johnny's opinion, the prettiest girl in his class. "I don't think she'd have much to do with somebody from my part of town."

"Let's hope she's not that way. She takes private music lessons from me, you know."

"I didn't know that."

"You have any interest in music, Johnny?"

"My folks want me to learn to play the guitar. . . sing that hillbilly stuff."

"It sounds to me like you don't like the idea."

"It ain't the kind of music I like. Truth is. . . I ain't sure it's music."

Railey laughed. "I can't argue with you there. What kind of music do you like."

"Something that's not sung through your nose."

Railey laughed again. "So you like soft music. . . popular music. . . maybe even classical?"

"Yeah. . . I guess you could say that."

"I teach piano, you know. Would you be interested in learning to play the piano?"

"Someday I might. I don't think I'd be much of a student right now. Just too many distractions."

"Well, when you're ready. . . you just let me know. We can work something out."

"You remember what you said about Mrs. Scott the other day? You know. . . about her and Mr. Thompson?"

"Yes. . . I remember."

"Well, I think I agree with you. She ain't what she seems."

"Some reason you reached that conclusion, Johnny?"

For a split second he considered telling Railey about what had happened the night before, but thought better of it. His concern was not for Marcie Scott, but rather for Bailey Thompson. He was worried that his admiration for Thompson had waned considerably as a result of what he and Bobby had witnessed at the Catholic Church. Until then he had thought of Thompson as strong and decisive, but saw that he was putty in Marcie's hands.

"No sir, nothing in particular," he said. "She seems to have forgot pretty quick that her little girl is missing. . . maybe even dead. Of course, I don't guess I've got a right to judge."

"You've got as much right to judge as anyone else. I probably shouldn't have said to you what I did about Marcie. I don't have a right to judge her, either. But, I am worried about Bailey. And, sometimes I tend to talk too much, especially when I have a good listener. Not too many people want to talk to me. . . even fewer want to listen to me rattle on. You're a good listener, Johnny."

He didn't know whether to say thanks or not. It was one of those offhand compliments that doesn't require a response. He couldn't help but wonder about Railey's interest in Bailey Thompson.

"I imagine you got lots of friends here in town. . . lots of people who like to listen to you talk."

Railey laughed. "You're a nice boy, Johnny. . . naive but nice. Bailey. . . I think he enjoys talking to me. Then there's Sol Bernstein and your friend Ben Jim Cade. They're about the only ones I talk to with any regularity. . . about anything that matters."

"Ben Jim ain't never told me anything about talking to you. But then, he ain't one to do much talking anyway."

"Ben Jim's a good man. I wish I had more work for him to do around here."

"You'd probably like talking to Father Ingram. He's a real smart guy."

"I've spoken to him. . . never had a conversation with him."

Johnny proceeded to tell Railey all he knew about the priest's background. He told him about all the books Ingram had and that he had borrowed some of them. "He's got a hundred times more books than Brother Baker. . . and they're not just on religion. He's got all of Mark Twain's stuff."

Railey laughed. "That doesn't exactly surprise me. . . the part about your priest friend having more books than Brother Baker. By the way, I have a pretty extensive library myself. . . and if you ever want to borrow some books, you'd be more than welcome."

Johnny had never been in Railey's house and was a little reluctant to go inside. He knew the man had a number of piano students, mostly girls, who took lessons there. But, despite having seen Railey at school and around town for years, Johnny felt he knew him slightly. "Well, I might just take you up on that," he said.

They talked for a few more minutes, then Johnny excused himself and went on to the Baptist parsonage to see Mrs. Baker. He knocked at the back door and she came back and pushed the screen door open. "Why Johnny Tobin. . . what in the world are you doing here?"

Marie Baker was a big, jovial woman who seemed to always have a smile on her face. She was testimony to feeling good about religion and, in Johnny's mind, was everything a Christian ought to be. She wasn't pretty physically but she was one of the most beautiful people he knew. He always wondered how she got tangled up with Brother Marvin Baker.

"Thought I'd come by and see you before church," he said.

"Well, I'm glad you did. Now you come on in here and sit down at the kitchen table. I just made some cookies and I'll get you a cold glass of milk."

"Well, I wasn't counting on eating."

"It doesn't matter whether you were counting on it or not. I was just going to have some coffee and cookies myself."

He knew it was impossible to argue her out of feeding him, so he went on in and sat down at the table. "This is mighty nice of you, Mrs. Baker."

"Oh, fiddle," she said, acting a bit embarrassed. "I'm just glad for the company. Marvin. . . he doesn't sit down and talk to me that much anymore."

You ought to thank the good Lord for small favors, Johnny thought. However, he said, "Been plenty going on to talk about."

"Ain't it the truth. Little Sadie missing and that colored family being killed like that." Then sadly, "Clarice Williams was one of the finest women I've ever met."

"I heard she used to work for you."

She put a glass of milk in front of him and set a cup of coffee on the table. Then she sat down. The cookies were already on the table. "Yes, Clarice did work for us a while. Then one day she just up and quit."

"That's funny. She tell you why?"

"Not a word. It bothered me. . . a lot. I think it bothered Marvin, too. . . and you know he's not that fond of colored people."

Johnny munched a cookie, washed it down with milk, and then said, "Yeah. . . I kind of got that impression."

Marie Baker laughed. "Sometimes I think you're way ahead of the rest of us, Johnny. I just wonder what's going on in that mind of yours?"

He grinned. "Ain't a lot. It's been too hot to do much thinking."

"It's been a scorcher of a summer all right, but I'm not believing that you aren't doing any thinking."

"People give me credit for a lot more thinking than I do," he said. "Truth is. . . I probably think about fishing and hunting more than anything else. And neither of them requires a whole lot of thought."

"One of the ladies at the church said you and Ben Jim Cade did a lot of the looking for little Sadie."

"I guess we did our share. We ain't quit yet."

"It must've been awful finding that little Williams boy in the creek."

"It was bad. . . no doubt about that. What made me mad, though, was Ruley Gaspard not letting us put the little boy in the funeral home until the Negro undertaker got over here to pick him up. Mr. Gaspard being a deacon and all. . . you'd think he'd have more feeling for people."

She sighed. "You know that's something my husband and I don't agree on?"

"No ma'am. . . I didn't."

"Someday that kind of stuff is gonna come back to haunt us. The way I see it the Lord ain't interested in the color of a person's skin. He's interested in what's inside."

"That's the way I see it, too, but there ain't many of us feels that way. I think maybe Mr. Railey and Mr. Thompson feel that way."

She smiled. "The more I hear about Winston Railey, the more I like him. I know he's different, but. . . well, being different isn't the worse thing in the world."

"I don't know him that well, but he seems to be okay."

Her eyes teared up. "You know, if you hadn't found that little boy in the creek. . . Clarice, her husband and children might still be laying out there in the woods."

"I imagine Willard Jordan would've found them."

"Willard Jordan? Isn't he the ex-convict who's kin to the sheriff?"

"Yeah. . . only he don't seem to like the sheriff all that much."

"What did he have to do with the Williams family?"

"He and Vernell built caskets together."

"Caskets?"

"Yeah. . . you know, coffins. Mr. Jordan builds them for the state prison."

"I had no idea. You know the man?"

"Yeah. . . just met him. He ain't a bad guy."

"Well, I don't know, Johnny. You probably ought not to be hanging around with ex-convicts."

"I figure he was probably framed."

"Any reason for you to think that?"

"Just a feeling I got."

She laughed. "There you go thinking again. Probably different than everybody else, too."

He grinned. "Probably. Anyway, Mr. Jordan said the Williamses didn't have many visitors. He said Brother Baker had been out there, but that's to be expected with Clarice working for y'all and all."

Her face went deadpan. "No, I didn't even know Marvin knew the way to their house. He never told me he went out there. Maybe Mr. Jordan made a mistake."

"Could be," Johnny said, not believing it for a second. "He said he saw Father Ingram out there, too."

"Clarice worked for Father Ingram when she was working for us. Marvin didn't like it one bit, either. She was working for us two days a week and was working two or three days a week at the Catholic Church."

"Why did her working for Father Ingram bother him?"

"Oh, Johnny. . . you know how Marvin feels about Catholics. He's pretty open about it."

"Yeah. . . I guess so. Only I don't think he ever told me why he doesn't like Catholics. There's got to be a reason."

She laughed. "He's my husband, but I have to say that he sometimes doesn't have reasons for the way he thinks."

"Well, I don't think Clarice quit working here because of you. She was going to work for Mrs. Scott."

"That's what I heard, but she quit here before getting the job with Mrs. Scott. And she wasn't suppose to start that job until September. There had to be some other reason."

Johnny had some suspicions, but sure wasn't going to voice them. "Everybody says Clarice Williams was a fine looking woman."

"Oh, she was. She was beautiful."

After the cookies and milk, Johnny decided to go home instead of going to church. He didn't tell Marie Baker, of course, but figured she probably wished she didn't have to go hear her husband preach, either.

TWENTY FOUR

Ben Jim Cade was arrested late Sunday night for assaulting Elmer Guerdat. When Johnny got on Billy Burton's case about it the deputy shrugged and said, "I'm just doing my job."

"When was it that Ben Jim was supposed to have assaulted Elmer? Tell me that."

"At the ball game."

"That's an outright lie. Elmer was about to smash my nose with his fist and Ben Jim grabbed his hand."

"I believe you, Johnny. If I hadn't left the game as soon as it was over I could've probably stopped you and Elmer from fighting. Then Ben Jim wouldn't be in any trouble. But I wasn't there and didn't see what happened."

"Well, a lot of people did. Mr. Thompson saw it."

"All I know is Elmer's daddy filed a complaint and the sheriff is as happy as a doodlebug about it. I warned you he was just looking for a reason to put Ben Jim in jail."

"The sheriff'll listen to Mr. Thompson, won't he?"

Billy shrugged again. "I don't know. Maybe he will. . . maybe he won't. You never know what the man'll do."

It was early Monday morning and Johnny had been en route to school when he ran into Billy in front of the donut shop. It was the first day and he wasn't ready. He felt like he hadn't done enough fishing during the summer. "Dang it. . . I got to go to school right now. But I'll see Mr. Thompson there and we'll be coming down to the jail to straighten this thing out."

"I hope you can. I don't want to see Ben Jim in jail. But you'd better hurry. The drunker the sheriff gets the meaner and uglier he gets with a prisoner."

When Johnny arrived at school he made a beeline to the principal's office. Bailey Thompson was shocked when he heard what had happened. "Well, yeah, Johnny. . . soon as we get things underway here I'll be glad to go down and see the sheriff. . . tell him what happened."

"When do you want to go?" Johnny asked. "I'm ready anytime."

Bailey laughed. "I'll bet you are. But you just go on to class. There's no reason for you to go. I can take care of this."

Johnny didn't like it, but felt it was best not to make an issue of it. "When are you going?"

"Like I said. . . as soon as I can get away. Why don't you see me after you eat lunch and I'll tell you what happened."

The morning's classes passed all too slowly for Johnny. When the bell rang for lunch he went straight to the principal's office. He couldn't eat until he knew what had happened.

"I tried," Bailey said, shrugging his shoulders. "The way the sheriff tells it, Mr. Guerdat filed a complaint. He'll have to drop it or Ben Jim stays in jail."

"I might've known," Johnny said. "I think Elmer's daddy is kin to the sheriff."

"Seems I heard that, too. The sheriff's got lots of kin around here, which is probably why he keeps getting elected."

"Was he drunk?"

Bailey laughed. "What's that old saying. . . is the Pope a Catholic? There'd be some doubt if you asked me if he was sober."

Twenty Four

"I'm worried. Billy said the drunker he gets the meaner and uglier he gets with prisoners."

Bailey frowned. "Well, Johnny, I wish there was something I could do, but I went down and told the sheriff the truth of the matter. I'll tell it again when Ben Jim's case comes to trial."

"There ain't gonna be no trial if I have anything to do with it."

"I don't know what you can do."

"It ain't what I can do, it's what my daddy can do."

"You think you ought to get your daddy mixed up in this? I know there's no love lost between your daddy and the sheriff, so there could be lots of trouble."

"Oh, I don't think I'm gonna have to get him mixed up in it. When he hears what happened he'll make up his own mind about what to do. I wouldn't want to be in the sheriff's boots, though."

Johnny took his sack lunch out on the schoolyard and found refuge in the shade of a large oak tree. Bobby joined him. He was just starting on a sandwich, sitting with his back to the tree, when Elmer Guerdat and a couple of his shadows came up.

"Well, well," Elmer said, "I hear they arrested that old nigger friend of yours."

Johnny didn't bother to get up. He deadpanned, "You're a jerk, Elmer."

"I ought to finish what I started yesterday. . . ought to whip your butt good."

Elmer's nose was red and so swollen that his eyes were slitted. Johnny couldn't help but laugh at the face before him, though the area around his own eye where Elmer had hit him was bluish black and awful looking.

"What are you laughing at?" Elmer asked, angrily.

"He ain't laughing at nothing," Bobby replied, nervously.

Johnny gave Bobby that I can speak for myself look and said, "When you decide to whip my little butt, Elmer, you'd better bring your breakfast, dinner and supper. . . because it's gonna take you all day."

"Ain't he the tough one," one of Elmer's buddies said.

"I'm tough enough. Why don't you two jerks try to help Elmer whip my little butt."

Elmer shook his head in a bit of resignation. "You're a crazy little jerk. . . you know that?"

Johnny took a bite of his sandwich, chewed and swallowed before replying. "That's something you ought to think about, Elmer. . . a lot. You're bigger and stronger than me, but you're sure not smarter. You can beat me within an inch of my life, but the only way you're gonna keep me down is to kill me. And. . . if you don't kill me. . . I'm gonna get you. One of these days I'm liable to bury an ax right between your eyes. So yeah. . . I'm crazy. All the Tobins are crazy."

Elmer looked at his two friends with dismay. "You believe this? I told you he was crazy."

The trio started walking away, but Elmer couldn't resist launching a parting shot. "You're a nigger-loving jerk, Tobin, but ain't nothing you can do about your nigger friend. He's gonna rot in jail."

Despite what he really felt, Johnny grinned. "I wouldn't bet on it, Elmer. Your daddy's probably gonna be getting a visit from my daddy. Who do you think is gonna have the last word?"

Elmer's face colored up as much as his nose. He had heard often enough that Jake Tobin was the meanest, craziest man in the parish. "He better watch his step coming around my daddy."

"He always does," Johnny said.

After they were out of earshot, Bobby asked, "Why did you tell them your daddy was gonna take a hand? You don't know that for a fact."

"When daddy knows the truth of it. . . he'll do something about it," Johnny said.

As soon as school ended for the day Johnny went downtown and found Billy Burton. The deputy was having a cup of coffee at the Walla Cafe. Billy bought Johnny a cup, which, after doctoring it with sugar and taking a sip, said, "I want to see Ben Jim."

"I ain't sure that's a good idea. The sheriff wouldn't like it if he knew I let you talk to him."

"Then don't tell him."

The deputy sighed. "You're a pain. . . you know that?"

"I been told often enough. I figure the sheriff is drunk on his rear somewhere."

Billy grinned. "That's pretty good figuring." Then his mouth turned down into a frown. "The sheriff. . . he gave Ben Jim a bit of a beating. Thought I ought to warn you."

"The jerk. He didn't have no right to do that."

"What he's got a right to do and what he does. . . that's two different things. I'll let you see Ben Jim for a few minutes if Chief Crossland ain't there. If he is you're gonna have to wait because he'll tell the sheriff."

Roger Crossland wasn't at the jailhouse, so Johnny got to go in and see Ben Jim. The older man didn't look like he was in the best of shape, though his eyes were as defiant as ever. "You being here. . . I feel like it's my fault."

"Ain't no way it's your fault."

Johnny didn't like looking at Ben Jim through the bars. There was something strange about a man like him being locked up, something that defied the freedom of the woods they both enjoyed. "If I hadn't gotten in that row with Elmer. . . "

"Then it would've been something else. The sheriff's been out to get me for a long time."

"Billy tells me he beat you."

Ben Jim gave a tired grin. "He did that right enough. But it ain't the first time I've been beat. . . and it likely ain't gonna be the last."

"When daddy finds out what. . . "

"Now don't you be bothering your daddy with any of this. He's got enough to deal with without worrying about some old colored man what got crossways with the law."

Johnny knew it wouldn't do any good to argue with Ben Jim about it. He would just do what he had to do. "What did the sheriff beat you with?"

"That ain't nothing for you to worry about neither."

"They feeding you all right?"

"They ain't fed me yet."

"Dang," Johnny said, angrily. "I'll go over to the cafe and get you something."

"No. . . don't you be doing that. It'll just cause me more trouble. They'll feed me before long. Mrs. Crossland. . . she'll see to it that I get something to eat."

Johnny talked to Ben Jim for five minutes or so, until Billy came in and told him he had to leave. Out of earshot of the cell he asked, "What did the sheriff beat Ben Jim with?"

"Piece of rubber hose. It don't mark up a colored all that bad."

Johnny said. "One of these days I'm gonna. . . "

"Get in lots of trouble," Billy said. "Just take it easy, Johnny. Ain't nothing you can do about the way things is."

"I ain't so sure about that."

When Jake Tobin got off work Johnny was waiting to tell him about Ben Jim being in jail, but his dad had already heard. He had also heard about Ben Jim's alleged assault on Elmer Guerdat, which had been embellished considerably. Johnny told him the straight of it, and told him how the sheriff had beaten Ben Jim.

Jake's sun-browned, leathery face turned beet red with anger. He left the house without eating supper. Johnny wanted to go with him, but got an emphatic no. There were times he might have quarreled about it. This wasn't one of them. He could read his dad's face well enough to know when to keep his mouth shut.

No one knew exactly what happened, Jake not being one to talk. And Wilber Guerdat and the sheriff were not exactly anxious to share what their roles were in the drama. There were, of course, a lot of rumors, all of which made much of Jake's violent temper.

One of the more believable tales was that Jake went to the Guerdat home and dragged Wilber away from the supper table. Dragged might well be the kindest word that could be used. Anyway, he stuffed Wilber in his old car and drove around until he found the sheriff's parked car. It was parked in front of a house that belonged to a woman the sheriff was courting.

The story is that Jake stomped into the woman's house without so much as knocking and dragged the sheriff out onto the front porch. He grabbed him by the nape of the neck and marched him right out in the front yard, then watered him down with a garden hose until he was satisfied he was halfway sober.

He sat the sheriff down on the front porch steps and made Wilber tell him the truth about Ben Jim's alleged assault on Elmer. Wilber told it right and was more than anxious to drop the charges against Ben Jim. Jake took the sheriff by the nape of the neck and marched him back in the house where Merrick telephoned Billy

Burton and told him to release Ben Jim.

Word is that Jake also told the sheriff that if he ever heard of him whipping another prisoner, colored or white, he wouldn't have any reason to be visiting a woman.

There were other versions of the story, more exaggerated, but this one seems more likely to be true. But, true or not, Ben Jim was released that Monday night. Wilber Guerdat wasn't interested in telling anyone why he dropped the charges, and the sheriff didn't have anything to say, either.

TWENTY FIVE

September was not the best of months as far as Johnny was concerned. Snakes started shedding their skins, getting blind and meaner. And, it was always tough to get back in the school groove after summertime, especially in a month that was just as hot as August. The school didn't have air conditioning, not even fans, and the open windows just seemed to let more heat in. Toward the end of the month there would be a hint of cooler days, which meant better fishing and the advent of hunting season, but it seemed that those days were never going to arrive.

However, it wasn't just the heat that bothered Johnny. School cut into important things like fishing and hunting.

Johnny had an English class with Marcie Scott, whom he considered a decent enough teacher. Looking at her was especially nice, but thinking about her extracurricular activities with Bailey Thompson made his attitude toward her one of confusion. That confusion was compounded because, to his way of thinking, she had completely forgotten about little Sadie. She seemed extremely happy, as though there was no grief in her for the missing child.

Vernon Scott seemed to be carrying the burden of grief. Johnny couldn't help but wonder if his sadness was for Sadie, or if he knew about his wife and the principal.

He had a math class with Scott and couldn't say his teaching was affected by whatever was bothering him. The man, he thought, had never been able to teach. The problem being that he didn't know anything to teach.

Johnny knew for sure the football team wasn't the reason for Scott's long face. It was off to its best start ever, three straight wins by convincing scores. Elmer Guerdat had been brilliant, running wild and averaging three touchdowns a game. He was having to wear a face guard to protect his tender nose.

There was plenty of talk that LSU couldn't wait to get Elmer in a Tigers uniform. Johnny figured it would be a whole lot easier to dress Elmer than to teach him anything, and wondered how the university was going to arrange for Elmer to pass any of its courses. At Walla High such things were arranged for him.

For the first time, Johnny had Winston Railey as a teacher. Johnny considered him a strange duck, but readily admitted he was a fine teacher. He challenged the minds of the students, which had Bobby complaining right from the get go. "That crazy old man is gonna work us to death."

Johnny, who had Railey's class after a math session with Vernon Scott, said, "You ought to just be grateful to be spending an hour with somebody who knows what he's talking about."

Bobby, though, was like a lot of the other boys in school. He was just biding his time, waiting until he was old enough to get a job with the sawmill or get drafted into the Army.

He'll end up working at the sawmill or in the logwoods, marrying some girl whose folks ain't got anything either, Johnny thought. *They'll have a house full of kids and will never have anything*. He found it depressing, but knew there wasn't anything he could do about it. He was just determined not to end up the same way.

Despite schoolwork and a myriad of other things crossing Johnny's mind, thoughts of little Sadie and the Williams family were always with him. He felt compelled to somehow keep at least their memories alive.

He wanted to find out more about Clarice Williams, why she had chosen to leave the employ of Brother and Mrs. Baker. He also wanted to know why she had quit working for Father Walter Ingram. He wanted to know if Aunt Bessie's allegation that Isaac Simpson had killed the Williams family was correct.

After Ben Jim had been released from jail, Johnny had cornered Billy Burton and suggested they find out more about Isaac Simpson. "Aunt Bessie. . . she's convinced Isaac's the one who killed the Williams family. She says he wanted Clarice. Don't you think we ought to check Isaac out. . . see if he's the murderer?"

"Do I think we ought to check Isaac out?" Billy echoed, laughing. "You're gonna pester me to death about this, ain't you?

"Seems to me the sheriff would like to get a colored in jail to take Ben Jim's place."

Billy frowned. "Well now, that's kind of a sore subject with the sheriff. Whatever happened between your daddy and him. . . well, it ain't made my life any easier."

Johnny shrugged his shoulders. "I don't know what happened. And if I wait for daddy to tell me, I figure I'll be waiting forever."

"Probably right. Jake ain't one to say much." Then Billy grinned. "But I'll bet he put the fear of God in the sheriff."

It had taken some real convincing on Johnny's part, but finally Billy had let him get in his car and they had gone looking for Isaac Simpson. They had cruised hangouts Isaac was known to frequent, mostly barbecue places that were fronts for illegal liquor and gambling.

Corn Squeezin's place was one where Johnny had been before. He thought the cook there made the best hot tamales in the parish, and suggested to Billy that they eat a few. "Course you're gonna have to buy, Billy. I didn't bring any money with me."

Billy laughed. "I always said you was a smart one, Johnny."

There was a screened porch on the side of the old ramshackle frame building where white people could sit at a worn table to eat barbecue and hot tamales. A sign above the door read in crude letters: *White Only*. It was kind of like the sign above the door at the back of the Walla Cafe that read *Colored Only*.

Twenty Five

More coloreds ate at the Walla Cafe than whites at Corn Squeezin's place. The place wasn't new to Johnny, though, because he and his dad had eaten there a number of times.

Billy and Johnny made themselves comfortable and ordered strawberry soda pops and a half dozen hot tamales each. The tamales were wrapped in real corn shucks. Johnny posed a non-question. "Good, ain't they?"

"I ain't never had none better."

"You ever ask Corn Squeezin's how he got his name?"

"No. . . never figured it was any of my business."

Johnny shook his head in dismay. "I can't figure somebody not wanting to know."

Billy laughed. "That ain't surprising. I bet you know. . . and I bet you're gonna tell me."

"I ain't gonna tell you unless you want me to."

"Don't get your rear in an uproar, Johnny. . . I wouldn't mind knowing."

"Me and daddy was here eating tamales one time and Corn Squeezin's came out here and I asked him about it."

"Somehow that don't surprise me none neither."

Johnny didn't pay any attention to the dig. "He said his grandpa was a slave to a man he didn't like. . . and you know how most slaves took the names of their masters?"

"Yeah. . . I know about that."

"Well, Corn Squeezin's said his grandpa didn't want to take the name of a man he didn't like, so he took the name of something he did like. He said his grandpa dearly loved corn whiskey."

Billy laughed. "You believe his story?"

"Ain't no reason not to. Even if it's not true, it's a good story."

They concentrated on the tamales and soda pop until the cook came out to say hello. She was almost a duplicate of Bessie Jackson and with good reason. Jezebel Jones was Bessie's twin sister. "How you doing Mr. Johnny. . . Mr. Billy?"

Johnny grinned. "Well, I was feeling kind of poorly until I started eating these hot tamales, Aunt Jez. They put a good feeling in your belly and head."

She chuckled and shook her head. "You won't do, Mr. Johnny."

"I wish you wouldn't call me Mr."

"Old ways is hard to break. Besides, you calls me Aunt and I ain't your aunt."

"That's different."

"Why do you think it's different?"

"That's what I call your sister, too."

Billy said, "Ain't no reasoning with him, Aunt Jez."

"Well, it don't matter none no ways, Aunt Jez," Johnny said. "Billy and me. . . we're looking for Isaac Simpson."

"What you looking for that no account Isaac for?"

"I need to ask him a few questions about the Williams family," Billy said.

"Well, it's sure about time."

"Why do you say that, Aunt Jez?" Billy asked.

"He the man that killed them."

"You know that for a fact?" the deputy asked.

"Well now, I ain't seen him do it. But he done had his eyes on Clarice and she wouldn't give him the time of day."

Johnny said, "Aunt Bessie. . . she thinks he killed them, too. I guess y'all been talking about it?"

"Sure we talk about it. That Clarice. . . she was a strange woman, but that ain't no reason to kill her."

"What do you mean strange?" Johnny asked.

"That ain't for me to say."

"You don't have any idea where Isaac is?" Billy asked.

"You go find you a dice game or a woman that's trifling on her husband. That's where you'll find Isaac."

After finishing their tamales they checked several other places, but with no success. It was like Isaac had disappeared off the face of the earth. "When the law's looking for a colored, other coloreds just naturally ain't gonna help you find them," Billy said.

"Aunt Jez would've told us if she had known."

"I ain't talking about people like Aunt Jez. I'm talking about colored men. Can't say as I blame them, neither."

The next day after school Johnny saw Ben Jim in town and solicited his help in finding Isaac. "I ain't got no cause to be hunting Isaac," Ben Jim said.

Twenty Five

"Fine. If you don't want to help, then I'll just look for him myself. I got some questions I want to ask him."

Ben Jim shook his head in semi-despair. "I expect you would, too. Well, I guess I better go with you, because Isaac ain't gonna take kindly to some little white boy asking everybody where he is. Not that you ain't done it already, mind you."

"I ain't a little white boy. I'm pretty big for my age."

Ben Jim smiled. "I guess you are at that."

With Ben Jim's help, Isaac was easily located. They found him behind an old barn-like structure near the railroad station. He was rolling dice with two other black men. He was not pleased to see them and said, "What you coming round here for, Ben Jim Cade? I ain't got no business with you."

"I ain't that pleased to see you, Isaac. But there are some questions you need to answer."

Isaac, who had been on his knees talking to, shaking and rolling the bones, stood. He was stocky, built low to the ground like a bulldog. Johnny thought he also had a bulldog's face, which was creased into a permanent scowl. "Who do you think you is, Ben Jim. . . coming round here to ask me some questions? I don't have to answer no questions for you."

"You sure don't, but you're gonna have to be answering to somebody. . . and it might as well be me."

"What you talking about?"

"Let's go over here where we can talk quiet like."

Isaac wanted to argue, but there was something about Ben Jim's manner that was akin to that of a commanding general. The younger man felt he had no choice but to follow Ben Jim and Johnny out of earshot of his companions. They settled on a shady spot near the end of the building.

With a touch of bravado Isaac asked, "Okay, old man. . . what's this all about?"

Johnny wasn't sure how Ben Jim was going to handle the situation, but immediately realized he should have been. His friend sort of specialized in being direct. "There's talk, Isaac, that you're the one who killed the Williams family."

Isaac's eyes registered surprise, but not enough to Johnny's way of thinking. "What you talking about. I ain't never killed nobody."

"I'm just telling you what some folks are saying. And, don't be telling me somebody ain't done told you there's been this kind of talk going around."

Isaac, who was trying to look shocked and angry, looked sheepish instead. "Maybe I heard some of this kind of stuff, but I ain't paid no attention to it."

"Well, you'd better start paying some attention because the law is looking for you."

"What law you talking about?" he asked, huffily.

"Mr. Billy Burton, that's who."

Isaac laughed. "Ain't nothing to that. The sheriff and me. . . we got an understanding. Mr. Billy must not know about it."

"I don't know about no understanding you've got with the sheriff neither. So you tell me, Isaac. . . are you the one what killed the Williams family?"

"It ain't none of your business, Ben Jim Cade, if I did or didn't."

Ben Jim's eyes turned to flint. "I'm making it my business."

Isaac, who didn't want his reputation further sullied by getting whipped by Ben Jim again, said, "I don't have to tell you nothing, but no. . . no, I ain't the one what killed them. Besides, I already done told you I ain't never killed nobody."

"You know who did?"

"Can't say that I do."

"There's talk that you had your eyes on Clarice."

Isaac laughed, nervously. "Ain't no secret about that. Lots of folks had eyes for Clarice, cause she was one fine looking woman. But eyes is all I ever had on her. That woman. . . she didn't know whether she was white or black. . . or whether she was a man or woman."

"What do you mean?" Johnny asked, his curiosity erupting.

"Now I ain't gonna be answering no questions for Mr. Johnny here. I know he's been going around asking people questions about me. A white boy ain't got no business messing with what happened to the Williams family."

Ben Jim said, "Maybe you want to tell Mr. Jake his boy ain't got no business asking questions."

Isaac's eyes flashed fear. "Now I ain't got no quarrel with Mr. Jake.

And don't you be telling him that I do."

"Then maybe you ought to just answer the question Johnny asked you and be done with it."

"It ain't a question that you answer for no young boy."

Johnny snorted. "I ain't that young."

Isaac looked at Ben Jim for permission and the older man nodded his head in the affirmative. "I done been told that Clarice done did some unnatural stuff with some of the white folks round here," Isaac said.

"Like what?" Johnny asked.

Again Isaac looked at Ben Jim, pleadingly. Ben Jim said, "Let's walk on down the road here, Isaac, and you tell me what you know. You wait here, Johnny."

"Hold on here. . . I'm old enough."

"I'll let Isaac tell me first. . . and if I think you're old enough, then I'll tell you."

Johnny knew there wasn't much point arguing. Ben Jim was as hardheaded as Jake Tobin. So he waited while the two men walked down the road apiece. After a few minutes Ben Jim came back alone. Isaac walked out of sight.

"Well?" Johnny asked.

"Ain't nothing for your ears."

"Dang it, Ben Jim, you ain't being fair. And, why did you let Isaac just walk off?"

"What are we gonna do with him. . . put him in jail?"

"We could turn him over to Billy."

"Isaac ain't hard to find. He ain't going nowhere. Besides, he probably does have some kind of deal with the sheriff."

"You think he was telling the truth. . . about him not being the one who killed the Williams family?"

"Maybe. Hard to say. I figure he was telling some truth and telling some lies. Hard to say which was which. Isaac tells so many lies it's hard for him to know the difference."

"What about Clarice Williams and the white people? What unnatural things was she doing with them? And what white people was he talking about?"

"Maybe that was all lies, too. Ain't no point spreading no gossip about the dead, especially since we don't know if it's the truth or not."

"You ain't gonna tell me the white people he was talking about, either. . . are you?"

"Ain't no point tellin' you something that may not be the truth."

"I know one of the people he was talking about was Brother Baker. I talked to Mrs. Baker not long ago and she told me some stuff that gave me some pretty good suspicions."

"And that's all they is. . . suspicions. You need to be careful what you say to other folks about people, Johnny."

"I know it, but. . . dang it, somebody needs to nail Brother Baker."

"Well, it ought not to be you. And, you ought not to be carrying around all that hate in your heart for the man. You want him to be wrong and you're out to prove that he is. That ain't the way the Bible tells us we're supposed to be."

Johnny knew Ben Jim was right. Finding fault with Brother Baker, while not yet an obsession with him, was certainly a priority. He guessed maybe he did hate the man, the fact that he took such license with the Bible. Johnny considered himself respectful of God's Word, though not a so-called "messenger of God" like Brother Marvin Baker.

The previous year Johnny's usual after-school itinerary in September was fishing beneath the trestle, playing gumball baseball with Bobby, or playing football with Bobby and a few of the other kids. Now he was absorbed with solving two mysteries: little Sadie Scott's disappearance and the murders of the five members of the Williams family.

The afternoon after Ben Jim had talked to Isaac, Johnny went to Bessie Jackson's house. She had just arrived home from her work at the Catholic Church and was surprised to see him. "Come on in here, Johnny. . . I've got a big glass of lemonade for you."

Bessie's house was small, the green paint peeling from its exterior walls. It was shaped like a railroad boxcar except for the slanted tin roof. The interior was sterile clean, the wood floor worn from years of being scrubbed with lye soap.

"I don't want to put you to any trouble, Aunt Bessie."

"You ain't putting me to no trouble."

The furnishings, like those Johnny's folks owned, were no great shakes. He had been there before and felt very comfortable. The house had been witness to a lot of pain, suffering and love, the latter overwhelming all the negatives.

Bessie and her husband Eroy had raised six children in the house, fed them, clothed them and prepared them for life. Then Eroy died, leaving Bessie to make it on her own.

Johnny sat down at the table in the back of the house. It was adjacent to the wood-burning stove where Bessie had cooked meals for some forty years. She opened the icebox, chipped off a few chunks of ice from the small block inside, and put it in two glasses. Then she put the glasses on the table and poured the lemonade. It was semi-dark in the room, but she did not bother lighting the lamp on the table before sitting down. The house had no electricity.

"Now what did you come to see Aunt Bessie about, Johnny?"

He grinned. "Maybe I was just in the neighborhood and decided to drop by."

She laughed and the lack of light didn't hide her large white teeth. "Now you tell Aunt Bessie the truth, because the one white boy in this town that she know better than all the others is sitting right here at the table with her."

Johnny took a drink of the lemonade, sighed and said, "Lots of things are bothering me, Aunt Bessie."

"What kind of things?"

"Well, it's got to do with little Sadie being missing and the Williams family being murdered. Seems nobody cares anymore."

"Excepting you?"

"Ain't nobody wants to do anything. Seems I'm the only one who wants to find out what happened."

"You're like any young boy. . . you think you the only one what wants to do anything. The truth is that lots of people care, especially colored folks. But what are people gonna do? You know the sheriff ain't interested in finding out who killed the Williams family. And he don't know what to do about little Sadie being missing. Ain't nobody knows what to do."

"Well, he could question people."

"Hmmmm. I heard you and Ben Jim done questioned Isaac Simpson yesterday."

"Word gets around pretty fast."

"You find out anything? Did Isaac tell you he killed the Williams family?"

"No. . . he didn't say that. He denied it."

"Course he did. What you expect him to do?"

"He told us. . . well, he told Ben Jim some other stuff. Only he wouldn't tell me everything Isaac said."

"There's probably a good reason."

"I'd like to know about Clarice Williams. . . what kind of woman she was."

"What good is that gonna do?"

"Well, it might help me find out something."

"I don't like talking about the dead."

"If she's the reason the whole family was killed, you've got to talk about her."

Bessie paused for a few seconds before responding. "Everybody. . . long as I can remember. . . has talked about what a smart boy you is, Johnny. I seen it a lot when I was taking care of you and your mama was having your sister and brother. What I'm saying is that I can sit down and talk to you about just about anything. But, there's some things you shouldn't ought to talk about to little boys."

"Dang it, Aunt Bessie, I ain't no little boy. And if you don't talk to me, I'm gonna go find somebody who will."

She sighed. "I can believe that. And you might just talk to the wrong folks. . . get yourself hurt. All right, you've got to promise me that you ain't gonna run tell your folks that I done talked to you. I ain't sure what I'm doing is right. . . and I sure don't want your mama and daddy mad with me."

"I ain't gonna say nothing."

"All right. . . what you want to know?"

"I want to know about Clarice Williams. . . what kind of woman she was. . . that kind of stuff."

She sighed again. "Ain't nobody around here know Clarice or Vernell all that well. They came over here from Mississippi."

"I don't know whether it was you or Aunt Jez. . . maybe both of you. . . who said Clarice didn't know whether she was black or white."

"Folks say Clarice was uppity. . . like she thought she was too good to be colored. She was a pretty woman. . . real light colored. They say she was messing round with white men. Just remember that I'm repeating what they say. . . that I don't know it for a fact."

"Do they say one of those men was Brother Baker."

She laughed. "They say he wanted to be one of the men she messed with. . . but that she wouldn't have nothing to do with him."

"I figure that's the reason she quit working for the Bakers, don't you?"

"I expect so."

"Why did she quit working for Father Ingram?"

Mention of the priest put Bessie on the defensive. "Now Father Ingram. . . he ain't that way. I ain't got any way of knowing why she quit working for him. He's one of the finest men I ever been round."

"I ain't accusing him of nothing, Aunt Bessie. I was just wondering why Clarice quit working for him. You know I like him."

"Sure you like him, but ain't nobody safe from your curiosity."

"Any other white men they say Clarice was messing around with?"

"Ain't nobody wanting to say no names. People. . . they just got suspicions."

"They've got suspicions about Father Ingram, don't they?"

"Ain't for me to say," she replied, huffily.

"Isaac said Clarice didn't know whether she liked men or women. What do you think he meant by that?"

"Ain't no telling what that no account meant."

"Mr. Jordan's the one who told me the Williamses were visited by Brother Baker, Mrs. Scott and Father Ingram."

She laughed. "Mr. Willard Jordan? He the one you said killed the Williams family."

"Well, I was wrong about him being the murderer. But the way you laughed. . . something wrong with him?"

"Nothing I know about. He's just a funny man. . . that's all."

Johnny grinned. "Well, I didn't find him that way. . . leastwise not at first." He then told her about his initial encounter with Jordan.

"I could've told you right off that Mr. Jordan wouldn't hurt nobody. . . unless it was the sheriff."

"He don't seem to like him much," Johnny said. "What's the

story there?"

"They're related, you know."

"That's what I heard."

"Well, I don't know what caused the bad blood between them, but there's plenty of it. Wouldn't surprise me none if Mr. Willard didn't up and kill the sheriff someday."

"Wouldn't be much of a loss."

"Now you quit your talking that way, Johnny Tobin. . . even if what you're saying be true."

"Just can't help myself, Aunt Bessie. If there's two people in town that chap me, it's the sheriff and Brother Baker."

"You don't need to be worrying about them none. . . just grow up and do something about them."

"What can I do?"

"Ain't nothing to keep you from being a preacher man or the sheriff."

Johnny guffawed. "People hear you say stuff like that about me and they're liable to come take you away. . . put you in the insane asylum up at Pineville."

She smiled. "You know I'm telling the truth. You can be whatever you want to be."

"Maybe so, Aunt Bessie. . . but if you hear me saying I want to be a preacher or sheriff you'd better have them lock me up in the asylum, too. But, you know what's funny to me?"

"What?"

"When I first told Billy Burton about Mr. Jordan, he didn't know there was bad blood between him and the sheriff."

"Lots of people don't know cause Mr. Willard. . . he ain't one to do a lot of talking. The colored folks round here more likely to know who like and don't like the sheriff."

He had another glass of lemonade before leaving Bessie's house. He figured she knew a lot more than she was telling him, but knew he wouldn't be able to pry it out of her with a stick. Bessie Jackson, he understood, would tell him what she wanted him to know and nothing more, except on her own timetable.

Johnny walked the dusty road to Bernstein's Store, marched up on the wooden porch, opened the screen door and went inside. The late sun coming through the windows made the interior hazy and ghostlike, but also silhouetted the millions of little particles in the air that most often were not seen. Sol Bernstein was in the back of the store behind the meat counter. Ruth and Ruta were up front.

Both girls smiled and Ruth asked, "Shouldn't you be home studying, Johnny?"

He grinned. "So far the teachers ain't assigned anything I don't already know."

Ruta shook her head in mock resignation. "I might've known you'd say something like that."

"Why didn't y'all go to the dance over at the Catholic Church? Father Ingram invited you, didn't he?"

The young women looked at each other in a way Johnny interpreted as sorrowful. Then Ruth said, "Daddy's not too keen on us going to the dances."

"And, we're not too keen on going, either," Ruta said.

"Why not?"

"We're Jewish, Johnny," Ruth said.

"So? What's that got to do with anything."

They both laughed. "We don't fit in," Ruta said.

"Seems to me y'all ain't trying. I happen to know Billy Burton wants to take one of y'all out, only he can't decide which one. And. . . he's kind of bashful, too, you know."

"Tell him to ask Ruta," Ruth said, laughing.

"No, no. . . tell him to ask Ruth," Ruta said, finding the possibility just as amusing as her sister did.

"Y'all don't like Billy?"

Ruth crawfished. "Well, it's not that we don't like Billy. He's a nice enough guy and all that. It just. . . "

"He's no Prince Charming," Ruta said.

Johnny laughed. "I don't think you're gonna find one of those in Walla."

Ruth said, "Let me put it this way, Johnny. . . you're not gonna settle for just what's here, are you?"

"You know I ain't."

"Then don't expect us to, either."

"You got me there."

"Besides, Johnny," Ruta said, "I'm just waiting for you to grow up."

He laughed. "I'm already big as you are."

"Then why don't you ask me out?"

He loved their teasing, the give and take. "I'd ask you out, but you girls ain't old enough for me."

Ruth and Ruta were in their mid to late twenties, beautiful, but with little chance of a normal married life in Walla. Sol Bernstein was quite set on not letting his girls marry, or even date, outside the Jewish faith. Since there were no other Jews in Walla, it meant he was either going to have to import husbands for them or let them leave the town for more promising surroundings. Sol was not inclined to be in any hurry to do either. He still considered them little girls, needed their help in the store and their company at home.

The death of his wife when the girls were teenagers had devastated Sol. Even when she was alive there had been, on Sol's part, what some considered an unnatural protectiveness and affection for the girls. The truth was that living in Walla the four of them were like outsiders in a foreign land, with no friends or family to turn to except each other. His protectiveness was a direct result of his earlier life when abuse, hatred and racism had victimized him because of his Jewish heritage. His outward affection for the girls, which really wasn't abnormal, was simply an effort to offset the terrible loneliness they all felt.

Most townspeople dealt with the Bernsteins because they owned the store. No friendship was involved. In fact, the invitation to attend the dance from Father Walter Ingram was a first. The girls had, of course, attended some school functions when they were students, but there had been a long drought in between. Some local boys, excluding the bashful Billy Burton, had on occasion tried to date them when they were in high school. But it hadn't taken long for the word to get out that they didn't date gentiles.

There was talk that the Bernsteins preferred the colored people of the town to the white population, though no one could accuse the family of ever being disrespectful to anyone. That may have been the reason for the talk. The Bernsteins were just as courteous to Negroes as to whites.

Johnny bantered back and forth with the girls before asking,

Twenty Five

"How well do y'all know Mrs. Scott?"

Ruth shrugged. "We know her. She buys groceries here, but you know that, Johnny. She usually comes in on Saturdays, which you also know. So why are you asking?"

"Just curious."

They laughed and Ruta said, "Oh, no. We know you better than that, Johnny."

He grinned. "Well, I have her for a class. . . figured anything you could tell me might help."

"She's a strange woman," Ruta said. "That's about all I can tell you."

"What do you mean?"

"Oh, I don't know exactly. Her mood seems to change so much. You never know how she's going to act."

He nodded. "I noticed that, too. It's like one day I thought she might've killed herself because little Sadie was missing and the next day she acted happy as a lark."

"Coach Scott's about as strange as she is," Ruth said.

Johnny laughed. "He's that all right. But he's pretty predictable. He's dumb as a doorknob."

The girls laughed and Ruta said, "Well, there's not a woman in town dresses any better than Mrs. Scott. She must go to Shreveport at least once a month to buy something new. I'd say she's a woman who thinks pretty highly of herself."

Ruth said, "Of course, there's nothing wrong with that."

"Wonder where she gets the money to make all those trips to Shreveport?" Johnny asked.

"I hear she gets money from her daddy," Ruta replied. "Daddy makes us work for ours."

"He just doesn't want to spoil you," Johnny said, laughing. "Ain't much chance of my folks spoiling me, either. But, I guess the Scotts do okay. . . him coaching and her teaching. You'll notice I didn't say anything about him doing any teaching."

The women laughed again and Ruta said, "Coach Scott may not be smart, but I don't think he's a bad man. He doesn't treat people mean or anything."

"You saying Mrs. Scott does?" Johnny asked.

"Well, she's had a hard time keeping help. . . especially getting someone to keep Sadie while she was teaching. Of course, that's not a problem anymore."

"Clarice Williams was gonna keep her this year, I think," Johnny said. "At least, that's what I've been told."

"Clarice wasn't looking forward to it," Ruth said, drawing a hard look from her sister.

The statement surprised Johnny. He had talked to them about the Williams family before, at least a couple of times after the murders. They hadn't indicated they knew Clarice at all, except as an occasional customer at the store. "She told you that?" Johnny asked.

"In so many words," Ruta said. "We just kind of knew Clarice in passing."

"She say why?"

The women looked at each other uncomfortably. "Not really," Ruth answered.

Despite his youth, Johnny could read people pretty well. He sensed Ruth and Ruta were lying. *But why*? he asked himself. The sisters, he thought, had always been upfront with him before. "Y'all aren't telling me for some reason."

"No. . . no," Ruth said. "We just don't know."

There seemed to be a lot that people didn't know about Clarice Williams and Marcie Scott, he decided. Or, they just weren't willing to tell him what they knew.

"C'mon now. . . I'll tell you what I know if you'll tell me what you know."

Ruta sighed. "We don't know anything, Johnny."

"I could tell you why she quit working for Brother Baker," he said.

"That one's not hard to figure," Ruth said. "Mrs. Baker's a fine woman, but Brother Baker. . . "

"You don't have to finish," Johnny said. "The three of us know what he is. I just don't understand why the rest of the town can't see it."

"Ever think the three of us could be wrong?" Ruta asked.

"Not in a million years," Johnny replied, laughing. "What's funny is that Brother Baker hates coloreds."

"Clarice Williams wasn't like any other colored woman around here," Ruta said. "She was real light colored. . . and one of the prettiest women I've ever seen."

Johnny slipped and said, "Don't guess I ever noticed her when she was alive." He realized immediately what he had said and wanted to cover up, but Ruth and Ruta, he decided, hadn't noticed. "Everybody says she was a fine looking woman."

"Your friend Ben Jim Cade sure thought so," Ruth said.

"Why do you say that?"

"Because he always looked her up and down real good when the two of them were in the store. He used to talk to her every chance he got."

"Well, I don't know about Ben Jim having a roving eye, but I know Isaac Simpson does. . . and Aunt Bessie thinks he might've had something to do with killing the Williams family."

Despite the heat, both women shuddered like it was cold. "Isaac can be a little scary," Ruta said, "but I don't know about him killing somebody. I think he's just one of those men who can't stay away from the ladies and likes to talk about it."

"Aunt Bessie sure don't like him," Johnny said.

"I don't know anyone who does," Ruth said, "except Mrs. Scott."

"Mrs. Scott?"

"He used to do some yard work for her. I don't know if he still does or not. But she seems to be pretty fond of Isaac."

"Well, that could have caused a problem if things hadn't happened like they did. . . and Clarice had started working for Mrs. Scott," Johnny said. "From what I've heard, Isaac really had his eyes on Clarice. Funny thing is that nobody seemed to have known Vernell all that well. . . except for Willard Jordan."

Both women laughed again and Ruta said, "Willard Jordan. . . now there's an strange man. Didn't know you knew him, Johnny, but I might've known you would."

"Johnny knows all the crazies," Ruth said.

He grinned. "He ain't crazy. At least, I don't think he is. Anyway, he was a good friend to Vernell Williams."

"We never got to know Vernell," Ruth said. "Oh, he came in here, but never said anything. Clarice. . . she did all the talking. Other colored folks, though. . . they told me Vernell was real shy, maybe a little retarded. Of course, they just said he was a bit touched in the head, but I think they meant he was retarded."

"He helped Mr. Jordan make caskets," Johnny said.

Ruta chuckled and asked, "Wonder what he puts in the caskets?"

Johnny shrugged. "Told me he makes them for the state pen."

"He probably does," Ruth said. "But, I'll bet he hauls bootleg whiskey in them, too."

"I don't know about that. I just know he told me Vernell was a good man."

Ruth nodded in the affirmative. "He probably was, but it was kind of hard to figure him as Clarice's husband."

"Why's that?"

Ruth replied, "Clarice was smart, Johnny. . . real smart. She read a lot and could do math in her head like nobody I've ever known. You just didn't figure her having a dumb husband."

"Book learning ain't everything," Johnny said. "Maybe he had a head full of common sense."

Ruta laughed. "I don't think so."

They talked for quite a while about Clarice and Vernell. Johnny was surprised at how much the women knew about the couple. He didn't want to press them, but thought they knew much more than persons who claimed to have had just a casual acquaintance with the victims. He figured he might have learned a lot more if Sol Bernstein hadn't come up to the front of the store and quelled the conversation.

Walking home he decided there was one thing he knew for certain. Clarice Williams had been an unusual woman, one who affected a great many people. There was no doubt in his mind that she was the reason the rest of the family had been murdered.

He also found himself hoping. *If Brother Baker is the killer and I can prove it. . . man, that would be the icing on the cake. Ben Jim wouldn't like it, though. . . me thinking this way.*

If the killer was not Brother Baker, he wondered if he had talked to him or seen him. *Yeah, I'll bet I've seen him,* he thought. *I may not have talked to him, but I'll bet I've seen him.*

He fantasized, daydreaming that the killer would be brought to justice and he would be responsible for his capture. He had begun to think of himself as the *Green Hornet* and *Mr. District Attorney* all rolled into one. There were those who said his imagination and daring would be the death of him, but he didn't believe it.

TWENTY SIX

Marcie Scott called Johnny aside after class to express appreciation for his efforts in trying to find her daughter. "A lot of people have told me you just refuse to give up looking," she said. "Bailey. . . Mr. Thompson says nobody has looked harder and longer than you and Ben Jim Cade."

Johnny shrugged his shoulders. "We ain't had much luck."

What she said next surprised him. "Well, it's time you stopped looking. God knows, you've done enough. We're not going to find little Sadie around here. . . and you're upsetting people with all your questions."

He looked at her with disbelief. "People been complaining to you?"

"Yes. . . they have."

"You mind telling me who?"

"It wouldn't serve any worthwhile purpose."

"I been trying to find out who killed the Williams family, too. I thought there might be a connection."

"There isn't," she said. "You're a smart boy, Johnny, but murder and kidnapping aren't things you ought to concern yourself with. You're just a young boy and this is something for the law to take care of."

He was having trouble believing the direction of the conversation. After all, this woman was the mother of little Sadie. She, more than anyone else, ought to have been grateful for help from any source. "I don't guess I have much confidence in the law around here."

"Well, you may not understand the way grown men do things. One of these days you're gonna grow up and realize you're not smarter than everyone else. If there's one problem with you, Johnny, it's that you think you're so much smarter than everyone else."

How do you know what I think? he wanted to ask. He didn't, of course, even though the fires of anger were raging inside him. "I'm sorry if my asking questions has caused you some problems, Mrs. Scott. I just can't figure who'd be bothered by my asking. And, I can't figure why it bothered them unless they had something to do with it."

"Lots of people are bothered by it," she said. "And if you must know, Isaac Simpson told me you had Ben Jim get all over him. . . even threatened him."

"Isaac?"

"Yes. . . Isaac. He's done some work for me in the past. . . still does some from time to time."

"Big and strong as he is. . . I can't figure Isaac being scared of a man twice as old as he is."

"Whether you want to believe it or not, lots of people are scared of Ben Jim Cade."

"They ain't got reason to be."

"That's not for you to say. Maybe they know a side of Ben Jim that you don't know."

"Ain't but one side to Ben Jim. He's a man who's honest as the day is long."

"I have nothing against coloreds," she said, "but you have a lot to learn, Johnny."

They talked a bit more and he decided that she, without actually saying it, was ordering him to quit looking for little Sadie. It angered him because he hated to be told what he could and could not do, but her attitude puzzled him even more. *Why this conversation? Why did she want him to quit looking? What right did she have to tell him what he could and couldn't do?* Hers were not the words of a loving, caring mother. It caused him to remember again what Winston Railey had said about her. Later that day he found opportunity to talk to Railey about the unusual conversation with Marcie Scott.

"I wouldn't attempt to try to tell you why Mrs. Scott talked to you the way she did," he said. "But, there are things about her that it's probably best you not know."

"I already know about her being Mr. Thompson's girlfriend."

Railey smiled. "That's not what I'm talking about."

"What then?"

"There are things that go on in that woman's mind that would probably scare the daylights out of the bravest man alive."

As his relationship with Railey had grown, Johnny had come to realize how much the man liked to talk. They'd had a number of intense conversations about literature and art, but he knew it didn't take much to get the teacher gossiping. He was, after all, a man with all kinds of knowledge stored up in his head with no one to share it with other than a twelve-year-old boy.

"She don't seem all that scary to me."

"Outwardly, she isn't," Railey said. "I'm talking about getting inside her mind, finding out what makes her tick."

"Well, I guess that's pretty much impossible to do."

"I guess it is, but some of her actions tell us at least part of what's going on in there. This thing she has going on with Bailey tells us a lot."

As he had come to know Railey better, Johnny had also become more and more convinced that the man was jealous of Marcie Scott's relationship with Bailey Thompson. It didn't make sense to him, but he got that feeling.

"I guess it tells us she can't be trusted," Johnny said, "although a lot of people around here don't seem to blame her for cheating on Coach Scott."

"How do you feel about it?"

"Well, I ain't that fond of Coach Scott. . . but he ain't given me any reason for not liking him. I guess I just get teed off at him because he's supposed to be a teacher. . . and a teacher ought to know something. But, it seems to me that football's more important to him than what we learn."

"You haven't answered the question."

"It's a hard one to answer. . . about my feelings, I mean. You know I like Mr. Thompson. . . a lot. And I've always liked Mrs. Scott okay. She's not a bad teacher. The thing is, I guess I've tried not to think about it. When I do, I know it's wrong. The Bible says it's wrong."

Railey laughed. "You'd be more definite if Bailey wasn't involved. If Marcie was running around with someone you didn't know, or with someone you didn't like as much as you like Bailey, then you'd have a stronger and more definite opinion."

Johnny grinned. "You're probably right about that. Liking somebody, even if what they're doing is wrong, kind of colors your opinion on what's right and wrong, doesn't it?"

"In this case, I'm not sure Bailey knows that what he's doing is wrong," Railey said. "I think he's a victim."

Johnny couldn't understand Railey's reasoning, figured Thompson was a grown man who knew what he was doing, but he didn't argue the point. Instead, he said, "You haven't told me why you think Mrs. Scott wants me to quit asking people about Little Sadie."

"I'm not sure I can tell you. Some people might say it's because the memory of what happened is so painful that she doesn't want to be reminded. . . that she just wants people to quit talking about it, especially to her."

"But. . . that's not what you think, is it?"

Railey shrugged. "I'm not sure what I think."

"The way Mrs. Scott was talking to me. . . it's like she knows Sadie's okay. Or, knows what happened to her."

"How could she know that?"

It was Johnny's turn to shrug. "Danged if I know."

Railey laughed. "Of course, you're going to do just what she says."

Johnny grinned. "Well, I ain't exactly gonna stop asking questions because I'm trying to find out who killed the Williams family. And, I think the same one that did it had something to do with little Sadie coming up missing."

"I don't know if that's true, but your logic's not that bad, Johnny. I can see where the two might be connected."

"Nobody else does."

"Nobody else wants to. If it was the same person, they don't want to draw the conclusions that would be demanded by that kind of logic."

"What do you mean."

"If it was the same person, then Sadie's dead."

Johnny didn't like Railey's statement, but knew he was right. "The other thing I can't understand is why Mrs. Scott got all over me about Ben Jim talking to Isaac Simpson. If you didn't know better, you'd think she'd taken Isaac to raise."

"I don't know what that relationship is," Railey said. "I just know that Isaac works for her on occasion."

"Aunt Bessie thinks Isaac's the one who murdered the Williams family. If he did, though, that pretty well ruins my theory about who took little Sadie. He probably wouldn't have taken her. . . him and Mrs. Scott being so close."

"Don't be so sure about that. Don't be so sure she didn't have him take little Sadie."

Johnny's eyes flashed surprise. "That doesn't make any sense."

"I'm telling you, Johnny. . . the woman's strange. There's no telling what she's capable of."

Winston Railey's words were still playing with his mind that afternoon after school when he found Ben Jim at the Walla Cafe. Johnny had dropped by the cafe because his mother had been called in to work for the regular cook, who was sick. Ben Jim was sitting on one of the stools in the back of the kitchen where Negroes were served. He was having coffee.

Johnny had his mother pour him a cup, too, and then he told Ben Jim about his conversations with Marcie Scott and Winston Railey. He talked softly, though his mother was too busy and too out of earshot to hear him.

Ben Jim pondered what he had been told, then said, "Ain't no doubt the two of them. . . Mr. Winston and Mrs. Marcie. . . don't like each other. That's why you've got to take what Mr. Winston says with a grain of salt."

Twenty Six

"I know that, but what do you think about what Mrs. Scott told me?"

"Hard to know what to make of it. Maybe the lady's just tired of hearing all the talk and nothing getting done."

"Well, it sure ain't gonna get done if somebody doesn't do something."

"I ain't arguing the point. The thing you've got to remember, Johnny, is that folks don't always think right when something like this happens. You can't blame the woman for not thinking right. . . her little girl being missing and all."

"What about her getting on me for you talking to Isaac. . . saying folks are scared of you?"

Ben Jim smiled. "It ain't hurting me none. Folks got a right to think what they want to think."

"What about Isaac?"

"The man has to answer to the Lord for what he does. . . he don't have to answer to me."

"I'm talking about him and Mrs. Scott."

"Ain't for me to say. Sometimes he works for the woman. . . that's all I know."

Johnny shook his head in resignation. There were times when Ben Jim could be so frustrating, he thought. Well, he wasn't about to give up questioning people about the murders and about Sadie Scott being missing. And, if Marcie Scott didn't like it she could just shove it.

TWENTY SEVEN

If Johnny's curiosity about Marcie Scott's attitude was working overtime, he had nothing on her husband or Bailey Thompson. Vernon Scott learned of her conversation with Johnny and didn't know what to make of it. Of course, it was not the first time she had thrown one of her weird curve balls, he decided, but figured this time she had hit a new level of strangeness.

She was the strangest female he had ever encountered. Early in their relationship he had attributed her quirkiness to a mystical intelligence. He had assumed he was simply too ignorant to comprehend it. He knew Marcie liked it that way, her being almost too brilliant to be understood and him being the poor dumb jock who didn't even know how to tie his shoelaces.

Vernon was quite aware that he was a little short in the brains department when it came to book learning, but knew he wasn't capable of being as dumb as Marcie wanted him to be. She would, he thought, prefer to be married to someone mentally retarded so her smartness could stand out all the more.

Early on in their marriage he had tried very hard to improve himself educationally, initially thinking that's what Marcie wanted. He had enough common sense to soon realize, however, that this effort on his part would drive a wedge between them. The way he came to interpret things, she would have much preferred that his ignorance be greater.

This attitude toward their daughter's disappearance, though, topped her strangest ever behavior, he thought. And that was saying a lot.

Vernon had done all he could think of to make their marriage work. It had been important when Sadie was with them. Now he wasn't so sure. The psychological abuse Marcie had heaped on him over the years was taking its toll.

He wanted to talk to someone about it, quickly considered and rejected the idea of talking to Reverend Marvin Baker, then asked Bailey Thompson to meet him at the Walla Cafe for breakfast on Saturday morning. Bailey agreed, not knowing what Vernon had in mind.

The principal worried about the reason for the invitation, of course, because his and Marcie's relationship had intensified during the football season. Vernon was late getting home from football practice, so after school Marcie would go immediately to Bailey's apartment and spend an hour or two. She was getting bolder, which worried Bailey and didn't escape the attention of Winston Railey or Brother Marvin Baker.

Other things about Marcie also worried Bailey, not the least of which was the way she seemed to have just written off her missing daughter as no longer being important. He worried that she might be losing touch with reality, that Sadie's disappearance might well be pushing her over the edge.

Lately, when he dreamed about Marcie, her face took on the shape of a poisonous snake, her eyes as black and cold as a serpent's. Such dreams startled him, caused him to get up with the chills. Often he would prowl the apartment looking for snakes, unable to stop the frantic pounding of his heart.

Bailey sat down across the table from Vernon and said, "Heckuva game last night. I didn't think our boys would pull it out."

The coach smiled. "I thought we'd blown it when we fumbled with five minutes left."

"Elmer Guerdat's one heckuva runner. I don't know how you're keeping him eligible. . . not sure I want to know."

"Elmer's not as dumb as most people think," Vernon said.

Bailey laughed. "You're right. He's dumber."

They laughed together and Bailey began to feel a little easier, though he was not completely relaxed. The waitress came over with coffee and took their orders.

"I'll just be glad when the cooler weather hits," Vernon said. "It's awful practicing in this heat."

"We should've had a little cool front by now," Bailey said. "Weather's strange this year. A lot of things have been strange this year."

As soon as he said it, Bailey wished he hadn't. He saw the sadness cloud Vernon's eyes. "Yeah," the coach said. "It's been strange all right."

"Anything new from the sheriff or the FBI?"

Vernon shook his head. "No, nothing. To tell you the truth, I don't think anybody cares anymore. . . including my wife."

The statement shocked Bailey, though he had begun to think the same thing about Marcie. "I don't think that's true, Vernon. I think a lot of people care. . . they just don't know what to do any more. I know I don't."

"Oh, I know that, Bailey. All the people around here. . . they couldn't have been nicer or helped more. It's just that after a while you kind of lose hope. And Marcie ain't helping things, acting the way she does."

"What do you mean. . . about Marcie?"

"Ain't you noticed the way she acts. . . like little Sadie never existed? The other day she told Johnny Tobin to quit talking to people about it and to quit looking. . . like she wants to put it out of her mind altogether."

"Well, Vernon, this thing's been real hard on her. I know she loves little Sadie."

"Not as much as she loves herself."

Bailey was surprised to hear Vernon say it. The coach was probably just as surprised that he said it. There was an awkward silence before Bailey said, "Little Sadie's disappearance has been hard on both of you.

I'm sure it's been a strain on your relationship."

Vernon sighed. "There was plenty of strain before Sadie came up missing. You just don't know Marcie, Bailey. Nobody around here really does. She's not what she seems."

"About really knowing her, I guess you're right," the principal said, just half-believing what had come out of his mouth. There were times when he thought he knew Marcie, yet at the same time he knew he didn't. Lately, she had been very confusing to him. "I don't guess any of us can really know a person totally. The human mind's just too complex."

The waitress brought their food, so there was a pause in the conversation while eggs were salted and peppered, biscuits were covered with gravy and cups were refilled with coffee. Then Vernon said, "As far as I'm concerned it hit the fan when she got on Johnny for trying to do what's right. When I found out about it, I talked to the kid. . . told him how much I appreciated what he was trying to do."

Bailey couldn't, of course, tell the coach that he had also talked to Marcie about her conversation with Johnny, how the very mention of it sent her off on an tirade. "I'm glad you talked to Johnny. He's a good kid. . . doesn't know the meaning of the words give up."

"Yeah. . . he's like a bulldog. Mean and tough as he is, I can't wait to get him in a football uniform. I just hope your weird landlord don't mess him up. . . teaching him all that art and music stuff."

Bailey laughed, uneasily. He liked Winston Railey, knew he was a good teacher who would never attempt to push his preferences on anyone. But, the social environment was such that he wasn't prepared to defend him. "I don't think you have to worry about that. Johnny's just got a mind like a sponge. He reads everything he can get his hands on. He's interested in just about everything."

Vernon forked a piece of biscuit saturated with gravy, put it in his mouth and washed it down with coffee. "Reason I wanted to talk to you, Bailey, is. . . well, how do you feel about divorce?"

Almost from the time their relationship had begun, Marcie and Bailey had talked about the possibility of her getting a divorce from Vernon. With the coach actually bringing it up, though, Bailey felt a kind of chill rush through his body. He knew the cold that raced through him wasn't because of the creaking ceiling fan overhead, that it was because he might soon have to make a decision about Marcie, one he wasn't sure he was ready to make.

"Well, Vernon, I don't know that I've given it that much thought one way or the other. I'm single, you know."

Vernon grinned, wryly. "You don't have to rub it in that you're smarter than me."

Bailey managed a wry smile. "I assume you're talking about you and Marcie. So I don't know that we ought to be having this conversation. You probably ought to be talking to Brother Baker."

"I ain't gonna discuss anything personal with that clown. Be all over town if I did."

Bailey thought Vernon's reference fit Baker perfectly. He had never liked the preacher, but had been willing to give him the benefit of the doubt. But that was before Winston Railey and Johnny had told him about Baker watching his apartment. When the time was right, he planned to confront the preacher about his spying.

"Well, I'm sure not gonna say anything, Vernon, but I'm no marriage counselor, either."

"I don't think I need a heckuva lot of counseling, Bailey. My mind's pretty well made up. I'm just wondering if I'm gonna have a job here if I do it?"

"Far as I'm concerned, you will. I can't speak for the school board."

"Marcie. . . she can be pretty vindictive. She's probably gonna try to turn folks against me, including you."

"Maybe you're misreading her. She doesn't seem that way."

"I told you. . . you don't know her."

"You sure y'all can't work this thing out?"

"Bailey, I could tell you stuff about Marcie that would make your hair stand up on end. In fact, I'd like to tell you if you wouldn't mind listening."

"I'll do whatever I can to help you, Vernon, but this stuff you want to tell me about Marcie. . . well, I'd rather not hear it. Both of you being teachers in the school. . . well, it kind of puts me in a bad spot."

Vernon sighed. "You're right, Bailey. . . it ain't right what I was asking you to do."

"Tell you what I think would be a good idea for both of you."

"What's that?"

"Why don't the both of you talk to Father Ingram."

"We're Baptists."

"I know, but you don't have any confidence in Brother Baker. And, from what I know of Father Ingram, he seems to be a pretty good guy. I've gotten to know him a little and I like him."

Vernon crawfished. "Well, I don't. . . "

"Just talk to him. It can't hurt anything."

"I hear Catholics don't believe in divorce."

"I don't think Baptists do, either. It's not something you believe in. . . doesn't matter what your denomination."

"Well, I might talk to him. . . doubt that Marcie will, though."

They were interrupted by a familiar voice. "You fellas mind if I join you?" The interloper did not, however, wait for an invitation, just plopped down in a chair and scooted it up as close as he could get to the table. The chair groaned with his weigh.

Both Vernon and Bailey gave Brother Marvin Baker a *What are you doing here?* look. Bailey spoke first. "Kind of early on a Saturday for you to be up and about, isn't it?"

"There's no timetable on the Lord's work."

"Didn't know the Lord's work was a platter of biscuits with gravy," Vernon said, sarcastically. Bailey was appreciative of the coach's perceptive remark.

Baker, however, didn't understand sarcasm any better than he understood humor, so he chuckled and said, "Got to keep my strength up."

Bailey asked, "Does that mean you're here to try to straighten Vernon and me out?"

Baker chuckled. "Oh, no. . . not at all. Surprised to see y'all here and just figured I'd join you fellas. See that you've already finished breakfast."

Knowing Baker had been spying on him, Bailey imagined the preacher was more than a little surprised to see him having a meal with Marcie's husband. He wasn't sure what Baker's game was, but didn't trust him as far as he could spit.

The waitress came, poured Baker some coffee, and he ordered a breakfast that was about double what Vernon and Bailey had eaten.

Vernon scoffed. "No wonder you're big as the side of a barn."

"Runs in the family," Baker said. "Mama. . . daddy, they was both big people. So's my sisters and brothers."

Bailey and Vernon exchanged glances, each knowing what the other was thinking. Baker wasn't just big, he was plain old fat, like a hog ready for market. His problem wasn't genetic. He ate like a pig and never exercised.

Turning to Vernon, Baker said, "Hear Marcie got all over the Tobin boy for all his meddling. About time somebody put him in his place."

"What place is that?" Bailey asked.

Baker shifted in his chair. "You know how he is. . . always bothering people with his questions."

"Nothing wrong with a kid being curious," Bailey said "If a man doesn't have anything to hide. . . he doesn't mind answering a few questions."

Baker looked at Vernon for help, but the coach said, "I agree with Bailey. Marcie didn't have any right to jump on the boy. He was just trying to help."

The preacher stuttered. "Well, uh. . . I. . . "

Bailey laughed. "Johnny been asking questions about you, Brother Baker?"

"He's been sneaking around asking questions about how well I knew the nigger woman who was killed."

Johnny had talked to Bailey about the preacher's relationship with Clarice Williams. He hadn't known anything about it, but was happy to see the youth had struck a nerve. "Well, how well did you know her?"

"She worked for us for a little while. . . that's all."

Bailey shrugged. "Well, I can't see what the problem is."

"It's the way he sneaks around. . . that's the problem."

"Who's he talked to?"

"My wife, for one."

Both Bailey and Vernon laughed. The principal said, "Well, that don't sound like sneaking around to me."

Baker grunted. "He's talked to other people, too."

"Who?"

Twenty Seven

"Well, I'm not sure just who."

"Why don't you ask him?"

"I may just do that."

The principal and coach knew the preacher was lying to himself. They knew he wouldn't confront Johnny over fear of how Jake Tobin might react if the kid told his daddy. They could understand, since Jake's always-volatile temper went to boil when someone bothered his children. At the same time the men were mentally applauding Johnny for upsetting the preacher.

Bailey, though, was reading more into Baker's fear than Vernon was, which probably had something to do with the preacher spying on Marcie and him. He wanted to nail Baker for invading his privacy. *Where there's smoke there's fire*, he told himself. *The preacher*, he thought, *was afraid of what Johnny might discover*, and what Baker might be hiding aroused his curiosity. He wanted, desperately, to find something to offset what the preacher had on him, some sort of defense against the man's intended use of it.

The waitress brought Baker's huge breakfast and Vernon excused himself. "I've got to go," he said, "got a lot to do. Thanks for your help and advice, Bailey."

The latter part of the statement got Baker's attention. "Don't know that I was that much help, Vernon, but you're welcome," Bailey said.

Vernon reached for the check, but Bailey stopped him. "No, I got it. You can get it next time."

When the coach was out the door, Baker asked, "What kind of help and advice were you giving Vernon?"

Bailey wanted to say, *None of your business*. He said, instead, "Just a school matter. . . wouldn't be of any interest to you."

Baker gave him a look that clearly indicated he thought he was lying. "Seems to me Vernon's acting a little strange lately. . . kind of uppity, like he don't want to talk to anybody. Maybe it's because the football team's winning."

"This hasn't exactly been a normal year for Vernon and Marcie," Bailey said. "Little Sadie being missing and all. . . the way it happened. I'm surprised either of them can act close to normal."

The preacher's mouth was full of biscuit, gravy and bacon, but that didn't keep him from responding immediately. "Can't see where Marcie's any different."

Bailey wanted to say, If you only knew. Instead, he said, "Human beings are different. They're not all gonna act the same. I'm sure they're both hurting more than we can imagine."

"Well, it's over and done with. They ain't likely to ever see the little girl again. . . ain't likely to ever know what happened to her. Be better if folks just forgot about it and went on."

"You're talking about Johnny Tobin?"

"That's right. That kid hasn't got any business upsetting folks."

"He hasn't upset me any. I don't think he's upset Vernon, either. I think Vernon appreciates what he's been doing."

"A twelve-year-old boy running around playin' detective. . . it ain't right."

"It's not wrong, either," Bailey said. "Johnny knows that someone around here knows who killed that colored family up the creek. . . or has some information that'll lead to the killer. And, chances are that information might also tell us something about little Sadie's disappearance."

"It's a job for the sheriff. . . not a kid."

"I agree with you. . . if we had a real sheriff. What we have is a drunk whose ability to reason went out the window a lot of bottles ago. He doesn't care who killed the colored family and finding little Sadie is way down on his list."

"Well, we see things a little different, Bailey."

The principal shrugged. "I guess we do. For one thing, I can't see why you're so upset about Johnny asking your wife about Clarice Williams working for y'all. He's just trying to find out a little about the woman. . . what she was like and why she kept changing jobs."

"Well, I don't see where it's any of his business."

"It's not. He's just looking for anything that might give him an idea about who killed the family. . . and who maybe also took little Sadie."

"You're saying he suspects me."

"No, I'm not. I'm saying that knowing more about Clarice might. . . Vernell, too. . . might give someone a better idea about who would want to kill them."

Twenty Seven

"And a kid's gonna be able to do what the law can't?"

"Where the colored victims are concerned. . . a white boy's all they've got. Nobody else seems to care."

The preacher stiffened with piety and said, "Well, I've always been one to say let the niggers take care of their own. I figure that's the way the Lord wants it."

Bailey shook his head in resignation. "That figures. But, since you don't want Johnny prying into why Clarice quit working for you, Brother Baker, why don't you tell me?"

There was a long pause. The preacher swished some coffee in his mouth before swallowing. "I never figured it was nobody's business, Bailey, but if you must know. . . well, Clarice wasn't that good of a worker. I fired her."

"That's strange."

"Why do you say that?"

"Because everybody I've talked to talked about what a good worker she was."

Baker cleared his throat. "That mean you been asking, too?"

"No, it just came up in the course of conversation. . . mostly just right after she was killed. They talked about what a fine-looking woman she was. . . and what a good worker she was."

"Well, she wasn't that good a worker for us."

"Your wife told Johnny she was."

"Mrs. Baker just doesn't like to speak bad about the dead."

"If she wasn't doing the job, why did you go down to the Williams place to visit her after you got rid of her?"

"Who says I did?"

"Willard Jordan. He told Johnny."

"You know he's an ex-convict."

"I guess everybody knows that. Are you saying he's lying'?"

"I don't remember going down there after we let her go."

"Willard says she quit. That's what he told Johnny. That's what your wife told him, too."

The preacher's face was flushed. "I told Clarice to say she quit. I gave her a little extra money to tell my wife she quit. I didn't want people knowing she was fired because it might've been harder for her to get another job."

Baker's words didn't ring true, especially considering how he felt about Negroes. Bailey tried to look him in the eyes, but the preacher's eyes were darting around the room. That's when he figured the time was ripe.

"Oh, while I'm thinking about it, Brother Baker. . . if you ever need to see me when Marcie Scott is over at my place, just come on up. We're just doing school business. . . and I'm sure she'd be glad to see you, too. Winston Railey and Johnny told me about a few times you've been sitting outside my place in your car. They figure you didn't come up because she was there."

Baker's mouth was agape, which opened another opportunity for Bailey. He picked up Vernon's and his check and said, "Been nice chatting with you. Enjoy the rest of your breakfast. . . I got a lot of work to do."

TWENTY EIGHT

Brother Marvin Baker and Father Walter Ingram had very few things in common. One common thread was that both had been interested in Clarice Williams.

The difference was that Baker had actually unsuccessfully attacked the woman, thinking a nigger ought to be grateful to be cared for by a white man. Ingram, on the other hand, had played the role of the sympathetic suitor, tempering his interest with a stated concern for her oppressed condition.

Neither had been successful. Both wondered about their failure.

Baker justified his failure with thanks to God for helping him maintain his purity of purpose, telling himself that Clarice did not deserve to be blessed with his love. But Clarice's rejection had angered him to a murderous rage.

Ingram truly could not understand Clarice's rejection. What had worked on sophisticated women in the East should, he thought, have worked on a simple Negro woman from the South. He was angered, too, but as much at himself as at her. This parish in the boondocks, to which he had been banished, was his last chance to clean up his act where women were concerned. The bishop had made that very clear.

Another bond the preacher and priest shared was that they feared Clarice might talk. That fear was eased only after she was dead.

Johnny Tobin was borrowing some books from Ingram early Sunday afternoon when the priest decided it was time to talk to the youth. "I haven't been completely honest with you," he said.

"What do you mean?"

"Well, I know you've been asking a lot of questions about Clarice Williams. . . that you know she worked here before Aunt Bessie. . . and you wonder why she left. I'm sure you're also wondering why, after we found the child's body in the creek, that I didn't tell you I knew the Williams family."

Johnny shrugged. "People say I'm too curious for my own good."

Ingram smiled. "You don't want to ever lose that. It's important to be curious. . . to ask questions. That's how you learn."

"Some folks think I ain't trying to learn the right things."

"That's probably true. . . to a certain extent. But making mistakes is the way we learn, too. Anyway, I want to tell you what I know, which might ease your mind a little. It may, at least, get you going in the right direction. You see, like you, I've read a few detective novels. I know how much time can be wasted on false leads."

"Wanting to know more about Clarice Williams. . . it's not like I'm accusing anybody of anything," Johnny said.

"Oh, I know that. But you've heard a lot and sometimes that creates suspicion. . . usually unfounded. Now, what have you heard about Clarice working here. . . why she quit and so on?"

"I ain't heard much. I just heard she worked here for a while and that she was gonna be working for Mrs. Scott this fall."

"That's all?"

"Well, yeah. . . and that you drove down to the Williams place a few times."

"Who told you that?"

"Willard Jordan. Him and Vernell. . . they made caskets together. Mr. Jordan. . . he makes them for the state pen."

"I think I did drive down there a couple of times," Ingram said.

Twenty Eight

"I was trying to get Clarice to come back to work. You see, I never knew why she quit."

"She just up and left, huh?"

"That's right. One day she was here, the next day she was gone."

Johnny grinned. "That's exactly what Mrs. Baker said. Maybe she just got sick of being around church folks."

Ingram didn't seem to think the statement was funny. "What do you mean by that?"

"She worked for Brother Baker before she worked for you. . . and at the same time. Working for him probably gave her a permanent pain in the. . . well, you know what I mean."

The priest laughed. "I hope I didn't add to the pain."

"I doubt that you did. There's something else, too."

"What?"

"Brother Baker. . . I think he tried to do some stuff to her. You know, like a man would do to his wife."

Ingram's eyes took on a pained look that Johnny could not interpret. "I can tell you that nothing like that happened around here," the priest said.

"Didn't figure it did."

"Anyway, I probably should've talked to you earlier about all this. When we found the little boy, though, then I went out to the Williams place and we found the other bodies. . . well, I was pretty shaken by it. To tell you the truth. . . still am. It's caused me a lot of sleepless nights."

"I ain't slept so well myself since it happened."

"That's certainly understandable. I have to say that after Clarice left, I was real fortunate to find someone like Aunt Bessie."

"Can't argue with you there. She's a jewel."

They talked a while longer in the library, then went to the kitchen where Aunt Bessie poured them some lemonade. The priest, Johnny thought, seemed overjoyed, as if a burden had fallen from his shoulders. He didn't understand. There was a lot he didn't understand, including Ingram's brief explanation about Clarice quitting and his reason for not saying anything about knowing the Williams family.

Johnny genuinely liked Father Ingram, but their conversation had aroused his suspicions about the man tenfold. Something wasn't right. There was more to the Clarice Williams story than the priest was telling.

When walking home Johnny saw a familiar pickup truck coming toward him. It braked to a stop right next to him. "Lots of books you got there, Johnny. Don't believe I could ever read that many the rest of my life."

"I like to read. How's it going with you, Mr. Jordan?"

"Can't say it's going real bad. . . can't say it's going real good neither."

"Cooler weather will help us all feel a little better. That and squirrel season."

"Squirrels is thicker than flies out around my place."

"Is that right? I don't believe we've ever hunted out that way. Mostly we hunt the bottoms south of your place."

"Well, you know you're welcome to hunt out around my place. And if you get tired and hungry you can come over to the house and I'll fix you something to eat."

"I really appreciate that, Mr. Jordan."

Jordan's mood suddenly darkened. "You still sniffing around. . . trying to find out who killed Vernell, his wife and all the kids?"

"Yes sir, I'm still trying to find a clue."

"Well, somebody's been sneaking around my place, watching my house. . . mostly at night."

"It ain't me."

Jordan chuckled. "I know that, Johnny. But somebody's out there. I figure it's the same jerk that killed Vernell. If I get him in front of my shotgun, I'll blow him to kingdom come."

"You told the sheriff. . . anybody else. . . about this?"

"No, I ain't told that jerk nothing. . . don't intend to. For all I know he might be the one that's out there."

"You saying he might've killed Vernell and his family?"

"Wouldn't put it past him. He'd kill them just because they were niggers. Ain't nobody sorrier than Nick Merrick."

He didn't tell Jordan that someone had been stalking him, too, especially when he was out at night. At first he had thought it might be his imagination, but then decided his senses weren't lying to him. He hadn't told anyone other than Ben Jim.

Jordan insisted on giving Johnny a ride. On arrival home he told the man to be careful, then carried the books into the house with the intention of doing some reading. But restlessness took hold of his mind. He decided, instead, to go to the trestle to do a little fishing. He and his dad had gone fishing earlier that morning at San Miguel Creek, so the trip to the trestle wasn't because he felt some great need to catch a fish. It was because he thought he did some of his best thinking under the trestle.

It was a lazy day, one where there's some indication summer is slipping away and no one is interested in blocking its escape.

Johnny baited his hook, then flipped it out near one of the trestle supports. The bobber sent out ripples and Johnny reclined on the slanted bank. He pulled a piece of sweet grass to chew on and half hoped nothing would bother his bait. For a good thirty minutes his wish seemed to be the fish's command, a period in which he sort of dozed and daydreamed.

What he had told Father Ingram about his inability to sleep since the murders was true. He couldn't close his eyes without seeing the murdered Williams family, which was one reason he might have been obsessed with finding the killer. Deep sleep might come, he thought, if the killer was brought to justice.

When he did sleep it was from sheer exhaustion. Even then he had hideous dreams that caused him to cry out and wake from his slumber. He had never shared those dreams, or the fears they caused, with anyone. This was, he believed, a road that only he could travel, a problem that only he could solve.

He did wonder if others who had seen the murder victims suffered the same sleeplessness and anxiety he did. He wondered specifically about those who had seen the little boy fished from the creek. He knew it bothered his father, despite what he had seen in the war. He wasn't so sure about the others. Many of them didn't seem to care because the little boy was colored.

He was startled by a voice. "I was hoping I'd find you here."

Turning his head he saw Billy Burton, who was carrying a couple of pops in his hand. "Ain't a bad place to be on a Sunday afternoon. . . especially since there ain't no baseball being played," Johnny said.

Billy handed him one of the pops. "World Series is just around the corner."

"Thanks," Johnny said. "Yankees will take the Dodgers. . . probably in four straight."

"Maybe they'll stretch it out longer. . . get more money."

"Dang it, Billy, I hear that kind of stuff all the time. Don't you know the players only get money from the first four games?"

"No. . . don't guess I did."

"Well. . . now you know. That's how things were set up so there wouldn't be any thought about doing what you're suggesting."

"Makes good sense."

"Of course, it does. The people who run baseball ain't a bunch a dummies. At least most of them ain't."

Billy, seeing Johnny was perturbed by his ignorance about the World Series, was anxious to change the subject. "Where you been hiding yourself? Ain't seen you much since school started."

"I been around. . . been questioning a lot of people."

The deputy laughed. "So I hear. I hear Mrs. Scott talked to you about it."

Johnny grinned. "News travels fast. Everybody in town must know by now."

"That's because it's so danged strange. Why would the woman want you to quit looking for her little girl?"

Johnny took a swig of pop, shrugged his shoulders and said, "Got me. Lots of people have been giving me a lots of reasons for her acting the way she did. Most of them are just trying to make excuses for her. She ain't the only one I'm making nervous, though. I think I'm making the guy who murdered the Williams family nervous. And there's lots of people around here who don't think it's right for a jerk kid to be asking questions the sheriff ought to be asking."

"Whoa now. You said something there that caught my interest. . . about making the guy who murdered the Williams family nervous. You saying you know who killed the Williams family?"

"No, I ain't saying that," Johnny replied. "But somebody's been keeping an eye on me. . . watching me, especially when I've been out after dark."

"Dang it, Johnny. . . if you know that why ain't you told me before now?"

"He's keeping his distance. I ain't actually seen him."

Twenty Eight

"Then maybe you're just imagining it."

"Ain't no imagining to it, Billy. I've stalked deer enough to know when somebody's stalking me. You just know. . . that's all."

"You told your daddy?"

"No. . . and I don't want you telling him either. There's no need in making him and mama worry."

Billy grinned. "You're just afraid they won't let you go out at night."

Johnny returned the grin. "What you say's true, but I don't want them worrying either. I can take care of myself."

"I know you think you can, but if some grown man's after you. . . "

"I shouldn't even have told you about it, Billy. Me and Ben Jim. . . we'll take care of the jerk."

"So you've already told Ben Jim about it?"

It was obvious to Johnny that the deputy was hurt that he had confided in Ben Jim before him. "You and Ben Jim are the only ones who know. I just told Ben Jim. . . would've told you first if I'd seen you."

Billy was pleased to be put in such select company. "I wouldn't mind helping you catch the guy."

"I thought about that, Billy. Then I decided it could get you in a whole lot of trouble with the sheriff. Best we take care of it. . . then bring the jerk to you."

The deputy, who initially had felt left out, found himself thanking Johnny for not getting him in trouble with the sheriff. Then he whispered, "You think he's watching now?"

"Probably. . . but from a distance. I don't think the man's out to hurt me. I think he just wants to know who I'm talking to. . . what I'm finding out."

"If the man's a killer, how come you think he don't want to hurt you?"

Johnny shrugged. "Can't say for sure. But, you've got to figure he had some reason for killing the Williams family. Now I think it had something to do with Clarice. . . her being so good looking and all."

"You asking all these questions. . . he's got good reason to kill you, too."

"Only if I find out who he is. . . prove what he did."

"I think you're taking a big chance."

"Maybe. . . but I figure I'm gonna be all right with Ben Jim watching my back."

"He can't be watching it all the time."

"Maybe he's watching it right now. You wouldn't know if he was. . . would you?"

Billy hesitated. "No. . . I don't guess I would. Is he watching?"

"I don't know."

TWENTY NINE

Marcie Scott gave Johnny another piece of her mind on Monday. When she had talked to him earlier, it hadn't occurred to her that the conversation would get such wide circulation. "Did you have to go tell everybody, Johnny?"

"No ma'am. . . don't think I did. I'm not sure who I told and who I didn't tell."

"Well, what you've done is make it seem like I don't care about my little daughter."

"Don't believe I ever said that, either."

"Oh, you didn't have to say it," she said, sarcastically. "You just implied it."

"Don't think I did that, either. I can't help the kind of conclusions people draw."

"What's your conclusion?" she asked, her voice as icy as a frozen Popsicle.

Johnny shrugged. "I figure you love your daughter a lot. I figure you and Coach Scott both love her."

"Well. . . thank you for that."

Marcie was angry because her husband and Bailey Thompson had called her to task. Both had taken Johnny's side. What she had said to Johnny, she thought, had been blown way out of proportion.

Then Bailey had also told her about his conversation with Vernon, which didn't set too well. If something was going to happen with Vernon, like a divorce, she wanted to initiate it. Marcie had a need for control.

She also couldn't understand why Vernon would talk to Bailey about it. And, she couldn't understand why her lover would suggest they get counseling from a priest. After all, a divorce would free her to marry him, though she wasn't sure that's what she would do. At least, not right away.

"Darn right, I'll talk to Father Ingram," she told Bailey. "There's no telling what Vernon might tell him."

So she made an appointment to see the priest late Monday afternoon, during the time she and Bailey were supposed to spend together. *That'll teach the jerk to interfere*, she thought. Angry with Bailey, she figured he, as well as Vernon, needed to be punished. And, what better punishment could there be, she decided, than not allowing him to be with her when expected. He would, she angrily decided, be clawing the walls before she gave him another opportunity.

During the lunch hour she went home to see Isaac Simpson, who was doing some yard work there. They had a lot to talk about.

She met Father Walter Ingram later that afternoon in the privacy of his study, which she had never before seen. Like Johnny, she was impressed with his library and told him so.

"I love good literature," Ingram told her. "I only wish there were more great books to add to my collection. Unfortunately, there's not much in the way of great literature being published today."

She agreed and they talked about books for a while, more as a way of getting acquainted than anything else. Then she said, "Well, you know why I'm here."

"I suppose so. I feel a little awkward about it. . . like I'm treading on ground Brother Baker ought to be walking."

"I've been a Baptist all my life, Father Ingram, but. . . "

Twenty Nine

"Please. . . call me Walter."

He smiled, she returned it, then said, "As I was saying, Walter, I've been a Baptist all my life. . . not always a very good one. . . but I'd have a little trouble talking to Brother Baker about marital problems."

"Why's that?"

She thought, *Because he's a fat jerk.* She said, instead, "I think it's because he's unrealistic. He would just quote a Bible verse or two and tell me to pray about it."

"How do you know I won't do the same thing?"

"I think there's more depth to you than that."

"You don't really know me. . . and I'm sure you know the Catholic stance on marriage."

"You're right, I don't really know you. And. . . yes, I know the Catholic view on marriage. But you're from up East. . . an educated man. You're bound to have more insight and good advice than a backwoods preacher."

Ingram was smart enough to know Marcie was playing with his ego. But, he was so intrigued, fascinated and aroused by her beauty that he lost practically all perspective. "I've learned," he said, "to never underestimate the power or knowledge of a backwoods preacher."

She laughed, the sound of it sweet to his ears. "Excuse me, Walter, but you don't have to pamper me like you do your parishioners. I only have to look around me here. . . to see the kind of books you read. . . to know that you don't believe half of what you tell these half wits."

"You, obviously, don't have much respect for the people around here."

"Do you? You could put all the brainpower in this parish in a bottle and it would be harder to see than a gnat in the dark. Present company excluded."

He smiled. "That may be a bit of an exaggeration, but I can see where a place like this would be frustrating to a woman of your intellect."

Ingram knew how to push all the right buttons. It had been obvious since they met that Marcie was obsessed with her perceived intellectual superiority. He had difficulty thinking of a woman in that way, but was game for whatever worked. He wasn't, of course, sure what he wanted to work.

"It's difficult," she said, sighing, "but I've had no choice but to make the best of it. Vernon, you know, is not exactly stimulating company. . . unless you want to talk about running around end or off tackle."

"I know your husband only casually," he said. "I've had coffee with him at the cafe a couple of times, but there was usually a crowd around."

"Your impression?"

He laughed. "I'd say it's pretty much the same as yours."

Support was what she wanted, which was exactly what she was getting from Ingram. She thought him quite handsome, was attracted to him. "So you understand our incompatibility?"

"I think I understand it, am sympathetic. . . but can't condone divorce. The Church doesn't condone it. . . and I'm bound by the Church."

"What would be your advice for saving this marriage?"

"We first have to discuss the problems you and Vernon are encountering. Can you tell me why you're not getting along?"

"There are lots of reasons."

"Name one."

She studied him before answering, then boldly replied, "He doesn't fulfill me. He tries, but it's not enough. Do you understand what I'm saying?"

Her eyes looked deep into his and he could feel a prickly heat coursing through his body. If pushed, Marcie, he thought, might say anything. There was a shamelessness about her that was exciting and dangerous. "I'm not sure I know exactly what you're saying," he said.

"Well, in plain English. . . Vernon can't satisfy me. But then, I haven't really found a man who can."

Ingram's face colored and he felt a tightness of breath. "I guess that's plain enough."

"There's another problem with Vernon. He always gets overly excited too quickly and that's frustrating."

"I see. I. . . well. . . I was thinking more in terms of mental, emotional things."

She shrugged. "I don't know how you can separate them."

Twenty Nine

"Uhhh. . . I don't guess you can when you come right down to it. But you're getting into an area that I. . . "

"Don't tell me it's something you don't know about, Walter. If you say it is, you'll be lying. I know you were interested in Clarice Williams. I don't know what happened between the two of you, but something did."

"That's not. . . "

"I know a lot about you, Walter. . . about the kind of man you are. I might even know more about you than you know about yourself."

He was sweating bullets. The caliber increased when she got up from her chair and came around to his side of the desk, then boldly sat down in his lap. His eyes tried to escape hers, but found no hiding place. They, instead, quickly devoured her. She kissed him then and he knew he was lost.

Sacred vows were terribly insufficient barriers to his desire for beautiful women. His resolve to never again allow something like this to happen was a futile mental exercise tied to the bishop's warning. And, what the Church offered was suddenly meaningless.

• • •

Marcie felt good about what had happened with Father Ingram. Breaking down any perceived sense of morality he might have had made her feel good. There was, she believed, no man who could resist her. And, it was especially sweet to break the resolve of one who allegedly subscribed to some higher power or purpose. It made her feel very powerful.

Though grateful for an opportunity to exercise her power over an alleged holy man, she also felt that she was punishing her husband and Bailey Thompson. Marcie blamed both for sending her to Ingram, at the same time feeling confident she completely controlled them.

A man, she had decided early on, was easier to dominate than a dog, which itself was an animal quick to attach to a human for whatever favors it could receive, whether food or affection. She saw herself more as a cat, willing to take the food and affection, but independent of any strong emotional attachment as a result of such favors. *Besides,* Marcie thought, *I'm the one with the favors to give, favors that no man can resist.*

She thought that if she really wanted to keep Vernon, there would be no problem doing so. *The only reason he seemed more interested in Sadie than me when she was around,* Marcie thought, *is because I chose to make him suffer.*

When she had first met Vernon, she had known immediately that he would be as easy as any other man to dominate and manipulate. The attraction was that he was big and strong looking, which at the time she had equated with prowess. *How wrong I was,* she thought, chuckling to herself.

While it was impossible for Vernon to satisfy her, things between them would have been better if he hadn't gotten her pregnant. She blamed him totally for that, was angry with him because she was afraid carrying a child might cause her to have stretch marks.

Pregnancy had not been a pleasant experience for her, because she alternated in blaming Vernon and Sadie for destroying her beautiful body. When the child was born, though, she experienced the closest thing to love for another human being that she had ever known. It was not, of course, complete or total love, because she could never truly love anyone other than herself in that way.

Sadie did no lasting damage to Marcie's body. Three months after giving birth, there was no telltale evidence she had ever been pregnant.

Problems with Vernon increased after the baby's birth. Suddenly, it seemed to Marcie, he was giving Sadie a lot more affection and attention than he was giving her. The truth was that she did not want his affection or attention anyway, but couldn't stand the idea of him giving either to someone else. She was soon looking at Sadie as a rival in her domination of Vernon.

In Sadie she saw a mirror image of herself. In fact, she was determined that the child be exactly like her in every possible way. The child, obviously, could never be as beautiful as her mother, but could have the same attitudes.

Sadie developed those attitudes rather quickly. Over a short period of time she became as hateful to her father as was her mother. So Vernon was belittled from two directions, but never seemed to waver in his affection for his daughter.

This bothered Marcie because she very much wanted to cause a deep schism between the two. She wanted both to love her totally, the other not at all.

When she arrived home it was dark. Vernon hadn't gotten in from football practice, but she knew he would be coming in the door in the next fifteen to thirty minutes. *He'll be wanting supper*, she thought. *Well, he can fix it himself.* She was tired, suddenly irritated. Her good mood had vanished the moment she entered the house.

She went in the bathroom and turned on the faucets to fill the tub. She added some bubble bath, took off her clothes and admired herself in the mirror. She liked what she saw.

When the tub was filled with warm water she submerged her body in it, leaned back, relaxed, and gave thought to the events of the day. She wondered what Bailey might be doing. *Probably eating supper*, she thought. *I'm going to have to do something about him.*

There were days when she saw herself as Bailey's wife, other days when the very thought of it bored her. A good reason for divorcing Vernon and marrying Bailey, she thought, was that it would shock some of the old church biddies in town. It would shock Vernon, too, to learn what she and Bailey had been doing behind his back.

If I marry Bailey, she thought, *maybe I'll start singing in the church choir. That'll really give them something to talk about. It'll make those few hairs on Brother Baker's head stand up on end.*

She liked playing mental games with herself, liked setting up scenarios and imagining what might happen, predicting to herself how people might react.

Then she thought, *What would they say if they knew about Isaac and me?*

THIRTY

While Marcie was soaking in the tub, Johnny Tobin was en route home from Aunt Bessie Jackson's place. He knew he was late for supper, but figured it couldn't be helped. Some things were more important than pinto beans, fried potatoes and cornbread.

He knew the stalker was close behind him, but figured if the guy was going to make a move it would be somewhere around the trestle. Because of the stalker, he had been avoiding going out at night. But this evening was planned, just like his route home. He planned to walk across the trestle, up the railroad spur, past the sawmill and then up the dark street to his folks' house.

Johnny wasn't stupid. He was smart enough to be scared, but brave enough to take a situation right to the edge. He had exceptional peripheral vision and thought he caught glimpses of the stalker moving ever closer to him, using trees and various other structures for cover. His heart was pounding and he wanted to run, but he kept a steady pace. Everything depended on the man thinking he was unaware of his presence.

He had been scared the night the little boy's body had been found in the creek and he had run for help. He'd been scared when he went to the Williams place to see the bodies of the other members of the family. He'd been scared at Willard Jordan's place when he thought Jordan was the murderer. He couldn't count the number of times he'd been scared by snakes. But this was different. This was really life and death scared.

As he got closer to the trestle, he sensed that the stalker was picking up his pace. Fear was choking Johnny, causing him to almost hyperventilate. There was a heaviness of breath he wasn't sure he had ever experienced before. It was like there was a big pine knot that was trying to explode out of his chest and up through his esophagus. He felt he might strangle before reaching the trestle.

The night was clear and warm, the stars bright, clouds blowing up from the Gulf and chasing each other across the face of a full moon. The tops of trees on the creek bank were swaying gently in the breeze, as if keeping time to a melancholy ballad. Lazy smoke from the mill's always burning sawdust pile was allowing the wind to carry it northward.

Johnny walked down the center of the railroad spur that led to the trestle that stretched across the creek. His entire body was sensitized, the feel of the gravel and crossties on the soles of his shoes traveling like icy fingers up his legs and to his brain. The closer he got to the trestle the greater his fear. The area around the trestle was one of dancing shadows and eerie darkness. The surrounding terrain seemed much brighter.

The trestle across Sandy Creek was much shorter than the one across the bottomland of San Miguel. It was no more than fifty yards long. He was no more than a half dozen crossties onto the trestle when the stalker rushed toward him. He turned, fearfully and saw something in the man's hand that was glistening in the moonlight.

Knife, his mind cried out just before he started to run.

Suddenly, hands came up from beside the trestle and grasped the stalker's ankle. The stalker screamed something indistinguishable as he was pulled off the crossties and went tumbling down the creek bank.

He rolled to the water's edge, then came up quickly with the shiny object still in his hand.

Ben Jim had followed the stalker's tumbling act down the incline. When the man raised up ready to fight, the brogan on Ben Jim's right foot caught him under the chin. The object fell from the stalker's hand and he went backward into the creek. Ben Jim plunged in. The water was only waist deep.

Johnny, momentarily frozen by fear, watched his friend go after the man. Then Johnny jumped down off the trestle and grabbed the bat he had earlier hidden in the weeds. He ran to the water's edge in time to see Ben Jim land a punch on the man's nose that knocked him back toward the bank and within range of the bat. Johnny took a good swing and the meaty part of the bat caught the guy just below his left ear.

The stalker screamed in pain and sunk to his knees, just in time to catch another of Ben Jim's punches flush on his nose. Ben Jim could have drowned him then but, instead, pulled him partially out of the water, the upper part of his body on the bank.

"Isaac," he said with disgust, while bending slightly to pick up the shiny object the stalker had dropped. It was a straight razor. "Now what was you planning to do with this, Isaac. . . cut my friend Johnny's throat?"

There was no response. Isaac continued groaning in pain, holding the bloody side of his head with one hand.

"Johnny, if you want to kill this coward of a man with your bat, ain't nobody gonna blame you."

At that moment Johnny wasn't thinking about killing anyone. His knees were trembling. He thought he might throw up.

"Why was you after Johnny?" Ben Jim asked, his voice demanding.

Isaac's only answer was a constant groan. Ben Jim put the cold steel of the straight razor to his throat and said, "Now Johnny. . . he ain't gonna kill you. But you can't count on me being that forgiving. I'd just as soon slice you from ear to ear as not."

There was something about Ben Jim's tone that made Isaac believe he'd do what he said. So he stopped his groaning and started crying. "I was just trying to scare the boy," he said.

Thirty

"Why was you trying to scare him?"

"He been going around talking to everybody about me."

Ben Jim pressed the razor against Isaac's neck until it brought a trickle of blood. "You're lying about just trying to scare Johnny, Isaac. You know what Mr. Jake Tobin would do to you for scaring one of his kids. You was gonna kill him, wasn't you?"

"No. . . I swear," Isaac said, his fear and tears intensifying. "I don't want to kill nobody. I just wasn't thinking because I sure don't want to rile Mr. Jake."

"You don't want to rile me neither, Isaac. . . and you done went and done that."

Johnny, who had regained a bit of composure, said, "Ask him if he killed the Williams family."

"I ain't killed nobody," Isaac said. "I swear to the Lord I ain't killed them."

"Stop your crying, Isaac. Man like you'd lie about anything. Ain't no way I'm believing what you say."

Isaac did his best to stop the tears, but he couldn't stop the fear. His eyes were unnaturally wide and focused on the razor. "I'm telling the truth."

"What do you want to do with him, Johnny?"

"I don't know. If we turn him over to the sheriff, he'll turn him loose."

"You're right about that. We can turn him loose as good as the sheriff can. Or maybe we ought to kill this nigger and let him float on down the creek."

Johnny was fairly certain Ben Jim wasn't completely serious, but couldn't be sure. There was a cold anger in his friend that he hadn't witnessed before. He suspected it only surfaced when someone tried to hurt a kid or one of Ben Jim's friends. He wanted to say, *Yeah, let's kill the jerk*, but was afraid Ben Jim might comply.

"I don't think he's gonna be bothering me any more."

Isaac might have gulped if he hadn't been afraid that any movement in his throat would cause the razor to cut deeper into his skin. "No sir, Mr. Johnny," he managed to fearfully say, "I ain't gonna be bothering you none."

Ben Jim relaxed the razor on Isaac's throat and said, "You're a lucky nigger, Isaac. I'm gonna keep this razor. . . and if I ever hear about you looking crossways at Johnny, I'm gonna cut you from the top of your head to the bottom of your toes."

When Ben Jim raised up and stood to his full height, Isaac remained with his back on the ground and his legs partially in the water. His hands and feet were quaking and his breath came in gasps. Ben Jim shook his head in disgust and said, "Get your black self out of here."

Isaac moved quickly, scrambling to his feet and sprinting up the embankment. He looked back once, to make certain Ben Jim wasn't following him. He was soon out of sight.

"The man was lying like a dog," Ben Jim said.

"About killing the Williams family?"

"About everything. Isaac wouldn't know the truth if it jumped up and bit him on the rear end."

"I don't know about that. You scared the dickens out of him. But are you saying you think somebody sent him after me?"

"Wouldn't surprise me none."

"I been stirring up some stuff here and there, but I can't figure who would've sent Isaac after me. I figure I've been teeing off the sheriff more than anybody else."

"Well now," Ben Jim said, "it wouldn't surprise me none if Isaac was working for the sheriff."

"I don't guess it'd surprise me, either. Only I don't think that's the case, unless. . . "

"Unless what?"

"You reckon the sheriff might've killed the Williams family?"

"It wouldn't hurt the man's conscience any. But I doubt that he's the one who did it."

"You think Isaac's the killer, don't you?"

"From what I hear, the man wanted Clarice Williams mighty bad. And she wouldn't have nothing to do with him."

Johnny shuddered. "Don't seem like that would be reason enough to kill all those people."

"Ain't nothing funny about what a woman can do to a man. Some women. . . they fall all over Isaac. Man gets used to something like that and his mind can go when it don't happen. Isaac. . . he's a man what's got a terrible temper, too."

Johnny laughed. "He didn't have much of a temper when you were holding that razor to his throat."

Ben Jim smiled. "Something like that do calm a man."

"You think he'll try anything else."

"Ain't likely. . . now that he's been caught. He's probably gonna stay hid for a while. . . afraid you done went and told your daddy about what he tried to do."

"I don't think I'll tell daddy."

"Probably best. . . unless you want Isaac dead."

THIRTY ONE

On Tuesday after school Johnny stopped by the Walla Cafe, hoping to find Billy Burton there. He wanted to tell the deputy about how he and Ben Jim had ambushed Isaac Simpson. He was surprised to find Carter Duncan drinking coffee alone. The FBI agent asked Johnny to join him.

"I was hoping to see you," Duncan said. "I guess you're kind of steamed at me for leaving town without talking to that suspect of yours. What was his name. . . Willard Jordan?"

"No skin off my nose," Johnny replied. "I talked to him. He didn't have nothing to do with little Sadie being missing or the murders."

Duncan laughed. "You don't give up easy, do you?"

"There's enough people around here who give up too easy."

"You talking about the sheriff?"

"You got to start before you can give up. He can't even get started."

Duncan laughed again. "You found out anything about the murders. . . or little Sadie's disappearance?"

"Nothing you don't already know."

The waitress brought Johnny a cup of coffee, which he doctored with sugar. Then Duncan said in a hoarse whisper, "You know we don't have any jurisdiction about the murders, but I might be close to a lead on what happened to Sadie Scott."

Johnny gave him a look of disbelief. "You joking me?"

"I wouldn't do that. I got more help from you and Billy Burton than I got from anybody else in this town. So I'm gonna be straight with you."

"You told Coach and Mrs. Scott?"

"No, and I'd just as soon you wouldn't either. No point in giving them what might be false hope."

"I don't see why you can't look into the murders."

"It's a local matter. But if it wasn't, I'll bet the sheriff has messed up the physical evidence to the point where no one could tell doodley squat about what happened. You're right about him being a stupid jerk. I'm tempted to use even stronger language than you do to describe the jerk."

Johnny grinned. "I take it you ain't gonna tell him you might have a lead?"

"I don't trust the man. I don't trust that jerk police chief, either."

"I figured an FBI man would be smart enough not to trust either one of them. This lead you may have. . . is the name Isaac Simpson connected to it some way?"

"No, but his name has come up in the investigation. In fact, I questioned the man because he does some work for the Scotts. Or, at least he did."

"I think he works for Mrs. Scott. I doubt the coach even knows him. If he does, it's just in passing."

"How well do you know the coach?"

"About as well as you can know a coach."

Duncan laughed. "I take it you're not all that impressed with coaches?"

"You could say that."

"Anything unusual about Coach Scott?"

"What do you mean by unusual?"

"I'm not sure. I just want to know if you've noticed anything different about him. . . the way he treats people. For example, how did he treat his daughter?"

"Far as I know he treated her just fine. Lots of people think he cared more about her than Mrs. Scott did."

"You find that strange?"

"I think Mrs. Scott's strange." He told Duncan how Marcie had gotten on his case for questioning people about little Sadie's disappearance. "She's still treating me like dirt. I'm probably gonna make an *A* in all my classes except hers."

"She's probably just overwrought because of what happened. She'll probably be thanking you before long."

Johnny laughed. "You, too. Everybody wants to make excuses for her. Especially men."

Duncan's face colored up a bit. "She's a looker, no doubt about that. But I was just giving her the benefit of the doubt. What she's been through. . . I think she deserves that."

Johnny sighed. "You're probably right."

"This Isaac Simpson. . . why did you ask me about him?"

"Because Aunt Bessie Jackson. . . do you know her?"

"No. . . she's one I haven't talked to."

"Well, she thinks Isaac murdered the Williams family. I thought the murders and little Sadie's being missing might be connected. . . them being so close together."

"It's a good theory. . . and I thought about it, too. But that's not the direction things have been taking me."

"Since you ain't been around here, I figured you'd just quit looking."

"I been talking to relatives of the family. Everybody around here's been talked to and nothing was happening. I thought maybe one of the relatives might know something."

"That must've been where you got this *maybe* lead."

"Yeah, but I can't tell you about it right now. I've still got some more checking to do. And, I've got to count on you not mentioning it to anybody."

Johnny shrugged. "Ain't got nothing to mention. You ain't told me nothing."

Duncan laughed. "I guess you're right. I just don't want anybody around here knowing I might have something."

"They won't hear it from me."

Johnny had a couple more cups of coffee with the FBI agent, during which time they talked about everything from baseball to fishing. He figured Duncan was okay, but didn't think it would do much good to tell him about Isaac making the attempt on his life. Like the man said, the FBI had jurisdiction when it came to kidnapping, but not for a local murder or attempted murder.

When Duncan got ready to leave, Johnny asked, "This *maybe* lead what brought you back to town?"

"Yeah. . . everything's circumstantial right now. I've got to question a few more people. Then. . . *maybe*. . . things will start making sense. I'll keep you posted."

"How long are you gonna be here?"

"Just a couple of days."

"Maybe I'll see you again."

"Maybe. I'll get your coffee."

"Thanks. . . I appreciate it."

"You leaving, too?"

"No, I'll hang around. Billy Burton will be coming in before long. He has to have his pie and coffee every afternoon."

Duncan laughed. "You can tell Billy what I told you. But mum's the word."

After the agent had left, Johnny started pondering what he had said. There wasn't a whole lot to analyze, but before he could really get started Ozzie Guidry and Mouse Malone brought their coffee cups over and sat down at his table. They'd been sitting at a table across the room. Their presence didn't exactly brighten his day.

"Seen you was talking to that FBI feller," Ozzie said.

"Always said you had good eyes, Ozzie."

The barber laughed and his sidekick grinned. "Thing I like about you, Johnny, is that you're such a kidder."

He knew, of course, that neither man liked much about him or his family. They were too close to the sheriff to have anything good to say about the Tobins. "Surprised to see you guys in here this time of day. Figured it would be a good time for haircuts and pumping gas."

"Kind of slow," Ozzie said, which Mouse verified by nodding his head. The barber was the talker of the two. "What's that FBI man doing back in town?"

"He didn't say."

"You two was talking for quite a while."

"Yeah. . . about fishing. . . baseball, the fact that hunting season is right on us."

"He say anything about little Sadie?"

"Said he's still looking."

"You'd figure the FBI would've found out something by now."

"At least they're looking, which is more than you can say for the sheriff."

That hit a nerve with Ozzie and Mouse. The barber said, "Now ain't nobody looked for the kid any harder than Nick. And he's still looking."

Johnny gave his best incredulous look. "Is that what he's doing now?" The time of day told him the sheriff was drunk.

"I can tell you this," Ozzie said, defensively, "ain't no time when Sadie being missing ain't on his mind."

Johnny knew that arguing with the two about their buddy the sheriff was a waste of time, but he was prepared to give it a go until Winston Railey interrupted them. When Railey sat, Ozzie and Mouse suddenly decided they had work to do. They paid their bill and left the cafe.

"Sorry I ran your friends off, Johnny," the teacher said, obviously amused by Ozzie's and Mouse's departure.

"They're no friends of mine, Mr. Railey. I'd just as soon have coffee with snakes or skunks. They just came over here and sat down. I didn't invite them."

"You didn't invite me, either."

Johnny laughed. "That's different. I like you."

"Well, I'm glad you do. Anything new going on in your world?"

"Nothing much. Same old seven and six."

"Well, I would hardly call last night the same old seven and six."

"Last night?"

"Ben Jim told me what happened."

"That surprises me. He's usually so closemouthed and all."

"We talk a lot," Railey said. "He's a good man."

The waitress came and took the teacher's order for pineapple pie and coffee. "Bring two slices. . . one for Johnny here."

"You want more coffee?" the waitress asked.

"Sure. . . might as well."

After she was out of earshot Railey said, "You took an awful chance. You could've been killed."

"I ain't saying I wasn't scared, but I figured Ben Jim could handle Isaac easy enough. We had a pretty good plan."

"Even the best laid plans often. . . "

"Yeah. . . you're right, Mr. Railey. I guess it was dumb, but it's me who's stupid. Ben Jim didn't want to do it. I kind of forced him into it. . . said I'd do it on my own if he didn't help."

"Ben Jim thinks the world of you."

"Well, I feel the same about him. . . I think the world of him, too."

The waitress brought their pie, which Johnny's mother had made. She made most of the pies for the cafe. They dug into the crust and gooey substance, mouthed it and savored the taste.

"If I was eating your mother's cooking all the time, I'd be big as the side of a barn," Railey said.

"She can cook all right."

Billy Burton came in and joined them. He ordered pineapple pie and coffee, too. Johnny knew he was curious about what had happened the previous evening, but was hesitant to ask because of Railey's presence. Johnny cleared that up right away.

"Mr. Railey knows about last night."

Billy looked at the teacher and Railey nodded. "Well, Johnny. . . you ain't even told me who it was."

"Isaac Simpson."

"I'll be."

"Ben Jim put a hitch in his giddyup. I'll bet Isaac looks like the dickens today. He didn't look all that good last night." He told the deputy how he and Ben Jim ambushed the stalker, giving particular details as to how Ben Jim had handled Isaac. He noticed Winston Railey was most interested in the details, too. He figured Ben Jim hadn't elaborated when telling him the story.

"Kind of explains a call I got a while back when I was in the office," Billy said.

Johnny asked, "What kind of call?"

"Mrs. Scott called and wanted me to arrest Ben Jim for beating up Isaac. I told her if Isaac wanted to file charges, he'd have to do it himself. . . that she couldn't do it for him. I think I made her mad."

Johnny and Railey exchanged glances. The teacher said, "That woman gets stranger every day."

"I can't figure her taking Isaac's part," Johnny said.

The deputy shook his head. "Neither can I."

"Gentlemen," Railey said, "it is difficult enough to understand any woman, but this woman defies any semblance of understanding."

"She always seemed okay to me. . . up until lately," Johnny said.

The teacher laughed. "That's because you hadn't been around her much until lately. . . and you hadn't bothered her. As long as you don't bother the woman. . . as long as she has use for you. . . everything is okay. But she's so self-centered no one else really matters to her. And she can turn on you like a poisonous snake."

The waitress interrupted them with Billy's pie, which he attacked with relish. "I still don't understand her taking Isaac's part," Johnny said.

"Maybe she don't know what happened," the deputy said. "I don't figure Isaac told her the truth, do you?"

Johnny laughed. "I just got on Carter Duncan about everybody making excuses for her. Don't make me get on you, too."

Surprised, Billy asked, "Carter Duncan's in town?"

"Yeah. . . he'll be here for a couple of days. He'll be looking you up. He's got something to talk to you about."

"I saw Mr. Duncan earlier," Railey said. "He asked me a lot of questions. . . mostly about Vernon Scott."

"He asked me a question or two about him, too," Johnny said. "What do you make of it?"

"I don't know. He didn't ask me any questions about Marcie. . . just Vernon."

"I don't know that I trust Mr. Duncan all that much," Johnny said.

Billy showed shock. "My gosh, Johnny. . . he's an FBI man."

Thirty One

"So? He wouldn't be the first one that was crooked."

"Dang," Railey said. "Now I may leave."

The reason for his statement was Brother Marvin Baker, who had just walked in the door. The preacher seemed to be looking for someone to sit with other than Johnny, Billy and Railey. Seeing no one else in the place he made a reluctant beeline for their table, except that he was more like a rhino than a bee.

"Hope they ain't out of pineapple pie," he said on arrival. "I heard Johnny's mother made fresh pineapple pie." The preacher disliked Mary Lou Tobin with a passion, but was like a pig when it came to her pie.

"You're in luck," Railey said. "I think they have three pies left. That ought to hold you until suppertime."

"Good, good," Baker said, completely unaware that the teacher was being sarcastic. He plopped down and gave Billy a look of disdain as the chair groaned beneath his weight. Railey and Johnny figured the look was for them, too. When the waitress came to the table the preacher ordered half a pie. "No point making her run her legs off."

"Save anyone today?" Railey asked.

"Don't know that I did, Winston, but I sure hope I did some good. That FBI man came by and questioned me again."

"Ask you any questions about Vernon?"

"Why yes. . . yes, he did. How did you know?"

"Oh, I don't know. It was just something that came into my head. It happens to me all the time."

"I didn't know that."

"I don't tell many people about it."

It was all Johnny and Billy could do to keep from breaking up. Johnny decided to keep things going. "You know, Mr. Railey, up until I really got to know you, I thought Ben Jim Cade was the only one around here who has visions."

The preacher grunted. "There you go, Johnny, talking about that old nigger again. One of these days you're gonna learn that a white boy ought not to be running around with a nigger."

His voice dripping with sarcasm, Railey said, "You listen to the preacher, Johnny. He knows what he's talking about."

Baker was surprised by what he thought was support. "Well,

thank you, Winston. I've been trying to get Johnny to see the light."

"Between us, maybe we can help the boy," the teacher said.

Johnny, who started choking to suppress his laughter, grabbed a glass of water and started drinking. "You see, Johnny," Railey continued, "the Lord is probably causing you to choke because you've been running around with Ben Jim Cade."

Billy had one of those silly grins on his face that the preacher was trying to ignore. He always tried to ignore everything about Billy. He despised him as much as he despised the Tobins.

The waitress brought a degree of order when she arrived with Baker's pie. The preacher started to dig in, but Railey stopped him. "Shouldn't we have a blessing, Brother Baker?"

"I usually don't say one when I come here just for pie and coffee."

"That kind of surprises me," Railey said. "Billy, Johnny and me. . . we said the blessing before we ate our pie."

Baker was looking at him with disbelief, but Railey wasn't ready to stop. "If you don't mind, Brother Baker, I'll say the blessing. Now all of you bow your heads."

They all complied, the preacher reluctantly.

Pompously and piously, Railey intoned: "God is great, God is good, let us thank him for pineapple pie. Amen. Now. . . if you gentlemen will excuse me, I have to go."

"So do I," Johnny and Billy said in chorus.

The trio left Baker sitting at the table, went outside and laughed until it almost made them sick.

THIRTY TWO

Johnny wasn't sure just when Father Ingram's attitude toward him changed. He just knew it wasn't a gradual thing. Things had been fine between them, then all of a sudden the priest developed a quiet animosity toward him.

He had no way of knowing, of course, that Ingram's attitude was the result of his relationship with Marcie Scott. He couldn't know that a change in attitude toward him by the priest was one of the conditions of that relationship continuing.

To say Ingram was smitten by the woman was an understatement. After their initial encounter, the priest soon found his entire life centering on the few moments they could steal together. The time she allocated was pretty much every other day after school. Marcie had decided to alternate between Ingram and Bailey Thompson.

Ingram hated himself for allowing her into his life, more for allowing her to toy with and tease him, which included telling him in great detail about her relationships with the principal and Vernon. She was always making him feel inadequate.

He did not, of course, know that she was doing the same thing to Bailey. And, if the priest hated himself for letting Marcie dominate his life, the principal was in even more of a quandary. There had been a time, he believed, when Marcie had been his alone. Now she was blatant about her infidelity to both he and Vernon.

Bailey had been accepting of the fact that she was Vernon's wife. He hadn't liked the idea, tried to keep it out of his mind, but he had been able to deal with it. And, she had massaged his ego by telling him nothing happened between she and Vernon because he was no longer interested in her.

But now, having to share her, and with a priest, was taking a mental toll on Bailey. He knew he should just walk away from the situation, tell Marcie to stick it where the sun didn't shine, but for some reason he couldn't do it. Maybe it was love, though he wasn't sure. If it was love, even he had some comprehension of how sick it was.

Just a couple of weeks earlier he had been wavering about following through and marrying her if she got a divorce from Vernon. Now she had taken the option away from him. And for some reason the more unattainable she became the more he wanted her. He couldn't stand the idea that she was often with Ingram, yet the dark side of him found it exciting. There were times he became so angry he would threaten to kill the priest. Marcie liked that. She would laugh and antagonize him even more. She was evil. He knew it. Yet he felt there was nothing he could do about it except become part of the evil.

He knew her influence was changing him. His mind had become putty in her hands. She molded and shaped it for her own purposes. He just let it happen, even though it was destroying him.

Marcie's attitude toward Johnny Tobin became his attitude. He and Ingram found themselves rapidly losing their identities, becoming mirror images of all that Marcie was and wanted. It was an unusual psychological twist, one that defied interpretation.

A few people other than Johnny noticed the changes. They attributed the change in Bailey to the fact that too much learning just wasn't good for a man. They were afraid to attribute the change in Ingram to anything other than God. After all, he was perceived to be a holy man.

Thirty Two

Brother Marvin Baker recognized the change in Bailey and was fearful of it. Maybe it was because he thought the Devil had gotten hold of the principal. He figured Marcie Scott caused some of what was going on with Bailey. And while he outwardly disapproved of their adultery in his one-way conversations with God, inwardly he envied the principal more than any man he had ever known. Baker wanted Marcie, too, much more even than he had wanted Clarice Williams. And the desire made him feel better because Marcie was white.

Of course, he didn't know about Marcie and Ingram. He didn't see any change in the priest because he avoided him like the plague. He was not willing to jeopardize his salvation by consorting with Catholics.

The air in and around Walla was filled with tension, so thick it could almost be cut with a knife. A little girl was missing, a family had been murdered, a priest and school principal were having an affair with a princess of evil, and the Walla High School football team was undefeated.

To some degree one or more of the aforementioned affected everyone in the town. Isaac Simpson was affected by all but the undefeated football team. He had been lying low, recovering from the beating Ben Jim had given him, but now he was ready to move again. The plan had been told to him and he was confident it would work.

THIRTY THREE

There was a lot to like about October. Days got cooler and squirrel season opened about the middle of the month, which was an eagerly anticipated time for Johnny. It meant days in the woods with Ben Jim and Jack, the sound of the dog treeing and suppers of fried squirrels, rice, gravy and biscuits.

While Johnny was not that enthusiastic about eating fish, he loved to eat squirrel the way his mother fixed it. She rolled the pieces in flour, fried it, and then smothered it. The meat would almost fall off the bone.

Early in October Ben Jim did something that touched Johnny deeply and caused him to be even more aware of how much the colored man treasured their friendship. He presented Jack to Johnny as a gift.

Johnny protested, of course, because the dog was Ben Jim's most valuable asset. A wealthy and avid squirrel hunter from Shreveport had, in fact, offered five hundred dollars for Jack, which for colored laborers at the sawmill represented about three months work.

"I ain't got no use for that much money," Ben Jim told Johnny. "And, I know how much you love this old dog. I ain't sure how the man from Shreveport would treat him."

"It's too much, Ben Jim. I can't take your dog. There's nothing I can give you that comes close to being what he's worth."

"I ain't wanting nothing from you. You and your mama and daddy have been awful good to me and Sally and Billy Boy. If you don't take this old dog that you done spoiled rotten, I'm liable to have to take him out here and shoot him."

Choked with emotion, Johnny had said, "You wouldn't do that. You love old Jack as much as I do."

"The way to make sure is for you to take him. Ain't gonna be no arguing about it."

Despite all his protests, Johnny wanted the dog. But, understanding the poverty in which Ben Jim and his family lived, he felt guilty about taking him. A major problem was that Johnny was a giver, not a taker. Even Christmas gifts made him uneasy. It was like, You've given me something and now I've got to give you something better.

"Dang it, Ben Jim," he had said. "I just don't have anything to give you."

"You need to get over that, Johnny. . . thinking that because somebody gives you something you've got to give them something back. That ain't the reason I'm giving you this dog. Besides, your daddy gave me something worth a whole lot more. I might still be in jail if it wasn't for him."

So Jack became Johnny's dog, which certainly didn't make him inaccessible to Ben Jim. Johnny figured he and Ben Jim would be hunting together for years to come. And he knew Ben Jim would never have sold the dog. Ben Jim took literally the scripture in the Bible that prohibited the sale of dogs.

Squirrel season was scheduled to open in the middle of the month and on a Wednesday. Johnny was glad because a workday would keep most hunters out of the woods. He planned to skip school and go, though Bailey Thompson and his dad had warned him of the consequences.

He didn't, however, mind a couple of whippings for a good squirrel hunt. Besides, because of his dad's love of squirrel hunting he knew Jake Tobin's heart wouldn't be into whipping him. He figured Bailey Thompson would ease up on the paddle, too, because he would give the principal a mess of squirrels.

Ben Jim, of course, always got on his case when he skipped school, but would go hunting with him anyway. Johnny knew his friend didn't want him roaming the woods alone, nor did his dad. That was especially true now, after what had happened to little Sadie and the Williams family. If he was bound and determined to go, Jake Tobin preferred that Ben Jim be with him.

That day before the squirrel season opened, though, Ben Jim was arrested again, this time for the murders of little Sadie Scott and the Williams family. The sheriff, who said he was acting on a tip, went out to Ben Jim's house and found some of Sadie's clothing and what was thought to be Vernell Williams' shotgun under the front porch.

Marcie Scott identified the missing girl's clothing. The sheriff found a couple of colored men who had known Vernell and who said they thought the shotgun belonged to him. It was distinctive because the stock was split a bit and Vernell had wrapped it with some black tape. Willard Jordan said it was Vernell's shotgun all right, but that there was no way Ben Jim was a killer.

Of course, nobody paid any attention to Jordan because he had been a jailbird. The evidence was all against Ben Jim.

As for the sheriff holding Ben Jim on murder charges that included the name of little Sadie Scott, her body never having been found, the attitude of townspeople was that it didn't really matter as long as somebody paid. There was little doubt that the child was dead. And, the entire Williams family was definitely dead. All murdered by Ben Jim Cade.

The truth was that few cared about the Williams family. But if in prosecuting a man for killing them brought justice for little Sadie that was all that counted. Ben Jim Cade was as good as tried and convicted.

"It's all a lie," Johnny told his dad. "The sheriff's been out to get Ben Jim for a long time. Ain't no way he could've killed anybody."

Jake Tobin agreed, but said, "From what I hear they've got a lot of evidence."

Thirty Three

"Sure they do. Somebody put it out there at Ben Jim's place. If he'd done it, he's smart enough that he would've got rid of the stuff. . . not left it laying around."

Jake sighed. "You're right, son, but the important thing now is for Ben Jim to convince a jury."

"A jury from this town? Might as well go ahead and hang him."

"Johnny, I'm gonna do all I can to see that Ben Jim gets a fair trial. Just try to hold your temper and let's see what happens."

After supper Johnny went to the jail to try to see Ben Jim. He figured Billy Burton would be there. Sure enough, he was. "I know what you're gonna say, Johnny. . . and there's no use getting on my case. I ain't had nothing to do with it."

"Didn't figure you did, Billy. . . figured you had more sense."

Billy was sitting behind the sheriff's desk, where he wouldn't have dared sit if Nick Merrick had been around. He knew he was safe after supper, though, because Merrick would be three sheets to the wind. "It don't look good, Johnny. All the evidence. . . "

"Somebody put it there. You know it and I know it."

Billy shrugged. "I just follow orders."

"Heard it was some kind of anonymous call. Didn't that seem a little suspicious to the sheriff?"

"Him feeling the way he does about Ben Jim, I doubt that he gave much thought to it."

"He's a stupid jerk. . . I'll grant you that. But you know Ben Jim wouldn't kill nobody."

"Well, I would've thought that. . . until I found out it ain't true."

"What do you mean?"

"Ben Jim killed a man over in Mississippi."

"I don't believe it."

"Well, it's true."

"There must've been a good reason."

Billy shrugged again. "That I don't know. Sheriff was checking on Ben Jim, though, and found out about it."

"You reckon he was lying about the anonymous call?" Johnny asked. "If he found out about Ben Jim killing a man in Mississippi, he might've put the stuff out at Ben Jim's place himself."

"Now I wouldn't put it past him, but I don't think that was the case this time. But he's so happy to have Ben Jim in jail. . . shoot, I thought he was gonna dance a jig."

"He's probably so drunk right now that he couldn't put one foot in front of another."

Billy laughed, then turned somber. "He beat Ben Jim pretty bad. I was afraid he might kill him."

"Must not have been a fair fight."

"Of course, it wasn't. He had him handcuffed and beat him with that piece of hose he used on him last time. He uses it on niggers all the time."

"One of these days I'm liable to use it on that jerk. Or hang him with it."

Billy laughed. "Wish there was something I could do, Johnny, but I'm caught in the middle. You know I ain't got nothing against Ben Jim. And I sure don't like staying down here at night guarding a prisoner."

"Can I see him?"

"I don't think I'm supposed to let you."

"Are you gonna let me?"

"Yeah. . . I guess so. The sheriff and chief won't be coming around again tonight."

Billy took him down the small hallway with a window at the end. About halfway down the hallway was a door, which he opened. They went into the rectangular room where the jail's three cells were located. Only one was occupied.

Ben Jim's cell was as tiny and nasty as the others, none of which had been cleaned in a long time. He was lying on a cot, his back to the door.

"Ben Jim," Johnny said, softly.

His friend turned and it was easy to see he was in pain. The sheriff had used the hose on his face as well as his body. The sight made Johnny even more angry and frustrated at the injustice that was being done.

"I'll leave y'all alone," Billy said.

He left and Johnny took an old wooden chair and pulled it up close to the bars and sat. Ben Jim sat on the cot, which was against the back wall, but they weren't far apart. "You okay?" Johnny asked, then angrily said, "Now that was a dumb question. I guess I just don't know what to say."

"Ain't nothing to say," Ben Jim said, "except this ain't no place for you, Johnny. They're liable to be coming for me anytime."

"What are you talking about?"

"The sheriff done told me there ain't gonna be no trial. He said there's some men who are gonna come get me and hang me."

"That's crazy. That ain't gonna happen."

"Ain't nobody to keep it from happening."

"There's me and daddy. . . and Billy and Father Ingram. . . and Mr. Railey and Mr. Thompson. . . and Mr. Bernstein. There's lots of people won't let that happen. Alto and Willard Jordan won't let it happen either."

Ben Jim smiled, faintly. It was hard to see because of the facial bruises and swelling. The swelling had almost caused his eyes to close. "Now don't you go getting mad at folks if they don't do what you think they ought to do," he said.

Johnny didn't seem to be listening. His mind was marshalling the little army that would protect his friend. "I just can't believe this happened. Who would put that stuff out at your house and then call the sheriff?"

"I don't know. I just know I ain't never seen Vernell Williams' shotgun. . . or that little girl's clothes before. I don't know why somebody would want to do this to me."

"Isaac. . . he probably done it."

"That's what I was thinking."

"Daddy and me. . . we'll find Isaac and beat the truth out of him."

"May not be time for you to find him."

"Now don't you go talking that way. I don't want you giving up. Heck, Billy was even telling me the sheriff's lying and saying you killed a man over in Mississippi."

"That ain't no lie, Johnny."

"What do you mean?"

"I did kill a man in Mississippi. He was a colored man that was going around hurting children."

"So he needed killing."

"Ain't nobody needs killing, Johnny. I didn't want to kill the man... just wanted to make sure he didn't hurt no more children. Killing him was an accident."

"What happened? I mean... with the law?"

"They put me in jail, but then all the coloreds told them what the man had been doing and they let me go."

"So they must've thought he needed killing."

"That still don't make killing right."

"Well, what happened then don't matter none. It's what's going on right now that matters. I'm gonna get some people behind you. We're not gonna let you rot in here."

"Just make sure Sally and Billy Boy is all right. That's all I'm worried about right now."

"Don't worry none. I'll make sure."

They talked for a while longer, then he yelled for Billy to come unlock the door. When he and the deputy were in the sheriff's office, Johnny said, "Ben Jim tells me the sheriff was threatening to let some people hang him."

Billy's brow furrowed with worry. "There may be more to it than just a threat. I heard a while ago that some of the people around here are talking about lynching Ben Jim... and the sheriff ain't gonna try to stop them."

"What about you?"

"You know I'll try, Johnny... but chances are I can't stop it. I'll be outnumbered. The sheriff did tell me that if folks came after Ben Jim I'm supposed to keep my pistol in the holster. He said he was worried about me getting hurt. You believe that?"

"When do you think these people might try to do something?"

"The way I hear it, there's a meeting later tonight over at the sawmill. They might come right after that meeting. In fact, you can dang near bet that's when they'll come. Ozzie, Mouse and Ruley Gaspard are the ones behind it... and you know they'll do whatever the sheriff wants done."

"How many do you think there'll be?"

"No telling. Probably fifteen... twenty. That's just a guess."

"Well, I'm gonna go get you some help... just in case."

"I don't think you're gonna have much luck."

Thirty Three

"You know daddy will come. . . and there's quite a few more that'll probably help out."

When Johnny got home Jake Tobin had already heard about the lynch mob. He had already taken his shotgun down off the rack and was planning to head down to the jail. Mary Lou didn't want him to go. She was crying.

"I don't see where I've got any choice about it," he said. "You can't let people take the law into their own hands."

She said, "At least get some help, Jake."

"I can't think of one white man working at the mill who'll stand up for a nigger."

"What about some of the coloreds?" she asked.

"They can't do it. If one of them stands with Billy and me on this. . . his life won't be worth a plug nickel."

"What about your life?"

He grinned. "They'll think twice before going against me."

"Jake," Mary Lou said, pleading, "if you're bound and determined to go, don't take the gun. I don't want you shooting one of our neighbors over this."

"I ain't planning to shoot nobody."

"I know you ain't," she said, "but it could happen. Think about it, Jake. What would happen to us if something happened to you?"

He didn't speak right away, just looked at her like he was pondering the situation. Then he took a deep breath and let the air out. "You've always been the voice of reason, Mary Lou. You know I tend to go off half-cocked. But I've got to do something. I can't let them hang Ben Jim."

It was Johnny's turn to breathe a sigh of relief. For a split second he had thought his dad was wavering in his commitment to protect Ben Jim.

"Why don't you reason with the men," Mary Lou said. "Go to the meeting. Talk to them before they get to the jail. They'll listen to you."

He shook his head in resignation. "Some of them will. . . maybe. But things have been simmering here since August. . . since little Sadie came up missing. A few troublemakers have probably been pumping people up about finally getting the man who took her. . . getting them real riled. They may not be in any mood to listen to reason."

"You've got to try."

"You're right, Mary Lou. And I will. But if worse comes to worse, I've got to go stand with Billy at the jail."

"I know that. But before you do anything go get Sally and Billy Boy and bring them here. You've got time. I don't want them alone in that house down in the woods with what's going on. You don't know where the craziness is gonna lead."

Johnny, who had quietly listened to the exchange, said, "I know some white men who'll stand with you, dad. I'll go get them."

Jake laughed. "You do that, son. . . and don't be disappointed with them if they ain't anxious to help. I'll go get Sally and Billy Boy. . . then go to the meeting. Then you tell Billy I'll be down to the jail to stand with him if things don't go right."

Johnny first went to Sol Bernstein's house, certain that the merchant would be willing to lend his support. He quickly told Bernstein what was going on, that his dad needed his help.

"I sympathize, Johnny, but I can't help. This is not something I want to get involved in. We have to live here with these people."

"But Mr. Bernstein. . . Ben Jim's innocent. You don't want to see an innocent man hanged."

"Of course not, Johnny. . . but I can't help. Don't you understand? I could lose my store if I helped save a Negro. And besides, there's evidence that he's guilty."

"Somebody put that stuff out at Ben Jim's house to frame him. You've got to know that."

"I'm sorry, but I can't be sure of that and I can't help you. Now please, you'll disturb the girls."

Johnny gave the merchant one of those looks of disappointment that aren't hard to read. He was crestfallen. Of all the people in town, he thought Bernstein would be the first to rally to the cause of a man unjustly accused.

Minutes later Bailey Thompson came to the door of his apartment with a book in hand. He interrupted Johnny's plea. "I know what's going on," he said. "I was invited to meet with the group who are talking about what to do with Ben Jim."

"Then you'll help dad and Billy?"

Thirty Three

"I can't take sides in this thing, Johnny."

"Dang it, Mr. Thompson. . . you know Ben Jim's innocent. Do you want to see him hanged?"

"Of course not. And maybe it won't come to that. The boys are probably just blowing off some steam."

"You know it's more than that. You know the sheriff's behind it. You know it's a lynch mob."

Bailey got irritated, mostly because he knew Johnny was right. "You've got no right coming here telling me what I know and don't know, Johnny. I told you I'm not taking sides. . . I can't afford to. . . and that's that. Now, leave me alone."

He shut the door in Johnny's face. For maybe a minute Johnny stood in frozen disbelief. He had thought he knew Bailey Thompson. He thought the principal was a man with brains, guts and principles. A man who would stand for what was right. *How could I have been so wrong?* he asked himself.

Shattered by the attitude of Sol Bernstein and Bailey Thompson, Johnny hesitated to even knock on Winston Railey's front door. After all, what good would a man like Railey be if it came to a fight? When he did knock it was half-hearted, not with any great conviction that Railey would be any different than Thompson and Bernstein.

But the teacher surprised him. "I don't know that I'll be worth much," Railey said. "But I'll stand with your dad and Billy Burton. And, by golly, if they get Ben Jim they'll have to walk over me to do it."

Railey's defiant attitude caused a flicker of hope in Johnny. The teacher said he'd head for the jail in a few minutes, so Johnny took off running to the Catholic Church. He had dismissed any thought that Brother Marvin Baker would aid a colored man, no matter what the situation, but was sure Father Ingram would stand between the lynchers and Ben Jim. He was important because some of the men would be Catholic.

Ingram was not pleased to see him, even less when he understood the reason for the visit. "There's nothing I can do. This is a legal matter."

"If some people aren't willing to stand and be counted, it ain't gonna get to the point of being legal," Johnny said.

"You're probably exaggerating the gravity of the situation,

Johnny. You have a tendency to do that."

"I ain't crying wolf just to see people run. People like Ozzie, Mouse and Ruley Gaspard are gonna hang Ben Jim if somebody doesn't stop them."

"How am I going to stop them?"

"You just being there might stop them. I ain't asking you to shoot anybody. . . though, I might."

The priest looked at Johnny and said, "I believe you would."

"You're right, I would."

"Well, I'm not going to the jail to be party to a situation that might get violent. I'm not going to be a party to murder."

Johnny shook his head in disbelief. "If you don't go there's gonna be a murder. They're gonna hang Ben Jim."

"It's the sheriff's job to protect him. . . not mine."

"The sheriff's all for the hanging."

"I find that hard to believe."

"This ain't the North, Father Ingram. Coloreds ain't even looked at as people down here. They ain't treated as good as animals."

"I don't care what you say, Johnny, I'm not going. You might as well just go on and leave me alone."

Johnny didn't cry right away at the priest's refusal. He waited until he was about fifty yards from the church to do that.

THIRTY FOUR

The men planning Ben Jim's fate were meeting at one of the sawmill's sheds where lumber was kiln dried. After Johnny made his rounds he sneaked into the shed, taking cover behind a stack of lumber. He knew his father wouldn't want him there, but felt compelled to see and hear what was going on.

The number of men milling around surprised him. He counted more than fifty, a far cry from Billy's estimate. His heart beat with fear because he knew there was no way his dad, Billy and Winston Railey could control a mob of that size.

Ruley Gaspard took center stage, calling the men to order. The greasy slob of a man was wearing a white shirt with big yellowed stains caused by sweat beneath his armpits. "All right men. . . you know why we're here."

"To hang a nigger," someone yelled from the crowd.

There was a chorus of approval, which caused Gaspard to grin. "Some people think we ought to give the nigger a fair trial."

"Hang him," someone else yelled. "He didn't give little Sadie a fair trial."

There was a lot of cursing and yelling, the consensus being that the no good nigger didn't deserve anything but a rope. The mob was in an ugly, angry mood and eager for vengeance.

Gaspard, flanked by Ozzie Guidry and Mouse Malone, smiled at his two cohorts and they smiled back. Things were going just the way Sheriff Nick Merrick wanted. The men were lusting for blood.

Jake Tobin made his way to the front of the crowd, up where the trio was standing. Seeing him caused their mouths to droop a bit. "Men, listen to me," Jake yelled, trying to be heard above the din. He had to yell several times before a degree of quiet prevailed.

"Men, you know this ain't right. If you hang Ben Jim. . . "

"Nigger lover," someone shouted.

That was all it took. There was no way the mob was going to give Jake a say. Gaspard, Mouse and Ozzie grinned at each other. Everything was working to perfection.

It didn't take Johnny long to read the situation. He slipped from his hiding place and started running toward town. He figured the mob would walk, shouting obscenities and building up their courage. Johnny knew enough about human nature to know it was one thing to talk about hanging a man, even a colored one, quite another to do it. The lynch mob would have to depend on each other for support and courage, each fearful that the other might doubt his manhood.

If anything, Johnny ran faster than he had the night they had found the little Williams boy in the creek. He ran down the sawmill's railroad spur and across the trestle, his heart pounding in his chest. He knew he had to warn Billy that the mob would soon be on its way, but felt he had to do more. There was no time for planning, only instinctive action.

For what seemed like an eternity, he ran. Then he literally crashed into the door of the sheriff's office, knocking it open and startling Billy. The deputy, his hand going to his gun, said, "What the. . . "

"They're coming, Billy. They're coming."

The deputy's face blanched with fear. He had hoped it was all just a bad dream, which would go away. Now the crisis had arrived and he had to face it. He hoped he didn't make a fool of himself.

Thirty Four

"Where's Mr. Railey?"

"He's back talking to Ben Jim. Where's your daddy?"

"He'll be here. He tried to stop them at the mill."

"How many you reckon there is?"

"More than fifty."

"My god. . . ain't no way we can stop that many."

"We've got to try."

"Ain't saying I won't try, Johnny. . . just saying there ain't much hope. Now you go tell Mr. Railey it's time he got up here."

Johnny did as he was told and said to Ben Jim, "I'll be back in just a few minutes."

When they were in the sheriff's office Billy said, "I figure we ought to lock the door and meet them outside. . . try to talk some sense into them."

Railey agreed and Johnny asked, "How many shotguns you got, Billy?"

"Don't figure we ought to take any guns out there," the deputy said. "And I don't think you ought to be out there, Johnny."

He thought about protesting but thought, *Maybe he's right. I can stay in here with a gun. And if they come through the door, I'll sure as the dickens shoot.*

Billy must have known what he was thinking, because before he and Railey went outside the deputy locked up all the guns. "Now you lock the door behind us, Johnny, and stay out of the way. I don't want you getting hurt. Where's your daddy, anyway?"

"I imagine he's on the way."

Jake was at the door when they opened it. Johnny figured his dad would make him go home, so he quickly shut the door and locked it as soon as Billy and Railey were outside. He could hear loud voices and shouting. The lynch mob was no more than a block away.

What Billy had forgotten to lock up were the keys to the cells. They were just hanging there on the wall, invitingly. Johnny knew what he had to do.

He grabbed the keys and ran back to Ben Jim's cell, found the right one and opened it. "Come on," he said. "Let's get out of here."

Ben Jim hesitated. "This is gonna get you in serious trouble, Johnny. You don't want to be doing something like this."

Johnny was crying. "Dang it, Ben Jim. . . I ain't got time to argue with you. They're almost at the door. Daddy and Billy and Mr. Railey. . . they can't stop them. There's too many."

Ben Jim followed Johnny out the door and into the hallway, then down it to the window in the back. Johnny pulled the window up and they crawled out. They could hear loud yelling, the sound of glass breaking and something battering against the front door. The mob, obviously, had overpowered Jake Tobin, Billy Burton and Winston Railey.

Johnny and Ben Jim disappeared into the night.

THIRTY FIVE

Johnny figured Ben Jim's only chance was to make it across the Sabine River into Texas and hope that if caught there he might have a better chance of a fair trial when transported back to Louisiana. Johnny also knew he was in deep trouble for aiding his friend's escape, but figured the law outside of Walla would take the circumstances into consideration. Surely, not everyone in Louisiana approved of lynching.

He had, obviously, acted on impulse, but didn't have a single regret. For the moment anyway, there wasn't time for it. There was only time for running and hiding, using all his and Ben Jim's wiles to elude the mob that was after them.

Johnny figured on traveling all night, putting Walla as far behind as possible. Come daylight, there would be a lot of good trackers and dogs on their trail. The problem was that Ben Jim had been really hurt by the beating the sheriff had given him. Merrick's favorite piece of hose had been used extensively on his legs, so he could do little more than hobble.

After crawling out the window they had made a beeline for the railroad tracks that led west to San Miquel Creek. Fear that they would be discovered was clawing at Johnny's insides. But, fortunately, they hadn't encountered any opposition to their flight because the crowd was in front of the jail.

They were not, however, out of earshot of the building when the mob discovered Ben Jim had escaped. There was yelling and cursing. All kinds of confusion was taking place.

Johnny was sure his dad would do his part to delay any chase on the part of the would-be lynchers. He was also sure the group would have trouble getting organized. He figured it would be at least an hour before someone decided Ben Jim might be heading for Texas, or that he might be heading west on the railroad tracks to get there. He couldn't even guess how long it would be before the mob discovered he was with the escapee.

Ben Jim, breathing hard because of the pain inflicted on his ribs by the hose, said, "I ought to go see Sally and Billy Boy. Ain't no telling if I'm ever gonna see them again."

"First place they're gonna be looking is at your house. . . or at my house. And that's where Sally and Billy Boy are. . . at my house. We just ain't got the time and can't take the chance."

Ben Jim sighed with resignation. "You're right, Johnny. But you go on back now. I'll be all right."

"There ain't no way I'm leaving you on your own. I'm going with you to Texas."

"I can't let you do that."

"Ain't nothing you can do to change my mind."

"Johnny, I'll turn myself in before I'll let you get hurt coming with me."

"Forget it, Ben Jim. . . and you ain't turning yourself in. If you care about Sally and Billy Boy, let's get moving."

They argued, but Ben Jim finally gave up. He knew how hardheaded Johnny was, how determined he could be. There were some arguments he could win with Johnny, but he realized this wasn't one of them.

"What about your folks?" Ben Jim asked. "They're gonna be worried sick. They ain't gonna have no idea about where you are."

"Dad will know. He knew I was in the sheriff's office and he'll figure out real quick we're together. And Billy'll have to tell everybody I took the keys to protect himself. He'll have to come after us, too, because it's his duty. Can't blame him for that."

They were moving as quickly as Ben Jim's legs would permit. Their feet crunched the gravel between the railroad crossties, sending out signals into the clear night.

"Wish it would rain. . . rain like the dickens and wash away our scent," Johnny said.

"They'll have the dogs after us real quick. You know that."

"Yeah, I know it. We can't just keep walking down the tracks. We're gonna have to go into the swamp. . . get in the water where the dogs can't smell us."

"They're gonna figure on us doing that."

"There ain't nothing we can do that they ain't gonna figure. We just got to keep moving. . . keep dodging them."

They came to the long trestle across the bottoms and San Miquel Creek. Neither had a light or weapon of any kind. The escape had been such an instinctive thing that Johnny hadn't thought about what they would need.

While they knew the lay of the land, going into the swamp at night without benefit of a light was risky and nerve-racking business. There was always the possibility of an angry cottonmouth sinking its fangs into human flesh, or a scared alligator taking a bite. The swamp was no place to be without light or a weapon.

Crossing the trestle, Johnny thought, took longer than usual. Maybe it was Ben Jim's condition, or maybe it was the fear clutching at his heart. He certainly didn't feel very heroic, not like a movie hero who had just rescued a friend. He just felt sick and scared. Fear ate at the pit of his stomach and made him nauseous.

Once over the trestle Johnny looked back toward town. The track was straight and level and he could see lights bobbing up and down a good two miles away. "Some of them are coming this way," he said. "I don't hear the dogs, though."

"It'll take them a while to get the dogs rounded up. . . and they ain't sure which way we've gone yet."

"We'd better get off the tracks. . . head into the woods and try to get to the swamp. It's a long way to the Sabine River."

The rugged terrain between Walla and the Sabine River was made up of wooded hills, creek bottoms and swampland. It was an obstacle course that some said had been laid out by the Devil.

They went down the embankment and into the woods along San Miquel Creek. It was cool but not enough, Johnny figured, for the snakes to be hibernating. They were, most likely, out prowling. The thought caused him to shiver.

As scared as he was of serpents, he still felt compelled to lead the way. He was quite sure Ben Jim was hot with a fever, another result of the beating by the sheriff.

"You're gonna have to slow down, Johnny. My legs. . . they ain't working all that good."

"How are you feeling otherwise?"

"Hot and sweaty. The sweat's pouring off my head and down into my eyes."

Johnny put a hand on Ben Jim's forehead and felt the heat. "You've got fever," he said. "You need to drink some water. I need a drink myself."

They went down the creek bank, scooped water in their hands and drank. "San Miquel water ain't half bad if you're thirsty," Johnny said. "Be better if it was colder."

Ben Jim washed his face in the creek water, scooped more and put it all over his head. "It helps," he said.

They began making their way toward the swamp, through briar patches and heavy brush. Thorns tore their clothing and scratched their skin. It was miserable and slow because they had no light to show them the best way.

Johnny figured it was about midnight when they heard dogs in the distance. The searchers had finally put the dogs on their trail. Reaching the swamp quickly was now crucial. They picked up their already frantic pace. But, no matter how fast they moved, it was quite obvious that the dogs were moving faster.

About an hour later, their breath coming in gasps, they reached the sloughs that made up the outer edge of the swamp. The dogs were no more than a hundred yards behind, so there was no time to worry about the snakes and gators that might be gliding around. They plunged into the slime-covered water, working their way between cypress trees with eerie Spanish moss hanging from them. The bottom muck sucked at their feet and caused pain to the calves of their already tired legs. But they kept going, from knee-deep to waist-deep water.

They knew their pursuers would not be giving up, that some would follow them into the water and others would take the dogs around to where the water gave way to land. That's the way the terrain was, one slough after another with spots of land in between until they reached the major part of the swamp. There they would find refuge in knee-deep to waist-deep slime-covered water that stretched for miles. Johnny began to fear that they would be cut off, not allowed to reach the refuge they were seeking.

Throughout the night they played hide and seek with the dogs and their pursuers, dreading the coming of the light of day, which, they realized, would give a definite advantage to the searchers. Johnny was experiencing terrible leg cramps and knew that Ben Jim's legs, given the beating he had received, had to be worse. He just wanted to lie down, to give up. But there was something in him that wouldn't let him do that. There was a spirit that could not, would not, accept defeat.

• • •

Billy Burton had been forced into the role of having to help lead what was now considered a posse. And he hated it. He was secretly praying that Ben Jim and Johnny would make it into Texas and find sanctuary there.

The sun's rays were just finding their way into the swamp, colliding with a foggy, rising ghostlike mist. There was a mystical look to the setting, a feeling of being lost in time. Billy couldn't help but think the searchers looked and moved like zombies he had seen in a movie.

To his left was Sheriff Nick Merrick, equipped with a rifle and a bottle. Surprisingly, he had not seemed all that upset by Ben Jim's escape. One of his cronies had rousted him from the bed. Astoundingly, he was about half-sober. Billy figured the sheriff had held off on getting blind drunk until he got word of Ben Jim's hanging. Then he would have celebrated until he passed out.

Billy figured the fact that Johnny Tobin broke Ben Jim out of jail helped to explain why the sheriff wasn't too upset about the escape. The sheriff probably thought Johnny's involvement would turn the town against the Tobins, which as one of his priorities ranked right up there with killing Ben Jim.

To Billy's right was a worried Jake Tobin, whom the deputy knew was there more to protect his son and Ben Jim than to catch them. He, Jake and Winston Railey had been overwhelmed, but not hurt, by the mob intent on hanging Ben Jim.

Elmer Guerdat, armed with a shotgun, came up to Billy and said in an almost whisper, "That Johnny Tobin's got guts, ain't he? Dang if I'd wade this swamp water at night with no light. I wouldn't be out here now if daddy hadn't made me come."

Billy managed a wry smile. "Thought you and Johnny was enemies."

"No. . . nothing like that. The kid and me. . . we got our differences, but I admire the little rascal. He's tough as nails. It's kind of nice to have a friend who'll put his rear on the line and break you out of jail."

"Maybe you won't never need to be broke out," Billy said, "but I know what you mean."

Contrary to what the sheriff thought, Billy figured a lot of the men hunting Ben Jim and Johnny had a deeper appreciation for the kid. After all, this was country where a man was measured by his willingness to put himself on the line. Johnny had done that and then some. They'd have difficulty admiring his nigger loving ways, but not his toughness and determination in doing what he thought was right.

Of course, Ozzie Guidry, Mouse Malone and Ruley Gaspard wouldn't be impressed by what Johnny had done, Billy thought, because they were too busy kissing up to the sheriff. And he wasn't sure about Elmer's daddy, Wilber Guerdat. But he figured the rest of the men were with him in secretly applauding Johnny's courage.

About that time one of the men came up to the sheriff and said, "I think we got them. I think they're on that little island about sixty. . . seventy yards to the left of us."

They were in water about thigh deep, so the dogs had been left behind. They started wading toward the little island and Jake Tobin said, "I'll go ahead. If they're there. . . I'll get them."

Jake moved some ten yards in front of the advancing men and

Thirty Five

Billy called out, "Don't be getting itchy trigger fingers now. Ben Jim ain't got no gun."

The words had no sooner left his mouth when there was the sharp report of a rifle, which echoed like a cracking whip throughout the eerie stillness of the swampland. All the men just froze. Then their eyes turned toward the sheriff, who said, "Thought I saw some movement in the brush."

Jake exploded, angrily shouting expletives. "You no good. . . "

He started wading back toward the sheriff, but Billy intervened. "Hold it, Jake. Maybe no harm's been done. Let's go on. Now dang it. . . no shooting."

Jake's eyes were like fire. Billy knew that if he had been carrying a gun the sheriff would have been a dead man. They turned their eyes back to the little island and saw Ben Jim walking toward them, crying. He was carrying Johnny in his arms and there was a big bloody splotch on the kid's chest.

Billy was standing next to the sheriff. He wasn't sure whether Merrick planned to use his rifle or not, but he saw the barrel move up. He brought his pistol down hard across the sheriff's nose.

THIRTY SIX

The weather was erratic in the spring of nineteen fifty, but no more deviant than the events that took place during the fall and winter months leading up to the season. Indeed, the populace of Walla was ready for a change from the shockwaves of the previous seasons, ready for the promise of new beginnings brought by spring.

The very day Johnny Tobin had been shot the previous October, FBI agent Carter Duncan had brought little Sadie Scott back to Walla. A maternal aunt who believed Vernon Scott had been molesting his daughter, it seems, had taken the girl. That, however, was not what professionals who questioned the child discovered. They were more inclined to think that any molestation that had taken place had been on the part of the mother, Marcie Scott.

As a result of Sadie's return, Ben Jim Cade was released from jail. The men who had planned to hang him seemed to have lost interest for a couple of reasons. First, the shooting of Johnny Tobin had directed the anger of most toward the sheriff. Second, Billy Burton said he would shoot any man who tried to take his prisoner. And, the deputy had suddenly become credible.

Sadly, the mob had burned Ben Jim's house to the ground the previous night.

Marcie, of course, who had learned a short time after Sadie was taken that it was her sister who had taken her, denied that she had molested her child. But all the evidence pointed in her direction, including Sadie's testimony.

Coach Vernon Scott wanted both his wife and her sister tried for kidnapping, but Marcie's knowledge of the child's whereabouts pretty well negated that possibility. The townspeople, who had suffered the trauma of the child's disappearance, turned against Marcie and called for some kind of justice. The only persons who stood by her were Father Walter Ingram and Bailey Thompson, who by doing so pretty well sealed their fates in the town.

With the sheriff laid up with a broken nose, fractured jaw and concussion, the result of more than one whack from Billy Burton's pistol, the deputy became a different kind of lawman. He arrested Isaac Simpson and charged him with the murder of the Williams family.

Just what kind of interrogation Billy put Isaac through is unknown, but there are those who say it made Sheriff Merrick's hose treatment seem like a picnic. Whatever happened inside the jail, Isaac confessed. And he also named an accomplice.

Marcie Scott, he said, had helped him do the killing. Isaac admitted that while he had lusted after Clarice Williams, Marcie had lusted more. People in Walla didn't know what to make of that. They also had trouble making sense of it because Clarice was colored and Marcie was white.

They had trouble with other revelations by Isaac, too, the primary one being that he and Marcie had been lovers. A white woman with a colored man was a bit hard for folks to swallow, though the opposite was somewhat of a tradition.

Isaac admitted that he lusted a whole lot more after Marcie than after Clarice Williams. And he further admitted to being angry that she was carrying on with Father Ingram and Bailey Thompson. Her relationship with Thompson was no surprise to many townspeople. The same could not be said about her relationship with the priest. It was, to say the least, a shocking revelation, one that Brother Marvin Baker would be able to use over and over again in discussing and preaching against the evils of Catholicism.

Initially, Marcie denied everything. But then she seemed to revel in all the destruction she had wrought. She openly bragged about how she had killed Clarice Williams while the woman begged for mercy.

And yes, she had been responsible for Isaac planting the gun and some of Sadie's clothing at Ben Jim Cade's house. She had then disguised her voice and called the sheriff, told him where to look. "I know how badly he wanted Ben Jim," she had said, "so I wasn't worried about him thinking it was a frame up. In fact, I wasn't worried about him thinking at all."

Marcie said she had also ordered Isaac to kill Johnny Tobin, and was angry with him when he wasn't able to accomplish the task. "Isaac. . . he's such a coward. He's always been afraid of Ben Jim Cade."

With the two killers telling all, the result of their separate trials was a foregone conclusion, except that Marcie's folks got some hotshot lawyer from Shreveport to come in to defend her. He got her off with a trip to the state mental institution. It wasn't difficult to convince a parish jury that the woman was crazy.

The flip side of the equation didn't work well for Isaac, who was sentenced to die in the electric chair.

Word is that Bailey Thompson went to Texas and got on with a pipeline crew. Father Ingram left the priesthood and got a job as an orderly at the mental institution where Marcie was sent.

Vernon Scott's football team won the state championship and he was named principal of the high school.

EPILOGUE

It was one of those spring mornings when the weather had seemed to settle. The sun was shining brightly, there was a light breeze from the south and the smells of the season were hanging in the air. Smoke from the mill's always burning sawdust pile was playing with the clouds.

Beneath the trestle Johnny Tobin was fishing, concentrating on his bobber, which was taking up residence near some brush protruding above the water's surface. He didn't even turn his head when Bobby Milam came down the embankment with his fishing pole and asked, "Having any luck?"

"Couple. They ain't biting."

Bobby baited his hook and then positioned it and his bobber the other side of the brush from where Johnny was fishing. "Y'all still planning on moving when school's out?" Bobby asked.

"Yeah. . . reckon so."

"How you feeling. . . you healing up good and all?"

"Doing fine. . . just a big old' scar where the bullet went in. Probably won't be the last time I'll be shot in my life. The Army'll see to that."

"You're gonna miss fishing down here under the trestle."

"Yeah. . . reckon I will. But I figure there'll be some pretty good trestle fishing over in Mississippi."

"I wish you wasn't going. Is your dad just bound and determined?"

"The whole family is. There ain't nothing for us here."

"What's over in Mississippi?"

"Different people. Dad's got a good job offered to him over there and he figures we don't exactly have a lot of friends around here."

"Everybody I know is sorry for what happened. And y'all always got me and Billy Burton."

Johnny smiled. "Us leaving ain't got nothing to do with you and Billy."

"Think you'll see Ben Jim over in Mississippi?"

"I don't know where he is over there. Sure can't blame him and Sally and Billy Boy for leaving here. . . especially after folks burned their house. I'd like to see him. . . like to do some hunting and fishing with him. But. . . well, I don't know if I'll ever see him again. No telling where he's at."

They didn't talk for a while, just watched their bobbers and drank in the peaceful sounds of the creek and the whispers the breeze caused in the treetops. Suddenly, Johnny's bobber disappeared beneath the water's surface. He arched his pole and felt a strength on the end of his line that was much stronger than that of a perch.

Bobby was quick to realize his friend had a good fish on the end of the line, too. Probably a catfish, he thought.

Johnny worked the big fish toward the bank. It rose toward the surface, its side flashing in the sunlight. "Bass!" Bobby shrieked. "A big bass."

After a hard battle Johnny worked the fish in close, then got its bottom lip between his thumb and forefinger. The hook was just barely stuck in the side of the fish's mouth.

Johnny lifted the big bass from the water and held it up toward the sunlight.

Epilogue

"My gosh," Bobby said. "That's the biggest bass I've ever seen. How much you think he weighs?"

"Six. . . seven pounds."

"Looks to me like he'll go ten."

Johnny laughed. He removed the hook from the mouth of the fish, admired it a few more seconds, then put it back in the water and let it swim away while Bobby stood there aghast.

"What did you do that for?"

Johnny shrugged. "Something fights that hard deserves to be free."